THE ORIGINAL OTHER
A COMPELLING WORK OF FICTION

BY

ALEXANDRA F. CLAIR

PublishAmerica
Baltimore

ISBN: 1-4137-0671-1
PUBLISHED BY PUBLISHAMERICA BOOK PUBLISHERS
www.publishamerica.com
Baltimore

Printed in the United States of America

This book is dedicated with love to my Aunt Mary for the inspiration of her encouragement.

Mary Kearin Richmond

Thank you to John Bailey, Rosalyne Vaccaro, Frieda Clement, Walt Overbey, and my husband, Brett Stancil.

PROLOGUE

It wasn't logical to believe that after all this time she was still alive, and yet he knew that somewhere she lived and had a life they could not guess at.

Late February sent a chill over the mountains and down the long sloping reach towards the valley where early mornings were slow to warm, even under the bright California sky. Dexter Arujo leaned his head over the veranda and fought off another wave of nausea. As though in pain, he lifted his head and looked out to where vines stood curved and knotted, but to his eye, pristine and perfectly tailored. Amidst cleared furrows, patches of mist clung to the ground and darkness lifted to a pale violet hue. For the first time in memory this familiar sight, which had occupied his family for four generations, failed to offer solace.

He thought of the photographs. They lay behind him, image down and scattered over the wrought iron table. Beyond the wide French doors Anya slept, oblivious to his turmoil. The love he felt for his wife was a stone of outrage so heavy that he felt physically weighed down by anguish, and it occurred to him that he did not deserve their happiness. He had systematically lied to himself, and now that ostrich retreat from reality could no longer keep at bay the mountain of inconsistencies that should have been obvious long ago.

With great reluctance he extended his hand and picked up one of the black and white photographs. What he saw burned an ugly stain into his psyche that no amount of denial would ever scrub clean. With effort he willed his breathing back to normal, spat out the bile that collected at the back of his throat, and struggled to silence an avalanche of thoughts. No doubt other photographs would follow and finally demands for money in exchange for silence. Isn't that how blackmail worked? Isn't that how the plot unfolded in countless books and movies?

Unable to sleep he had wandered out to the screened section of the veranda, settled into his favorite wicker chair, and snapped on a reading light. Not appreciating these last seconds of peace, he had reached for the battered canvas duffel that served as a brief case, and his hand closed on the large

7

manila envelope. He had slit the flap with the tip of a pen, withdrawn the contents, and felt a shock so profound that his mind had momentarily become numb. This was the depraved, amoral side of life that only occurred in the lives of fictional characters and strangers, but then his eyes made out her features. It struck him with swift and painful clarity as entirely plausible that his wife should be cast as a central figure, for he could no longer suppress all the suspicion that had built up over time with subtle, sneering persistence.

He let the porch door close behind him and walked into the bedroom just as the sun lifted off the eastern ridge, casting slanted tentacles of light across the width of the veranda. She lay sleeping, her red hair a ribbon stain against the stark, white sheets. With her features reposed in sleep, Anya looked very unlike the aloof young woman the western press had dubbed 'the ice princess.' The controlled, sophisticated facade that she presented to the world was nowhere in evidence and it was like this, when she truly slept, that he could almost imagine that he knew her.

Anya had been an orphan, a natural athlete with a dancer's grace who had outshone the other children and so, in a seemingly odd quirk of fate, had been placed in a state-sponsored skating program. This was the story she told, which in the years before her defection to the United States, mirrored precisely the promotional bytes put out by her country's government. Why hadn't he noticed that when she spoke of her childhood she sounded like a walking press release? Why didn't he pursue more details when she claimed she couldn't remember? He was a fool.

Dex pulled the light blanket over Anya's shoulder before returning to the veranda. One last time he forced himself to examine the photographs. He had recognized her face immediately. How old was she in this photograph? How old in that? He thought of his young female students and guessed she would have been six or seven. Even now, faced with such irrefutable evidence, he longed to convince himself that this was not Anya, not his wife; but there was no mistaking the defeated slump to her shoulders that only he saw when her guard was down, nor her habit of clenching her thumb with her fist. He recognized the lock of hair that would not be tamed as it fell forward over her brow and the absent stare centered on a place where he could never go.

Dex fought to separate his feelings from his intellect. He needed to examine the photographs with care, searching for any clue to their origin, but he could not avoid the frozen look of utter revulsion on Anya's face and then the forced smile that grimaced in pain. Nothing would ever wipe from his memory that child's stare of stark terror and humiliation as she was brutally accosted and raped. Instead, Dex forced himself to concentrate on the face that the entire skating world would recognize in a heartbeat, and another that stood back and watched. This man could also be easily recognized.

The third man, poised over Anya, kept his back to the camera, even when his stance was awkward. It was evident to Dex that this man had made a conscious decision not to assume the risk that the other two believed would never be compromised. Dex examined the camera angles and realized they were too deliberate for a tripod. A fourth person had to be operating that camera. Perhaps this was the person who had handed the envelope to Hillary in the overcrowded rink at an out of town competition. "Was that Boston?" He'd have to ask to be certain, but the innate cautiousness that had served him well through most of his life caused him to hesitate, even as he forced himself to reach for the phone and dial the rink number.

"Tell her it's important," he told the mother who answered the phone. Hillary would be on the ice for the first patch lessons of the morning and would ignore the summons unless she knew who was calling. When she finally came on the line, irritation and concern mingled in her voice to jar his nerves.

"What's wrong, Chief?" She had begun calling him Chief after they had stayed up late one night to watch a marathon of old Superman reruns, and Dex knew that behind his back the children had taken up her habit. His relationship with his assistant coach had begun as an affair that ended after Anya came into his life, but for a while it seemed they might not be capable of continuing the working part of their relationship, which had brought them both success. It had taken Hillary a long time to get over her jealousy of Anya, and Dex had nearly lost his patience, deciding to fire her more than once but failing to follow through. Hillary's new boyfriend was a coach from Arrowhead who visited as often as their respective schedules allowed, and Dex noticed that they had begun signing their students up for the same out of town competitions so that they could spend additional time together. He hoped the relationship would last.

"That large manila envelope you gave me yesterday? Remember?"

"Sure."

"There isn't a postmark. Where did it come from?"

"From that competition last week."

Hillary had accompanied a large group of younger skaters and parents along with several junior and senior level girls who would never be competitive but were being groomed as potential coaches. Dex, who ran the program and owned the facilities, concentrated on fewer, more select students, "Who gave it to you?" he asked.

"I really don't know, Dex. It was after the junior long program. You know how crowded it gets. Someone passed it to me while I was trying to check scores. I put it in my bag and later in my suitcase, and then I forgot about it until I unpacked, but was careful to keep it flat. Photos, right?"

"Yes, that's right."

"The only reason I didn't open it myself is because it was labeled confidential. Was it important?"

Dex noticed that a note of curiosity had crept into her voice. "It seems there is no return address and I'd like to respond. Think about this Hillary. Did a man or a woman give it to you?"

There was a short pause. "For all I know it might have been a child. There were so many people in that lobby area. You know what it's like. Pandemonium, with everyone crowding around to read scores and see who placed and really Dex, as I think about it now, it may just have been slipped into my bag."

"I don't understand, Hillary. How can you not remember something like this?" As soon as the words escaped he regretted them. He didn't want Hillary too curious.

"Well, Dex, that would be because you haven't had to handle more than four students at competition at any time in your life, while I am left with all the rest, some of them on new ice for the first time in their lives."

Dex swallowed the retort that sprang to mind and not for the first time regretted their past intimacy. "If you remember anything at all Hillary, no matter how trivial, I'd like you to call immediately. Will you do that?"

Hillary hung up without saying goodbye. She was a good coach and gave the children a solid base. People new to skating often thought that past medal contenders made the best coaches, but this was not necessarily true. Hillary's years of frustrated competition resulted in a thoughtful and patient coach with an analytical edge that served her well with parents. No one could calm a crying child faster or put defeat back in perspective with more humorous pragmatism. Their philosophy and teaching methods, although different, complimented one another, and only after they abandoned their more personal relationship had Hillary begun to irritate him.

Dex replaced the phone. With exaggerated care he gathered the photographs and slipped all but two into the envelope. Anya was usually up for morning practice by six, but the night before she had flown in from a charity exhibition in Palm Springs and would indulge the rare luxury of waking slowly. As the sky lightened, Dex knew he had little time to compose himself. Anya was an astute observer and would suspect immediately that something was wrong.

Dex walked across the wide hall into what had once been his parents' bedroom. Built into the floor was a safe. He spun the dial, opened the heavy door and slid two of the photographs into a large leather binder. He then walked back into the bedroom he shared with Anya, clutching the other photographs in a fist so tight that his hand hurt. Kneeling by the hearth and knowing that he solved nothing, he struck a match on the gray fieldstone.

"What is that, Dex?" Anya asked, surprising him. She had a disconcerting habit of moving without making a sound and actually seemed to enjoy startling him. If he complained, she would laugh in ironic detachment and remind him, "But I am an angel. Angels can do such things."

"You are an angel," he would agree. "You are my angel." The term had become for Anya an endearment that she could never quite accept as a compliment, and now he understood why. Now he understood so much more, and he dreaded the prospect of having to reevaluate all those ill-conceived notions that had held his marriage together.

Anya had loosely belted a green satin robe with ivory trim. As his eyes locked on hers, he felt a fierce protective emotion, completely new and almost foreign for its zealous intensity. This, he thought, must be how one feels with home and hearth, farm and country in great peril. Mistaking his look, she moved forward but Dex turned away. He placed a log over the last of the black and white photographs and caught a final look of utter humiliation staring back at him from the curling edge of the paper. Quickly he reached for kindling and fed the narrow pieces of wood into the glowing embers until the log flared in sudden hungry avarice.

"In an hour it will be too hot for a fire," she said, but Dex knew she loved the warmth of an open flame, claiming it reminded her of that first time they had made love in an isolated cottage in the wilds of Maine. She was in a good mood and yet her moods had an unsettling habit of shifting with a speed that was difficult to keep up with. The night before, she had skated flawlessly. Her show program, skated to a fifties rhythm and blues tune, had brought the crowd to their feet. She had turned professional only after intense pressure from him, and now her dynamic presence on the ice made her a more popular figure than any one expected.

Dex recalled how difficult it had been in the beginning to get Anya the right exposure. Her amateur career had been cut short by her defection. The bronze medal she had won at the Olympics was one of the few she could claim, and she lacked the sort of record that normally caught the attention of the professional circuit, but now there was no shortage of opportunities. Dex had managed to gain his wife a dramatic agent. As a result she'd been cast in a plum role that would soon make her more famous than ever. She was slowly becoming a familiar face and was due to make the promotional rounds of talk and morning shows to promote the film's release.

It didn't hurt her celebrity that Anya was married to one of the most celebrated male figure skaters in history. Her dramatic story of rescue and defection made good copy, and the two would appear next month on the cover of *People Magazine*. During the interview Dex had deliberately promoted Anya over himself, and he hoped the actual copy would read that way. When he had doubts about Anya's happiness, he told himself that she thrived on her success, but now he wondered if he were the only one thriving in their personal and professional relationship. At times Anya seemed uncomfortable with the attention and even a little contemptuous. She was slow to make friends among the other professional skaters, even though life on tour often forged quick and lasting friendships. Sometimes she appeared unreasonably dependent on him and at other times protective of her individuality, but always and right from the beginning she had been guarded and secretive.

Anya's surprise at her notoriety and the humble way that she received public attention was an endearing trait that only he saw. When the cameras were aimed in her direction, a metamorphosis took place and she was transformed. It was clear that she possessed that indefinable star quality that spoke through lens and image in a provocative and compelling language that drew or repelled, but always captured attention. He had guessed correctly at that wide gulf between Anya's public persona and deep insecurity that defined a personal reality. He had guessed, but chosen not to probe for understanding. He had committed blindly to his own selfish agenda for Anya and now they would both pay a price.

Dex turned from the fire and watched as Anya raised her hand to smooth back her long lustrous hair. He noticed how the green satin of her robe fell over her narrow hips. The slightness of her body and her long legs were as deceptive as her public persona. She was physically strong and could launch her body into high, beautiful jumps with an athletic grace that was stunning to watch. "Why don't we have breakfast before the fire?" he suggested.

"A good idea, Dex. We haven't done that in a long time. You call the kitchen and I'll be with you shortly," she called over her shoulder, already halfway across the room and striding toward the bathroom. He listened to the sound of bath water running and turned his face toward the fire, letting the heat evaporate the tears that fell down his cheeks.

Dex sat on the veranda and watched the late afternoon sun drift toward the rim of the pine-covered ridge. Anya bent to kiss his forehead. She was dressed in purple tights and an oversized white shirt tied in a knot at the waist, and she had yet to drop her skating bag. It came around and hit his shoulder as she bent once more to kiss his lips, her long burnished hair enclosing his face like a tent. She tasted of juicy fruit gum, a favorite American product.

"What is wrong?" she asked. "Rosa tells me you haven't moved from this spot all day. Are you sick?" She reached out to lightly place the back of her hand on his cheek in a way that reminded him of his mother.

"You didn't even come to watch me practice, and my triple-lutz is over-rotated," she scolded. "I needed you, and Hillary is useless. That woman will not help me. And beads are falling off my new dress. Imagine Dex, three thousand American dollars for one yard of fabric that falls apart. Can you imagine that, Dex?"

She looked at him, waiting. She had dropped the heavy skating bag and stood with hands on hips inviting him to share her exasperation, knowing that he would only be amused, but today she could not raise even that response. "Three thousand American dollars. You pay too much, Dex. We pay too much."

Anya could not grow accustomed to the high cost of skating after having all such expenses met by her former country. She had grown up poor. The only clothes she had were either gifts from her former coach, Sasha Eymrnov, or provided by the state for her skating.

Dex looked at her face. A lifetime spent in cold ice arenas had slowed the aging process, and her skin was virtually unlined. Her cheekbones and wide green eyes gave the impression of endearing youth. She wore makeup only when competing and otherwise seemed not to care for artifice of any kind, traits totally out of sync with her public image.

"Come here," he said and held out an arm. She nestled beside him in the wide chair and he pulled her close. They sat like that, comfortable and still for a few minutes.

"You will come to my practice tonight?" Anya asked turning her face up to his. She knew he was thinking about something that worried him, something he had yet to confide, but he was not a secretive man, her Dex. He was not complicated in the bad way she had grown accustomed to shielding herself from. He was open and honest with an endearing vulnerability that made it possible for her to trust him. Soon he would tell what was on his mind, and she could depend on the problem being easily rectified. Perhaps another fight with Hillary or a script for another movie that he knew she wouldn't be interested in. His life was too firmly rooted in routine and his way of thinking and behaving entirely predictable, which was precisely what made her presence in his house and his life possible. How long that would last she couldn't say.

"I'll come to your practice and I'll even sew those beads back on your dress," he announced.

Anya laughed again. Like most skaters Dex could repair a costume, but she knew he hated the task. "Crystals," she corrected him. "They are Austrian crystals at three dollars each and two of them are lost forever."

They sipped from the same glass of Kanelli. "This is certainly a great tragedy," he agreed and put up an arm to block her punch.

"You are making fun of me again," she laughed, but he did not laugh back in his usual way. Nor did he return the light jab that often sent them wrestling to the ground until locked in a passionate embrace. Anya looked at him intently, again sensing a guarded wariness, but she let it pass. She felt content and safe when Dex was near, and she had learned to let the feeling envelop her rather than send her into a roaring panic as it once had.

Dex finished the wine while Anya fished a bottle of water from the top of her equipment bag. She would shower and rest before dinner and then both would drive to the rink for her last practice. She looked at her husband and could not escape the feeling that some innate part of him had shifted. Whatever affected him would eventually impact her. In the beginning he had meant nothing to her, only a means of escape, but time had brought the unexpected. When she looked into his face and saw happiness there she actually found a little for herself.

Despite the fact that she was skating when she really preferred not to and had far more notoriety than was safe for those Others, she was sleeping and sometimes even straight through the night. And she was eating and enjoying the physicality of her body and even his. More important still, that feeling of not being real, of being absent from her consciousness, had ceased to plague her as often. She was far more present to herself and to their marriage than she had ever intended and only when she examined herself and thought about the unexpected bonus of his love was she frightened.

If he stopped being what she needed, they would have to go. Anya thought of the partially packed suitcase and stash of cash. One of the Others had packed that suitcase and there it was, waiting in the back of a closet in a little used room of his large house. There was now plenty of money. She didn't need her husband for a place to live and for food to eat, and so why did she stay? Perhaps it was true. She really did love him. He used that word like he truly knew the meaning and yet, when the time came to leave, she wouldn't hesitate.

Anya watched the light flicker as the late afternoon sun drifted behind a cloud and shadows climbed like fingers from the depth of the valley. In the last year, lulled by the barrier of security that Dex offered, she had neglected her investments. More important still, she had neglected the list compiled by one of those Others. That list was her reason for returning to this country and she mustn't forget for long their purpose for living.

Anya lifted her face and looked into her husband's eyes. "What are you thinking about?" she inquired and held her breath, fearful of the answer.

Dex paused before speaking. "I'm thinking about my mother. I'm thinking that she did a good job of protecting me when I was young, and I'm wondering about you. Who," he asked, "protected you?"

She didn't know the expression on his face. Was it pity? She stood abruptly and hoisted her heavy equipment bag as though it weighed nothing. The question had to be innocent. She cautioned herself not to be alarmed. Her Dex did not and could not know anything. It was true that he had asked questions like this before, but they had lacked the focused bite of curiosity that she now heard in his voice. He foolishly expected an answer, and she would have laughed if she hadn't been compelled to change the subject, as she always did when questions presented as slippery slopes of entrapment.

For the first time since Dex had known her, although he had heard it many times before, he only truly heard it now. Her tone was evasive, faintly defiant, and false. He shivered.

"I think I'll take a bath. Rosa is having the cook try a new recipe from her book, and I'm suddenly starving. Don't think too much about your mother, Dex."

"Why not?"

"Because maybe she would not have liked me." "Maybe," Anya added silently to herself, "she would have hated me."

"She would have loved you," he said knowing that it wasn't true and besides it was already too late. He had spent the afternoon thinking about his mother and those early years when he had hated skating and looked for his father to take the initiative to rescue him from long, often painful, practices.

Dex laid the palm of his hand on the place beside him that Anya had newly vacated. He thought of his father's guns. There were two gun cabinets in the house and a display of antique pistols, but he had never learned to load and shoot. "I'll learn," he told himself and felt oddly stirred by the idea. "I'll get Joey to show me later tonight after our wives have gone to sleep. We'll go out past the fallow fields where no one will hear us and I'll learn."

CHAPTER ONE

He was the last person to see and speak with her on that day that she had disappeared. He was the older boy, and she had smiled up at him as her melting ice cream cone brushed his arm. Details of that day were indelibly imprinted on his consciousness, and many years later he continued to grieve the betrayal of his senses. He never guessed that evil stood in broad daylight, wearing a benign disguise and blending in with all the fabric of normalcy.

Irene Arujo entered the office of her son's coach and settled her large frame into one of two newly upholstered club chairs. Glen Winston looked up from his desk inquiringly. He glanced at his itinerary for the day and saw that Irene's name did not appear.

"What can I do for you?" he asked, failing to disguise his annoyance. He hadn't invited her to sit, but already the dense foam of his new chair sank to a thin sliver beneath the weight of her massive thighs, and not for the first time, Glen wondered how someone with her gene pool could have produced a specimen like Dex.

"I've told Dex that he can pack his things. We'll be leaving this afternoon," Irene said, offering no other explanation.

Glen had noticed that most communication between mother and son came from her vast repertoire of looks and shrugs, which Dex seemed to interpret without difficulty.

"Leaving?" Glen laid aside a heavy folder, processing her statement. Even before learning that Dex's former coach was ready to retire, Glen had campaigned to acquire him as a student. The boy was far too valuable a prize to give up without a fight, and yet Glen was not worried. The boundless ambition of most figure skating parents was easily manipulated, and he was a master at serving up just the right confluence of censure and validation calculated to keep even the most astute parents off balance.

Irene took an audible breath as though it pained her to speak. "My son is not happy," she pronounced and waited.

"Happy!" Glen's smile was a smirk of condescension as he lifted his head and looked Irene full in the face for the first time since she'd entered his office. He could summon no enthusiasm for another whining exchange with one more insecure mother seeking assurance that they were valued.

Glen was not having a good day. The very expensive custom boots and blades he'd ordered for his most promising female skater had arrived wrong, meaning that the delayed replacement would not be properly broken in before the upcoming national competition. To make matters worse, one of his assistants was threatening to quit if not allowed more authority. Glen noted the stiff set of Irene's jaw and felt a momentary stab of uneasiness. Smoothing the feathers of a disgruntled parent was as much apart of his job as introducing a new jump, so he forced himself to appear attentive.

"If you're worried about Dex's program you should know that I hired the best choreographer money could buy, and at no expense to you," he added.

Even as he spoke Glen considered the circumstances that had brought Irene to his office, unannounced and threatening to remove her son. Obviously the brat had complained about the altercation they'd had over Dex's wish to alter certain elements of his program. Inwardly Glen bristled. He still had a thing or two to teach that boy about how things were done under his tutelage.

Just yesterday he had looked out one of the two windows at each end of his office that afforded him a full view of both Olympic-size ice surfaces. A smooth, pristine surface gleamed until Dex had burst into view, an explosion of energy, remarkable after a full day of training. Glen felt pleased that one of his two prized students should be working long after the others had disappeared into the lobby or locker rooms. This was not unusual for Dex. He was nearly always the first on the ice in the morning and the last to leave.

Glen was about to turn away when he noticed that Dex was doubling his triple jumps. This allowed him to concentrate on the changes to his program that Glen had clearly stated could not be made. Judging by the fluid ease with which Dex skated, it was apparent that he had been practicing these changes behind his coaches back, imagining correctly how each turn, jump, and footwork sequence would flow into the next. Glen was infuriated. What was this boy trying to prove, making unauthorized changes only a month before the first qualifying competition that would lead to nationals? Dex had been at the prestigious Winston Skating Center barely a year, and Glen could not allow his authority to be challenged in such a way. Only Ryan Campbell could get away with that sort of rebellion.

In a fit of rage Glen had bounded down the stairs and out a private door that led directly onto the ice. Student and coach met at the music booth where Dex was about to key up his tape for another trial run.

"What do you think you're doing?" Glen erupted as he ripped the tape out of the machine and squashed the plastic casing beneath the heel of his boot.

"I have a couple of ideas about changing my program," Dex began, but Glen cut him off.

"When I need your help, I'll ask for it. And let's get something straight right now, Arujo. You have a reputation as a mama's boy, but she's out of the picture because we're sending her packing. When you step foot on my ice, I'm your mother and your father. Are you listening to me?" Glen had shouted, inches from Dex's face as he pounded a finger repetitively into his chest, but Dex had refused to step back and now they had an audience. Some of the other skaters, hearing the commotion, had found excuses to wander back into the rink area to witness this very public confrontation. Glen was gratified to see that Dex appeared truly mortified. An additional dose of humiliation could only cement his authority.

Warming to this tongue-lashing, Glen noticed his student scanning the faces of the other students. Enraged that he did not have Dex's full attention, he followed Dex's gaze even as he continued his ranting and noted that only Ryan Campbell appeared at all sympathetic.

Over the last months Dex had heard his coach mercilessly berate other students while escaping the experience himself. This was not because Glen had not looked for opportunities to put Dex in his place, but because he was a model student who did little wrong. Glen's eyes narrowed even now as he thought of how Dex's gaze had sought out Ryan. He had done his best to keep the two apart. Figure skating was not a team sport, and as far as Glen was concerned, the two boys should hate one another. Yet Dex showed no animosity and seemed to go out of his way to be cordial to Ryan, a response that baffled Glen.

Glen appeared oblivious to the undercurrent of intense dislike that impacted his dealings with his students. Whether love or hate, he counted on that energy to drive a fierce compulsion that matched his own ambition to win at any cost. As far as Glen was concerned, winning was what skating was all about, and the tender age of his youngest students mattered not at all.

Even as he watched Ryan turned abruptly, scooped up his skating bag, and walked away. This infuriated Glen. Ryan's angry exit contained an element of hushed drama, not missed by the younger students as they made room for him to pass, and now Glen had the kind of captive audience he liked best.

While some of Glen's students came from the immediate metropolitan area, most boarded at the center, leaving behind family and friends. Glen and his staff had encouraged Irene to return home, but a nagging sense of caution restrained her. It didn't matter what the staff said. She had been too immersed in Dex's career to suddenly believe that her presence was counter-productive to his progress.

Glen in no way regretted yesterday's incident that had brought Irene to his office to ruin his morning. As he scrutinized her face for some clue as to how to proceed, he eased himself back in his chair, resisting an uncharacteristic urge to cross his arms over his chest in a defensive gesture. He didn't like mothers in general. He particularly did not like this mother, but he had learned from experience not to allow dissatisfactions to fester. It was what he could not guess about Irene that irritated him the most. Unlike the other parents, she did not crave his approval. As Glen opened his mouth to speak he could not conceal his dislike of her, yet his voice was intentionally soft.

"Perhaps what we have here is a slightly spoiled young man and an overindulgent parent."

"If you'd had the opportunity to meet my husband, Mr. Winston, you would realize that you should never threaten Dex. Never raise a fist, or in this case a finger that in any way connects with my child's physical person. Am I making myself clear?"

In all the years that he had jealously watched Dex compete and wished he could be the coach guiding that talent, he had never actually seen Mr. Arujo at any event. Sometimes if he could keep the parents arguing, they had less time to interfere with his own plans.

"Does you husband agree with your decision to remove Dex? Perhaps I should call him," Glen said, making a move to reach for the phone as though he and Dex's father talked often.

Irene continued as though his words and manner had not insulted her intelligence. "Dex is not happy," she pronounced with a simplicity that exasperated Glen. As usual her few words gave him little ammunition.

"What do you expect?" Glen asked, summoning his best facsimile of martyrdom. "I've gone out of my way for Dex, and there were some, Elliot included, who said I shouldn't take him on because of Ryan."

Irene had never been impressed by Elliot Smythe, as others were. Sports commentator and journalist for a major network, Elliot and Glen seemed to have a solid friendship. Elliot often flew in from New York to spend his free time with Glen, and the younger children adored him since he generously passed out sporting equipment and footwear autographed by the media's latest sensation.

"You can't say that Dex is not progressing very nicely," Glen continued. "I imagine you watched him skate last Friday. I'm quite pleased."

As competition season loomed, the students ran through their programs each Friday in full costume for interested observers and other skaters. It was the one opportunity for parents to observe progress, also providing a dress

20

rehearsal without the option to re-skate a program because of falls or missed timing.

Potential problems could also be identified, such as costumes that distracted the skater because they failed to stretch comfortably or faulty choreography and fatigue. Changes would be made, and the skater would learn that recovering quickly from a fall was just as important as delivering the flawless program that so rarely happened during those few, brief moments when it counted most.

As a rule Glen barred parents from attending practice sessions, so Irene looked forward to these Friday performances, her one opportunity to gauge her son's progress. Despite the atmosphere of polish and professionalism, Dex had failed to learn anything new. Worse still, the triple-axel he had just learned remained entirely unreliable, and other jumps he had been landing without difficulty seemed to lack flow.

In the last years the standards for male skaters had been steadily rising, and Irene suspected that some day even four revolutions in a jump would be required by men, but today the triple jumps and especially the triple-axel was crucial to staying competitive. Unless Dex had a consistent triple-axel he could not move up to the senior level of competition, and despite Glen Winston's opinion to the contrary, Irene had not planned on her son remaining a junior for any longer than a year.

"You may be pleased, Mr. Winston, but I know that Dex should be doing better. Too much time and money have been invested to see any one person interfere with our goals."

Ignoring her comment, Glen continued. "Perhaps all that you see is the pressure of Dex adjusting to my regimen, which demands more than most. If I may say so, Irene, I believe you are over-reacting."

Irene's next words clearly revealed what was most on her mind. "I notice that Ryan Campbell has a solid triple-axel. Why is Ryan still a junior with that jump? Dex was beginning to land a few before he arrived, but now it's not in his program. I believe that he'll do better in another less constrained, may I even say, less political environment."

Glen understood Irene's statement. Either he'd been too transparent or Irene was smarter than he realized. Both possibilities made him decidedly uneasy. It was true that he had undermined Dex's triple-axel. He had his reasons, but he was certainly not about to explain them to this obese cow of a mother. But, despite her challenge, he felt certain that he had managed to divert her attention away from replacing him as Dex's coach. Even as he made a mental note to ask his assistants to pay her more attention, he launched into a recital of the number of his students that had competed at nationals over the years, including those who had finished high enough to make a world team. Of these, five held Olympic titles and three could claim gold medals. The statistics were impressive because Glen had also trained more national champions than any coach in world history, and with good health, could continue coaching another thirty years.

Employing an excellent staff, Glen accepted only the best students and had a long list of families anxious to defer to his every wish in the belief that he could win their child acclaim, prestige, and riches. Glen was confident, warming to the subject of his many accomplishments when Irene stood abruptly, actually interrupting him in mid sentence. She had heard all this before.

"I've asked Dex to pack his things."

Glen opened his mouth to protest, but once again Irene interrupted. As far as she was concerned the conversation was ended. "Unfortunately, my judgment was clouded by your reputation, and I was unduly flattered by your interest in my son."

It had been Glen's record as a champion builder, combined with what she suspected of Ryan Campbell, that had convinced Irene that Glen would be the right coach for her son. Now she bitterly regretted that decision and especially the very valuable training time that was lost and could not be recovered.

"Is it Ryan Campbell? Are you actually pulling Dex because of Ryan?" Glen blurted out. Damn Ryan, he thought to himself. He would fix that brat if he had sabotaged his plans for Dex. "Because if you want us to start working on the triple-axel and put it back in Dex's long program, we can do that, although you must realize it's a little late for changes."

"I asked you to have Dex work on that jump and get it added as quickly as possible. You have not done so. Why is that, Mr. Winston?"

They both knew there was a threat implicit in that question. Usually the top competitors did not meet until the end of the season, when they took the ice at American Nationals. If Glen planned to replace Ryan with Dex when he actively sought to take on another high profile, male skater of the same skill level, then no one could fault him. Ryan was rumored to have a substance abuse problem, and Irene believed that he could self-destruct at any time, leaving the field open to her son. Although immensely talented Ryan, would not have the longevity in skating that would place him in direct competition with Dex in the important years to come for those precious few spots on the world team. When she allowed Glen to coach Dex, Irene assumed that he agreed. Now she knew better.

Irene had always admired Ryan's ability as her son's chief rival, believing him to have more raw talent than any other male skater, including, she had to admit, her own son. Given the tricky dynamics, Glen had made a point of keeping both boys away from one another, making certain that they rarely practiced on the same surface at the same time.

Glen had proposed keeping Dex a junior for two years while he moved Ryan up to the senior level of competition as soon as the season was over. It was clear that Glen expected and even hoped that Ryan would come in first at the next nationals. Irene had vigorously objected, and Glen, more accustomed to parents conceding to his every whim, appeared to agree. Now Irene had come to see that in not pushing the triple-axel and keeping it out of Dex's program on the pretext that it was not consistent enough, Glen was deliberately manipulating his two most promising skaters to serve his own ambition. And she had to admit that he nearly succeeded. If she had gone home as they advised.... Well, she didn't want to think about that.

By reining Dex in and not presenting him in the best possible light, Glen was insuring that the following year he could conceivably end up with the junior and senior national champions respectively. If accomplished, this would be a great coup. Carried out at Dex's expense, it would capitalize on what everyone feared would be a short skating life for Ryan, while enhancing Glen's sterling reputation as a champion builder.

"I've made up my mind, Mr. Winston, and Dex has agreed. If he liked or respected you at all...." Irene turned to go.

Glen could hardly believe she was actually leaving. "You'll have trouble finding another coach, you ungrateful cow! By interrupting Dex's training you've ruined his best chance of medalling at nationals. Think about it! He'll never finish in the top ten."

Forgetting his pride, Glen ran after Irene as she disappeared down the stairs that led to the lobby, not wanting to believe that he had lost a student of Dex's caliber. "No one will look at you the same way after they hear how difficult you are to work with," he yelled after her. "Count on it! You won't be viewed the same after today. I'll see to that!"

Irene heard this last as the heavy metal door that opened onto the lobby slammed behind her with a rush of cold air off the ice. Suddenly she felt a stab of intense pain radiate to her lower back and up to the base of her neck. She was standing in the lobby, and the expression on her face drew the curious gazes of the other mothers. Some had heard from their children about Dex's argument with Glen, and they had waited with great anticipation for the scene that would surely follow. One of the mothers guessed that Irene was suddenly in physical pain and rose to offer assistance, but Irene waved her aside.

For a short span of seconds she doubted herself. Against her doctor's advice Irene had delayed a course of chemotherapy so that she could see her son securely settled elsewhere. To switch coaches and alter costumes and choreography with the first qualifying competition little more than a month off was a slap in the face to those of skating's elite who had paved the way for Glen to coach Dex in the first place.

Despite the gloss of professionalism, Irene had felt uneasy from the first day that she entered The Winston Skating Center. She reminded herself that even if she could control how Glen related to her son, she could not control how he treated his other students. Glen had a way of confusing her. Except for today, he had always known the right words to say to calm her fears, but now Irene felt grateful that Glen had revealed himself so clearly.

As she headed in the direction of the ivy-covered dormitory building, where Dex was even now gratefully packing his possessions, Irene looked about her with fresh insight. For the first time in his career Dex had been offered nearly full financial sponsorship when he entered The Winston Skating Center. Located on the grounds of a former college, there was a dance studio, a state of the art weight and work out room, a full time masseuse and whirlpool, along with two full ice surfaces, insuring that those who practiced figures did not interfere with those doing freestyle.

Wealthy patrons had gravitated toward Glen, and his students enjoyed the best of everything. When sponsors visited, Glen made a point of parading them through the lobby and introducing them to parents as a subtle reminder of the control that was lost because of the financial help they'd accepted.

Irene had briefly met Howard Maple and the well known broadcaster Elliot Smythe, and like the other parents, she could not help noticing that they paid particular attention to Ryan, often taking him off the premises for dinner and giving him gifts, which tended to make the younger students jealous.

The best coaches were well known and worked out of select skating centers, across the country. There could be no delay in replacing Glen. Without consulting her son, Irene had already decided on Susan Eberly. All that remained was for them to make the confirming telephone call.

There was no doubt in Irene's mind that it was well within Glen's power to poison the minds of judges and officials against her son. All too often little internal accountability, gossip and the exchange of favors determined the outcome of a close competition. At times the problem was so pervasive and so well known that it was openly talked about by parents, only to be quickly ignored for fear that their child would pay a price. Susan Eberly could claim only one national champion, but she had a stable personal life and a solid reputation for honesty that Irene felt would counter some of Glen's slander.

Irene took comfort in knowing that Dex would be back in California, but still far enough away that she could conceal her illness, at least long enough to see him settled with what she hoped would be the last, best coach of his career. This time, when Dex left home, she would not accompany him. Irene knew that she was dying, but had determined that no one would use her illness to undermine her son's career for their own selfish purposes and especially not her husband Thierry, for in Irene's mind he was as much the enemy as Glen Winston ever was.

As she left the rink Irene was in no hurry to face her son. She lowered herself to the cool slab of a marble bench and lifted her face to the sun. A robin hopped about the ground and had only fluttered a short distance away at her approach. Two red squirrels raced up a tree trunk and jumped onto a smaller branch, causing it to sway. Soon the robin was back, nearly at her feet. He seemed to watch as she shook into her palm two yellow pills and swallowed them dry. Dex, she determined, would be protected from the truth of her illness for as long as possible, and his career would go on undeterred. She would see to that.

CHAPTER TWO

He opened his Bible and read: "The race is not to the swift or the battle to the strong, nor does food come to the wise or wealth to the brilliant or favor to the learned; but time and chance happen to them all" (Ecclesiastes 9: 11).

Despite Glen Winston's predictions of disaster, Dex Arujo came in first, winning the coveted gold medal as a junior competitor at American Nationals. This accomplishment was often cited among the many accolades of his career, but even before this first place win could be recorded in official record books, Dex knew something different about this event that would trouble him for the remainder of his life.

There was no more difficult or important competition than American Nationals. Just getting there was an accomplishment, and every decision a serious skater and coach made during the year built toward this one event.

After practicing on the same ice and sharing the same coach for nearly a year, Dex realized that most of what he had believed about Ryan Campbell was wrong. There was no boasting or posturing, no sabotaging of equipment, or secret measuring of tracings to see whose jump was higher. It seemed that Ryan almost wanted to be his friend but did not know how to proceed. After all the years of fiercely competing against one another for gold medals, they should have accepted the premise that so permeated competitive skating, that cooperation and getting to know one's chief rival undermined success. But Dex felt that he could detect in Ryan's practiced reserve a kind of sympathy that almost felt like pity, and an awkward silence hovered in the air between them whenever they met.

Both boys had heard the glib analysis many times. Ryan was the more artistic, purer athlete, while Dex worked harder and longer and had better stamina. If Dex came in first, it was luck; if Ryan won, it was skill. Going into American Nationals, it was the consensus of skating insiders that Ryan Campbell, coached by Glen Winston, would come in first. Given a clean program and Ryan's riveting presence, few expected any other scenario so that the event itself had lost some of its luster.

If both boys could manage the required elements, there would be little excitement. Those who knew skating, when they finally sat down to watch, were almost bored. Too many people owed Glen favors and disapproved of the way that Dex's mother had recklessly switched coaches. Glen's reputation and his contacts would carry the day and only a freak infusion of blind luck could win Dex anything more than third or fourth place.

Glen had been Ryan's only coach, while Dex had four during his long career. The first was discarded after only a few months when his mother caught the skating virus of obsession and began to view figure skating as something more than mere recreation. The second coach retired and the third was Glen Winston. Susan Eberly was to be Dex's last coach taking him on as a junior competitor, just before the same American Nationals that would forever shatter Dex's insular view of himself and others. He had just turned sixteen, had never attended a school dance, never been on a date, or had the dubious distinction of being challenged to a fight on a school playground. Rites of passage experienced by most young men of his time and his age had eluded him and real life, he imagined, would happen after the skating ended.

Glen's threat of ostracism had not materialized, but Dex's satisfaction in winning the gold medal had quickly soured. Only a fraction of a point had separated the first and second place ordinals when Ryan fell on what should have been a simple jump. If he had recovered quickly and moved on, he might still have come in first because the judges could easily have cited his superior artistic delivery. But he had hesitated, prolonging the agony of that fall into an eternity of suspense, all the more painful because it was so rare a reaction in such a predictable athlete. Ryan never reclaimed the earlier momentum of his program so that this mistake left an indelible impression in the minds of those who watched.

With the last event completed and his gold medal firmly in hand Dex was too elated to be tired. He had prepared all year for this one evening upon which so much hinged, and despite the set back of switching coaches he could not have wished for a better outcome. The top skaters had been held back for additional photographs and Dex was further delayed when a friend of Susan's, a prestigious official had some advice to offer about his future. When Dex finally got around to showering and changing out of his costume the locker room was deserted.

Dex pulled on corduroy trousers and felt the slap of the gold medal against his chest. Despite its weight he would leave it in place a little longer as he anticipated the satisfaction he would experience each time he looked at it, feeling a certain vindication for both his mother and his new coach. As he reached for his shirt the locker room door swung open and a loud metallic crash reverberated through the room.

27

"What was wrong out there? Are you on drugs again? Do that again and your career will be over. I'll kill you myself. Are we finally clear on that?"

Dex recognized the voice. He had witnessed Glen lose his temper many times, but never with such fury in his tone and never accompanied by physical violence. Suddenly he recalled the incident when Glen had repeatedly stabbed a finger into his chest and there had actually been a bruise. He hadn't wanted to back down then, and he didn't want to do so now. Dex knew it could only be Ryan that Glen addressed with such rage. Believing that they were alone, Glen had let slip the public face of unruffled ease, entirely different from the private face he showed his students.

"What were you thinking of? You just can't cut it, can you?" Glen ridiculed. "We both know you can land that jump sleepwalking, so why not now? That medal was in the bag, and all you had to do was skate clean!"

"Maybe I fell on purpose," Ryan taunted. "Maybe I did it to make you look like a fool after all your smug boasting about Arujo ruining his career because he fired the great almightily coach. You can't stand it that Dex skated well in spite of you. That's right, isn't it? You're jealous! I can see it in your face. And you know what? I'm sick and tired of your face."

Dex heard the unmistakable sound of a fist connecting with flesh and then a loud noise that could only be a body thrown against one of the lockers.

"You touch me again and I'll kill you," Ryan hissed back at Glen. "Do you hear me, you pervert. I'll kill you. Because unlike everyone else I know who you are. I know all about you!"

"Are you threatening me? Because if you are...."

"I'm not afraid of you. Not any more because I hate you. Only God knows how much I hate–" Ryan's words were abruptly cut short as Dex heard the sound of another blow and then a scuffle. He knew he had to intervene. Leaving his things behind, he exited the cubicle to find Glen gone and Ryan on his knees, bent over and holding his stomach as he gagged involuntarily in violent heaves.

Ryan seemed unaware that he was not alone, and feeling awkward, as though trespassing, Dex brought him a moistened towel. In response Ryan tore the towel from his grasp with unexpected fury and tried to stand. Dex reached out a hand to help, which Ryan pointedly ignored as he gingerly lowered himself to a bench.

"Are you all right?" he asked, clearly worried.

"What do you think?" Ryan rasped.

"Should I call someone? My mother and Susan are just outside," Dex offered, already starting for the door.

"No! Not unless you really want him to kill me?"

"You have to get another coach! Tell your parents!" Even as he said the words Dex realized that he had never seen Ryan's parents at any of the countless skating events they had competed in through the years. He wondered what it would be like to have two disinterested parents instead of one, and if that was truly the case, what kept Ryan skating?

"In your world that would be the thing to do, wouldn't it? You could actually tell good old mom and she would do something about it," Ryan said with biting sarcasm. "You're lucky, you know. Glen's a master manipulator. I've seen it over and over again. Another few weeks and Irene would have been silly putty in his hands no matter how you complained."

"You don't know my mother. If you'd seen her stand up to my father, you'd know that she could handle Glen."

"Yeah?" Ryan's tone was doubtful, but Dex thought he detected a note of jealousy at his escape from Glen. Dex leaned close to look at Ryan's eyelid. It was quickly swelling and would soon close without some attention. He went to his equipment bag and retrieved an ice pack. "You don't have to stay with him. Everyone says that some day you'll win a medal at the Olympics."

"Yeah, well they say that about you too, and they've said that about lots of skaters no one ever hears of again."

"I have to work a lot harder than you. Even I can see that," Dex said over his shoulder as he filled the bag with ice and tossed it to Ryan. Now it was his turn to feel a tinge of jealousy. "So why not leave? There are lots of coaches who would kill to have you."

"Not if they know what's good for them. Glen has a long reach, but I will get away!" Ryan vowed. "I have a plan."

"Did you really throw the competition?" Dex had to ask. As he waited for the answer, a heavy stillness settled over his chest. He almost found it difficult to breathe.

"Don't worry. You won by a slim margin, but a fair one. I like winning too much. I'm addicted to the spotlight, I live for the applause, and much to everyone's distress, I'm destined to be the next media darling. Isn't that what they say about me?"

As much as Dex did not want to doubt Ryan's words, he found that he did. Ryan could be as flamboyant and spontaneous, as he was composed and predictable. While he personified the ideal for a male figure skater, Ryan pushed constantly at the parameters, but always with an air of nonchalance that others found conversely charming or irritating. Ryan wore his hair well below the collar line until just before the first qualifying event of the year and was the first male skater to pierce his ear and then have the audacity to leave the gold hoop in place as he actually competed.

Ryan's trademark costumes tended to be severe, almost stark, and it was known that he and Glen fought long and hard over what he would wear. He refused music reminiscent of any of the old skating standbys, as well as movie sound tracks which required him to re-enact a dramatic role on the ice. When Ryan took the ice, he skated as himself, which never seemed to disappoint his audience.

Glen was reduced to bribing Ryan to gain his cooperation and was openly criticized for failing to control him as he did his other students. Appearing to make the best of a difficult situation, Glen coolly capitalized on Ryan's bad boy image, leaving many to conclude that he possessed immense patience to suffer repeated rebellion with such élan.

The older, more conservative judges and officials almost found themselves wishing that Ryan Campbell would fade from the scene because of their fear that once he reached the senior level of competition and received more media attention, he would tarnish the clean cut image of skating. Despite Glen's record of churning out a solid parade of superior skaters, there was not a judge on the panel who would not have been more comfortable with Dex receiving the gold medal. Glen had noted the tide of opinion turning against Ryan and thought that with Dex in his pocket he could work the images of both boys to his advantage. But first he had to separate them, and the best way to do that was to keep one a junior while the other moved up. But his plans had failed, and he was still reeling from the disappointment, an emotion that Glen never handled well.

Still, Ryan's superior athletic ability and engaging style could not be ignored. On the ice he was a riveting presence and had a mystifying following of loyal fans, particularly those young girls at the intermediate level who admired Ryan as others did rock stars. Dex would never generate that same raw, almost palatable excitement that Ryan exuded with seemingly limitless energy.

After what he had just overheard, Dex suspected that for one moment of sweet revenge Ryan might have made a calculated slip, giving up his first place standing to the skater his coach least wanted to win. Ryan had been the last skater to take the ice. Unlike other skaters who could not tolerate the stress of watching those who competed ahead of them, Ryan was always a careful observer, coolly listening to the scores of his competitors as they were announced. The knowledge that someone else had skated a flawless program had never seemed to affect his performance, as it had tonight with that one careless fall on what had always been his most consistent jump.

Just before he skated, Susan had reminded Dex to play it safe, concentrating on a clean program and omitting the unreliable triple-axel, since he and Ryan were the only junior competitors planning to attempt that jump. Dex realized that Susan was thinking of Ryan, who had not yet skated, but whom she hoped would make mistakes. Even now as Dex thought about it, he knew the judges could have given Ryan the higher artistic scores that would have secured first place despite his fall. When he saw the play backs, Dex suspected that he would see what he always saw. Ryan was superior to every other male skater, and this should have compensated for that one fall at the end of his combination because Dex too had made mistakes.

"I saw you go into that double at the end of your combination. It looked good but your body just wouldn't cooperate," Dex probed.

"Yeah, it's a muscle thing. Your brain says, 'perfect' and your body says, 'no.' Or is it a mind thing? Your mind says, 'yes' and your body says, 'screw you man.' Which comes first?" Ryan asked in a perfect imitation of Mr. Rogers that made Dex smile. "The chicken or the egg?"

"It's happened to me a lot," Dex offered.

"Yeah, but it didn't happen to you tonight, did it champ?"

Dex picked up Ryan's large silver medal, which had fallen to the floor during his altercation with Glen and lifted his own from around his neck. He compared the two, weighing each in one hand. "Which one belongs to you?" he asked, searching Ryan's expression for an answer.

Ryan's all black costume was ripped at the sleeve, and vomit splattered the elegant velvet vest. His longish bangs fell over his swelling eye, and blood splattered the knuckles of his left hand but there was an air of dignity and even pride in Ryan's manner which Dex could only admire.

"Well?" Dex prompted. A helpless expression washed over Ryan's face. Coldness resided there and even a hint of something like despair, until suddenly, as though humiliated at this tiny fissure in the plaster of his face, he looked away and Dex thought he had his answer.

"There's nothing wrong with second," Ryan offered, pulling his shirt off over his head with a grimace of pain.

"Yeah, right," Dex said. The two looked at one another knowingly, each understanding the harsher reality that no one in skating ever remembered second or third place very long.

"Why don't you join us for dinner? My mother and Susan wouldn't mind."

"I should. It would send that paranoid sleaze-bag screaming, but I can't. I've got a date. Why don't you come along? I'm sure she has a friend. No complications. That's what we need tonight."

Dex was embarrassed and suddenly grateful for the excuse of his mother and coach waiting outside. His parents were not religious and attended church services at the Catholic mission only on Holidays, but he had been drawn to the Bible from a young age and had adopted those principals for his life. He planned to be a virgin when he married and imagined his wife would be one as well. Only now that he was older and observed his peers did he realize how idealized his views would seem to others. There was no one, it seemed, who had similar values, including his father who had been repeatedly unfaithful to his mother, which made Dex want to lead a different kind of life. But Dex had learned not to care that he was different, and that willingness to stand apart contributed to the decision he now made. With Ryan's head averted, he dropped the gold medal in the pocket of Ryan's skating bag.

"Will you be all right?" he asked, hesitating at the door.

"Yeah, thanks. By the way, if you see a blonde in a white jag outside tell her I'm running late. And don't say anything about tonight. It will only make things worse."

"I don't know."

Ryan was instantly alarmed at Dex's hesitancy. "Don't worry," he said. "If Glen stays true to form, he'll be kissing my feet for the next few weeks and anyway, I don't plan on being with him much longer. If you say something now before I have everything set, I'll never get away," he added, his tone almost pleading.

The two boys regarded one another until Dex nodded in agreement. "What will you do?"

"If I want to keep skating, it has to be in an area Glen can't influence as much. I thought of pairs."

Dex was stunned. He couldn't imagine not having Ryan to compete against, and to have him switch to pairs at this late date seemed a terrible waste of talent. Although more dangerous than any other area of competition, the highest skill level in jumping required for pairs was one side-by-side triple jump, and Dex knew that in practice Ryan could already do a quad, as yet unheard of in men's skating. Although he knew some part of him should be glad to see his chief rival no longer a threat to him making a future world team, Dex suddenly felt furious. Furious that Glen Winston could get away with such egocentric cruelty while every one else in skating looked the other way. Dex understood very well that no one would bother much with Ryan after he went against the grain of all the subtle manipulation by the skating establishment. Some would do all they could to be sure he never bounced back.

"So we're agreed, "Ryan said stopping Dex at the door. "You won't say anything?"

Dex nodded, even as the knowledge that he was somehow taking the cowardly path prodded him to a better course of action. Suddenly he was certain that he had a gold medal that he didn't deserve. He had the status and the goodwill of the skating establishment that rightfully belonged to another, but worse still he was leaving Ryan to battle Glen by himself. Dex knew what was at stake. Glen had already lost one carefully groomed contender who could compete for a spot on the world team, and now he couldn't be expected to give up Ryan without a bitter fight. Ryan's loss would leave him without a student ready to compete at the senior level and might remove him from the limelight, which fueled his ambition and filled a hungry craving.

Skating talent of Ryan's caliber did not arrive on the scene prepackaged and ready to skate. It took years and luck and the right family dynamics, and especially a boy who couldn't be persuaded to substitute football or basketball in order to cement a masculine image in question to peers who did not understand the sport. No, Glen would not give up Ryan without a fight and especially not after he'd already lost his replacement.

Dex no longer looked forward to having dinner with his jubilant coach and his mother. There would be no explaining the absence of the medal that they would both want to see and gloat over. Instead he wished he could have spent more time with Ryan, wished he was privy to the details of his plan to leave Glen, and that in some way he could help. Suddenly Dex didn't care about the medal. Ryan and Glen had threatened to kill one another, but that was only talk. Dex was filled with a sense of dread for Ryan, which he felt was exaggerated, but on some level completely reasonable.

Before he walked away he could see that Ryan's facade of haughty amusement was firmly back in place. It made him feel sad and a little unsettled.

"Good luck," he said.

"Yeah, good luck, Arujo."

CHAPTER THREE

Sometimes he felt he was the only one who believed she was still alive. It was a lonely burden that drew him to pray. "Lord Jesus, make me as full of your love as a redeemed sinner can be, let me pray according to your will".

Dex leaned against the frame of the bathroom door and watched his mother remove the eye makeup one could barely detect, with a generous scoop of cold cream. She looked tired and was preparing for bed earlier than usual, which meant that he would be free to look for Ryan, who he already knew had not yet checked out of the hotel.

So far Irene had not asked to see his gold medal, but Dex knew that when they returned home she would expect to include it among the collection she kept in a glass case situated conspicuously at the center of his father's home-office and library. Over the years the case had been expanded, but Dex no longer viewed the location of his mother's shrine to his skating career as benign.

"I've been thinking about Glen," he began.

Irene's wide eyes shifted in the mirror as she regarded her son expectantly. This was his cue to continue, but Dex was still attempting to frame his words with just the right tinge of indifference. If either too aloof, or too transparent she would know that he had something to hide.

He had done a lot of thinking since the incident with Ryan the night before. He recalled that Glen's behavior toward his students often fluctuated between fawning attentiveness and biting rejection. There was no middle ground, and the younger students especially waited anxiously at the start of each day until his mood could be assessed. If they happened to be one of his favorites, they enjoyed a brief respite but fully aware that when they least expected it that cherished approval might be withdrawn. Glen's message was clear. "If you complain to your parents, there will be a price to pay."

"They say that Glen is the best coach around, but we fired him. I know we're not supposed to use that word, but I can't think of any other, so why did we?"

Irene shrugged her massive shoulders under the pink satin robe, nearly identical to all the others she had worn over the years. "Tell me," Dex urged.

Irene's failure to articulate beyond short clipped sentences was a source of frustration, and while he hated to hold any opinion in common with his father, he knew that in this they did agree. Dex knew that his mother could express herself quite well when she wanted to, and it was this element of choice that most irritated him. Now she took an audible breath as though talking depleted secret energy reserves, and he guessed correctly that she was about to indulge him with a particularly long declaration, the words strategically arranged to stifle further conversation.

"I sat in that lobby barred from practices and both of us prevented from making decisions, and I listened to the other mothers. After they finished assuring themselves that Glen was wonderful and their child lucky to have him for a coach, they gossiped about his former students. Marie was anorexic, you know," she said, not pausing for him to answer. "And also that sweet girl from Milwaukee who died last year. Two have been in and out of drug rehab centers more often than you've celebrated Christmas, and another tried to commit suicide when she couldn't skate anymore. Those who have married fall prey to quick divorces. I know gossip is a problem in this sport, but I did not hear of one former student who went on to have a happy and productive life. I decided we could accomplish our goals without you paying that price, and if we couldn't, well, I guess we'd find something else for you to do."

She turned to scrutinize his face, but Dex looked away. When he was younger, he was convinced that she could read his mind and he would devise ways to test that ability.

"Why is this on your mind, Son? You wanted to leave Glen long before I recognized the depth of the problem."

Dex hesitated. "If someone we knew needed a safe place to live for a while, could they stay with us?"

Having a mother who talked very little had taught him to read her almost as well as she did him. She gave him a look of inquiry over the steaming edge of the thin hotel washcloth, knowing that she had focused on his use of the word 'safe'.

"I can't discuss it right now. I promised not to," Dex said, fending her off.

She gave him an icy stare and plunged the same washcloth into equally frigid water before laying it like plaster over her face. He had watched this nighttime ritual many times.

"Well, yes," she said, the sound of her voice muffled by the dripping wet square over her mouth. "You could offer that person our help but," she said, letting the washcloth drop, "if this is Ryan Campbell we're discussing, we might have to find him help elsewhere. Assuming only half the gossip about that boy is true, then he has more problems than you and I are equipped to handle. I also think a close association would tarnish your image, and you know what people say?"

"Maybe you're wrong about Ryan. Maybe everyone is."

Irene didn't care if she was right or wrong. She knew that she had just attended her last competition and felt a deep, pervasive weariness, far more debilitating than the pain. Just getting ready for bed required a supreme effort, and she wanted nothing more than to sleep.

"I know you're disappointed in my answer, Son, but I can't help that right now. If we opened our home to Ryan, it would look like we had some agenda. Right now is just not a good time for any more negative attention."

"You're thinking about skating. You can't think about anything else. Well, people are more important than winning all the time."

Irene didn't answer. She simply could not afford a friendship to develop between her son and Ryan. She feared that Ryan's freedom and lack of restraint might begin to seem attractive to a boy as protected as Dex. Whatever Ryan had learned about life had come too fast and too early, and now he was growing up at the expense of those adults who had failed him from the beginning. It didn't take a genius to see that much, but Irene would share none of this with the son she loved. Even that could seem like an invitation, and she couldn't afford to start a conflict that she would not have the stamina to see reconciled.

Dex had expected something more from her. He had expected compassion and a willingness to reach out. She turned, knowing that she had not said enough, but Dex had already left, and it struck her that he had forgotten to kiss her good night. She could not recall a time when he had failed to kiss her goodnight.

Dex had rung Ryan's room and left a message, but he hadn't responded. The next day, as he and his mother checked out of the hotel and Dex organized their luggage, Ryan breezed into the lobby, laughing raucously and flanked by two female skaters. Ryan lifted his chin in greeting, and as he smiled it struck Dex that only the black eye and the angry swelling of one check suggested anything amiss.

"I have something that belongs to you," Ryan whispered as he pulled Dex aside to speak privately.

"Keep it. There'll be other nationals, and maybe next time I'll get the medal I deserve."

"You don't understand," Ryan whispered. "I don't want it."

"Then throw it away because I don't want it either." Dex had found it increasingly more difficult to conceal the flood of guilt he felt each time he was congratulated for winning.

Ryan nodded and once more Dex glimpsed that haunted, almost desperate expression, which swept Ryan's features in a wash of sadness. "I don't know how you plan on getting away from Glen, but I spoke to my mother and.... No," he rushed to assure Ryan when he saw a flash of abject panic. "I didn't tell her anything. But she did say you could come to stay with us at the vineyard for a while," Dex lied.

Ryan grinned, and Dex understood how that smile could disarm the worst of suspicions. It was radiant and wide, showing perfect teeth, and would sell anything. No wonder he had already been approached to do several television commercials.

"Does it hurt?" Dex asked. He'd never had a black eye. Only the day before he might have secretly envied Ryan for all the tantalizing mystery that his injuries implied.

Ryan touched his cheek, as though just reminded. "I guess people are talking?"

At breakfast Dex had overheard those at the next table say with certain authority that Ryan had been in a drunken brawl the night before over his disappointment at finishing second instead of the much lauded and expected first. There was no one to defend Ryan, and Dex had felt a frustrated inadequacy over his promise of silence.

"I haven't heard anything," he now lied.

"Well, you can be sure the gossip mongers, or should I say the gossip mothers, are at work." He looked about in a parody of furtive paranoia. "I guess the legend grows whether I want it to or not," he said as the two girls, impatient to be off, interrupted them. "See," Ryan said in parting. "All you need to attract girls is a bad rep and a black eye. Believe me, Dex, it's a magnet." The two boys smiled at one another, sharing what for Dex was a rare moment of alliance with another boy his age.

Dex Arujo could well remember when he had hated skating. Caught between two equally strong personalities, with differing ambitions for their only child, his participation in this expensive sport became the single most damaging source of friction between his parents.

He was seven when his mother got him started after his father demanded Dex be involved in some sort of organized activity as a means of toughening up their undersized child. Irene announced that Dex would skate, and Thierry approved. Skating for a boy could only mean ice hockey, and although Thierry didn't actually make the time to follow sports, he approved. Ice hockey was clearly a masculine endeavor bound to reinforce manly attributes.

Thierry was an expansive man who did nothing with restraint, but he was far too busy with the vineyard and other farming duties to attend practice. He failed to notice the absence of hockey equipment and did not scrutinize the bills his wife presented for payment. Not until eight months later, when Dex was measured for his first costume, did Thierry discover there was another altogether different dimension to skating.

The last thing Dex wanted was for his father to see that first costume, for unlike his mother, he suspected the scope of his father's ignorance. But Irene had insisted, and so like a lamb before the slaughter, he was paraded out in the mock military uniform, a light blue polyester blend with sequined epaulets at the shoulder and gold fringe that swayed with the slightest movement. As if that were not enough, Irene had insisted on matching sequins at each cuff and down the outside seams of his trousers. Thierry's reaction of stunned disbelief, followed by booming protest, in no way fell short of the expected tirade.

Thierry attended that first competition with the express purpose of telling his wife, "I told you so!" After that he never came to another. There were five boys in all, a small group compared to the girls, at a one-surface rink in Orange. As Dex stood in line waiting to compete, he did not care if he won or lost. The other boys all skated better. They had been landing their axel longer and even started on double jumps, while he had just mastered the single-axel in time for this first event. Dex observed how nervous the other parents were. They smoothed back hair, fussed over costumes, and whispered last minute instructions that overrode the coaches.

"Don't be nervous," the parent would whisper. "Make the nervousness work for you," the coach would say. "Leave out that new-double toe," the parent would advise, thinking of the relative they had brought along to watch, who would not comprehend the level of difficulty between jumps. "It doesn't matter if you fall. You'll get points just for trying it," the coach would counter, knowing that the judges would realize their student was landing that jump in practice or it would not be in the program.

Over the years the details of other competitions would blur in monotonous continuity, but he would always remember that first skate in Orange. This was a daunting experience, one destined to repeat itself time and again. Dex left the parameter of the ice and glided to his starting spot in the middle of the arena. A subdued hush fell over the crowd. Fraught with terror, Dex waited for the opening cords of his music. That first note signaled the grateful release of his muscles so that the skating itself had a quality of fleeing that terror and defeating it in the over-rehearsed, mindless explosion of his program. Commentators would often remark that he skated with boundless energy.

Even then Dex was a handsome boy who had inherited the best from both parents. His straight thin body, so unlike theirs, suggested a burgeoning masculine athleticism. With his father's nearly black hair and his mother's heavily lashed blue eyes and dressed as he was, the young Dex resembled a miniature version of the Prince Charming depicted in children's fables.

The sound of his blades as they skimmed the surface of the ice came to him with exaggerated clarity, and an automated sense of unreality took over. He welcomed the sharpness of the cold, which cooled the hot flush of his face, as he propelled his small frame from one end of that long surface to the other, barely a synapse behind the running image in his mind.

There was no doubt that Dex had the crowd's full attention, and the energy he absorbed from that approval was an adrenaline rush, greedily savored. As he improvised, substituting a jump here, adding a jump there he told himself that only his mother and coach would know that he was not skating the program he had practiced over the last few months. If he skated badly they would return home, and his father would yell at his mother in a tone reserved for the hard of hearing and yet entirely normal for Thierry. "Now that you've humiliated this family are you willing to admit what a mistake this has been?" And as his father raved on, Dex would retreat as he always did by wandering off unnoticed until that booming voice, which precluded any meaningful discussion, could no longer jar his nerves like spatters of burning grease from a frying pan.

As he skated on that day in Orange, Dex only knew that whatever the outcome he did not want his mother to lose the battle she was really waging with his father. He knew that he was a pawn in a conflict he could not name, and suddenly, in the complicated web of a child's reasoning, a fall seemed the ultimate humiliation. Dex skated not for his father, who wanted him to fail, or for his mother who hoped to be proved right, nor for the onlookers oddly riveted to his performance. Instead there was firmly planted in his mind the unique notion that the ice was something for himself, an island whose happenings he could control beyond the reach of that angst that dug a wedge between his parents and a pit of loneliness for himself.

Dex came in first, not because he was better, but because the ice had become an emotional refuge. A talent for judging choreography, even before he understood the meaning of the word, and the discipline to leave anxiety at the guardrail, were great assets that would see him through many more competitions often in a field of far more accomplished skaters.

Feeling an odd mix of doom and triumph, he stood on the shabby podium behind the hockey lockers that smelled of sweaty socks and disinfectant. He stood taller than the other boys, a step down on the second and third place pedestals to receive his medal, and it occurred to him that he should have fallen at least once. That second axel was overkill. He needed it to win, but he had fully expected to lose. The other boys hung their medals around their necks and paraded through the crowded lobby, but Dex slipped his in his pocket, for the look on his mother's face of almost greedy pleasure as she smiled from behind her camera was totally arresting. Never before had she looked at him quite like this, with an adulation that made him feel more an object than her child.

A week later he had a new coach who charged twice what the former did for lessons. The used skates were traded in for two sets of custom boots and blades, one for freestyle and the other for figures. The exotic appearance of winter clothing began to arrive from New England catalog companies. There were crash pads and tights to wear under his skating pants and insulated jackets in several colors and styles. It was an out-of-season Christmas, although he received nothing he actually wanted and yet was expected to feel enormous gratitude.

Thierry Arujo complained about the expense. "Five thousand dollars in one month," he thundered, waving a fist full of bills in Irene's face, but soon Dex was too tired by day's end to pay much attention, and the sound of his parents arguing faded to a dull, incessant hum. Banished forever were the three hours a week of ice time which had launched his skating career. Now he was up at five each morning and on the ice for fifty minutes of school figures, referred to as 'patch.' Then after a quick change into his freestyle boots that left painful sores on his feet until they were properly broken in, he was back on the ice for another two sessions of freestyle followed by others into the evening.

With few exceptions this schedule was repeated six days a week for the remainder of his amateur career. His mother's scrutiny became a burden as she monitored any competing interest that might distract Dex from skating. Each night he fell into bed utterly exhausted. With a great sigh he would push his face against his mother's white sheets, sun-dried on her circular clothesline. They smelled to him of grapes in season, and newly mowed grass, and the lavender toilet water that the help sprayed the pressed linens with. The combined scent hinted of lost, leisurely afternoons playing catch until dinnertime, until soon the ease of those cherished freedoms became no more than a distant memory.

Before she died Irene had seen her son win two national titles, while Thierry had remained intentionally oblivious to these accomplishments. When Dex qualified for the world team and was to compete at the Olympics, it dawned on Thierry that his son had accomplished something beyond his reach, and his first urgent thoughts were for the winery. People he barely knew from town began to stop him on the street to ask about Dex, and even more disconcerting, complete strangers began to offer advice. *As though,* Thierry inwardly raged, *ice skating could actually be a career.*

For the first time Thierry realized that his plans for Dex might be permanently jeopardized. When Dex returned from Europe, where he had been assigned a competition representing the United States, Thierry was primed for confrontation. Dex parted from his coach at the airport and joined Joey Santos in the red Jeep with the farm's name and logo emblazoned on the door for the ride home.

Jose Santos, called Joey by Dex's father, was a good friend, and the two had known one another since they were boys. Unlike his parents Joey was an American citizen. His mother had gone into labor during picking season, and she had been rushed by Thierry to give birth at the charity clinic near the mission. Cut off from other children because of his training schedule and frequent trips away from home, Dex had counted on Joey for the occasional game of catch or trip into town for ice cream and a movie. Both boys loved to fish, and it was a rare luxury for Dex to pack a lunch with squirming bait in the bottom of his tackle box and disappear with Joey for a day of fishing on the nearby Gallant River.

Joey's parents had been migrant workers who came to the vineyard each harvest. One year after the grapes were safely fermenting in their huge vats, Joey's father had mysteriously moved on, leaving his wife and son behind, and Joey had taken to trailing after Thierry, making a general nuisance of himself. Accustomed to taking charge and compulsively shaping objects and people alike to fit his own private vision, Thierry soon had Joey attending school and joining them at meals, becoming a new fixture that Irene tolerated but never quite accepted.

"I hear the old man gave you a promotion," Dex said to Joey once his luggage was stowed and they were settled in the car.

"Yeah, man, he gave me the promotion he wanted to give you. He told me it was only temporary." Joey laughed and gave Dex a sidelong glance under thick eyelashes.

He was almost as tall as Thierry with glossy straight hair that he wore in a ponytail, tied with various pieces of tooled leather. Tourists often stopped to talk with him, and soon he was offering advice on the best wines for them to purchase and send home in cases. Noticing his natural sales ability, Thierry moved Joey into the store, where sales soon tripled. Then he began sending Joey to various wholesale markets, expanding the gift shop and increasing their drop-in trade. At Joey's suggestion a string quartet from the local college came in each week, and they sponsored an afternoon of wine tasting and a tour of the old chapel, which predated the house. Try as he did, Thierry could not convince Joey to cut his hair, and, although he disapproved, Dex knew that his father would accept such behavior from a man he sweated and worked beside that he would openly berate in his own son. It was obvious to Dex that the two seemed to share an easiness and tolerance of one another that would never be his in any comparable measure.

"As far as I'm concerned the job's yours forever," Dex said, surprised at the note of bitterness that had crept into his tone.

Joey gave him a sidelong glance. "You okay?" he asked.

"Yes. It's not your fault, but I sometimes think he likes you more than me."

"Likes, not loves. That's the operative word, Dex, because there is a world of difference. He just doesn't understand what you're about. He can't relate."

"Doesn't understand or doesn't choose to understand?" Dex countered. "Because there's a world of difference there too, and I think we both know the answer."

"Yeah, well, don't get into it with him this trip. I've been a little worried about the old man," Joey said with obvious affection. "He can't do everything himself anymore, and he hates it. You know his energy level. Can go forever, but lately he's been getting tired out quickly. He brought my mother in to be his housekeeper and even she's noticed it."

Before she died Irene had always had help with the large sprawling house, but never live-in help. Dex knew the two were probably lovers and perhaps had been even before his mother's death. There was even talk that Joey was his half brother. Dex didn't think so, and although both boys knew that Joey's parentage was a topic of gossip, they never discussed it. Although it did his mother no good, and she was now beyond caring, Dex experienced a sudden stab of jealousy on her behalf.

Even before Dex walked across the worn and scarred threshold of the large Spanish style mansion of stone and adobe with the red tile roof and the weathered companario of burned brick, he experienced his usual sense of foreboding, only this time a little stronger. Joey's mother took his suitcase and reached up on tiptoe to kiss his cheek. "Your father's in the library," she said ominously. "Don't fight with him tonight, Dex. Just agree with him if you can."

Dex felt a flash of defensiveness at her words. Why did his father believe he could wear him down with his constant demands? Never one to concede defeat, he seemed to think that skating was the last bastion worth fighting for, a last obstacle to the son emerging from the father's mold. With Irene gone Thierry refused to understand that his son's life was not his to manage. Dex gave in when he could, each time more and more ashamed at his own cowardice. Fighting with a man who saw no agenda but his own proved an emotionally draining experience, and Dex had begun to feel that no relationship was preferable to continuing under the immense weight of his father's limitless disapproval.

Like a condemned man walking the last few yards into the gas chamber, Dex counted the hollow rhythm of his steps over the polished wood floors and wished he could be any other place in the world. He thought of his upcoming itinerary. There was an exhibition to do at Lake Tahoe, and then in a month he was off to Oslo before the American season began. Perhaps he could use that as an excuse to cut the planned two-week stay at home to a few days.

The library was a combination study and office with ceiling to wall bookcases encased in glass. It had always been his father's retreat, the place he did his planning and ordering for the farm. Irene had been laid to rest in a small family churchyard just down the private lane that ran across the valley.

Thierry stood as Dex entered the room. He had a full head of white hair, complimenting the rough-hewn features of a distinguished face. Perhaps because of Joey's warning, Dex thought he could detect an odd pallor beneath the tan, and despite the athletic build and overall impression of health, a disturbing hint of frailty.

"How'd you do?" Thierry asked in a gruff approximation of a greeting as he seated himself across from his son.

"Fine," Dex said, understanding that Thierry did not want to know the details of his second place finish. Details that his mother would have been avid to hear. Dex felt a grip of anxiety. He could see in the set of Thierry's face that chomping-at-the-bit gleam of avarice that lit the strange pallor of his face and was always a precursor to unavoidable conflict.

"I'm not going to beat around the bush, Son."

"No, I don't imagine that's possible."

"Don't be flip with me, boy. This is important."

Dex understood that his father had already rehearsed what he would say, and it was now his job to agree regardless of how he felt or what he thought. Joey and his mother had both advised him to tread lightly. Well, this time he might not accommodate.

"You know this skating business cannot be a career. If you continue, the best you can hope for is touring in some fairy skating show, and you know what people will say about you then."

"I know what you would say. Not everyone shares your view." Dex felt that familiar grip of tension constrict his stomach muscles. His father had called him a boy, but he wasn't a boy any longer.

"Well then. I've had Joey doing your job until you got back, but now you can call that coach of yours, what's her name?"

"Susan Eberly. You know her name, Dad."

"OK, that's right. Call Susan and tell her to cancel anything she has you down for."

There was a haunting ring to his father's words. Almost against his will Dex remembered a recurring childhood fantasy, in which his father rescued him from the grueling monotony of long, sometimes painful practices. "Enough, Irene," he would thunder to the unfailing hope of a boy's imagination. "Dex is my child too, and I say no more skating." In this fanciful revelry his suddenly docile mother would look at her husband in loving submission and agree and the skating would end. He had been disappointed in his father then, and now oddly, he was even more disappointed. Thierry had never rescued him, and yet, that perpetual disapproval had pervaded their lives and sapped the joy from each accomplishment.

The pressure to stop skating had been building almost since the day of his mother's funeral. Dex had rarely been openly defiant of his father, but as he looked into that stubborn face, an overwhelming rush of resentment washed over him. Even now, after all the trophies and accolades, Thierry would not appreciate the accomplishments, the very great ambivalence, the discipline, or finally the determination to rise above it all. As he glanced about the room Dex realized that the trophy case his mother had been so proud of was missing. Where had his father removed it to? Its absence unveiled the truth of his father's disdain, which Dex could no longer excuse.

As Thierry spoke of his responsibility to the Arujo legacy and his new role as the-heir apparent, as though the vineyard were a small country, Dex wondered how he had evolved from hating his craft to loving it. There was not one particular incident that he could recall and hold up as the crisis point of change, and yet a love of skating had seeped into his blood and burrowed a place in his heart, quietly tilting a subtle balance from one extreme to the other. Now he was symbiotically tied to the sport and there was no going back. Dex looked into his father's determined face and saw his features relax in smug victory. He had taken his son's silence for agreement.

"Now whatever it is you have coming up next. What is it? Some exhibition somewhere? Cancel it!"

Dex stood and placed two shaking hands on the desk, which filled the space between them. "Dad," he began tentatively.

"You need to get that so-called coach of yours, what's her name? Susan, is it? Get her on the horn and tell her to cancel everything else too. There'll be no more trips to Europe for you for a while."

"Dad," Dex spoke a little louder.

"And while she's at it tell her to call that damn skating association and tell them you're out. You hear? You're out," he shouted with undisguised glee.

"DAD," Dex nearly screamed. "Will you PLEASE listen to me? I'm not going to stop skating. I'm training for the next Olympics. That's eighteen months away and I could come home with a gold medal. Don't you understand what that means?"

"Your life is here. Now I've got Joey doing your job, but he'll step aside." Thierry picked up the phone and held it out to Dex. "You are no longer a child. It's time to grow up and have a real life. Here," he jabbed the phone toward Dex's face. "Call that damn coach of yours and cancel."

"Cancel what? Cancel my life? The only life I have? If you force me to make a choice between you and skating or the vineyard and skating, you'll be making a huge mistake. It's not that I don't appreciate all you're trying to do. And maybe later–"

"I don't understand you. Your grandfather nearly lost this place during the great depression, and my father and I built it back up for you. This farm is your heritage. You'll have a son and it will be his. If you can't feel it now you soon will. You are the only son I have."

Dex looked into his father's face. "That's not what I hear," he said, immediately regretting the words.

"What did you say?"

"I hear that Joey is your son. And he loves this place."

"Gossip! Tell me who has said such a thing and I'll kill them."

"I want you to see how hard you are to talk with. I point out something that you don't choose to admit, and rage is your only response. Well, sometimes you just can't rewrite history."

"Your mother would roll over in her grave."

"My mother believed it was true, and now you have that woman living under her roof every night."

"You'll believe gossip and not your own father. Get out!" Thierry's face was contorted in an ugly parody of rage. It was all he could do to restrain himself.

45

"You don't mean that, Dad. Just for once let's have a rational conversation. One where I speak and you actually listen."

"You get out of here, until you're ready to accept real responsibility. See how you get along without a monthly allowance and someone to subsidize this very expensive hobby of yours. Your life is here."

Thierry pounded the desk and sent a crystal paperweight flying with the sweep of his hand. The jagged edge came so close to Dex's shoulder that he felt it whiz by.

"Do you think you're better than your ancestors who struggled to make a living picking someone else's grapes in Portugal? But you dishonor their memory."

Dex knew from experience that to argue with his father was to lose. He turned his back and walked slowly toward the door, unable to deny a liberating sense of release. He wouldn't give Thierry the satisfaction of seeing him cry because his father hated such weakness, and yet there was something profoundly sad and even wrenching about leaving the only home he had ever known.

Thierry had never forgiven Irene for sacrificing their only son to her obsession, and now it seemed he could not forgive Dex for preferring it. His father was already near the end when Joey called to tell him. With Joey pacing outside, Dex sat in that whitewashed hospital room and held the large beefy hand, scarred and wrinkled from years of hard physical labor and recalled how as a young child he had loved the feel of that hand cuffing his cheek, ruffling his hair.

They had never said, "I love you," to one another, and yet even as he watched, Dex could not quite grasp that this seemingly invincible man could leave the world forever. In the sterile arena of the hospital Joey was fearful and awkward, already grieving for the surrogate father who had given him so much. Joey was decidedly uncomfortable lingering in the room and yet refused to leave the corridor, while Dex was happy to hold a grieving son's vigil by the bedside, even helping the nurses change the linens and bath his father. Secretly he hoped his actions would somehow alleviate any residue of guilt in the years ahead for that last argument and ensuing estrangement.

At the end Dex leaned his elbows on the narrow bed and held his father's hand to his cheek. Silence seemed to encase the small huddle of their bodies, as choked by expectation, a final opportunity slipped beyond reach without the healing balm of what each knew should be said. That call to apologize, those words of reconciliation, overtures well within their power to make and often on their minds, would never come. In stunned disbelief Dex felt his father's hand relax in his. He watched the stillness of Thierry's chest as life emptied from his face, and for some time he sat paralyzed in the grip of that mysterious absence. He knew that he should wake Joey, who was sleeping in a recliner in the corner of the room. He should ring for the nurse and think about arrangements, but his only thought was to postpone any intrusion that would spoil this last goodbye, hollow in its finality, a goodbye that was no goodbye at all.

Dex expected to feel a similar loss that could ambush him, even now when he thought of his mother, but only a numb parody could be dredged up from that place where dormant emotion hibernates and waits. Like a visitor intruding where he least belonged, Dex organized the funeral and played the role of grieving son. In those weeks he often thought to pray, but pushed from his mind that subtle, gentle call to talk with a loving God. He felt guilty for the love he could not feel and for the joyful surge of relief over his father's absence that he could not deny. In a daze of self-hatred he moved through the formality of what was expected of him, convinced that the final failure of a last parting was his entirely to bear. Friends and family only thought him brave.

CHAPTER FOUR

Today he prayed for those who might someday intercept her life.

Fresh from his father's funeral and pointedly ignoring any and all references to grief and sympathy, Dex met the only girl he would ever love, at a skating competition in Sweden. This was to be his last amateur season. He was nineteen and destined to win the coveted gold medal at the Olympics, and Anya Szcepanik was thirteen and had just emerged on the international scene.

Like everyone else, he was stunned at the triple jumps she executed in practice, which at that time were unheard of for a young woman, let alone a child just entering adolescence. She looked younger than her years, and for the first time the western press took notice and began to predict a great career.

In spite of this Anya did not skate well. The triple jumps, executed flawlessly in practice, did not materialize in actual competition, and her standings plummeted well below the first twenty contestants. Dex sat in the stands and watched her compete, embarrassed for her, and like all skaters, cringing at the humiliation that could so easily have been his.

With the ladies' event over, Dex had pulled the last practice of the evening, which was sparsely attended. Most of the judges, who attended practice in order to become familiar with the skaters and promote their country's hopes for a medal, had wisely stayed in their hotel rooms. A large storm was predicted, and already snow blanketed the narrow streets where the complex was situated. Dex had arranged to meet friends in the hotel bar as soon as he was finished, and to save time he came prepared to shower and change into blue jeans and a flannel shirt at the rink. Overall he wore a bottle green, Hard Rock Café, Amsterdam jacket that Ryan had brought him the night before, and it was Ryan he thought of as he took a wrong turn exiting the American locker area.

Although the truth was carefully guarded, Dex knew that rumors of Ryan fighting a drug habit were true. American hopes for a medal had been pinned on Ryan and his partner to unseat the eastern Europeans, and especially the Russians at the upcoming Olympics. Ryan's coach had sent him to a private clinic for a fast and secret cure before the trip to Sweden, but it proved difficult to hide a figure skater of Ryan's reputation. Rumors abounded, although no one pressed for the kind of confirmation that would dash all hopes for a medal.

Following an argument with his partner and her parents, Ryan had stormed off to Amsterdam, where drugs were freely bought and sold. Behind the scenes a frantic search was launched to bring him back. The team doctor stood by, ready to conduct a discreet and unofficial drug screen. If America's most celebrated pair team needed to withdraw from competition, then whatever illness was currently making the rounds would be cited as the reason and all rumors to the contrary glibly denied.

"Hey Dex," Ryan had called with his usual polished élan. "This is all I had time for; one for you and one for me. Which color do you want, blue or green?" he said tossing the jackets on the bed. It was three thirty in the morning, and Dex fought his way awake to see the association president, Elizabeth Cannon, enter their hotel room, followed by Ryan's coach, his partner's father, and the team physician in tow. No one looked happy.

"I know we can count on you not to say anything about this," Elizabeth said to Dex. She looked grim-faced, and Dex realized she was convinced that Ryan would have to be withdrawn from competition, a humiliation to them all.

"Damn partner," Ryan drawled in a mock Texas accent. "These marshals work too fast for me." Dex smiled as he recalled Ryan rolling up his sleeve for blood to be drawn and then being dispatched to the bathroom for a urine sample, nonchalant, as though he did this as often as he brushed his teeth. "And no privacy either," he lamented and turned to flash the huddle in the doorway.

Ryan's parents, both celebrity attorneys, lived in Los Angeles and Dex worried about the holiday break that was coming up. If Ryan returned home after the competition, the temptation to resume old friendships and party with the spoiled and indulged young people he associated with when not in training might prove irresistible. Dex had just decided to invite Ryan to the vineyard for a few weeks when he realized that in his haste to get back to the hotel, he had made a wrong turn.

An additional surface for the competition had been erected and a complicated labyrinth of tunnels was constructed to accommodate travel back and forth between the newer and older facilities. Open grillwork loomed overhead and nothing looked familiar. Dex was about to turn back when he heard the unmistakable sound of a cry, which seemed to emanate from above.

"Who's up there?" he called. As he spoke the lights snapped off, replaced by a dim glow from the auxiliary system.

"It's me," a small voice, still choking back tears, sounded from above. The accent sounded almost American, but Dex could not remember that any of the coaches had brought along a child, and none of the skaters sounded quite this young.

"What are you doing up there?" Dex struggled to keep his voice clear of irritation as he peered into the darkness of the open ceiling. The pressure of preparing and training for this important event was beginning to show, and tonight would be his last opportunity to relax with friends until all was over.

"I'm hiding."

In spite of himself Dex smiled. "And how, may I ask, did you manage to get up there?"

"Like this," came the reply, and suddenly Anya Szcepanik dangled before him. He recognized her instantly as he guided her descent to the floor.

"I'm sure there's a pretty interesting explanation for why you've been hiding, but I don't have time to hear it. They're closing the place down, so if we don't hurry we may find ourselves locked in."

"I'm not going anywhere!"

Dex studied her small upturned face. Stubborn determination was evident in the set of her jaw. He could not entirely hide his impatience. "Don't you realize that people will be worried about you? I'm surprised they're not tearing this place apart right now."

"I failed to skate well, so NO, they won't care," she replied and actually stamped her foot in childish defiance.

"Now you know that's not true," Dex cajoled. Up close he could see that her hair was bleached, and while usually it was pulled back in a tight bun, it now hung loose about her shoulders, the ends splintered and uneven from too many chemicals. With the competition makeup scrubbed from her face, Dex could see that blonde was totally wrong for her coloring. Her pale skin had a washed-out and almost wizened quality that seemed unhealthy for one so young. She wore black tights with matching practice skirt and a bright yellow sweatshirt emblazoned with her country's flag. On her feet were cheap slippers, comprising the incongruous detail that typified her country's teams, whose equipment and dress could range from the very best to the most decrepit he had ever seen in serious competition.

Dex recalled the silver medallist at European Nationals who, despite blades over-sharpened until there was almost no edge to skate on, finished second when he might otherwise have managed first. Because his upset had not been anticipated and because he was not the political choice his equipment had been virtually ignored by an inflexible and unimaginative regime.

When he assisted Anya in her drop to the floor, Dex was surprised at how light she was and found it difficult to imagine that a girl of her size could throw her body into triple jumps with such controlled ease. Her face was tear-stained and her restless eyes red and swollen. Dex knew very well what it was to have one's confidence shaken after a disastrous performance, but to be so young and to have it happen in front of an international audience with so many expectations was brutal.

"I know who you are," she said, interrupting his thoughts. "You are the American skater, Mr. Dexter Arujo." Once again Dex was puzzled by her odd accent, which lacked the British inflection of most East European language programs, but was still surprisingly flawless.

"Come on, I'll take you back to your hotel."

"But you've forgotten. I'm not going back."

"You have to, or they'll think you've defected." She did not speak but looked at him with an intense expression of concurrence, which surprised him in one so young.

Irritated, Dex looked at his watch. It was getting late, and he knew Ryan would not hang out with the other skaters if he were not there. Forever restless and looking for excitement, Ryan would be off in search of his own brand of fun, and Dex knew his friend could not afford any more controversy.

"You're too young to defect. As it is you'll get into enough trouble. I've heard about your coach, Sasha Eymrnov. I had a coach like yours once, but if possible yours might actually be worse."

What Dex refrained from saying was that Sasha had a reputation for being entirely focused on success to the extreme of ignoring entirely the humanity of the skaters he trained. It was not unusual for him to confront a judge if he disagreed with a score, and he seemed to have inexhaustible contacts and influence in the international skating community, where he was looked upon with a disturbing mixture of fear and respect. While others in his country had their travel restricted, Sasha often showed up in the decadent cities of the west: in New York or Los Angeles, London or Paris. Little of importance happened in the skating world without his being among the first to know, and although no one took it seriously, it was rumored that he sometimes acted as unofficial courier or even spy for his government.

At the sound of Sasha's name Anya looked frightened. Ignoring her reaction, Dex took her hand and led her back the way he had come. Only in retrospect would it occur to him how defeated and sad she seemed, and this, his first opportunity to pursue the truth, flew by with no more than a whimper of uneasiness. Years would pass before he would torture himself with regret as he wondered how many squandered opportunities there had been to

51

unravel the complicated mesh of Anya's life.

The storm had intensified, and as they opened the door hard pellets of snow, whipped by the wind stung their faces. Dex could see how inadequately dressed Anya was, and he comforted himself with the thought that her decision to defect had never been a plan but was probably just an impulsive act by a distraught child too disappointed in her performance to face her coach. It seemed obvious to him that she had taken off running on impulse, for she had nothing significant with her. No coat, no boots, and even her skating equipment was missing. Dex removed the jacket Ryan had given him and settled it about her thin shoulders. As she pushed her arms into the sleeves, he placed on her head the Bruins cap he'd picked up while passing through Logan Airport. He was grateful to note that the car he'd ordered was still waiting, and once settled in the back seat he told her how talented he thought she was.

"Who are the Bruins?" she asked, ignoring the compliments and removing the Bruins cap to study the name.

"They're a Boston hockey team," Dex said, trying not to sound distracted, but calculating how long Ryan would wait. Without him to run interference, Ryan would be bored to distraction, and ignored by the other skaters who would have been warned by coaches and parents that it might not be prudent to be seen socially in Ryan's company, he might decide to strike out on his own.

"I know Boston, Massachusetts," Anya offered in the clipped, almost breathless way she had of speaking.

"Good," Dex replied absently as he suddenly recalled her country's tight security and the number of guards, carefully dressed goons really, that watched the athletes with hawk like attention. He wondered how she had managed to elude them. "It doesn't appear that anyone's been looking for you," he prodded.

"They don't care about me. I failed them, you see," she repeated, as though explaining something very elementary to a novice. "I fell three times and now they hate me and I must give up skating. My life is over." She began to cry, this time quietly, as she buried her face in her hands. Feeling awkward, Dex patted her shoulder and fished a tissue from his pocket.

"Listen," he said. "I'm an excellent judge of skating talent. You do believe that, don't you?"

"Yes," she said solemnly. "I believe you."

"You're very talented and you have a lot of success ahead of you. No one gets this far without a lot of both. Sasha might be angry because you didn't skate well, but no other girl has the jumps that you have. Your country is well

aware of this. Talent, in our world is power. Capitalize on it while you can."
Even as he said this, Dex knew that many skaters could deliver the goods in
practice but not when it counted in competition. He hoped that this was not
the start of one of those heart-breaking patterns for Anya.

"But I want to go home," she said, and her voice sounded profoundly
weary.

"You will," he soothed.

"No," she whispered in hushed exasperation. "I want to go home with you,
to America."

"They wouldn't have you. You're a minor without parents." Everyone
knew her story of being orphaned and then sponsored by Sasha into the state-
sponsored skating program. "You do understand this, don't you?"

"I know. I must wait. I must always wait," she said almost in a wail. "And
I may never have another chance. You do understand that, don't you?"

Dex knew that she spoke of defecting. He looked nervously at the driver's
profile. A broken window separated the front and back seats, but the driver
appeared to ignore them as he skillfully maneuvered the car through the
snow, which was accumulating at an alarming rate on the roads and
embankments as they passed.

"Look," he said, opening the inside flap of the jacket he'd lent her and that
Ryan had given him only the evening before. "See this patch? Only the
American team has these, and each has a name on it." Under the light from
the passing street lamps Anya traced the letters of his last name with her
finger. Carefully Dex ripped out the stitching that he had sewn around the rim
only hours before and placed the patch, symbolically in her hand. "Someday
we will be at another event together, you and I. You'll be older, and if you
want me to help you defect, you can send me this patch as a signal and I'll
know. I'll know and I'll find a way to help you."

"You think I'm just a child and you're trying to appease me," she
countered.

"No. I mean what I say. I'll help you."

Instantly she smiled, and the transformation was so complete and
unexpected that impulsively he grinned back. "And you do mean this, Mr.
Dexter Arujo?" she demanded buoyantly, but with a formality to her tone that
made him realize she was entirely serious.

Thinking her pretty for the first time, Dex nodded. She was dwarfed by the
size of the jacket, which extended below her knees. Snow had settled in her
hair and made him think of fireflies as they glistened under the shifting glow
of street lamps and shop windows as they passed. They were almost at her
hotel.

Like all athletes he had been briefed on how to behave in certain situations, and he had already broken several rules, but he could not concern himself with that now. Dex believed that he would never hear from Anya again. She would evolve from skating to coaching, produce several children who skated and forget entirely his promise of future help once puberty set in. He did not reveal his thoughts to her, for this was no more than a transient meeting, and she, just a little girl who needed his encouragement. He had no inkling that just knowing her would one day put both their lives in grave danger. And that he had no hint of her future importance to him would one day seem an unforgivable breach of insight.

Dex opened the door. She stepped from the car clutching tightly his patch in her hand. "This is a solemn promise you have made," Anya reminded him in the overly-dramatic stance that childhood can sometimes assume. Appearing both vulnerable and cute in the baseball cap and jacket, she turned all the force of her intense stare on him, and Dex fought hard to stifle a smile. He had let her out a block from her hotel, and now he attempted an expression of equal seriousness as he nodded in answer.

Anya turned and walked away, but suddenly concerned for whatever repercussions might follow on the heels of her aborted defection, Dex directed his driver slowly forward. As Anya approached the door of her hotel a man stepped from the shadows, and confirming his fear, grabbed her slender arm, nearly lifting her from the ground with a force that seemed excessive for such a little girl. Dex opened the cab door to follow, but already Anya had disappeared into the bright lobby, and he knew that he would be prevented from going any further.

As the cab drove away, Dex could not ignore a hollow feeling in the pit of his stomach. There would be no enjoyment in the evening ahead. He wished he could have done more for Anya, but what that would be, he had no idea. Still her almost desperate neediness would continue to haunt him in the days ahead.

Ten days later, after figures and a strong technical program, Dex was first in the standings and ready to skate the final freestyle event. He had picked by lot what most skaters consider the worst possible placement, slated to skate first in his elite group.

No matter how well he skated the judges must be conservative, leaving room for any better performance that might come after his. This could tilt a slender margin, until what might be a first-rate performance among a field of relatively clean programs, could now emerge almost anywhere in the top six. Upon learning that a skater would compete first a coach could often be heard to tell the media, with false bravado, that this was the position their student preferred. It was always a lie.

With Susan near by, Dex sat by himself and composed his thoughts. He wore headphones and was absorbed in the music from his program as mentally he skated through the best possible performance, carefully visualizing how each jump and spin would unfold. The headphones blocked all conversation and background noises, but nothing could diminish the excitement and sense of expectation that clenched the backstage atmosphere in a tight grip of frenzy. As he tied his skates and stretched out his long legs in order to gauge the feel of his boots, Dex reminded himself to allow that peripheral energy to work for him and not against him.

Dex lifted his head and spied Susan, who had wandered off to speak to an official. Beyond her he was startled to see Sasha Eymrnov striding toward him, with a murderous scowl on his face. On Sasha's head was the same Bruins cap that Dex had given Anya only days before. Instantly he knew that he was about to be confronted and that Sasha, who had a student slotted to compete behind him, had strategically chosen this very moment. With unexpected force Sasha bent down and snatched off the earphones, dislodging the foam attachment and causing a sharp edge to scratch his face, leaving a thin welt of blood.

"We know what you did with that child," Sasha whispered venomously into Dex's ear, sounding more like a jealous lover than a protective coach.

Sasha could not have chosen a more inappropriate moment to have a conversation. All of Dex's carefully constructed focus was instantly shattered. Even the great Sasha Eymrnov would have difficulty explaining his actions should either Dex or Susan decide to file a formal complaint. With concentration lost, Dex could slip significantly in the standings and Sasha's own student could end up with a medal.

A lifetime of watching his mother be bullied by Thierry had left Dex scornful of such manipulation. With skates on he towered over Sasha, as he stood with menacing slowness and retrieved the headphones, which had broken free of the cassette player. He glared into Sasha's face and was gratified to see that this was not the reaction Sasha expected.

"I don't know what you're talking about," Dex said, allowing his voice to rise in anger. "I simply escorted Anya back to her hotel. She was scared because she was afraid you would hate her for not skating well. Maybe you should have taken better care of her yourself. Maybe you should even thank me for taking the time to get her safely back in that storm."

A swift change came over Sasha's face. Dex was not intimidated nor was he matching Sasha's whispered tone, which invited a curious expectation of secrecy. Something was not quite right, but Dex had no time to explore the possibilities. Still there was an unsettled aspect to their exchange, which nagged at his sensibilities. He couldn't help wondering why Sasha would risk attracting attention if he had something to hide. And why must he conclude that Sasha had something to hide?

Susan looked their way. Sasha's back was to her, but there was no mistaking the expression on Dex's face. It was the epitome of poor sportsmanship for a rival coach to speak with another student minutes before competition, but to do so at such an important event was tantamount to being criminal. Already several officials and volunteers had looked curiously at Sasha, wondering what the two could possibly have to discuss at such a time. As Sasha turned away Dex swept the cap off his head. "I do believe this belongs to me," he said.

Sasha turned back, and his words belied the look of abject hatred on his face. "But of course, and I am simply returning it," he added for the benefit of Dex's coach, who now stood between them. Susan Eberly was a small woman with gray hair and a penchant for dressing always in black. She had an unassuming manner, but when it came to protecting her students, she was like a mother bear with new cubs.

"What's happened here?" she asked Dex, staring incredulously at Sasha's back as he sauntered away. Taking out a handkerchief, she dabbed at the trail of blood that marred his face. "I'm going to file a complaint as soon as your program is over. That man has finally gone too far."

"No," Dex said. "I'll handle this."

Susan knew that now was not the time to argue. Dex's name had been called more than once, and now he was frantically being waved forward. He stepped up to the rim of the ice and removed his guards as the signal was given to announce his name over the arena. With difficulty he attempted to empty his mind in an effort to regain the concentration that was lost, but he could not shed the uneasiness he felt at his encounter with Sasha.

An image lingered in his mind of Sasha's cold gray eyes and skin stretched tightly over careful, deliberate features. As he glided to the far corner of the arena to await the start of his music, Dex brushed the place on the side of his face where Sasha had snatched off the earphones. Suddenly Anya's desire to escape no longer seemed melodramatic, and he felt truly sorry for her. As the first notes of his music filled the stadium, Dex vowed that if the patch ever made its way back to him, he would keep his promise to help Anya escape. If not from her country, then certainly from her coach.

CHAPTER FIVE

Over the years he had heard many theories about how she died and why she died, but because there was no corpse to autopsy and no suspect to condemn, some blamed the families. He was always willing to listen. Someone would say, "You were there," inviting conversation. And he would nod his head but say little, hoping to hear something never heard before. He was desperate for the truth. It was this very desperation that drove him to his knees and led him to embrace the role of intercessor.

Dex would not have remembered Anya but for that odd occurrence of fate that lodged her forever in his memory. Seven years later he watched her take the ice at the Montreal Olympics and could not quite reconcile the image he had carried in his mind of a waifishly thin, almost gawky pre-teen to this stunning beauty that bore her same name and credits.

Head bowed, hands on hips, she paced like a caged animal before the gate, as her coach, Sasha Eymrnov, looked on. Dex knew just what she was feeling, and when her name was announced and she erupted onto the ice in an infusion of energy, he could almost feel himself skating with her. The restlessness that had marked her pacing just seconds before was gone, and she lit up the arena with a spontaneous smile that drew people in as she glided to her starting spot. A metamorphosis had taken place, and Dex found his eyes riveted on her face as she lifted her arms and moved smoothly into the first notes of her music, eager to embrace whatever fate delivered.

Few recalled in any detail the thirteen-year-old wonder that had stunned the skating world at practice seven years earlier, with her flawless triple jumps. Anya had continued to compete but her record was sporadic, and it was generally believed that she could not deliver except in practice where little counted. With a less than spectacular showing at the European Nationals, Anya arrived in Montreal by default when another skater had suffered a stress fracture.

Ryan Campbell was covering the Olympics in Montreal for a new cable network and was slated to join the better known Elliot Smythe as commentator on the dance and pair events. He had sent Dex tickets and back stage passes, followed by a phone call from his New York Office.

"Come on, Dex. It'll be fun. Just like old times."

"I guess three weeks in Montreal could qualify as a vacation. I could use a break."

"And you've got Hillary to take over your students," Ryan finished.

"Yeah, but you'll be pretty tied up."

"I only look like I work," Ryan said. "Making Elliot, that relic from the dinosaur age, look foolish in front of millions of spectators has become my sole purpose for living."

"Well, if that's all you have to look forward to, then you're in trouble," Dex laughed.

The generation of skaters who had suffered most under Elliot's biting commentary had now grown up and remembered well his ungenerous, often caustic remarks. Dex himself had suffered as a result, although no skater more than Ryan. To all appearances Ryan had turned his life around, but Elliot never missed an opportunity to remind others of the past and seemed to find sadistic joy in fostering Ryan's bad boy image. Teaming up the younger, more dynamic Ryan with the polished and sophisticated Elliot was considered a mistake in the skating community. But the network that brought Ryan on board was impressed with his popularity and growing reputation as an authority on skating, and saw only ratings, while those aware of the history remained wary.

Threatening to hire a lawyer and emancipate himself, Ryan had packed his belongings and moved to an obscure town and rink in Stoneham, Massachusetts, in order to skate with a partner much younger than himself, under a pair coach who had never produced a medal holder beyond the regional level. Ryan's sudden unexplained departure became a slight that some in skating would not forget. Rumors of drugs, promiscuity, and outbursts of temper became subjects of speculation, and Elliot made certain that, at least in print, Glen was portrayed as the surrogate father, overly generous and patient, his trust betrayed by an ungrateful student.

With more people wishing him ill than good, Ryan and his partner had gone on to win silver at the same Olympics that saw Dex take the gold in men's figure skating. Ryan had an unbeatable combination of looks and charm, wit and intelligence, which he projected on and off the air. Younger generations of skaters believed that Elliot, who was thirty years older and had always been vain, was jealous.

"You win," Dex said, accepting Ryan's invitation. "How could I possibly turn down the opportunity to witness you and Elliot politely decimate one another in front of a national audience."

Ryan and Dex sat in reserved seating with easy access to the back staging area to watch the last ladies' event. Dex was glad he'd come and enjoyed meeting former competitors now as coaches, judges, and officials. He had not been present for the ladies' technical program and was surprised to learn that Anya was being touted as the stunning upset, now in third place. If she finished the evening with a medal, any medal, she would be the dark horse winner at a time when there were very few upsets in skating. Still it was only as her name was announced and she pushed out on to that frigid surface that their former encounter came back to Dex in any detail.

Along with the other spectators he was mesmerized by her unique presence. Her simple red dress with the handkerchief skirt and square neckline lacked the intricate bead and sequined look of the other costumes and reinforced the image of a skater not expected to be competitive. In the opening minute of her program Anya two-footed a triple and then doubled the second jump in what was intended to be a triple-lutz, triple-toe combination. Knowing that she was short a triple jump Anya spontaneously added another toward the end, insuring that her presence was strong enough to move her into first place, with four other competitors still to skate.

Almost immediately those spectators seated around Dex and Ryan complained that her scores were higher than they should have been, as they shuffled through programs for the bio section and reminded one another of who she was. Anya had soundly captured the spotlight from her teammate who was the actual favorite to win a medal. Some close by murmured that the judges had been distracted by her beauty, complaining that she did not deserve the bronze medal that she ended the night with.

While it took the western press a heartbeat to adjust to the unexpected, it would take her country a bit longer. Having just turned twenty, Anya was young enough for the next Olympics, and for the first time in her career would become a useful commodity to her coach and her country.

As Anya finished skating, Ryan got up to leave. He had a few prearranged minutes to interview the Canadian expected to come in first, just after she stepped off the ice to hear her scores in the area known as 'kiss and cry'. It was an interview he had wrested from Elliot, who was furious.

"If you see Anya Szcepanik back there, tell her I said hello."

"You know her?" Ryan was clearly surprised.

"From a long time ago. She probably won't remember me."

Dex watched Ryan's live interview on one of the big screens set up around the arena. Just as the last skater took the ice, Ryan returned.

"Here," he said, feigning an indifference that Dex knew was not genuine.

Dex looked down at his hand. The patch was worn and so faded that it was difficult to make out the insignia of the World Skating Team.

"Where did you get this?" Dex asked, somewhat astonished as he traced out the letters of his name to be sure the patch really had belonged to him.

"The question is, where did Anya Szcepanik get your team patch?" Ryan responded. "She asked me to give it to you, and in the process I was nearly roughed up by her bodyguard, who happened to be twice my size and not at all charmed by my press credentials. I think he thought I was trying to interview her. From what I could see they're watching her more closely than anyone else. Can you tell me why?" Ryan asked, now openly curious.

"Perhaps, but later. Did anyone see her give this to you?"

"Maybe. I don't think so," Ryan considered.

Still gripping the patch Dex walked to a phone booth. He knew he must at least make an attempt to see Anya and felt a rush of excitement at the prospect. The skinny little waif had turned into a beautiful young woman, and there was no doubt that he had felt an instant attraction. Feeling somewhat guilty, he made an obligatory phone call to his assistant coach, Hillary Nagle. The two had been a couple for almost a year, and now they talked briefly before ending with the automatic, "I love you."

Already those words were not ringing true for Dex, but to Hillary they meant everything. Just before leaving to join Ryan in Montreal, he had tried to articulate his doubts, but she had assured him that she loved him enough for both of them. At Hillary's instigation they had talked marriage, and already friends had referred to them as being engaged. Impatient for a proposal and a ring, she had let him know what shape of diamond she preferred and Dex had begun to feel a nagging resentment at the pressure.

Although he had once planned to remain celibate until marriage, Dex had failed to live up to that standard of moral purity. Moral purity, he had decided, was an impossible goal in today's world. But now, as he thought of Hillary and the entanglement of their relationship, he realized how wrong he was to sleep with a woman he didn't love. He had not taken the time to test that attraction in a boundary-defined relationship over time, and now they would both be hurt.

Dex cancelled his plans for dinner in order to attend the final party held for all of the skaters, their families, and coaches. This was the one place where he and Anya might exchange a few words in relative privacy. Security was tight at this function in order to keep away press and fans alike, and as a non-participant Dex had not been invited. Still, he knew that as soon as he was recognized he would be welcomed.

An elaborate buffet was served, and the sound of music filled the air as couples gathered to dance. Dex expected to invite Anya to dance and then laughingly remind her of their previous meeting. He thought it unlikely that her purpose in sending the patch was a reminder of her wish to defect. Few skaters would turn their backs on the opportunities afforded by this night's performance, even if politics would let them. Although he thought she deserved better, the judges held up two other skaters who had done well at Worlds, giving Anya third place and the bronze medal. Next time, if she skated well enough, it would be her turn to be 'held up', pushed to the forefront by the judges, a highly political practice in skating, which many of the younger athletes had begun to openly deride.

Dex was no longer as readily recognized by the general public as he had been, but here in the skating community he would always be famous. As he walked through the crowd some of the younger athletes and their parents asked for his autograph, which he signed and quickly moved on. He could see that Anya's country was well represented, and yet there was no sign of Anya herself. With the exception of Sasha, their group stood nearly isolated from the frenzied social atmosphere against a far wall with several nondescript gentlemen, clearly not athletes, coaches, or parents in attendance. Of all the eastern block countries, this one appeared the most paranoid as well as the most repressive. Defection was often a possibility.

Ignoring the looks of the bodyguards he walked boldly in their direction. "Would you like to dance?" he asked, not waiting for an answer as he reached for Sophie's hand. Sophie had been the favorite to win a medal but had actually finished behind the first ten. Through the years he and Sophie had been at several competitions together and had a nodding acquaintance. An accomplished athlete, Sophie was a small blonde girl with powerful legs, and although she lacked the grace and presence that Anya exemplified, she was a seasoned competitor with an impressive record of wins.

"I've admired your career," she told him as they danced. Dex was aware of being eyed suspiciously from the sidelines, and in a burst of defiance he pulled Sophie tightly to him and watched over her head for the predictable reaction.

"And I've admired yours," he returned the compliment. "I know you expected to do better. Sorry about what happened."

"Thank you," she nearly spat out the words. "I would have if not for Anya. She was not even supposed to be here, you know. She barely made alternate and would never have come this far without Sasha manipulating behind the scenes."

Dex was surprised at the bitterness of Sophie's comment. The music stopped, but he kept her on the dance floor. The next song was fast, which prevented them from speaking. Afterwards he offered to get her something to drink. She looked over her shoulder in obvious discomfort. "I can't," she said pointedly, and so they danced again.

"Why isn't Anya here?" he asked.

"She is unpredictable. Crazy, as you Americans like to say. They don't let her go anywhere."

A photographer walked by and snapped a picture, and Dex realized that by tomorrow people would speculate that they had managed an affair, despite her country's grueling security. He could also expect a thinly disguised call from Hillary, who seemed to have a limitless supply of girlfriends who plied her with news of his every move whenever they were separated.

As he held Sophie and moved in time to the music, he imagined that it was Anya he held and wondered at the strong attraction he felt for a woman he didn't know. He had not thought of Anya much in the intervening years. Perhaps, Dex cautioned himself, what he really wanted was an escape from the relationship with Hillary that had begun to make him feel almost claustrophobic. He reminded himself that he didn't need the pretext of another relationship to break up with Hillary. It was something he should have done a long time ago, and the pain she would feel because he had procrastinated for lack of courage would be entirely his fault. He had to find a way to get himself back on ground that didn't undermine his self-respect.

"Under the circumstances it would be difficult for you to share a room with Anya," Dex probed, feeling more guilt at yet another manipulation.

"She stays in Sasha's suite. They always travel together. He can keep a close watch on her that way."

"It doesn't look like we'll be seeing one another again."

"No," she agreed. "This has been my last year to compete, and I'd hoped to finish better." She lifted her head and looked into his eyes. "I didn't know you liked me so much."

The music started again. He was about to lead her into another dance when one of the muscled men from against the wall stepped between them, having clearly decided the two had spent enough time together.

Dex danced with an old friend, a former skater who was now an association employee. They made small talk as he scanned the room for Sasha Eymrnov, finally seeing him at a corner table with numerous other coaches, including Elliot and Glen Winston.

Dex disliked Elliot, believing him to be a phony. Because of his friendship with Ryan, the one person in skating that Elliot actually seemed to hate, Dex knew the famous broadcaster would have preferred to ignore him as well, but this was not possible. Dex's gold medal, and now his growing reputation as a coach, made it unwise for Elliot to snub him, and so, overcompensating, he went out of his way to be cordial, often feigning a closeness that did not exist. Dex recognized Elliot's congeniality for what it was and avoided him whenever possible. Now Elliot smiled and waved Dex to join them, even as Sasha deliberately turned away.

It didn't seem that Elliot's party would break up soon. Clearly they were celebrating Sasha's success with Anya's performance. As he watched, Glen leaned forward to whisper something into Sasha's ear, even as they both looked in his direction and smiled. As they did so, Dex felt an almost physical stab of revulsion. There was something so very wrong with these men, and this thought prompted a sense of urgency. Why, he wondered, should men like this always win? Why should there not be consequences, and why was no one holding them accountable? Dex turned his back on Elliot and his friends and went in search of the service elevator. It was close to midnight, and the small area off the kitchen was deserted. Placing empty cups on a tray he covered all with a napkin, and reaching for a wall phone was instantly connected to the hotel operator. He asked for Sasha's room number.

"I can't give out that number. You know that. You kitchen people are so lazy. Look it up yourself; you haven't lost the room roster, have you?" she accused without pausing between sentences. "You'll lose your job for that."

"I'm temporary," Dex said, knowing that the hotel would have hired extra help to accommodate the influx of activity as a result of the Olympics.

"Okay, but don't bother to ask again. I'm not going to break the rules, just so you can screw up twice." She recited the room number. "But you better have your ID or you won't get off the elevator. You do remember that much from orientation, don't you?"

Dex returned the wave of the housekeeper who passed in the hallway and replaced the phone. The automated numbness, which typified his competition days, had taken over, and he felt the familiar burst of controlled energy. Going to the wall of lockers he searched through pockets, finding nothing of use but a pair of glasses and a baseball cap. From close observation from the inside of many such competitions, and weeks in hotels too numerous to count, he knew that security was often no more than bluster and appearance. The glaring inconsistencies were often a source of amusement to Dex and his friends, who as young boys could not resist exploring behind closed doors and odd corridors labeled, "no admittance" or "employees only." Any such sign was a magnet, and sharing stories and boasts of being nearly detected or chased from a restricted area created a bond among young competitors that the coaches would have disapproved.

Dex sat at a metal desk and searched through drawers. In the back, in an open shoe-box, he found what he was looking for. He examined the photographs. Moving quickly he smeared the one that most resembled himself with a layer of ink and attached it to the lapel of a white waiter's jacket. Along with the tray he grabbed a gift basket, which contained a collection of cheeses, chocolates, biscuits, and nestled in the center, a bottle of wine.

The service elevator opened on the eighteenth floor where a guard met him, while two others stood idly about the row of passenger elevators. Struggling to focus out of the thick glasses, Dex handed over the basket before anything could be said.

"Compliments of Sasha Eymrnov, for doing such fine work," he announced, hoping that all that would be understood was the coach's name, as he gestured to include the others at the end of the hall. The men smiled with obvious skepticism, as indecipherable comments flew back and forth, none sounding the least bit grateful. It seemed that even among his own countrymen Sasha Eymrnov was not popular.

Dex tried not to think as he walked to Anya's door and knocked. He had so poorly thought out his actions that it suddenly occurred to him that Anya might not be there or, worse still, might not be alone. He reprimanded himself for such stupidity and knocked once more, the sound jarring his facade of calm. Turning he made a helpless gesture toward the door as one of the guards reached around him and slipped a key into place. With obvious impatience, which Dex guessed was not directed at him, the guard flung the door wide and called a sharp command into the darkened room before stepping back into the hallway.

Even as his eyes adjusted to the dimness he saw her. She sat alone and motionless on a purple sofa. Wet hair had deposited shadowed patches over the shoulders of an oversized white blouse, and with a hairbrush suspended in midair, her eyes locked on his. Dex felt mildly ridiculous and had just placed his tray on a nearby table when Anya threw herself into his arms with such force that they nearly toppled to the floor.

"You came," she said. "I prayed that you would remember. I dreamed you would help me, and now here you are," she marveled, clearly amazed at her luck as she kissed his face in tiny, fevered pecks, impulsive tears smearing both their faces.

Her reaction brought him abruptly to his senses. Clearly he should not have come, and yet he had made a promise to a distraught child years before. That she remembered and even counted on the seriousness of that promise, and he had not, suddenly struck Dex with potent alarm. What, he wondered, had he gotten himself into?

"We do not have any time," she said breathlessly and rushed into the adjacent room for a sweater, socks and boots. She pulled the sweater over her wet hair. "What is our plan?" she demanded.

He shrugged his shoulders and felt foolish. "I have no plan," he admitted. "I came to say 'hello' and tell you how well you skated. I thought we might dance, but it seems you've missed the party."

Anya stopped her frantic activity and regarded him with astonishment. "You did all this for foolish sentiment," she said, and then recited a few epitaphs which he recognized only from spending so much time backstage at foreign competitions.

She began to pace. "But you got here. How did you manage?" she asked and turned abruptly to face him.

He told her, mildly impressed at his uncharacteristic daring, explaining that his actions had been impulsive. "I imagine if I'd actually planned to help you escape I'd never have gotten this far."

"Planned or not, you are late. Sasha will be back any moment."

"What do you suggest?"

"This is fate," Anya pronounced decisively. "We must do something to distract them. We must get to the elevator right away. Sasha will be back," she continued, shoving her feet into leather boots.

Her sense of urgency and even fear infused him with new resolve. He had known all along that her purpose in sending the patch was a cry for help, a cry he must heed. Dex felt a new rush of adrenaline pump through his body. If she chose to escape the repressive restrictions of her country, who was he to stop her? For once in his life he would not overanalyze or even think about the consequences. This was just the sort of impulsive action Ryan was famous for. The kind of mad spontaneous exploit that no one would ever connect with him, and this alone might buy the time they needed.

Dex watched as Anya shaped pillows under the sheets to look as if she were under them. She then opened a bottle of what he supposed were sleeping pills and placed a half empty glass of water on a tray beside the bed. He thought her actions amateurish and forced himself to think. Dex could not help notice that Sasha's belongings were everywhere in evidence. He glanced behind her into the second bedroom and saw that it remained unoccupied. Somewhere along the way coach and student had become lovers, and yet Anya had absolutely no qualms about leaving Sasha.

In any sport which relied on the performance of a single athlete, the relationship between coach and student could often be intense, but this was certainly crossing a line. Dex had observed a culture in skating that tended to dismiss serious problems rather than risk intervention and the possibility of bad publicity. As long as a secret remained securely in the dark, it was best left ignored, even as insiders gossiped among themselves, resulting in a high casualty count of kids who left the sport feeling bitter and unfulfilled.

"I have an idea," he told Anya and quickly removed the loose waiter jacket and trousers that covered his clothes. He explained as he helped her pile her hair under the baseball hat and settled the glasses over the bridge of her nose. He then picked up a bottle of vodka and spilled some over his shirt.

"This is too dangerous," Anya asserted when he finished explaining. "How can they not catch you, and then what will happen to me?"

"That's the idea. And what can they do anyway? I'm drunk and in love and for what we hope will be at least an hour Sophie will be shrouded in romantic mystery." He stood back to look at Anya. The loose chef's trousers hid her figure and the back of the white jacket would be all anyone would see as she walked to the elevator. "Not very convincing," he mused. "If they see you at all, let's hope it's only a short glimpse."

"Wait," she said and returned seconds later with the same jacket he had given her in Sweden seven years before.

"Looks like you've hardly worn this," he said as he slipped his arms into the sleeves, mildly surprised that it still fit.

"Sasha hates that jacket, but it's good luck. I take it to every competition, but I've only worn it once," she said softly and looked him fully in the face for the first time. Something was there when their eyes met, something he could not name, and yet now, for the first time, Dex could no longer regret the risk he'd taken.

"Here," he said and handed her the key to the hotel room he shared with Ryan. Their hands touched and his almost involuntarily lingered seconds longer than necessary. He then gave her money for a taxi, instructing her to have the cab drop her off at the Hilton, before walking the four blocks back to his hotel.

"Give me forty seconds. Forty seconds and then walk, don't run, to the elevator. I'll meet you at the hotel within the hour. Once you're in that room, whatever you do, don't leave, don't answer the door or pick up the telephone. If I don't come back, you can count on Ryan Campbell to help you."

At the mention of Ryan's name an expression of what could only be fear crossed Anya's face. "You do remember Ryan? He met you backstage and collected the patch from you."

She nodded her head and turned away. "And this is your good friend?" Her voice was halting, full of tension. He wished he could see her face.

"He's my best friend, almost like a brother. I know there's been a lot of gossip about Ryan, but you can trust him. He's a different person today." Dex walked up behind her. He placed his hands gently on her shoulders and turned her to face him, but her head remained down. Placing his hands on her face, he gently forced her to look at him. "Don't worry. This will work. We'll get you away safely, but we have to move quickly." There was an inscrutable expression on her face that suddenly made Dex uneasy. "Is this really what you want? Because...." he asked, wondering if she had changed her mind.

"No, no!" she asserted. "I must get away from here."

Dex guessed that far too much time had already been wasted. Flashing a last smile of encouragement, he walked to the door and opened it. Her whisper came to him like a kiss. "Thank you," she said, so low and soft that he almost did not hear.

All three guards were congregated out of sight, huddled over the huge basket with rainbow paper strewn about their feet. They passed between them a gift card, which Dex had overlooked. He could hear them painstakingly sound out the English inscription and knew that time was short.

Wishing he had the power to make himself invisible, he ducked around the corner toward Sophie's room, now in full view of the guards but still unnoticed. Without hesitating, he began to knock loudly at the door until the sound of running converged on him and he was pinned roughly to the ground. "You can't be up here," one guard shouted in his ear. "How did you get up here?" With his arms pinned behind him Dex nodded toward the stairwell. The four guards regarded one another.

"What did you think you wanted?" they demanded in such broken English that only because he anticipated what would be asked, did he understand.

"I'm meeting Sophie."

"Sophie is downstairs and you are not to be here!" Silently Dex counted out the seconds as the muscle-bound guards argued among themselves. By now Anya would be exiting the elevator and just entering the service room off the kitchen, where she would rid herself of her disguise. Visualizing her progress, as though his thoughts could guarantee safety, he imagined her walk to the side entrance and around the building to the line of waiting cabs.

With his face still pushed into the carpet Dex heard more conversation back and forth on a portable phone, and he recalled that the bodyguard who had cut in on him and Sophie had worn one at his belt. "You are Dex Arujo, is that not right?" one of the guards demanded, pleased at his stellar detective work, as two others jerked him to a standing position. They were all larger than he was and he guessed armed. Dex nodded, trying his best to look compliant.

"You are a stupid man," the guard finally pronounced after more words were exchanged over the hand-held receiver. "Now you may go and do not please, come back."

They regarded Dex unsympathetically and escorted him to the elevator. He suspected they wanted to be rid of him as quickly as possible. If they had decided to report the incident to Sasha, he would have been detained longer. Sasha would certainly have recalled his connection to Anya and would have discarded the notion of a drunken Dex Arujo pursuing a woman he hardly knew. He glanced at his watch. It was now after midnight and the party downstairs was breaking up. Sasha would return to his room, and Dex doubted he would be fooled into believing that Anya had taken a sleeping pill and retired for the night. As he pushed his way out of the elevator, a group approached.

"Dex, how are you doing? Nice to see you here. You should have joined us for a drink. Did you see me waving?" It was Elliot Smythe. Resisting the impulse to turn and run, Dex nodded at Elliot and Glen, who blocked his path to the lobby. "You've met Sasha, haven't you?"

Unable to do otherwise, Dex extended his hand, but Sasha rudely turned away and bounded ahead of Glen and Elliot into the waiting elevator.

"I am sorry," Elliot apologized. "Sasha is usually very friendly."

"Sasha has many traits, but friendly is not one of them," Glen laughed. "Nice to see you again, Dex. I'll shake your hand even if my friend won't. I hear you're coaching full time."

"Yes. You had such a positive influence on my young life, I decided to follow in your footsteps," Dex said. "How are you, Glen?"

"Great," Glen said, obviously in rare good humor about something. "I have a couple of promising students, so I imagine we'll be seeing a lot more of each other."

"Good. Well, I must be going. It's been a pleasure. I'll tell Ryan I ran into you."

Obviously drunk, neither Glen nor Elliot appeared to notice his sarcasm. As the two followed a last group into the waiting elevator, Dex's eyes locked with Sasha, who remained standing at the back.

"We'll have lunch when all this is over," Elliot called with his usual polished buoyancy, just before the doors began to close. "Call me when you're in New York."

"Next time I'm in New York," Dex agreed, comforted by the fact that he had no immediate plans to visit that city. Still his eyes were on Sasha, whose contrived expression of boredom suddenly disintegrated like shattered glass! As though in slow motion, Dex could discern the exact moment when Sasha's mind registered the bottle-green, Hard Rock Café jacket that he had given Anya in Sweden and which he now wore. As full comprehension dawned, he had a last glimpse of Sasha frantically pushing his way forward to the closing

68

door of the elevator. But Sasha was a small man blocked by those in front, and forgetting to speak English, his drunken demand to let him pass was not understood.

The lobby was congested with the overflow from the party. Family members, escaping the loud blast of music, waited with coats in hand as a persistent cadre of photographers hovered about, hoping to snap one of the medal holders. Abandoning the casual demeanor that would not attract attention, Dex moved swiftly out the lobby door, brushing aside the doorman's offer of a cab and ignoring those who attempted to speak with him. Running to the end of the line, he thrust a crisp hundred-dollar bill into the palm of the driver as they sped off in the direction of his hotel.

Dex unlocked the door, half expecting the room to be empty and recent events no more than a dream. Despite the seriousness of what had just transpired, he was pleased with himself and inexplicably happy at the thought that there was no going back. Now he was responsible for Anya and for her safety.

Wasting no time, Anya had pulled a valise from the closet, tossing in a random mixture of his and Ryan's clothes. As she indiscriminately emptied the contents of the bathroom into Ryan's leather duffel, Dex scribbled Ryan a note. "Gone fishing," he signed off, hoping that his friend would pick up the reference to a past vacation they had spent together as boys.

"You can stay here, you know," he hesitated at the door, giving her one more opportunity to change her mind. "Once we call the authorities and get the Canadian government involved you will be safe."

"No," she nearly screamed. "Sasha will interfere. They have prepared for such an event here in Canada. He will not let me go. We must get away from here. Please," she pleaded and dug her fingers desperately into his arm. "Now! We must go now."

He decided not to tell Anya of Sasha's recognition of the jacket or his frantic attempt to push his way out of the elevator before it closed. Once in the hotel room it would take Sasha only seconds to piece together an accurate picture of what had actually transpired. Still he was surprised at the intensity of Anya's outburst until he recalled his own run-in with Sasha in Sweden years before. He opened his mouth to reason with Anya, but stopped when he saw the raw, abject fear gather over her features. Nothing he had to say about democratic governments or how past defectors had been treated in Canada and the United States would ease her fear.

"We'll buy ourselves some time. We won't give Sasha a chance to complicate the issue without significant distance between us," Dex soothed, gathering up the two suitcases she had packed in his absence.

Ryan had leased a jeep, which they hardly used due to the shortage of parking in the city. He found the car keys and tossed Anya a jacket. Once again he was loaning her a jacket, but this time the fit was considerably better.

He had to remind Anya to walk, not run through the lobby, but only after the urban lights had been left far behind and they hit a stretch of dark, deserted road did she refrain from looking over her shoulder every few minutes. Dex had a destination firmly in mind, but for now Anya was quiet, almost withdrawn as she rested her weight against the passenger door appearing to sit as far away from him as possible. "She doesn't trust me," he thought.

Dex reasoned that once Sasha had confirmed that Anya was not in the protective custody of the Canadian Government he would expect them to go directly south into Vermont. With the advantage of knowing Anya was with him, Sasha might also search west, looking at many of the obscure and unmanned border crossings closer to California, and so he had decided to head east into Maine.

It had begun to snow during the night and as sunlight slanted through the canopy of firs onto the forest road Dex was struck with the beauty of his surroundings. He looked toward Anya, ready to comment but she had dropped off to sleep. The color reflected off the snow was a wash of pink with a layer of yellow, iridescent and clean. The black pine boughs were laden with heavy drifts of snow, and their spidery configuration seemed perfectly balanced in nature's random paradox.

Once more he glanced at Anya, wanting to share this moment of serene beauty. She was still asleep, her forehead pressed against the window and her long hair draped like a curtain over one shoulder. Without thinking, he reached out and touched the back of his hand to her cheek. She needed him, and he realized suddenly how drawn he was to that helplessness. It was the same inclination that had propelled him into a relationship with Hillary, which he now so much regretted.

Lacking a map Dex scrutinized the occasional country roadways for that one that seemed familiar. The road he wanted would be obvious only for the long drift of white, unmarred by tire tracks or footprints, as the narrow lane disappeared into two rows of maples banked by evergreen. Ryan's former pair coach owned a cabin on Flagstaff Lake near Stratton, and Dex and a few other male skaters had spent a memorable vacation there.

After several wrong turns they arrived, and Dex was relieved to see that the place remained much as he remembered. The key was still hidden in a false bottom at the base of an old iron milk-bucket. As Anya removed covers from a few pieces of furniture, Dex went to check the kitchen. It was well stocked with canned goods and looked as though the caretaker who was supposed to come from town on a regular basis had forgotten the location.

Dex fired up the generator and built a fire. They piled pillows on the floor and wrapped themselves in woolen blankets and old quilts as he told her of the restless teenagers who felt like men as they grilled their catch each evening. She seemed to be put at ease by his aimless conversation, and so he related how they had gone at night to the local bar at the back of a small grocery store. No one had asked their ages, as beer was served up on demand, and they found themselves giving up their cash in game after game of darts to the local clientele.

Time not strictly accounted for was a luxury, and this rare break from routine was exactly what was needed. Dex was seventeen and occasionally recognized from his recent win at Worlds. In a few weeks he would begin preparing for what would be the defining moment of his career. A gold medal at the Olympics.

Anya listened to his story as though she could read something more, beyond his words. She had avoided answering anything but the most routine questions concerning her own life, and once they arrived at the cottage had seemed reticent and wary. Other than that one frantic embrace at the hotel, they had barely brushed hands, and so he was surprised when she leaned forward to kiss him. Without intending to do so, his lips parted hers.

He was drawn to her but baffled by this sudden change of demeanor, and yet the contact was sweet. They had all the time in the world to get to know one another, or so he reminded himself as he stifled his first inclinations, and prepared to withdraw. He expected her to follow, grateful for his restraint, but instead, as he moved back she slid forward. Almost immediately her kisses shifted with devouring fervency as all thoughts of retreat fled. Still a quiet, but certain instinct warned that something was wrong. This was too sudden to be at all meaningful. She couldn't and didn't care for him. But if they had time to get to know one another, then there was hope for a future relationship. He had to stop this flood-tide of desire before their emotions overwhelmed them.

Only later would he realize that Anya had ambushed him with a skill he was too stunned to analyze, and now she was firmly in control. Once more Dex pushed her back and looked into her eyes. He saw there an odd mingling of emotions he could not discern. But the time to question had passed.

As the sun slanted through the trees, invading daggers of light slid across the barren plank floor. Dex studied Anya as she slept. Twice during the night she

71

had struggled awake and seemed disorientated as she wildly surveyed her surroundings in obvious fright. Each time he'd gently reminded her of where they were, speaking quietly until realization relaxed her features, and he could see that she believed him.

Now that daylight had more fully infiltrated the room, she slept soundly. Dex watched the shadows flee from the surface of the old quilt tucked tightly about her and grew increasingly uneasy. He was disappointed with himself for giving in to temptation. He didn't want to be controlled by lust, but now the haunting echo of a similar mistake had trapped him once more. How, he wondered, could man control the urge to sin and did God just keep forgiving. He hadn't picked up a Bible in years, and yet he knew that he should. He was a man controlled by passion, just like any other, and he could not reclaim this mistake and start over with Anya. And where, he wondered, would that lead them?

Sasha did not have a reputation for losing gracefully, and Dex felt certain that he would not give up looking for Anya until they had found refuge with the Canadian or American authorities. Ryan's former pair coach, who owned this cabin and had graciously lent it to them years before, had also been in Montreal. When he heard that Dex had helped Anya escape he might even now think of Stratton and its proximity to the Canadian border. This alone was reason enough to move quickly, and yet he hesitated to wake her.

Dex thought of Sasha's contorted expression of hatred as he tried to push his way out of the elevator and felt a perverse thrill of pleasure. Let the chase begin, the game proceed, he told himself as he relished Sasha's loss of a talented student and felt the adrenaline rush of the hunted.

"Wake up," he whispered in her ear and kissed her lightly on the forehead. She was an enigma, and yet he almost felt that he loved her. As she stirred and shook the tight quilt off her legs, he lay down and drew her against him. But her body, unresisting and pliable in his arms the night before, now stiffened as she pushed a space between them.

Dex looked at her confused. Didn't she remember the night before? "Time to wake up," he spoke and buried his face in her hair. He had never felt so drawn to a woman, such desire and admiration in such equal measure. He thought her fears were exaggerated, but in deference to that very real state of panic he would avoid detection for as long as possible and as a result he would have her all to himself a little longer.

But she sat up abruptly brushing back her hair with a defiant gesture. "Don't touch me again. Never touch me under any circumstances unless I say you can," she announced with a chilling aloofness that startled him for its formality.

"But I thought … last night that.…" Their eyes met and he saw in hers a sudden influx of fear and confusion. Pain wrinkled her face and she put a hand to her temple as though she had a blinding headache. Then her shoulders slumped and she looked away. When she engaged him again, he noted a slight change in the tone of her voice and the expression on her face was one of sweet compliance. "What did you say?" she asked politely.

"I'm sorry. I really need to apologize. I don't know why I can't learn this lesson. It's so wrong to be intimate so fast. It undermines any hope for a solid relationship. And I really want to get to know you better, Anya. I know this isn't logical because we've just met and we don't know one another, but I really feel that I could love you and.…"

He looked at her. The blank expression on her face almost frightened him. "Don't worry," she said innocuously.

"It's just that last night I thought maybe we had something."

"Of course I remember. I'm just tired. You are right. I didn't sleep well." Had he said that? He knew he didn't, but let her statement pass.

"Do we have a plan for today?" she asked in a sing-song, well-bred tone, deftly changing the subject in a way that would become all too familiar.

Leaving the rented jeep in Durham, New Hampshire, they took a bus to Troy, where they purchased a car from a high school student, convincing him that they would attend to the legalities of title and plates later. Careful to stay off the main roads, they took three weeks to reach Southern California. Anya seemed thrilled by her newly acquired freedom, which Dex found intoxicating. What had previously masqueraded as love in his relationship with Hillary now seemed a tarnished imitation of what he felt for Anya. There was nothing he would not do for her.

The honeymoon ended as they drove the beat up Ford Falcon through the iron gates of Arujo Vineyards. He had planned to call the authorities as soon as they arrived, but the authorities were already present, none-too happy with the long delay. Although it was suggested he stay behind, Anya insisted he accompany her to Washington. Dex was glad to oblige, for suddenly her former enjoyment of new experiences wilted into a fragile, almost childlike fear at the thought of being interviewed and debriefed by American officials. Once again her fear struck Dex as exaggerated, but she would not be comforted, despite his reassurance that she was now in a democratic country.

Dex had known of several athletes who defected and was somewhat familiar with the process, but almost from the start Anya was treated differently. That she might have difficulty acquiring anything more than a temporary visa had never once entered his mind. When she verbalized the possibility, he was quick to minimize her fears even as he managed to convince himself that there was only some elaborate combination of bureaucratic misunderstanding which could easily be explained. Hiding his misgivings, he stayed by Anya's side, encouraging and supporting and waiting for her to share with him her thoughts and feelings. But Anya remained guarded and secretive, and her few confidences were coolly delivered, revealing nothing significant.

As he thought back, Dex wondered why he hadn't demanded more from his wife. Perhaps she had stayed with him precisely because he had never pressured her for more than she was willing to reveal. He had felt certain that with time, the consistency of his love would make her feel safe, inspiring the honest give-and-take of sharing in a healthy marriage. Now, in light of those photographs safely tucked away in the safe, he suspected that the truth would not come easily. He couldn't wait any longer for her to confide in him. The luxury of time had just run out.

CHAPTER SIX

God had given him a charge to pray, not as an occasional impulse, but as an established discipline. The call to pray was felt with compelling intensity. With divine authority it transcended his very human selfish inclinations and silenced many distractions. He prayed for her nearly every day.

As far as Thierry Arujo was concerned, the promise of an Olympic medal was a divisive wedge that had robbed him of the perfect successor to a legacy far more enduring than a few seconds of fame. With crushing reluctance he understood that Dexter would never willingly give up the insular skating world to farm and had generously provided for Joey Santos, under the stipulation that he never leave his position as general operating manager. Thanks to Joey, Dex could pursue his career in the way he wanted.

While the endorsements lasted, Dex had invested his money wisely and the winery continued to show a profit. Joey's wife, Rosa had a contract for her first cookbook and was planning on launching a gourmet mail-order business, capitalizing on the winery name. They had worked out the details to the benefit of all, and because of Joey, Dex had no concerns for the family business. But he did worry about what to do next. There had been invitations to judge, but often his scores were out of sync with the judging elite, who appeared to enter a competition with their favorites already chosen, and despite the technical strength of a program, tended to reward the traditional over the innovative.

The professional skating circuit had not caught the public attention as it would in the future, and except for the opportunity to meet up with old friends and reminisce, touring held little appeal. For a while Dex concentrated on the marketing end of the winery, leaving the farming to Joey, but after years of disciplined training every sinew of his body cried out for more of the same. A rink had been constructed close enough to the winery for a manageable commute, and he was offered the opportunity to build an elite skating program from the ground up. But Dex had other ideas. He wanted the benefits of skating to be affordable for a struggling family, and so he turned his considerable fund-raising talent toward that end and had already been

75

coaching successfully when Ryan called with the invitation to join him in Montreal.

The vineyard had always been a haven for Dex. It did not occur to him that Anya would not view its lush manicured setting in the same way, but almost immediately she had fallen into a deep depression, which he, Joey, and Rosa had worked hard to reverse, and then, without explanation she had disappeared. With her absence Dex felt as though he had lost an important appendage, and although he waited and prayed for news of her, there was none.

Reluctant to petition emigration for a current address, Dex had thrown himself into the work of the vineyard with a zeal never before witnessed by Joey. He turned over more and more students to Hillary until she too talked of hiring an assistant, and he came less and less to the rink, actually spending time in the field with the workers and helping to prepare the huge vats for the next harvest.

Dex had never known true loneliness. After his parents died he had Susan, who remained devoted to him, and he had the friendship of Joey and Rosa as well as a community of good friends in skating. But nothing could fill the hole left by Anya's departure, and until he found her again, there was no escaping the gnawing void of loss left by her absence.

Dex recalled Anya's meetings with state department and immigration officials behind closed doors. Frustrated at his helplessness and wanting to do more, he could only wait out the process as each time Anya emerged from long interviews with her face set in a grim stare. There were so many questions that sprang to mind, but soon Anya would fall into a coma like sleep that he dare not interrupt.

"They want to know about Sasha," she uncharacteristically confided after one particularly long meeting, "and they want to know who I am." Dex was alarmed at the near hysteria in her voice. "How can I know everything when I am an orphan," she cried, her voice breaking.

"Just explain," Dex told her.

"I explain and explain and they ask me again. Always the same questions and something they do not believe. And I can not tell them. I can not answer their questions," her voice trailed.

"You need a lawyer. I can call Ryan's parents and they can recommend someone here in Washington. Maybe you need someone to sit in on these meetings."

Anya was clearly alarmed. "No lawyers! Everything will be fine." As though burned by his suggestion, she never again complained.

Once home, emotionally and physically exhausted by her ordeal, she seemed to collapse, going to bed only to rise in order to wash and make trips to the bathroom. The brittle blonde of her former hair color had begun to grow out to reveal the rich, auburn red that she was born with. Anya seemed particularly fascinated by the process and Dex wondered how anyone could have preferred that false color to the natural beauty of what was slowly being revealed. On one occasion he found her sitting before her mirror with her hair parted as she studied the new color. In her hand was a sharp pair of scissors. Something about the way she gripped the handle and the blank stare as she studied her image, almost as if she did not recognize the face that stared back, gave him pause. Frightened, Dex walked up behind her. When he reached for the scissors he found that her grip was so tight that he had to peel white fingers off the hilt one by one.

Perplexed, he spoke to her gently. "Anya, did you want to cut your hair?" Stiffly she nodded her head in assent, never shifting her gaze from that of the stranger in the mirror. Fearful that she would harm herself, Dex trimmed off a narrow row of over-treated hair, speaking in soothing innocuous words that later he could not recall. "Rosa can take you into town and you can have your natural color matched if you like. You don't have to wait for this entire blonde to grow out."

With coaxing, Anya sipped the healthy soups that were Rosa's specialty, but otherwise wanted nothing more than solitude and sleep. Rosa had already suggested that a professional evaluation was needed. Something was seriously wrong, but Dex resisted.

"She's in a depression, Dex. I doubt we can help her. She needs a psychiatrist or at least a good evaluation by a medical doctor. Maybe even medication," Rosa stated.

"She won't go. You know I've tried."

"You didn't try hard enough. You wouldn't ask a sick child if they'd like a little something to bring down a raging fever. You give it to them, even if they resist."

"She just needs a little more time."

"One week, no more; if there's no change, I'll make the appointment myself. We have an excellent psychiatrist at St. Patricks' and I've already talked with him about Anya. From what I described he agrees that she needs help."

Rosa insisted Anya sit on the veranda part of each day and supplied her with sports publications, fashion magazines and Bible leaflets with inspirational sayings from her Church. Joey informed her that he was short handed and soon had her exercising their most predictable mare up and down the long drive. One day Dex came home from the rink and found Anya in the kitchen chopping vegetables as she laughed with Rosa. A sound was never more welcome, but so sudden a change seemed almost unnatural until he forced the disquieting thought from his mind.

It seemed to him that Anya's questioning by immigration officials had brought to the surface immense inner turmoil. She was apparently better, and yet their relationship was firmly altered. Her sudden disinterest in the physical side of their relationship seemed abrupt and final. Although they continued to occupy the same bed, she no longer turned to him for whatever solaces their coming together had previously satisfied. Her retreat from him almost made Dex feel that Anya was another person entirely, and yet, apparently oblivious to his confusion, she neither explained nor apologized.

Once again her sleep was restless. She often cried out or spoke in her native language words that he did not understand. She seemed to truly sleep only when he held her in the tight restraint of his arms, and so for long hours he lay with her, feeling her thin, highly-muscled frame against him, almost grateful to avoid that combat-like passion that had been equally unsettling.

Under pressure from him, she resumed a training schedule and continued to improve. He was surprised at how little she had lost in her months away from skating and when she was invited to perform several exhibitions, he accepted on her behalf. After a television special, in which she was a last minute replacement, Dex laid out plans for a professional career.

This resulted in their first argument. In no uncertain terms she told him that she would never skate to her former level again. Dex had heard that old lament too often and did not believe her. He knew many skaters who, with every good intention, left the sport only to find that they could not shed the discipline and focus of those formative years. As he watched her perform, he was struck at the instant rapport she established with her audience. From the moment she took the ice, the excitement and energy she inspired was electric and that genuine smile which lit up her face as the audience erupted in applause made him think that this could provide the much needed healing that would give their life stability. But this was not to be.

With no premonition of impending loss, he returned from the rink to find Anya gone! Leaving nearly every new possession he had bought for her behind, she had borrowed a suitcase from Rosa and called a cab. Bewilderment was followed by hurt and finally anger.

"Where did she go?" he demanded accusingly of Rosa.

"How should I know?" Rosa was defensive. "She packed a few things and called a cab."

"And you let her do that," Dex demanded. "Without calling me!"

Rosa was a graduate of Penn State and a third generation Mexican

American. She had married Joey, who had struggled to obtain a high school education and had spent his entire life working at the Vineyard. Only in the last year had her family begun to forgive her. Now she leveled a stare at Dex and took a deep breath as though weary of having to explain a basic and obvious truth.

"She is an adult, Dex. You can not keep her prisoner just because you feel compelled to indulge a rescue obsession."

"Is that what I've been doing?"

"Maybe not entirely, but any fool can see that she's unstable. Maybe you've told her what to do too often and not listened enough"

"I only want to give her a safe haven," Dex said, hurt. "Time to recoup and get strong."

"But you didn't give her much time, did you? You got her right back on the ice and out there in the spotlight, when she told you very clearly that this is not what she wanted for herself."

"She has only a very slim window of opportunity to rebuild her career. She doesn't know what she wants."

"Will you listen to yourself? She doesn't know what she wants!" Rosa repeated. "No woman will tolerate being treated like a child forever." Dex turned away, and she came up to touch his arm. "Sleeping with someone is not a bridge to intimacy. I just think she's complicated, and maybe none of us really know her as well as we think we do."

"What do you mean? I know her very well. I was going to propose marriage. After everything we've been through, how can you believe that it's right for her to go without even saying goodbye?"

"If she loves you, Dex, she'll come back on her own terms. And despite what you say, she is not well. I didn't major in psychology, but I suspect there may even be something clinically wrong with her, and that you haven't noticed is stupid."

Today, in light of those photographs, Dex knew that he should have listened to Rosa. Those wicked, evil images had changed everything, and now he could not passively wait to be blackmailed, especially when they had shown him very clearly where to start. Upstairs, locked behind the heavy door of a safe, they taunted him to make a move. It seemed now a terrible lapse that he had never forced Anya to explain her long absence after their return from Washington. Many pieces of a disjointed puzzle waited to be fit together, and his failure to read the signs and seek the truth had been cowardly.

Dinner would soon be ready, but he was not hungry. Anya would eat lightly, as she always did, and then they would drive to the rink for her last practice of the day. She expected her husband to join her and fill the role of coach as she practiced the jump she was having difficulty with. This wasn't new. She'd always had difficulty with this jump because she tended to drop her shoulder as she came around, throwing herself almost deliberately off balance. That the correction needed to be persistently relearned was an oddity of technique that many skaters experienced, to the great frustration of their coaches and themselves. Almost, Dex thought, like a character flaw that persistently reared its ugly head.

Dex stood before the gun cabinet in his father's study and wondered where he might find the key. He heard the gentle sound of the dinner bell that his mother had installed in the kitchen to ring throughout the house. It was intended to remind his father that now was the time to tear himself away from whatever he was doing. Rosa seemed to enjoy using it for any number of reasons, but tonight it called Joey, Anya, and himself to the long authentic monastery table in the high-ceilinged dining room flanked by twin fireplaces at either end of the room.

As Dex studied the contents of the gun cabinet he regretted that he had not allowed his father to teach him to load and shoot. "Every man," Thierry had asserted, "needs to know how to protect his land and his family." The statement alone was enough to turn Dex away. "What," he wondered, "did Thierry think this was, the Wild West? When, in this time and this culture would it ever be necessary to take up arms in defense of one's family?"

Rosa would know where the key was, but Dex had already decided not to ask her. She was too smart, too inquisitive, and he had to admit, correct in her criticism of him on that day that Anya had disappeared.

Maybe, Dex now acknowledged, he was more like his father than he had ever imagined. Thierry had wanted to write his own script, ignoring the realities and never admitting defeat. He would not recognize his son's accomplishments in skating because they did not coincide with his egocentric view of his only son as an extension of himself. Dex wondered if he had reenacted the same crime in refusing to believe that Anya did not want to skate. He had discounted her statements when they went against his own plans for her and for their coming marriage and life together.

Dex acknowledged that some part of him had always believed his father evil for that selective view of reality that seemed to give him carte blanche to manipulate. Thierry had never given up on the idea that he could force his son into a mold of his making. The great wound of Dex's life, in the rare moments when he allowed himself to dwell on the past, had been that his father had never made an attempt to know him. How could a parent really love a child whose individuality they refused to acknowledge? And hadn't he done the same? Even as he claimed to love Anya he refused to hear her conflicting thoughts and persistently ignored the very obvious fact of her pain!

He'd never once confronted Anya on where she had gone during that time that she had disappeared soon after their return from Washington and before they married. Instinct told Dex that at least a partial answer would be revealed in the genesis of that question that he had been too afraid to ask. Was he afraid of the truth and how that might shatter his hopeful fantasy of what their life would be like together as husband and wife?

Dex thought of the blackmail photographs he had not destroyed, as he ran his hands under the base of the gun cabinet in search of a key. He had already checked the desk without luck.

He could not indulge the luxury of being reticent any longer. Tonight he would ask Anya where she had been during that time away. He would demand an answer, for finally he had no choice. Not if he wanted to save her, and perhaps save their marriage in the process. But even now, even after viewing those photographs, he would not admit the possibility that his wife was mentally unstable. Rosa was wrong. Anya was fragile. She was sensitive and mercurial, but mentally ill? Certainly not that!

The dinner bell rang again, but Dex ignored it. He ran his hands behind the pediment of the walnut cabinet and felt the cold shape of a key. Now all he had to do was figure out a way to travel with a weapon.

Anya put her arms around his waist and rested her head between his shoulder blades. He hadn't heard her enter the room, but he wasn't startled this time by her unexpected presence.

"What are you doing here all alone and staring at these horrid guns? Come, Darling. Dinner is getting cold." She took his hand and he allowed himself to be led away. There was a lot to do. He had a plane to charter, a decision to make about which man he would confront first, and a few pointed questions to ask his wife. This time he'd wait for an answer. She couldn't avoid confiding in him forever.

CHAPTER SEVEN

There were times when he felt her danger so surely that he had to turn his back on the business around him and shut his office door to pray. He hadn't known enough on that hot July day to take her hand and return her safely to the others. But he trusted God for the kind of miracle that would someday bring her home.

Dex forced himself to smile and look concerned when it seemed called for, but he was finding it difficult to follow the conversation going on around him. Joey joined them late for dinner, and seeing that Dex was preoccupied, he turned his attention to engaging Rosa and Anya in conversation.

Joey and Dex had become more like brothers than Thierry Arujo had ever intended. Under the terms of the will, the Vineyard was to stay intact for future generations, but Dex had never seriously considered children, and now he wondered if that too was a kind of passive rebellion against his father's perpetual disappointment in him. And what about Anya, he wondered? Anya had never mentioned children, and suddenly Dex thought it significant that they, a married couple, had never once broached the subject with one another.

Anya looked at him and furrowed her brow even as she continued her conversation with Rosa. They were discussing the cookbook that Rosa was writing. She slid her foot over to touch his, and he returned the pressure as he checked off in his mind all that needed to be accomplished before he could leave for New York the following morning. He would have to revise the rink schedule and then phone Hillary and arrange for her to take his students. He recalled Hillary's reaction when she learned from Rosa that Anya had left him. She had wasted no time in letting him know that she was willing to forgive him. She wanted him back on any terms, but there was no going back for Dex.

"I thought we meant something to each other," Hillary demanded in tears. Once again the same argument was replayed, although this time with far more animosity. The next day when he saw her at the rink, Hillary took him aside to apologize. "I'm sorry, Dex. I want you to be happy, and if that means another woman, I can accept that." For the first time Hillary sounded genuine.

"Are you sure?" Dex asked. "You wouldn't rather stop working together? I know you've had offers and maybe you'd be happier with more distance between us."

"No. I've helped you build this skating program from the ground up, and I'm proud of what we've accomplished. I can keep my personal feelings separate. But Dex, do you realize that Anya may never return?"

"It doesn't matter, Hillary. Whatever happens I want you to understand that our relationship is over." Dex made a point to hold her gaze. He was wary. Always before she had failed to take him seriously, and when Anya returned and began to train at the rink, Hillary could barely be civil. Shades of that same jealousy remained even today in how the two women related to one another.

During Anya's absence the march of days fell together in empty succession, followed by long, interminable nights. Dex considered hiring a private detective, but after he ran the idea by Rosa and Joey, he immediately discarded it. Only Ryan seemed to understand his feelings and promised to let him know if he learned anything at all about her whereabouts.

Joey and Rosa headed east to spend the holidays in New England with her family, and with Anya gone Dex faced the prospect of spending Christmas alone for the first time in his life. They had not been intimate since her return from Washington, and yet Dex had found himself melting toward her in a way that he had never experienced before. He longed to provide her the comfort she needed to feel better and yet now he considered the possibility that his presence had mattered little. Imprisoned by withdrawal, Anya had been absent from him and present only to a place he could not go, and to a grief he could not imagine.

"Are you sick?" Anya's question brought Dex sharply back to the present.

They were still seated around the old monastery table gleaming from layers of polish. Anya reached across to touch his hand. "Are you not feeling well?" she repeated, "You've hardly touched your dinner."

To cover his discomfort Dex reached for his coffee cup and took a sip of Rosa's specially blended herb tea. The pattern of the cup was 'Chinese Tigers' which Anya had glimpsed during the opening scene of a movie they had watched together. It was the first and only time she had asked him for anything, and so he had been happy to track down a full service, although the pattern itself was discontinued. They used the china each night that Anya was home, and Dex could see that she derived a certain pleasure from looking at and handling the pieces. He could not help wondering if the pattern reminded her of happier times in her life, but when he asked, she only thanked him again for the gift.

Dex agreed that he was not feeling well. Still he insisted on driving Anya to the rink, hoping for just the right moment when he could question her on where she had gone during that time away, just before they finally married. He could not escape the conviction that this was information he needed in order to protect her. Leaving his own skates untouched, he sat in the bleachers and watched her land her jumps and run through her program without his usual enthusiasm. There would be no instruction or calls of encouragement, for he had to think. He had to decide what to do next, and yet as usual, when Anya skated, he could not take his eyes off her.

Dex thought of what a skilled lover she was. At the Stratton cottage she had stunned him with the abruptness of that first passionate encounter, for she did things and knew things that he had never thought of. At the end he had felt completely sated and exhausted, but robbed of some vital element that should have been present in the act itself. Despite the flawless execution of that skilled and heightened dance, he could not entirely shed a lingering impression that she, as a real woman, was profoundly and mysteriously absent.

In a painful flash of insight he recalled how Anya would tense at the moment of penetration and even seemed to prolong the inevitable for as long as possible. He saw himself seeking unconsciously to ease that moment and always failing. What a simple process it was, in the heated press of the moment, to convince himself that all was imagined. And yet he knew that he would never again make love to Anya with the same blind and careless excess. Those black and white images had shattered an illusion, and in the process revealed his inadequacy. He asked himself the hard questions. Was she only giving him what she thought he wanted? In the midst of pleasure was there remembered pain? Was their love-making truly reciprocal, and why had he not seen and known and sought the truth? Without honesty, the act itself was no more than a deceitful parody.

Dex's eyes followed Anya's graceful form as she flew over the ice below. He knew that she, like all skaters, loved the feel of the wind on her face as she lifted off and glided out of a jump for a perfect landing. There was no better feeling in the world. She was due to go back on tour shortly and was always the perfectionist, demanding and unreasonably critical of herself. It was a common trait among successful competitors.

"Take the jump back to the beginning," he had suggested. "Work on a single and then a double and don't try the triple until you've reminded yourself of how it feels to do it right." Dex had missed all of his lessons for the day, allowing Hillary and her new assistant to pick up the slack. A couple of the parents started towards him, but changed their minds as they drew closer. "Not tonight," he had said to others and, "Ask Hillary." Normally generous with his time, tonight he was distant and even abrupt.

Anya followed Dex's advice and took the jump back to basics. She was the only professional on this high freestyle practice limited to half a dozen junior and senior level competitors. Mirrors lined one wall, and when it grew dark, starlight gleamed from the overhead skylights, an architectural feature of the building that Dex had designed. The familiar sights and smells eased the sense of dread as he watched the skaters line up their jumps in the same corner, wearing deeper and deeper tracings into the hard surface. To the untrained eye the crowded practice session looked like a series of narrow misses and near collisions but was in truth a deliberate dance of grace and courtesy, which Dex never tired of watching. Classical program music played in the background, interspersed with popular, rock, and even country music.

It occurred to Dex that if he had not been so busy trying to reconstruct Anya's life, she might have confided in him, and then perhaps she would never have left. The abruptness of that ten-week separation, as he agonized over her safety, was a torture he never wanted to experience again. He had filled his days with any mindless activity designed to postpone real evaluation until she no longer occupied his thoughts with the same masochistic vengeance, but not always with success.

Joey and Rosa had invited him to join them for Christmas, but nurturing a secret hope that Anya would return for the holidays, he had declined. As Christmas and New Year's passed without so much as a phone call from Anya, Dex became despondent. An unexpected call from his agent was most welcome. Several board members of a company intending to launch a new electrolyte drink had extended an invitation and suddenly the prospect of flying to New York and mixing business with pleasure appealed to Dex.

He was accomplished at socializing with people he hardly knew and exuded a polished charm that drew others to him. But tonight, as he played the role of seeming to enjoy himself, he could not shed his disappointment at Anya's absence. The party had spilled over into several rooms and every so often Dex looked for Ryan, who had also been invited, but had not yet shown up. Feeling stranded, Dex knew he could persuade Ryan to make a quick exit as soon as he arrived. They had not talked in any depth since the day Anya left, but Ryan had promised to call if he heard anything. The prospect of having a drink with Ryan and catching up on what had been happening in their lives was preferable to this vivid party atmosphere, so contrary to the self-pity which held him in an unaccustomed grip of introspection. He could confide in Ryan who would not feel sorry for him, but would bring him up sharply with a challenging mixture of truth and humor. Dex suddenly felt the need of such emotional surgery.

As he glanced surreptitiously at his watch, Dex bristled with well concealed impatience. He had been cornered by a woman who held him captive with a string of comments on the potential crop of skaters for the next world team, as if she were pronouncing judgment on racehorses rather than humans. He hated her sort of flip analysis which demonstrated little comprehension of the sacrifice and determination it took for one child to reach the senior level of amateur competition. Dex thought of his students. As far as he was concerned any child who reached that level was already a champion.

Trying not to be too obvious, Dex glanced beyond his companion in search of Ryan, and then he saw her. Stunned, he blinked and looked again. She was changed. There was a sophisticated polish to her appearance that he had never seen before. This near stranger gave no hint of ever having suffered from a paralyzing depression and was difficult to reconcile with the needy and lost young woman who had fled his home without so much as the courtesy of a goodbye. Her hair had fully grown out and she wore a simple dress of hunter green with sequined straps and diamond earrings.

This was not the reunion he had envisioned as he watched her intently, uncertain of his reception. He had imagined her walking into his office at the rink or looking out from the veranda that surrounded three sides of the house and seeing her drive up in a taxi through the iron gates of Arujo Winery. He had envisioned every scenario except a party such as this. A party he would never have thought to attend, except to escape some measure of his own pain.

When he first arrived, Dex was surprised to note that a number of financial benefactors of skating were present as well. Presidents of corporations and boards who funded various projects as well as individuals, like the woman who still held him captive as she prattled on, apparently oblivious to the fact that his attention was intently riveted on another woman just across the room.

The host of the party was Howard Maple's son, Peter. Howard's name and reputation, despite rumors of a debilitating stroke, remained compelling. No one in the history of figure skating had raised more money for the sport or prepared so well for what would eventually erupt into a marketing and licensing bonanza. Howard was credited with anticipating and preparing for the future in such a way that the old guard and their organizations were protected from infringement.

To drop the news that Howard Maple had entertained you was, in the insular skating community, the equivalent of an invitation to dine at the White House. Knowing that Howard lived with his son, and was even now under the same roof of this weathered brick mansion, caused some to feel disappointed that he had not been paraded out in his wheel chair. The speculation concerning his health, and especially his state of mind, had been intense, and many were avid to confirm the rumors.

As Anya's eyes locked with his, Dex recognized the same fleeting shock and uncertainty that must have been evident on his own face seconds before. Once again he felt that familiar, blind infusion of lust rush through his body. It was a torrid, primitive energy that Anya rarely failed to recognize, and now she smiled in return; an unguarded and open smile that promised everything but assured nothing. Anya turned from her companion and unceremoniously walked to meet him.

"Where did you go, why did you leave?" He hated himself for asking. He hated the agony that drove the question from his lips without so much as a greeting of hello.

"I had to go, Dex. You must try to understand," she said in that breathless way she had of speaking when excited.

"Of course," he said, touching her cheek. "I do understand. I was smothering you. Making too many decisions without taking your feelings into account. Can you forgive me?" Even as he apologized and said that he understood, Dex knew that he did not, but he would not risk an argument. Not now. The mood shifts and never knowing what to expect was the impetus that set his pulses racing. Sometimes she was like an entirely different person, and his life when she was gone seemed dull and pale in comparison to the stimulus that she brought to every encounter.

"Dex, I have a favor to ask of you. An important favor," she said getting right to the point. "I would have called but I was afraid to ask. Afraid that you would say no. But now my situation is desperate."

"You can ask me anything. Don't you know that? I love you."

"I may not be able to stay in this country. They think I know something about Sasha and money missing from my country." This was the first real information concerning her ongoing immigration problems that she had ever confided.

"Everyone knows your country is run by a group of paranoid madmen."

"Well, yes, that is true," she replied impatiently. "What I need, Dex, is a husband. If I marry you, no one will send me back."

Dex looked at her stunned. Marriage had never been discussed, and only he had ever said the words, "I love you." But he had thought of marriage many times and assumed that she too had anticipated marriage as a normal progression of their relationship. They were standing in the middle of a crowded room, and the moment was awkward. Dex longed for privacy as someone called Anya's name and she turned to wave and smile in return. Out of the press of bodies a woman asked for Dex's autograph.

"It's for my daughter," the woman said. "She won't believe I met you here tonight."

Dex scribbled his name on a monogrammed cocktail napkin. "Now if you'll excuse us," he said abruptly and took Anya's hand, leading her out into the hallway. When the next person stopped him, Dex could no longer control his impatience. "Can't you see we're trying to have a private conversation?" he snapped, forgetting that his purpose for being there was to be charming and accommodating, while his agent lobbied to keep his name on the narrowing list of candidates considered as spokesperson for the new sport drink. On impulse he opened a closet door and pulled Anya in behind him. They could smell damp wool, and fur tickled their faces. Dex found the overhead light so that he could study her expression.

"I love you," he said. "But I won't marry you unless we agree to have a real marriage." He hesitated. He was afraid to suggest that she love him in return. Love could never be demanded, so he said instead, "I won't marry you unless you have feelings for me."

She leaned against him, encircling his body tightly with her arms.

But Dex stopped her. He would not be distracted. "And you must confide in me, Anya. There is no real love without trust. It can't be the way it was. You must tell me everything so that I can help you."

Dex held his breath and waited. He could not quite believe that he had found the courage to give her an ultimatum, when in truth, he would gladly take her back under any circumstances.

Anya looked at him, a serious expression on her face. "I won't lie to you. I love you very much, but I don't know if I am capable of the kind of love you deserve. There are circumstances. Particulars that you cannot know, Dex. It is because you are good and generous that you do not see. It is I who will never deserve you. Not at all!"

"Nothing you can say will alter how I feel about you. Don't you believe that I love you and that I can never stop loving you?" he pleaded.

"Then I will marry you," Anya asserted and smiled in that radiant way that never failed to bring a surge of infectious joy to his heart. It struck Dex that she had forgotten that the proposal had originated with her, and for a moment he felt confused and inclined to question that odd shift of focus. But the old Anya was back. She stepped closer and like an addict hungry for a fix he buried his face in her hair. She turned her lips up to his, and they fell together. It was a deep, hungering kiss that blotted out the memory that she had ever left him. Once again he was whole and complete simply because he held her in his arms, and the truth of that greedy need was as blatant and palatable as the physical space they stood in. He could no more control his obsession with all that she had awakened in him than he could stop breathing.

"Let's get out of here," he said. "I came with my agent, so I'll call a cab."

"I have a car and driver," she said and kissed him again. "There is just one little thing I need to do. You go on and I'll meet you outside in fifteen minutes," she urged.

Dex sat in the darkened limousine and watched the snow drift under the lamp light. Anya's driver offered him a drink, but he declined. Instead he sank into the comfortable leather and watched white flakes, thick and heavy, accumulate on the drive and settle in a white line over the ink-black branches of the trees. The night reminded him of their first meeting in Sweden. Fifteen minutes turned to thirty. With growing anxiety Dex watched the front door. He had just decided to go in search of Anya when from the opposite direction a cold blast of air permeated the car, and she slid onto the seat beside him.

"Where did you come from?" he asked. He had not seen her emerge from the house, but noted a flash of color as she slipped something into the pocket of her coat. They fell together and kissed. Her hands on his face felt cold and her face hot. The scent of her perfume came to him from the open neck of her coat, and he failed to wait for an answer. Eventually a million questions would come to mind, but tonight they would make love, and there would be a new beginning.

Dex remained on the top row of the darkened stadium. He watched Anya glide around the parameter of the rink as she lined up her jumps with graceful ease, and he thought of what A. E. Housman had written, just before war enveloped England. "The thoughts of others were light and fleeting, of lovers meeting, of luck or fame; mine brought trouble, and I was readying when trouble came."

They were married in January just after they returned from New York. Anya seemed convinced that she was in danger of being deported if she did not marry quickly, although Dex saw no indication of this.

The ceremony was held in the chapel on the grounds of the winery. Once an outpost to one of the network of missions to spot the California coast, the building had been restored by Thierry and often brought tourists to the winery. Only Ryan, Hillary, Rosa, and Joey were in attendance as a local justice of the peace officiated. Joey and Rosa were pressed into quick service as attendants, and Anya wore an off the shoulder dress trimmed with Mexican embroidery and lace that Rosa had helped her select. Settled in the strands of her burnished hair was a cascade of gardenias, and she carried a bouquet of white tulips, gardenia, and rosemary. Afterwards they had a barbecue on the lawn and invited all the farm workers and their families, as well as friends from the town and rink. Dex thought it the happiest day of his life even paling in comparison to the day he won gold at the Olympics.

Now, as he thought of that day, Dex felt a stab of pain. He had loved Anya and believed his love was returned. He had ignored the truth and replaced his doubts with a fantasy marriage in order to stave off a deluge of fear. He should have heeded those instincts and had the courage to demand the truth, for nothing else could have armed him better for the arrival of those loathsome photographs. Now it struck Dex that the survival of their marriage, and perhaps Anya's life, depended on his willingness to fight this battle for their protection.

Dex watched Anya turn her body for the backward approach into the double-lutz. She shifted her weight onto her left foot, and using the toe pick of her right skate as a spring, she propelled her body into the first revolution. After two rotations she exited the jump on her right foot. Now she would try a triple. It was the jump she was having difficulty with, but there was no hint of that now as he watched her come around for a second try. Her speed was good and as she pushed off with her toe pick, her leg came up and she flew into the final spiral, gliding out in perfect form. She looked up at the stands for his reaction. She needed his praise and he accommodated, gesturing thumbs up and forcing a return smile.

Dex watched Anya leave the ice. Although skating required great physical exertion and skill, she seemed more relaxed on the ice than any other place. In many ways she reminded him of Ryan. Locked within the perimeters of the boards and isolated on that frigid surface, they were both focused inward and aware of little else, seeming to skate for that unconscious freedom rather than for skating itself. It was enough to 'be out there', on that private island. He suspected that if Anya had never turned professional, she would still have skated, as Ryan did now, for a sort of release.

As usual she was the last skater to leave the ice. As she reached for her guards, he joined her below. "Here, let me do that," he said and bent to unlace her skates. Anya extended one leg and leaned back against the row of bleachers. He could feel her eyes studying him, and as he slid off her second skate she leaned forward to kiss his forehead.

He avoided looking at Anya as he wiped down her blades and slid the terry cloth protectors into place. How many times had he performed this mindless ritual for himself, for his younger students, and now for Anya? There was comfort in the familiarity until a swift dart of an icy presence, a premonition of what might come intruded. It made him want to freeze this one act of sheer and utter normalcy forever.

"Soon you must tell what is wrong, Dex?" Anya spoke softly. With reluctance he studied her face and knew that he could not protect her forever. Rosa would even say it was wrong to conceal vital information she had every right to know. Just not now! Not until he had a plan. Dex passed Anya a towel. She dabbed at her face and took a long swallow of water.

"I'm going away for a week," he told her once they were in the land rover and heading north on 101. He didn't look at her but studied the road ahead.

"Where are you going?" she asked, curious.

"Our agent wants me to meet with a potential sponsor." The ease of this lie as it slipped off his tongue surprised him.

"So it is an endorsement you've been worried about," Anya said, relieved that this was all that was bothering her unusually subdued and withdrawn husband. "We don't need the money. This is what you always tell me, so why should you worry?"

"I know, but still it would be nice. Good exposure for you and especially combined with the People Magazine article that will be coming out. But we'll talk about it. You'll be out of town anyway, so I thought as long as I was in New York, Ryan and I might head into New Hampshire or Maine for a little fishing. No more than a week, maybe a few days."

"I love you," she said. "You deserve a break." She leaned across to kiss the hollow of his neck.

This would be their last night together. She was going on tour and he would fly to New York. Dex found it difficult to grasp the concept that Anya and the anguished child of those photographs was in fact the same person. That thought alone, as she was overpowered and violated, enraged him and each time he connected that terror stricken face to hers, he closed his mind to the onslaught of pain. Dex knew that he could not make love to Anya tonight. He must find a way to avoid the intimacy that she would expect, for in that instant that she turned to him, she would certainly know that something more was terribly wrong.

Dex realized that the photographs represented only the tip of the iceberg and that Anya, who had withheld so much, would fight him at every turn in his effort to learn the truth. He was on his own. This thought wounded him. Rage burned behind his eyes. Now was not the time to indulge in self-pity or anger. He knew he must maintain self-control and whatever pain he was feeling, was nothing to the torture endured by her.

The inevitable blackmail demand was sure to arrive at any time, and he could not wait passively by wondering where the next set of photographs might surface. Unless he wanted to involve the authorities and risk a media circus he had no other option than to discover the truth on his own. It was fortunate that he did not need Anya to tell him where to start. The photographs had shown very clearly that Elliot Smythe was his first logical choice.

Dex could think of no two people who held on to a grudge longer than Glen Winston and Elliot Smythe. The two remained good friends and now Anya was about to join the same tour that Glen had promoted and now managed. For some reason, which had not been clear at the time, Glen had not wanted Anya. Dex had assumed it was Glen's way of punishing him for the year that he had come in first at nationals ahead of Ryan. Knowing of Anya's insecurity, Dex had not told her, but he was no longer an immature teenager. He now had as many contacts and more clout than his former coach, and unlike Glen, he was genuinely liked and trusted.

As it turned out the sponsors did not need Dex to point out what a draw Anya had become, but he still made a point of reminding them of Glen's attitude toward having Anya join the tour. A recent poll had shown her surprisingly popular, even with segments of the American public that previously had no interest in figure skating. With Anya's performance in the children's fantasy movie and the cover of People Magazine, Dex was well aware that he too would experience a resurgence of his own career. As soon as Anya finished a round of talk shows and interviews, she was due to pick up Glen's tour in Kansas City. They would now depart on the same day.

Dex thought of the long-standing relationship between Glen and Elliot and could not avoid the conclusion that Glen was one of the two men who could not be recognized in the photographs. The two had sat on numerous boards and committees and shared many judging assignments before Elliot began his very successful broadcasting career and Glen founded the Winston Skating Center, devoting himself exclusively to coaching. Dex only hoped he could persuade Elliot to talk without first sinking a fist into that pompous face, for Elliot Smythe was the man who watched as the child Anya Szcepanik was raped. His Anya! Dex rolled his hand into a fist and rammed it into the seat. Beside him Anya jumped, startled by the force of the sudden blow. She looked at him astonished.

In a squeal of brakes Dex cut across two lanes of traffic. Behind him a horn blasted at the abrupt swerve and dust rose as tires spun onto the shoulder. He turned in his seat. "I want you to tell me where you were before Christmas. I want to know what you did after you left California!"

Anya looked at him wide-eyed, and as often happened when there was a sudden shift of mood or topic; there was a pause, a certain interlude of blankness as she prepared to answer. "I'm sorry," she said finally in a childlike tone that undermined his anger.

"You've told me nothing. I want concrete answers, not vague phrases about being alone in order to think. I want to know where and what you did during those weeks that you disappeared."

When Anya spoke again, her accent was more pronounced, and she pressed one hand to her forehead as though in pain. "This is important to you, Dex?" The little girl voice was gone, her words now collected and cool. She was stalling and he knew it.

"We agreed to have a real marriage and now it seems you still can't trust me. Not even enough to share minor details and answer simple questions with a straight reply."

"You are being very tiresome and melodramatic," she said. "I went away. We were reunited and got married just as you wanted, and aren't we happy together, Dex? Isn't this enough for you?"

This was his cue to reassure her and apologize, for he always had relented in almost every confrontation. But this time he could not accommodate her fears, whatever they were. He had to know. "What are you hiding, Anya? I asked you a simple question that you seem unwilling or unable to answer."

"What question?" she asked and looked around as though suddenly unsure of her surroundings.

"I want to know what you did during that time that you left me without so much as a thought for how I would worry. It was just a fluke that we met at Peter Maple's party after the Holidays. We discussed marriage and you agreed that we would not keep secrets. That you would tell me everything, but the fact is, Anya, that I know nothing more about you today."

Anya reached over and shut off the air conditioner. She rolled down the window and looked out at the Pacific. A pale sickle moon hung overhead. He followed her gaze. Above on the hillside of a jutting peninsula houses clustered on the sloped landscape, giving the appearance that they might slip into the sea. The manner in which she held herself erect, as though in readiness for flight, revealed how tense she was, although her face remained an impenetrable mask of neutrality. Dex waited. As always, he waited in vain.

CHAPTER EIGHT

He was always able to pray for her with confidence. She was alive, and someday she would be coming home. He felt this was true, as surely as he counted on the softening thaw of the earth heralding spring after a particularly cold and long New England winter.

What had she done and where had she gone? Imprisoned in the claustrophobic closeness of the car, as traffic flew by and that sickle moon hung overhead like a distracting slice of lemon rind, Dex demanded answers to those questions. Anya formed her thoughts and opened her mouth to speak, but nothing came out.

How could she explain that she had not lived alone for a very long time? That in the throes of their most intimate moments, Others took over and in the midst of heated words Others spoke. They had not expected love and weren't ready to be changed by love, and yet cruelly and without consent, the process had begun. If she could not explain in the beginning, why did Dex suddenly imagine she could do so now?

It angered her that when it came to their careers Dex was never satisfied, always striving, planning, and pushing. The very qualities that drew her toward him in the beginning were those she now spurned. If she went to the local rink and skated twice a week and gave a few lessons and could have him in the bargain, that would be enough.

She regarded her husband critically. He was handsome. His glossy hair was neatly trimmed, and even when he woke in the morning it hardly ever looked ruffled. His dark blue eyes had a purple tint that reminded her of the velvet depth of violets just before that color merged with the yellow core.

She tried again to say the words, but found herself incapable of speech. It was she who was often silent. Anya was the only one who truly loved him, and yet the risk of doing so was enormous. The order of his life, the predictability of his kindness, the faithfulness of his actions had rarely altered, although she had tested and questioned and many times tried to provoke a different response.

Anya had begun to fear for her husband. She didn't trust Mocking or Lie to want the best for him, and she could not trust the Other not to hurt him. If Dex knew, really knew, he would be horrified and think her insane and a waste of that love he so eloquently claimed to feel for her, and she was jealous. Yes, she acknowledged, startled at the accuracy of that term for the emotion that she now claimed. She was truly jealous and could barely tolerate sharing her beloved Dex any longer with those Others.

Dex had never been entirely hers. She had seen the bruises on his hard strong body and knew that she would not have inflicted them and that he, loving her, would never raise a fist in self-defense. That Original Other, who actually hated wet, filthy coupling with the same degree of rapacity as the Lie craved it, while knowing nothing of love, but only the demand for immediate gratification, was responsible. When making love Anya had become almost successful at fighting the imperative to switch, refusing to let that Other take her place, but in consequence she could feel a frenzy mount under a canopy of rage at her presumptuous usurpation of what, until Dex, had rarely been her territory. She reached across and touched Dex's cheek, but he tilted his head away and gave her a steely look of determination that wounded her.

"Okay," Dex had finally relented. "By the time I've finished in New York you'll be in Kansas City for the tour. I'll meet you there, but I must warn you, Anya. This time I expect the full story. I can't settle for anything less."

As so often happened, Dex took her silence for agreement and maneuvered the car back into traffic. It was unlike Dex to brood, but he remained troubled and failed to pick up the threads of their argument as she expected he would. He hated to have her angry with him, and one or both of them would always apologize before they retired for the night, but this time he stayed late at his desk working out a schedule for Hillary to adopt in his absence. As the pearl gray of dawn infiltrated the darkness of their bedroom, he lay down beside her. She rolled into his embrace and he held her and stroked her hair, but did not sleep. Even as she dozed she felt his eyes on her face and marked his sleeplessness like a dog worrying a sore, relentlessly licking, licking. She tried not to dream. She mustn't allow herself to dream, but as so often happened when she least wanted to, she dreamt of Sasha.

Days after her disastrous performance in Sweden, the Other informed Anya that soon Sasha would no longer desire their body in the same way. Anya was afraid to hope and did not immediately recognize the greater danger. The Lie and its twin Mocking expressed it for them, in that unabashed way they had of stating the obvious without reserve. "Now that Sasha no longer wants our body, it is murder he'll require. Need I remind us? It's our murder I speak of. He'll need us dead."

All was reduced to a simple question of who would survive. A massive overhaul of their multiple existence was required in order to destroy Sasha before he destroyed them or touched the blindness of those silent cowering little ones that resided in the dimness of a formless existence. Anya, the Twins, and that Other had been together a long time.

"But he loves us."

"Even as he once claimed to love us, he will now hate us with a vengeance."

"But he has always hated us," Anya argued. "As soon as he turns his attention elsewhere, we'll be safe."

"We will never be safe. We will be a constant reminder of the danger his compulsions have placed him in," the Lie asserted as Mocking echoed.

"And yet," the Other said, "he cannot get rid of this body. The state has great expectations for Anya's career, even after that disastrous performance in Sweden. You will not usurp that skating body again," the Other turned on the Twins in sudden fury. "It was your fault that we did so poorly."

"You sound just like Sasha," they asserted. Anya agreed. A subtle balance had shifted, and a collective thread of fear was experienced when dealing with the Other's autocratic ways. The State had leaked the news that they had a skater who would land the first triple axel by a female in competition. They had been humiliated by Anya's performance and must now redeem themselves. Anya was their only hope. Sasha would receive the credit, but that mattered not at all. Only at a foreign competition would there be the opportunity to escape.

While Anya practiced, the Others became indispensable. The Twins mothered Sasha and commiserated even as they breathed secret poisonous ridicule. The Other matched that macabre humor and sometimes slept with him, no longer as a little girl but as a woman, while Anya did her best to fine tune those dual skills of avoidance and flight. The alters had not worked so well together for a very long time. It proved easy to assuage Sasha's anger with his great appetite for slavish dependence. He had never stopped thinking of Anya as his thing, his something to possess and control. Not until the very end would that illusion be irrevocably shattered.

The Other, perhaps recognizing certain traits in common with Sasha, saw that his greatest weakness lay in that vast, egocentric conviction that he was beyond the ordinary flow of consequence. His view of Anya changed as she grew into a woman, for now her very existence became a sort of perpetual reproach. Once more survival demanded change, but a chameleon-like response to life was something Anya had fine-tuned to a craft of superior sophistication. The alters began by inserting themselves into his affairs under the pretext of easing his ever-complicated life, and as it turned out, he needed a lot of help. For one thing there was far too much money and few places to spend it in that communist regime without attracting undue attention. Secrets bred secrets, and that ever widening mire of deceit was exacting a price that even Sasha was beginning to fear the burden of. Anya and a select number of alters set out to know him in order to destroy him, and to their immense collective amusement, he actually appeared grateful.

The following morning Anya and Dex drove to LAX. Anya let her head recline against the seat and looked out the window as Dex maneuvered the Land Rover through the morning rush. He checked their bags and escorted her to the gate before departing for his own.

His kiss of goodbye had been all too brief and his words perfunctory. Anya watched him walk away, and almost it seemed he would turn back. When he did not, she wanted to run after him, throw her arms around him, confiding everything. He was her knight in shining armor, her protector, and defender. It was in his nature to help and to love, and yet the prospect of trusting him bred confusion and rage. It was as if trusting him, or anyone for that matter, brought the certainty of betrayal. Far better not to exercise that failed muscle. It would almost be a relief to get it over with; to have him finally reject her forever. Crazy wasn't eating at her face and tearing at the top of her skull, as she sometimes imagined. No, crazy was the reality that lived within and from what she could tell, wasn't going anywhere.

Anya found her first-class seat and hoped that no one would sit beside her. As the airplane aligned its nose on the runway she made up her mind. The decision came seemingly from nowhere, and she was grateful. She would tell him. Inviting rejection and maybe even death, she would tell him everything.

Like any good actress who learns her lines as well as those of her fellow actors, she ran those weeks in question through her mind like the dailies from a disjointed day of shooting. She had to practice. What she could not say by rote might not be said at all. The fact was that she could never entirely know everything. There would always be missing time and information that could never be retrieved, but she could ask for help.

Anya grabbed a pillow and rested her head against the seat, feigning sleep. She hoped that those Others, whose memory she did not know, would share their thoughts, planting words in the collective consciousness of a multiple existence. In her exploration Anya made a monumental effort to keep still and small. Doing so could render her an invisible observer. Today this talent prevented disturbing ripples of alarm from reaching that Original Other. If her search was known, "it" would bring all to a crashing halt and she couldn't have that. Thanks to Dex, compartmentalized oblivion was no longer a luxury she could afford. She would start, not at the beginning, but at that place he asked. The day she left him.

By Boston standards it was a mild winter day. The sun shone and the streets were clear and dry with snow piled neatly along sidewalks and streets. Still the contrast from sunny California was stark and yet more like home, and she felt almost happy. She found her way to Filenes. She knew the building and across the street Jordan Marsh and down the block and around the corner the Boston Globe. She bought herself a winter coat, boots, gloves, and hat. She strolled up to Court Street and smiled at the huge teakettle, which hung off a grappling hook and sent a flow of steam up the overhang of the building. She knew that as well and the traffic and the subway stations. She recited some of the names, gratified by the memory.

From Court Street Anya turned down Boylston Street toward the Parker House to the old Boston State House. Sights and smells and thoughts were stirred out of the vast numbness of her being until an avalanche of memory assailed her, and it almost became too much. And it was too much and that's all she remembered until....

Significant time had been lost and so she did what she always did on those occasions. She couldn't rush the procedure. It happened of its own accord and in its own way. She came to herself slowly still feeling heavy and cumbersome and weighed down, the absence of herself fixed far from that space that her physical body occupied and yet reaching and yearning for that return to place. Sight was a rainy windshield obstructing her view, and so she squinted into a winter sun and waited to see more clearly. Her mind felt as though it were wrapped in cotton batting which muffled the sound of her own voice as she asked, "Where am I?" The answer was always unexpected and sometimes cruel. So she sat small. She sat quiet, in no hurry to learn her circumstances and especially because she didn't seem to be in any immanent danger. She concentrated on her breathing. She was breathing. She concentrated on her heartbeat until she felt herself filling the space of herself more fully. She imagined physical pain and reached for the awareness that would tell if she felt any. No, she didn't. That was good.

She had a routine that helped to smother the panic. She was nothing if not practiced, and prided herself on being able to handle these dense situations, dense with the unknown and fraught with risk. She continued the inventory looking down at her hands and whispering off the checklist. No blood. Good. The nails. No manicure. Not good, but not too bad. They weren't broken and she could see the remnants of the last, which told her ten days.

Approximately ten days out and counting.

What was she wearing? A coat. A winter coat. Yes, it was cold and she needed warmth. She was no longer anywhere near her home in southern California, but now she recalled leaving and the plane landing at Logan and the coat she'd bought at Filenes. But then she'd missed time and couldn't count on any of the Others filling her in. Most would be cowering somewhere, waiting for the Ferris wheel of ignorance to right itself.

Panic wanted to come. She heard the mounting echo of that irritating, whiny little voice, but she refused to listen. It was her job to take charge, and she would not allow Panic to step in. That had happened once before while in this country, and she'd landed in an emergency room with a doctor telling her he wanted to admit her to a closed psychiatric unit for observation and expecting her to sign some papers. The Twins had stepped in and while Mocking told him "NO!" the Lie said, more sweetly and contritely, "No" again. She'd had to pay cash for the visit so that Dex wouldn't see the charges. No, she could not panic.

The overriding physical sensation was hunger. She hadn't eaten, but she'd think about that later. Fingers trembling, stiff from cold, she reached for a purse that wasn't there. Instead there was a brand new soft leather briefcase stuffed with papers and blue plastic file folders all neatly arranged. That gave her a clue as to who had been preeminent during that missed time away. It could only be the banker, the money manager who had made them very rich, knowing everything there was to know about business and finance so that they could finally deliver a fatal wound to Sasha where it most counted: his pocketbook. That's what the Lie had said. "Let's hurt him where it most counts, in his pocketbook."

There were some whose actions were highly specialized and who performed only in certain high-risk circumstance. But for now the blood was the main thing. She examined her hands once more with studied determination. No. Thank you, Jesus. There was no blood.

Anya left the park bench, and heavy briefcase in hand, much too heavy to contain just papers, she moved to the window of a store filled with bric-a-brac and an antique mirror low in the center. She bent to see her reflection. Her dark red hair was caught back in a tight low ponytail, but at least her hair was clean and neat. It wasn't cut and her scalp hadn't been shaved and there were no bruises on her makeup-less face. Makeup-less. That was good. No makeup meant no abusive sex with strangers. She breathed a sigh of relief. That was good.

Another face appeared in the mirror beside hers. Anya tried to see that other face clearly, but her eyesight was still somewhat clouded. "Do you live around here?" she asked, more to see if the face was real than for an answer.

"Yes, Deary, all my life and look what I've come to. Stand up now, I'm an old woman I can't bend over like this for long. You going to buy that mirror?"

Anya shook her head. She looked back at the shop window. "No, I don't think so."

"You look like you could spare a twenty. Twenty dollars for an old lady who's come to nothing. Ten if you don't have it. Five will do."

Anya struggled to bring the woman's expression into focus. Dirt was caked in the lines of her wrinkled face, and her steel-gray hair peaked out from a low cap, which fell almost to her eyebrows.

"I may have lived there, in a big house," Anya pointed, the arm still feeling heavy and unfamiliar. As soon as she said the words she knew that it was true, and she knew what town it was that she'd come to and why.

"They tore it down, Deary, and the rest on this block too. Urban Improvement, don't you know? It's the latest thing," she commiserated. "And displaces the likes of me and you. I used to live in an apartment over there," the woman said and pointed also. "And a snug place too. Had a fire escape with plants and a place for my cat to sun." Anya let her gaze follow. She could almost see it. A brick apartment building with ivy on the walls and an intricate wrought iron canopy that sheltered the door. Anya smiled at the memory. The memory was hers alone, and she knew this to be absolutely true. The windshield was clearing, the cotton batting was melting away, her heart was still beating, and there was no blood embedded in her fingernails. She was grateful.

"I don't have the cat anymore." The woman's gray coat was threadbare, and her gloves were missing fingers. She seemed to like having someone to speak with. The odor that emanated from her person was atrocious, but Anya was just glad that it wasn't rotting corpses or her own stale urine from days of isolated confinement. She thought of walking away, but had no idea where she would go. It couldn't hurt to stand here on the sidewalk and listen to this harmless stranger. It was like listening to someone else's background music while she skated her own program. She would let the woman talk, and she would think as she came back to herself, more fully filling the arms and legs of the body that would be hers for at least a while.

"Would you join me for lunch?" she asked the woman.

"You must be daft, Deary. Blind or retarded. They wouldn't let the likes of me in any restaurant, and besides that they all know me. They know I can eat at the church. But they do have a cafeteria in that building. It's only for employees, but dressed like you are they won't know the difference. They have high turn-over. I hear things sitting at that bus stop there. Why don't you just march over there and get us something to eat. I like tuna on rye with dill pickles." Anya saw that her mouth was watering.

"Where can we eat?"

"There." The woman pointed to a transit shelter where a young mother and her child waited for a bus. There was something familiar in that scene, and she caught the sharp pain that clenched her heart before recognition could tear at her flesh. She wasn't ready to know.

"The very minute we sit down, they'll leave. They always do."

Anya decided. "Wait here. Watch my briefcase." With knowing fingers, fingers that knew what her conscious thoughts didn't, she reached for a small slim wallet of red alligator, and she caught site of the matching red gloves and looked down at her feet. Yes, matching shoes, and the colors of her coat softly blending with the artfully coordinated silk scarf.

"And don't forget cake."

Anya crossed the street, entered the building, and returned a short time later with two Styrofoam containers and her pockets stuffed with extras. She could see that the woman had fully expected her to return. She sat alone in a corner of the transit shelter hugging Anya's briefcase to her chest with a fiercely protective expression on her face.

"Lordy, what you got in here?" she asked as she put the briefcase at her feet. "A gun or something?"

Anya handed over one of the two Styrofoam containers into avid, outstretched hands. Immediately her companion was absorbed in her food, while Anya forgot that she had ever been hungry.

"Did you get us something to drink, Deary?" Anya passed over two cartons of milk. "Chocolate! How did you know?"

"I used to live over there," Anya recited softly. "It was a big house. White stone, I think, with a tall stained glass window on the second-floor landing. Do you recall this house?"

"I remember. The family lived there a long time."

"That's right," Anya agreed, a small thrill of excitement racing from her stomach to her throat, causing her heart to constrict. The feeling scared her. She didn't want to feel. Not yet. She only wanted to know.

"What happened to them? Where did they go?"

"I used to make better tuna than this. I had a kitchen once. Why you interested, Deary?" The woman looked at her fully for the first time. Her wizened eyes squinted into the sun beyond Anya's shoulder. Her tone was sympathetic.

Anya didn't answer. She knew the value of silence. She knew how

101

stillness unsettled curiosity, and guarded secrets worth keeping. She picked up the briefcase and hoped she could know the contents without looking. She thought about the gun. The Original Other would never own a gun that wasn't cleaned, primed, and loaded.

"I'll tell you if you want to know. There was a tragedy. They lost a child, I think." A stab of electricity shot through Anya at the old woman's words.

"Something happened to that child. I forget. But the mother went to live elsewhere, and the father stayed and worked during the week in Boston. He was a handsome man. Movie star handsome. I liked him."

"Why?"

"Oh, you know. You just like some people that you don't know well. He'd ask about my Judith, my cat. He was nice to everyone and he loved his two little girls. He played with them in the park on winter evenings, pulling their sleds and they'd watch out that window for him to come home." She paused and pointed across the street to the precise place where the window would have been. Anya knew that window well. She saw it clearly. "He was older than his wife and he walked with a cane. After he died they tore down the house to build that ugly monstrosity, and I lost my home too. I haven't been on my feet since."

Anya glanced at the woman's feet. She wore sneakers with several layers of socks to make them fit. "What would it take to get you on your feet?" she asked.

"More money than you have, Deary. Food is expensive and the landlords want references and first and last month deposits. I haven't collected a social security check in two years because I don't have an address. The priest said he'd help me, but I won't go in any shelter. As dangerous as the streets. A woman I know was raped there, and she was older than I am and uglier too. You wouldn't know this, Deary, but I was pretty once. I held down a job and I had a life. I miss my Judith."

Anya lifted the briefcase. She slipped knowing fingers into the zippered side compartment that was stuffed full, as wide as it could be with some of Sasha's money. She counted out the bills without removing them. "Do you have a place to hide this until you can get to a bank?"

"I got lots of places to hide things, Deary. I've been on the street a long time."

The woman looked at the money and hoped there was as much as two hundred dollars there. She watched as Anya walked from under the transit shelter.

As one bus approached and another pulled away, Anya breathed in the scent of diesel exhaust. That too was familiar. She had ridden this bus with her mother. It was the first bus that would eventually take them to Copley Square and the Boston Public Library. They went there for children's hour each Tuesday, rain or shine, and then took a taxi to North Station and rode the train home with father. The memory came in a cruel wave of grief that stung her eyes with salty tears.

As the bus pulled away the woman counted the zeros on the first bill. Was it real? Yes, the paper, the ink. It all felt real. She'd get another Judith. She'd have a kitchen and a little room with a comfortable bed. She was too happy to smile. So she cried instead.

Anya found him at the Boston Public Library. His face looked back at them from the glossy cover of *Legal Jargon*. There was something about his expression. She recognized the overdone polish of one committed to function and capacity rather than substance. He believed in the role that he played more than he believed in himself. Some of the Others were adept at spotting this sort of putrid ooze, that very ooze that seeped from this man's pores and would flow from his mouth with dangerous disdain. The Twins began to argue and almost made them walk away, but Anya thought that perhaps she had seen that face before and there was something compelling about his name. She repeated it to herself over and over again. Maple, Peter. Peter Maple. Maple....

In a professional register in the third floor gallery Anya found it again. Maple, Peter Howard. His reputation seesawed between notorious and respectable, and he had recently been up before the bar to combat charges brought by a disgruntled client, but somehow had managed to walk away unscathed. In his world money was the eternal lubricant, and denial, when cloaked repeatedly in the timely phraseology of politics, the great salve.

The next morning Anya boarded the shuttle to New York. Christmas decorations lent a festive air to the hazy winter light. The sight tugged at Anya, but the Others had no memory of Christmas in the midst of family, and it struck Anya as sad and then she thought of Dex. Like her he would be alone for Christmas. She knew he would miss her and wondered if he would come here, to the very city she looked out at from the window of her cab, to spend the holiday with Ryan. It occurred to Anya that she should call Ryan, but a chorus of Others warned against it. There was work to do and she knew this all too well, and yet, she would phone Ryan anyway. There were things that he could tell her that no one else could.

Anya took the cab directly to Peter Maple's building and then the elevator to the top floor office, where she walked the length of the Persian runner to the reception area, unannounced and without an appointment. Peter looked at her with an inward tug of curiosity that prevented him from sending her away.

Peter often acted on what he liked to term his 'lucky hunches', and after he learned how rich she was, and especially how unencumbered by family, he congratulated himself for having the good sense to have heeded those instincts. But he also felt that he knew her and there was something more. An odd confluence of disquiet merged with a strong feeling of déjà vu, which irritated and nagged at him.

Now, some weeks later he was not so sure. In moments of complete honesty he could almost admit an underlying tug of fear, although he felt completely foolish for indulging such a sentiment, and by then the serpent's head of greed had reared its ugly head, and he was determined to acquire something more than his usual fee from her.

There was very little to do really, although he did his best to make his work look as complicated as possible. He transferred money, and made a few investments that he explained to her in overburdened detail. She was maddeningly conservative and agreed to almost nothing he suggested, as though completely uninterested in making a profit. He was suspicious of her strategy, for he suspected she had one, but couldn't figure it out.

A few things became clear. She, or someone else, for he didn't think she could have done this on her own, had been deliberately obscuring a money trail. Some of the off-shore accounts had not seen activity other than interest accruing for ten years or more, which would have made her ten or twelve years old at the time that they were opened.

"What happened to this fund?" he asked, as he tried to access an account.

"It was closed," she said simply.

"Closed? Why closed?" he asked, alarmed, for he had grown to feel proprietary. He couldn't help it where money was concerned. He liked to imagine all money to be potentially his.

All his usual tactics to gain the upper hand failed. In the beginning, still grossly underestimating Anya, he tried to make the process complicated, until she phrased the legalese back to him with perfect ease. Peter even flirted with her though, as pretty as she was, she left him cold and when that fell flat he treated her like a daughter and finally, at the end of his rope, like an equal. Finance was not Peter's area of expertise. New York was the financial hub of the world, so why, when there was real cutting edge advice to be had a block away in any direction, had she sought him out?

It drove him crazy how she roamed his office, walking the perimeter like a caged animal and exhibiting an appalling lack of reverence for all the decorative investments he was so proud of. They had been chosen with great care to send just the right message of power, sophistication, and wealth. Above twin fireplaces at opposite ends of the room she paused only briefly before the original Turner that faced the more contemporary Stobart. She peered at the faces in the silver-rimmed photographs and displayed only courteous interest in his priceless collection of antique military miniatures.

Peter would invite her to sit, and she would drop into the nearest chair, often located across the large room so that he was forced to walk from behind his desk to sit opposite her. Then, just as he was again feeling comfortable, she would rise unexpectedly, often in mid-sentence, and resume her same circular stroll. With eye contact lost and focus disrupted, Peter seethed in barely suppressed exasperation. He could see that she was distrustful and that absence of trust, although completely justified, affronted his senses like fingernails across the surface of a chalkboard.

It was an office worker who finally recognized her. He was both astonished and relieved now that he could set aside the nagging suspicion that they had once personally known one another. And with figure skating in common he could build a little trust and perhaps end up managing her celebrity as well as her fortune. He had, in fact, never made so much for doing so little.

There was only one photograph of his father present and that was a black and white still taken during Howard's studio days of brief movie star fame.

Of course she had noticed that photograph in her forays about the office, but not until Peter mentioned his father's name did she really see it. Did the color of her skin plummet to a paler shade of ivory? Were those beads of sweat on her brow, and did he imagine that she slid her hands in her pockets because they trembled? His curiosity was piqued. Perhaps his father's fame and reputation would be the leverage he needed to forge a new bond with her. She had to be a fan. Anyone who knew anything at all about the history of figure skating held his father in high esteem.

"I know of your father," she admitted when he questioned her. "But of course in my country we have very little contact with that part of the figure skating establishment."

While her English was nearly flawless, it was her syntax that was slightly off. Sometimes he had actually forgotten that she was not an American citizen.

"We don't travel like skaters do in this country. Not unless we are in a competition. It is not like here, where everyone has access to what they choose. This is why I defected. I wanted freedom, you understand?"

He hadn't asked for an explanation, and yet, secretive and guarded, she was now offering him one. He felt good. She had picked up the small silver frame and was peering with intensity at the face.

"And this is your father?" she prompted. He had already said so, hadn't he? But this was more conversation unrelated to business than she had ever allowed, and so he answered. Later when he considered their exchange, he wondered if it was a glance of sympathy that she cast in his direction, but that shuttered window behind the blankness of her eyes opened but a faction, if it opened at all and he could not be certain.

"My father and I didn't know one another well. I lived with my mother and Howard was never really involved in my life," Peter offered.

"Your parents were divorced?"

Peter nodded his head. "Howard had a stroke almost two years ago and my wife wouldn't hear of him going into a home. He lives with us now."

She looked at him carefully, scanning his face. "Very admirable."

"Yes," Peter said, liking the compliment. During their brief exchange he had even thought of extending an invitation to lunch, but Anya changed the subject, and once again there was only the mechanics of their business dealings between them.

As usual she was dressed in what seemed to Peter a painfully nondescript manner. Her hair was up off her neck and pulled away from her face. She was dressed in gray flannel trousers and a white sweater with an oversized raincoat to hide her figure.

"Don't you ever wear your hair loose?' Peter asked without thinking. The question clearly caught her off guard. She turned her back and walked to the mirror over a console table. He watched her study her reflection as though she needed a reminder of how she had dressed that morning. He couldn't know that she was remembering rough hands and burning chemicals poured over her scalp for the first time. He couldn't know how she'd watched the stark platinum color being chased off by a rich strawberry red that she had almost forgotten was hers. The natural color had become like a badge and a symbol, but she failed to notice how it strengthened her delicate features, enhancing the green depths of her eyes.

Anya turned from the mirror and wordlessly regarded Peter. She could tell that her stare and especially her silence made him uneasy. But now, suddenly, she no longer enjoyed playing him. Instead she felt sorry for him. He too had once been a child and to have a father like that....

As Peter led Anya to a conference room, he knew she would prefer he not speak until they were alone, but he could not resist disguising his nervousness with talk as they walked past his secretary and down a long hallway. Anya's

106

refusal to reply to superficial banter with anything more than a nod or shake of the head seemed to him rude. Under the ballooning raincoat she wore a straight gray skirt and matching sweater with her hair caught in a tight bun. The absence of jewelry in view of her vast wealth was a glaring particular that irritated him, and he wondered. *Why not red? Why not a limousine rather than a cab that smelled of stale cigarettes and last night's drunk?*

Peter had searched through his father's collection of skating magazines and programs until he came upon a photograph of Anya standing on a podium in a glittering blue dress with silver sequins. Her hair was blonde, and because she was young, the overdone makeup made her look far less attractive than she actually was. He admired her legs and the outline of budding breasts, which she seemed bent now on concealing beneath loose, colorless clothing. Anya, he realized, did not want to be admired or even noticed, and this grated against every conception he had of women in general.

By three in the afternoon they were finished. There was no repeat of the previous meeting in which they had all too briefly discussed his father. Anya seemed committed to a polite and distant protocol. As usual she had her gloves on before she would shake his hand and appeared to deliberately avoid the nicety. He wondered if that wasn't because she disliked the clammy wetness of his palm, a symptom of anxiety that surprised him and that he hadn't had to concern himself with since adolescence.

He reminded himself that he did not know Anya well enough to hate her, and yet he was surprised to discover that his feelings, although unreasonable, certainly bordered on that emotion. Like a runaway train his frustration had progressed quickly toward loathing, and yet conversely, he felt compelled to show her more courtesy and attention than any of his other clients. As the elevator door closed off her face, he calculated how soon they would meet again. Why must they meet so often? Peter felt an inexplicable surge of repugnance that was nearly physical, and decided, as he had decided several times in the past, to end their association. Let her find another lawyer.

Anya sat or reclined against the low stone wall. Before her was the house, at her back the cemetery, and then the sea. As the sun came up from behind to reflect off the tall narrow windows of the second floor, she maintained her vigil. The wide shutters could be fastened and secured in the event of a hurricane and were still painted the same shade of bright green. The burgundy window boxes, which overflowed in summer with impatiens and wayward sprigs of ivy, were now packed with snow.

At Anya's back the pull and thrust of the waves rolled over the yellow sand of Front Beach, obscured now by a sculptured wall of layered, frozen spray. Overhead, flocks of gulls took wing on currents of frigid morning air, their clear, penetrating screech a haunting reminder of summer. From June through Labor Day, during the first years of her life, Anya had fallen asleep in a bed, under the eaves of this house.

She'd caught the train from North Station and arrived in Rockport in late afternoon. It was the same train her father caught each Friday night in summer so that he could spend his weekends with the family. Anya had a vague memory of going to meet that train and being caught up in her father's arms, lifted high above his shoulders, and she could close her eyes and almost hear the infectious thrill of that child's innocent laughter.

From the station she had walked up King Street and then down the hill toward the beach. Many of the summer businesses and restaurants were closed. She studied the wood sculpture of the pirate perched above the sign before the shuttered windows of Peg Legs, and she strained her eyes to read the fare of last summer's menu. What surprised her most was that nothing at all was changed. The trees looked no larger and the houses no different, and as night fell she walked the narrow, twisting streets until she found herself on Mill Lane.

When she saw the house she felt a great tumult of confusion. She smiled and cried simultaneously; great tears warm under the scarf pulled up around her face. When night fell the lights came up, spilling across the snow a welcoming glow of yellow. A single shadow moved within, and she dared not wonder whose as she waited, locked within the long-cloaking comfort of darkness until dawn. After a time the hall light came on, and during the pause she counted the steps from the second floor to the first. Precisely on cue the kitchen light filtered through to the front. It was gratifying to be right, and she could almost smell the coffee brewing and the tea steeping, and her mouth watered at the thought of her grandmother's raisin scones.

Anya thought of going in. The door was never locked. She walked a few steps forward and stopped. A bicycle came up Mill Lane from the direction of the pond that the winter children skated on. She had been a summer child, staying only in season, but if the old woman's memory could be trusted, her parents had moved here. Where else would they have gone?

The pond was covered now under a pristine blanket of new snow, but today was Saturday, and soon the boys would arrive to shovel off a hockey surface, and then the girls, to compete for their own space. Sleds would line up just beyond her view at the edge of the hill that ran down to the pond and over the bridge to the foot of the old mill. There had been a painting of that scene at the house in Belmont. Seeing the town draped in winter jogged that memory which slashed at her heart with biting cruelty.

The layer of new snow over the cobblestones gave the bicycle traction as the boy tossed his newspaper in a wild arch in the general vicinity of the few houses that faced the cemetery wall. The paperboy of her childhood had been the son of a fisherman. His wife hauled the lobsters up a barnacle encrusted wall, to huge boiling pots in her kitchen and sold them out the front, wrapped in waxed paper with Dixie cups of butter.

For a moment the boy's eyes locked with hers. She wondered how she must appear to him in the first light of a pale dawn. Obviously startled, his bicycle swerved and he averted his head and moved as far as possible toward the curb. With a last look over his shoulder, he peddled faster until soon out of sight.

Anya looked at the second house. Compared to her grandmother's, it was small and low, painted a deep red that looked almost black in the emerging light. She stepped up to the curb and let herself in the gate and walked around to the back. It was difficult to tell beneath the layer of new snow, but the garden seemed larger and there was a greenhouse, which had never been there before. These changes nagged at her and for a long moment she hesitated, but soon she had regained that even, emotionless veneer that served them so well when that Original Other was preeminent.

A short time later she emerged through the front door. She was in no hurry. There was no need to run and hide, for she knew that as long as she remained in that moment she was invisible and immune to any harm. By now the newspaper was gone, and she looked at the indentation in the snow bank where it had been recovered. She breathed in the crisp morning air and stepped into the painting she had earlier recalled. She followed in the tracks of the bicycle down the hill, over the stone bridge, by the old mill toward the railway station.

CHAPTER NINE

Some claimed that she had gone swimming and drowned, and yet not a soul had seen her return to the beach. Others said she had been kidnaped and was dead, and yet no ransom note ever arrived. He didn't believe either theory. Her family wasn't wealthy enough to attract a kidnapper, and like him, she had learned to swim in the fickle ocean and not the safer stillness of a pool.

Nora placed the coffee cup down in its saucer with a clatter and reached for the indestructible coast guard jacket of indeterminate years. For as long as she could remember, the jacket had hung by the door and was present even in photographs of times before she was born. Letting her pink flannel nightgown trail over the tops of her black Wellingtons, Nora Fothergill walked out to retrieve her newspaper. Once again the boy had missed the landing and failed to enclose the Boston Globe in plastic.

Although it had snowed quite a bit this winter, Nora had never once shoveled. With skill she picked her way over the little that could be seen of her front steps. Trying not to get caught up in her trailing nightgown she found the newspaper in a mound of snow, which when melted, would blur the print and stain her fingers.

"Hello, Paul," she called to her neighbor as in unison they bent to retrieve their newspapers. Her short red hair fell over her eyes, and she pushed it up, over her forehead, in the unconscious gesture that had been hers since girlhood. "How's Herb this morning?"

"The same," Paul called, which meant he was worse. As though his optimism could stave off death, Paul tended to exaggerate Herb's real or imagined improvement. For sixteen years they had been together, and now Herb was dying of a new and frightening disease called AIDS.

"Come on over for breakfast," Paul called.

"Can't. I have a shipment due at the Gallery. Why don't I cook for you tonight? I'll bring it over," Nora quickly added, knowing that Paul rarely left the house since Herb had returned from the hospital and was now bedridden.

"Hey," Paul called as an afterthought. "There was someone out here last night. Did you notice her?" Nora was alert to the tension in Paul's voice and his emphasis on the word 'her'. Later she would recall the icy feel of the doorknob in her hand and the prickly wool of the jacket lapel, which brushed her cheek as she turned her head in his direction. She had been thinking of spring and the sight of redbuds lighting the rim of the wet forest and anticipating the first whiff of thawing soil, but now she put those thoughts aside and looked at Paul.

No more than a few yards separated the houses. Each sat perched at the curb and belied the fact that behind was a sweeping yard that meandered toward the edge of a wood. Paul stood at the foot of his carefully swept steps, dressed in jeans and a Red Sox sweatshirt. His house was smaller and simpler than Nora's but much better kept, and he had gone to the trouble of hanging a wreath with garland about the windows. The house was painted a dark shade of red, and in summer the back was filled with flowers and shrubs that were the envy of all the county garden clubs.

"Did you get a look at her face? Was she young or old?"

"Don't know. If she comes back, we'll call the police."

Paul and Nora were comfortable with one another in the way of long time neighbors and friends. Nora's house had been her grandmother's before her parents moved to Rockport from Belmont. Paul's home had belonged to his mother. They attended Rockport High School together until Paul went on to Harvard and Nora across the Charles to Emerson. The last year of college they shared an apartment. His mother, Brenda Maple, had expressed disapproval, but was secretly relieved, assuming they were lovers, and took her last breath comforted by that fallacy. At fourteen Paul confided to Nora that he was gay and then had to explain to his naive friend exactly what that meant.

"Probably just another tourist watching for ghosts in our famous graveyard," she soothed. The graveyard was one of the oldest in New England, and tourists often came by to decipher and trace the inscriptions off the worn headstones.

"I don't think so. She looked to be watching the house. If not for Herb, I would have chased her away. When I finally decided to do so, she was gone. Herb hates it when people loiter about, and I didn't want to upset him."

"I'm sure it was nothing. See you tonight," Nora called and let the door slam behind her.

Nora felt an unsettled disquiet steal past her defenses. A cold wind swept off the ocean and stirred the windows in their frames. Suddenly that first whiff of spring seemed a long way off, and she wondered what it would be like to stand out in the cold lane with the cemetery at one's back all night. What would motivate someone to do such a thing? Nora walked into the living room and gazed up at the oil above the fireplace, oblivious to the melting snow that pooled round the heels of her boots.

Josiah Porter had painted the portrait, at his farm in Bucksport, Maine, when Lydia was five. Nora was taller, and older than Lydia. The two sat with their arms touching and their long, windblown hair, two different and distinct shades of red, intertwined as the bright, fractured sun gleamed off the whitewashed barn behind. Nora was in a cotton sea-foam sun dress with tiny daisies so small they looked like dots, and Lydia wore the same dress but in pink.

The portrait was not staged. Lydia's ribbon was half out of her hair and Nora's trailed from her lap. Their socks were soiled from an afternoon of play and their white Buster Brown sandals hopelessly scuffed. The portrait had just been returned to Nora from a twenty-city tour of the artist's work. As she looked at it now, Nora decided she could not part with it again. When the portrait was gone, the house seemed truly empty.

Nora was the last of her family. Her mother died first and then her father and last of all her grandmother. She no longer kept help except to clean once a week. Her grandmother's rose garden was overgrown but still produced stubborn blooms. There were no scones, no Earl Gray Tea steeping, and the breakfast china of Chinese Tigers had not been removed from the breakfront since her grandmother had lain in her casket in the living room for a traditional town wake.

As though just making up her mind, Nora walked to the kitchen. His phone number was still there, tacked behind a lobster magnet on the refrigerator door. Nora kicked off her boots and slid up onto the antique butcher-block in the center of the kitchen. Although it was hopeless, she lifted the lid of a cookie jar in search of a forgotten cigarette. It had been six months since she had stopped smoking. She counted the rings and let the pea jacket fall in a heap on the floor.

It was when the portrait was at The Museum of Fine Arts in Boston that he first phoned, identifying himself as the nephew of Josiah Porter. Although he seemed to remember her and Lydia quite well she barely remembered him. Reverdy Porter, or Rev as they had called him, would be younger than she but older than Lydia.

"I'm not surprised you don't remember me," he said in that first unexpected conversation. "If memory serves, I hated girls and resented your visits. I pretty much holed up in the barn and spied on you from a distance."

They spoke of the friendship between Nora's mother and his grandfather. One of Josiah's biographers had speculated in a recent New Yorker article that the two had become lovers that summer, but both agreed that this was not true. Nora's mother had been commissioned to sculpt a bust of Josiah and it was during that summer that the first sketches for the portrait were completed. After Lydia disappeared, Josiah had made a gift of the portrait to their family.

"What are you doing now?" Nora asked, feeling awkward. She wasn't good at aimless conversation.

"I'm a homicide detective. I live in Boston."

Nora's guard came up. Why did she have to be so defensive, and yet she could not help herself. "Forgive me for being blunt, Rev, but I'm guessing you did not call to reminisce about my mother and your uncle and a summer in which we hardly talked to one another. Exactly why have you phoned?"

Nora only half listened as Rev told her about the work of two MIT scientists who had recently developed an age progression computer program designed to produce a high resolution image of how a missing child would look as an adult.

"What does this have to do with me?" Nora demanded, already resigned to the answer.

"I was invited to the reception that kicked off the museum tour," he said, seeming to change topics. "I thought you might have come since you allowed them to borrow the portrait."

Nora recalled the invitation. She had fully intended to go, but somehow the date had come and gone without her noticing. "So what do you want, Rev?"

"I saw the portrait of you and Lydia as children. I thought maybe I could help."

"And how could you possibly do that?" Nora asked, failing to keep the sarcasm at bay. She had begun the conversation with caution, distant, but polite. Now she no longer made an effort.

"I thought I might go over the case. Review the evidence," he said. "I have some unexpected time on my hands."

"And you'll want photos of Lydia so you can have this age progression thing done. Isn't that right?"

"Well, yes."

"We've done all that."

"This is different, Nora. By seven a child has seventy percent of their facial growth, and Lydia was six when she disappeared. We should be able to come up with something close to accurate with little guesswork involved about which feature Lydia inherited from which parent. What the police did was a series of sketches by a composite artist. Just educated guesses, really. People do not study or remember a drawing in the same way they do a photograph, and that is precisely what this computer program can produce. A photograph."

"Do you really think, even in your wildest dreams, that after all this time my sister could possibly be alive?"

There was a pause on the other end of the receiver. Rev was taken aback by her tone and especially her attitude. Nora knew he would be far more accustomed to families desperate for any shred of evidence, no matter how far-fetched the possibilities.

"I must tell you that I am profoundly weary of well-intentioned people with useless suggestions which inevitably come to nothing," Nora stated bluntly.

"I am sorry if this opens old wounds for you. Lydia's disappearance inspired me to go into police work. I've never forgotten her."

"Neither have I, but that doesn't mean I want to relive the events of her disappearance each time some well-intentioned person gets the idea in their head that they can accomplish what the local police, private detectives, and the FBI could not."

"I thought you might like to see the results of the age progression photograph."

"You mean you've already had it done? Why do I feel manipulated? Again!"

"I'm sorry."

"Well, you didn't actually call for my permission then, did you?"

"I've contacted a volunteer group that mails out postcards of missing children. It's been a long time so they won't send one out on Lydia alone, but they are willing to add her picture to a group of several others in a flyer. I also took the liberty of getting a copy to a friend at the FBI."

"When my neighbors see Lydia's photograph on the wall of the downtown post office, or a milk carton, or wherever else you choose to place it, they'll feel compelled to console me all over again. My phone will start ringing. The weirdo freelance journalists and every budding writer with their first laptop, obsessed with crime, will crawl out of the woodwork expecting me to fall at their feet just because they offer to peel away the scabs. Don't you see? It's all just too hard, too hopeless, and pointless. Nothing can change what happened."

"Listen, Nora, we didn't have this kind of technology when Lydia disappeared. We didn't have a central computer or the kind of resource network we have today. It may be too late to find her alive but not to discover the truth and perhaps bring a criminal to justice. Someone out there knows. Someone always knows, another talks, or slips up. Wouldn't you like to know the truth?"

Rev sounded sincere. His voice had adopted an imploring sort of eloquence, which reminded her of her parents. They wanted so desperately to know the truth, but every shred of hope had ended in bitter disillusion. Although there was no accusation in his words, Nora imagined one.

"And I suppose you'll want to interview me?"

"Well, yes."

"I'll call you," she had said, her voice breaking, despite her best effort to maintain control. "If I decide it's worth a try, I'll let you know."

It had been four months since Reverdy Porter first phoned with his offer of help and Nora had not called him back. Now she was sorry for how she had come across. It was true that she would like answers. After starting therapy Paul had adopted a new vocabulary. He would call this closure, but Nora doubted if such a thing was possible. Lydia's disappearance had driven both her parents to an early grave. The authorities concluded that Lydia had been a victim of a stranger abduction and held out little hope. Still her family had always believed Lydia to be alive.

Only Nora had doubted as she witnessed firsthand the burden and ensuing cost of all those unanswered questions. The uncertainty and worse still, imagining Lydia's fate, had tortured each waking thought. The attic was full of gifts from missed birthdays and holidays in the hope that Lydia would be recovered. Just the thought of all those unopened presents, which sat under the Christmas tree each year, made it impossible for Nora to enjoy the festivities.

In their anguish over Lydia, it often seemed her parents had forgotten they had another daughter, and Nora felt a responsibility to be strong and endlessly solicitous of their sorrow. In that Rockport cottage, grief had become a stoic shrine to hope, and in defense, Nora had ceased to feel obsessed with the need for answers. Her sister was dead.

Nevertheless, here she was, dialing the phone number of another crime-obsessed outsider. Why must she put herself through this? Nora's ear began to throb, and she realized how tightly she pressed the receiver to her face. She was ready to hang up when a male voice answered. Rev, as he was called, was on medical leave, but a message could be got to him. Nora felt immense relief. Even as she left her name and number, she did not expect a return call.

Nora replaced the receiver and thought of Paul. Not wanting to open up old wounds she had not told him of Rev's original call. With Herb's illness he had enough to worry about, but at dinner tonight she would tell him about the age progression technology and about Rev's offer of help.

Although he did not say so, Nora knew that Paul was thinking of Lydia when he mentioned the girl who stood outside in the lane for much of the night. Like her parents, Paul fully expected that one day they would learn the truth and was quick to encourage Nora not to abandon hope, but after all these years they had both settled into a quiet acceptance of what could not be altered.

For Nora and Paul life ceased to exist on a certain level. Even routine and ordinary experiences were viewed or shaped by that one past event that made them acutely aware of how fate could combine to strike at the heart of peace. They no longer tortured one another with long conversations that revolved around the endless 'what ifs' of that day. If they had only waited, if only they had not argued, if only they had gone back for Lydia sooner, then perhaps that one trigger which propelled the events of that summer afternoon might not have exploded to result in tragedy. Forever lost was the ease of innocence, which no longer cloaked their lives in an insular facade of safety.

CHAPTER TEN

She had been so very young when she disappeared. How had she coped and what kind of damage had been done? Through prayer, in the depth of his spirit, he sensed the great confusion of her wounds. And so he prayed that she might remember. "Lord, do not allow her to forget her home. Do not let her believe the lie that no one wants her back. Return her to family and to those who miss her."

By the time Christmas was over Peter had almost forgotten his dislike of Anya. She had cancelled her last appointment and cancelled again the first week of January and what business there was, was conducted succinctly over the phone. Convinced that Anya had begun to trust him, Peter could not resist once more to scheme. Putting his investigator to work he learned that she lived in a single room in a run down building on Marlboro Street in Boston and that she had flown into that city directly from the Los Angeles airport. It was further reported that she had been living with Dexter Arujo and that he was acting as her agent, but there was some kind of conflict and she had left.

When his investigator persuaded the landlord to let him see Anya's room, it was discovered that she lived austerely, with no more than a bed and a table and little clothing. For this reason Peter was fairly astonished when Anya announced that she was buying a condominium that overlooked the Charles and a small cottage on Sanibel Island in Florida. Clearly help was needed if she was to furnish both places. From habit and to be polite, he recommended his wife's decorator and was flabbergasted when, a week later, the decorator called to thank him for the referral.

"Darling," his wife Cynthia oozed, during one of her late morning calls to the office, in which they discussed the logistics of two equally busy schedules and weighing the merits of one invitation over another. "Why didn't you tell me that Anya Szcepanik was a client?"

"Who told you?" he asked, having adopted Anya's wariness, at least where she was concerned.

"Well, you must know, Darling. You recommended Helen, who claims she has exquisite taste. Not mine or yours, you understand. Far too simple a

117

penchant for negative space and less is better and all that rot. But she may authorize Helen to bid for her at the Richmond auction, with no ceiling, if you can imagine."

Peter's thoughts spun ahead. He had not seen a withdrawal from any of the funds he monitored. Did that mean Anya had even more money? Money that he knew nothing about? The thought of her seemingly endless resources set his pulses racing. With effort he brought his thoughts back to the present.

"We ought to get to know this girl, and I've just had a thought," his wife was saying. "Let's have her to dinner and especially in light of your father's skating connections."

Peter groaned inwardly. He didn't want to hear any more, but Cynthia continued as though she'd just come up with a completely novel idea. "We do already have that party planned, Darling. We could include more skating people and wheel your father down for a brief introduction if he is alert enough. Dexter Arujo's agent has already replied and we'll include that young sports commentator who visits father so faithfully."

"Believe me when I tell you, Cynthia. Anya Szcepanik is not a client to entertain. She is a recluse of sorts and most decidedly not at all inclined to be social. Do not invite her anywhere."

"But she doesn't sound like a recluse, Darling. If she's buying a house and decorating she plans to see and be seen."

"You must tell Helen that she is wasting her time. I can safely assure you that Anya will never buy a thing from her. Why, she doesn't even wear jewelry or makeup."

"But how can you know that, I–"

"Enough, Cynthia!" Peter cut her off and the subject was mutually shifted to more benign topics.

Cynthia had not disputed his judgment, and so Peter was surprised when he opened the door that snowy January evening to see Anya standing under the foyer lights. The house was overflowing with guests. He called them his wife's charity crowd, for they mostly sat on boards of educational institutions, museums, and various other non-profit organizations. Peter had gleaned many clients for his firm from Cynthia's social involvements and had learned it was wise to be on hand whenever his company was required.

The moment Peter looked into Anya's face, he regretted not leaving the door to the help, but he had been passing when the bell sounded and now he was required to play the reluctant host. One look at her impassive face and all joy evaporated from the evening. To make matters worse, Peter was convinced that Anya was acutely aware of his discomfort.

For a heartbeat he failed to recognize her. Her luxurious hair glowed with highlights pulled up with tiny curls let loose at the hairline. She wore a green sequined shift, and he could not avoid noticing that her skin was milky smooth, with arms visibly muscled. At her wrist was a thick band of diamonds, with matching earrings; and as though oblivious to the plunging temperature, a mink coat was draped carelessly over one shoulder. The unexpected shift from deliberate understatement to stunning elegance made for a dramatic transformation. Peter looked over her shoulder to see a limousine parked at the end of the curving drive and blocking the walk.

"Your man can move the car around back," Peter said when he noticed more guests gingerly picking their way around the vehicle in the snow. He waved in the general direction of the back drive as he took her coat, but she looked beyond him and said nothing. Peter suppressed an urge to slam the door in her face.

"I won't be staying long," Anya retorted as though reading his thoughts.

Despite that assertion she did stay. When later he checked, her car remained inconveniently blocking the front walkway. Peter could not help noticing that Anya visited with uncharacteristic animation, feigned interest in various charities, and smiled as though she might actually be happy. He found that smile disturbing. She even accepted an unlikely invitation to lunch with Joyce Meadows, the elderly wife of Brian Meadows, financier. As much as he disliked Anya, the thought of all that money being handled by someone more capable set Peter's heart racing at a fast clip, and he rushed Cynthia over to charm her way into the conversation, wrestling Anya in another direction.

Peter remained silent as Cynthia greeted Anya like a newly garnered prize, introducing her to others with a smug satisfaction, that only because he knew her so well, did he recognize. Soon his duty as host required his presence elsewhere, and for a time he lost track of Anya, but that absence proved more disconcerting than the task of keeping tabs on her. She was like a different person tonight as she moved from one group to another, laughing and talking with that odd edge of an accent that came and went, the one subtle reminder that she was not American. This new Anya seemed the antithesis of the severe and composed young woman who was his client. The abruptness of her transformation did not seem to him quite normal. Peter felt anxious. He walked into the dining room and checked the buffet area. He waded through the crowd in the drawing room and then the living room and breathed a sigh of relief as he concluded that she had left. Now he could return to enjoying his guests.

It was a successful party, and Peter experienced a burst of pride in

Cynthia. No one knew better than she, how to combine the right mix of personalities, the right professions, with the current and popular proclivities and trends. Cynthia always claimed that she counted a party productive when people overstayed and became informal, as they did tonight. Guests had spilled into the cavernous foyer, draped themselves over the wide staircase, conversing with enthusiasm, occasional raucous laughter drowning out the music.

Peter caught sight of Lawrence, his English trained butler. The man spoke with a Bronx accent but performed his duties with élan. "Did you see Anya Szcepanik to the door?"

"Who, sir?"

"The redhead in the green dress."

"Oh, her, sir." Lawrence nodded in the direction of the guest coat closet. "But I wouldn't go in there if I were you," Lawrence suggested politely when he saw Peter step forward.

"Why not?"

"The lady is not alone, sir, if you get my drift."

Peter was astounded. The implication was clear, but he could not imagine Anya experiencing passion with any man. His own attraction had been so fleeting that he no longer remembered it and had actually come to think of her as asexual.

"Get them out of there. People will be leaving soon. They'll need their coats!"

"The door is locked, sir."

"As you well know there's a master key around the place somewhere; I don't care how you do it. Just get her out of there and out of the house entirely if you can do it without insulting her." He thought of telling Cynthia, but he knew she would only be amused at his reaction. "By the way. Who is she with?"

"Miss Szcepanik is with Dexter Arujo."

"The gold medal, the coke commercials, and the winery!" Peter was astonished. Why had he not recognized Dex? Did Cynthia go entirely against his wishes? He was furious. All that remained for Cynthia to do was to parade his father out in the antique wheel chair with a bib tucked under his chin to catch the drooling.

Howard Maple was a skating icon. Often when the history of skating was a media subject, footage was shown of Howard skating in a Hollywood movie or executing the jumps, that compared to today's level of expertise, seemed paltry. His father had retired on family money and spent much of his life traveling as a world-class judge. He was founder and frequent president of the

International Skating Alliance and had helped to draft many of the rules and regulations now adopted by most amateur skating leagues. Despite Cynthia's suggestion of bringing Howard out to meet the other quests, Peter knew that she would not. It was in their best interests to keep the state of Howard's health and especially his feeble and confused mind a secret.

Occasionally people called Cynthia to have her ask Howard's opinion on a subject, and she would promise to speak with him. It was a small, select group that actually held the power in skating, and, always an elitist Cynthia enjoyed getting to know these people. She used the opportunity to learn about the skating world, which she found fascinating and fraught with unusual stories and endless gossip concerning details of people's lives not normally available. It almost made her wish she had a child who skated so she could stay in the loop after Howard died. It was only a question of time, although she hated to think of that happening, since Howard had certainly enriched their lives. He had not only brought her husband business but also given her a new area of interest for what she freely admitted was a fairly useless life. If only she'd had a child of her own, she might have been a different person. Maybe, she thought, she and Peter would find a young child to sponsor in skating. A child whose parents would allow her to pull the strings.

Taking these requests for Howard's opinion seriously, Cynthia took detailed notes and promised to call back as soon as she had an answer. When she did, it was her own opinion she rendered, although she did certainly discuss the matter with her father-in-law, who could not even grunt in response. But often, when she talked of skating, an intelligent gleam stirred the cloudy surface of Howard's eyes, and she almost felt him straining toward her, actually seeming to listen intently and taking in each word.

While Cynthia knew it was only her imagination, Peter seemed to believe his father understood far more than the doctors admitted was possible. Outside of staff and family members, Howard had only two regular visitors. Both men had known him well through the years, and although she was doubtful in the beginning, she now knew she could trust them to maintain the image of Howard as disabled, but in no way mentally-incapacitated.

Peter stomped off to look for Cynthia, and Lawrence, following instructions, raised his hand to knock on the door just as it opened. Out stepped Anya and Dex. Anya looked at him as though it were entirely normal for her to have locked herself in a closet with the guest everyone else had been looking to meet. Trained not to react, Lawrence returned the courtesy.

Three hours later Cynthia and Peter Maple closed the door on the last of their guests. Cynthia looked at Peter with an expression of deep satisfaction. From her perspective the evening was a great success.

"Well, I do believe we are responsible for rekindling a love affair. Did you recall that Dex Arujo was the man who helped Anya escape to this country? Lawrence tells me they left together. How charming," Cynthia congratulated herself.

Peter did not answer.

"Darling, do say that you are not angry with me for including her. She was a great success. Everyone loved her."

But Peter was reluctant to forgive.

"When I invited Anya here I intended no harm. I don't understand how you could possibly dislike such a delectable creature." Cynthia kicked off her heels and sighed. Automatically Peter bent to pick them up and their hands touched. They never stayed angry with one another for long, and although Cynthia often appeared to defer to Peter, she was actually the stronger personality.

"Come," she said and led him down the hall. It was their habit to retire to the library, filled with books they rarely read, and sip brandy as they gossiped over a successful evening.

"First let me check on father."

"Let me," Cynthia soothed. "You've been upset, and you need to relax or you'll never sleep tonight."

Howard was seventy-two and had lived with them ever since he'd suffered a stroke and required nursing care. Peter walked to the row of decanters and selected one. Slowly he poured just the right amount of rich amber liquid into each glass. He placed Cynthia's on the federal walnut table and settled himself in one of the twin chairs that faced the fire. He wrapped his hands around the glass and thought of his father.

They had spent more time together in the last few years than all of his life. Peter's parents had been divorced when he was a child, and he had spent his school days at Choate and then Harvard and summers near Gloucester, Mass. The Maples had a mansion that overlooked Rockport Harbor, and after it was lost by fire, his mother continued to return for an annual vacation, staying with her former sister-in-law, who was also divorced.

Rockport had never been a fashionable place to summer. The coastline was rocky, the beach modest, and the town crowded against the sea had no place to grow beyond its origins. Peter hated the visits. Most of his friends were at the Cape or traveling, and he had nothing in common with his younger cousin Paul. Despite his objections his mother was committed to a stay each summer at the rambling cottage on Mill Lane. She spent hours in whispered conversation with his Aunt Brenda, and he and his cousin Paul were left entirely to their own devices. Not until Paul was old enough to sail did Peter resign himself and stop complaining. The two shared a passion for sailing and this alone redeemed the visits.

Peter would never follow in his father's footsteps to take up skating, either as an athlete, judge, or benefactor. He had to wonder if his mother had not deliberately set out to insure that father and son have nothing in common. Howard Maple had been a true intellectual. Committed and passionate were words often used to describe him. He had played tournament chess and collected stamps as a boy and had only begun to skate at the doctor's chance suggestion after contracting a mysterious illness that left him bedridden for nearly a year.

Peter, on the other hand, collected nothing. His mother kept him busy during the summer with camps that emphasized outdoor activities, and his interests rotated randomly with the seasons. Fall was football, winter was basketball, and summer was golf and sailing. From the time he was young he had a personal trainer who taught him the fine points of various sports, and if he had any physical ailments, his mother refused to respond unless he was vomiting or had a raging fever.

She never spoke of her former husband, and Howard never attempted to visit his son. Only as an adult, after his mother had died and Peter unexpectedly became responsible for his father's affairs, was he confronted with a first objective view.

While sorting through the New York apartment, that had been his father's principal residence for thirty years, it was immediately evident to Peter that, even with no foreknowledge of the stroke that had so suddenly incapacitated him, Howard's affairs were meticulously organized. Through the years Howard had kept everything, including tax records from the first year he made an income, to every shred of documentation pertaining to his divorce.

Feeling like an intruder, Peter read the terms of his parents' divorce and realized for the first time the lengths at which his mother had gone to gain complete and total custody. Interpreting the legalese that he had grown so good at weaving himself, he concluded that his mother was privy to some sort of unsavory information and may even have resorted to blackmail.

As he pored over the initial documents between his parents' respective attorneys, he was surprised to learn that Howard had begun by insisting on equal custody, a novel idea at that time, when mothers were considered by the courts and society to be the only care givers for children. Howard modified his demands, asking for alternate holidays and summer vacations, which seemed only reasonable; but his mother's attorney responded with a flat refusal. Then, after more ambiguous correspondence, and just before they were about to go to court to fight a bitter custody battle, everything was settled.

Howard now gave up all claims to his only son. Inexplicably he doubled his child support payments and agreed to lifelong alimony and maintenance, which would not terminate even if the former Mrs. Maple decided to remarry. Peter was curious, but an inward tug of fear prevented him from investigating further, and he was unable to ask his father, who, as a result of the stroke, had lost the ability to speak.

It was a pleasant surprise to learn that Howard was in possession of a sizable estate, including his choice apartment that overlooked Central Park. In contrast, his mother had spent every cent she got her hands on. After her death it was a bitter disappointment for Peter to learn that he was broke. The two homes his mother maintained were heavily mortgaged, and by the time creditors were paid and almost everything sold, nothing remained. All was compounded by the fact that Peter was about to enter law school, and for the first time he took out a school loan and was required to work just to purchase essentials. Peter had no time for his former social life, and only because of Cynthia and her support was he able to keep up appearances.

During that autumn that his mother passed away and as he wrestled with the reality of his new circumstances, it occurred to Peter that he should contact his father and ask for help. He started several awkward letters, which he quickly abandoned, and then impulsively he boarded a train for New York. Train fare back and forth was all he had. He had already walked and hitched several rides down Massachusetts Avenue, over the Charles River toward South Station. Now arriving at Grand Central he began the long walk to his father's apartment, but the closer he came to his destination the more reluctant he was to continue. It was a fine fall day. The sun was shining, the air was crisp, and only the thought of his total lack of resources propelled him forward.

When he came to his father's building, several leather suitcases were lined up on the sidewalk. A boy about his own age grumbled about how difficult it was to obtain a taxi in New York, as he ineffectually waved from the curb whenever he saw a flash of yellow amidst the oncoming traffic. Peter was immediately repulsed by his appearance. His hair was colored a most unnatural shade of mustard and his dark eyes smudged with traces of what could only be liner. Above his thin lip was a small black mole that made Peter think of a fly, and the gleam of a thick gold bangle between cuff and jacket flashed in the sun.

"Where's the doorman when you need him?" the young man complained and lifted a finger haplessly into the air as though checking wind direction.

"You'll never get a cab with that gesture," Peter mumbled and walked to the door.

"Can't get in without a key or 'less the doorman is standing there. This is an exclusive building," the young man offered. Peter felt contemptuous of the explanation, acutely aware that he was being looked over in a way that made him feel decidedly uncomfortable. They were about the same height, but vastly different in appearance. Peter wore chinos and an Oxford shirt with his monogram on the cuff. On his feet were loafers, no socks, and he had slung over his shoulder a cordovan leather jacket.

"Just wait and he'll be back. Went up to get more bags. We're off't Europe. Paris and Rome," he offered proudly and then scrutinized Peter's face for a reaction. Disappointed that there was none he turned away and once more gestured for a cab, this time already a block beyond the curb.

Disgusted, Peter walked between two parked cars. Putting two fingers between his lips, he whistled and lifted his arm as a cab stopped at the curb. Behind him the door opened, and the doorman, dressed in his mock military uniform, emerged. Following close behind was a tall man with graying hair and finely defined features. There was a feline grace to his bearing, and his manner of walking was both elegant and regal.

"He got us the cab," the young man said, motioning in Peter's direction. Howard placed a hand on the young man's shoulder, and some aspect of this possessive gesture both alarmed and repelled Peter. He watched intently as Howard smiled as though indulging an underling and glanced only briefly in his direction. The Maple family resemblance was evident. Howard was taller than he, but the cut of the jaw and the eyes were the same. There was little doubt in Peter's mind that he was looking at his father.

"Thank you," Howard's tone was dismissive as he pressed a ten-dollar bill into Peter's hand. Peter was so stunned that he did not protest, as Howard slid into the back seat of the cab. He stood at the curb and watched the car disappear into traffic and wondered why he had not introduced himself. This first sight of his father had come and gone so quickly that it hardly seemed real. He thought of his mother's years of silence on the subject. Shrugging his shoulders as though he could just as easily shake off his bitter disillusionment, he turned and walked away.

Peter spent the money on two chili dogs and a large coke, purchased from a street vender, and with the food he choked down a profound sense of disappointment. For the first time in his life he felt like an orphan. His mother was dead, and the father he hoped would claim him not only did not recognize him but was also homosexual.

When Peter got the call years later that his father was in the hospital after suffering a severe stroke, he could only wonder why they were calling him. Would his father have put his name down as next of kin? The thought was astonishing. He wondered what to do. It was Cynthia who took over, dutifully conferring with the doctors and Howard's attorney and making daily trips to the hospital to monitor his care.

Both were stunned at the number of letters and cards and hundreds of gifts of flowers that began to arrive at the hospital. The wealth of contacts made that first year as a result of Cynthia's management of her father-in-law's care began to send Peter more business than he could handle, and he added two young attorneys to his practice. Howard's many friends and acquaintances, unaware of any previous estrangement, quickly embraced Peter and his wife as one of their own, all too glad to endear themselves to Howard through this handy conduit of a son.

Peter was amazed to learn from Howard's attorney that under the terms of the will he was named nearly sole beneficiary of a sizable fortune. The one exception was a plot of land in Rockport that had contained the family home before it burned, which was curiously left to his cousin Paul. When it became obvious that therapy would never restore his father's mental faculties, Peter was appointed legal guardian and given power of attorney.

Peter and Cynthia decided to sell Howard's isolated summer home at Martin Point in Maine. They sold his Austin Sloop, the log cabin in Aspen, and donated his extensive collection of skating memorabilia to the Skating History Museum in Colorado Springs. He and Cynthia kept the Manhattan apartment, which Cynthia determined was outdated and wanted immediately to overhaul and redecorate. Peter felt such a project was premature and so they put the furnishings in storage, making only superficial changes. But slowly the twelve-room apartment filled back up with Cynthia's antique and auction finds. Now they used the premises for entertaining and Peter stayed over on weekdays when he could not get home to Southampton. It was a convenience he had come to rely on and only last week he had given Cynthia the go-ahead to begin the renovation project that would put their own stamp on the place.

The introduction of a father into his life evolved into more than an opportunity to own a valuable piece of New York real estate. Peter actually liked having Howard under his roof. On Sundays they took breakfast together and Peter read the Times aloud, imagining shared interest, and he rarely went to bed, no matter how late, without looking in and planting a kiss on that sandpaper brow.

Peter convinced himself that Howard liked his company and looked forward to that private time together. He enjoyed having others ask after

Howard. "My father," he would say, liking the sound of those words and with a vague sense of how not having that parent had left a hole in his heart, now partially filled by the possessive utterance of a child's desperately coveted phrase.

He and Cynthia hired round-the-clock nursing companions and refitted one of the guestrooms for physical therapy. They hung a lift over the pool so that his flaccid body could be lowered into the heated water for his daily constitutional. Peter even installed an elevator that went directly to Howard's third floor quarters. In some way that he could not explain, the old man with the impaired faculties and faulty, aimless attempts at speech became the child he and Cynthia never had, and his dependence and presence added a new dimension and even depth to their marriage.

It seemed to Peter that Cynthia was taking a long time. His own brandy was nearly gone when she walked into the room. He did not allow himself to think much of the past and his thoughts had evoked a discomforting state of mind. Peter was relieved when he saw that Cynthia had changed into a dressing grown before going in to father. This, he decided, was what kept her so long, but as she stepped into the light there was an odd, unfamiliar expression on her face. Time seemed to slow for Peter, and he wanted to stand but could not. Cynthia came to him immediately and knelt at the edge of his chair. Peter felt the first infringement of fear curl an icy grip over his thoughts. He almost knew what she would say.

"I'm sorry Darling. I am so sorry for you, but father has left us. He is now in heaven and no longer suffering. You must think of him in this manner, Darling. Do you understand what I am saying, Peter?"

"But he was fine," Peter choked. "The doctor was just here and said his heart was strong and he could live another twenty years, and where was his nurse? Why didn't he call us?"

"Father was put to bed and thought to be sleeping. This is how painlessly and simply he left us. I myself believed he was sleeping until I kissed his cheek."

"But why? How could this have happened?"

"He was not well, Peter. You know that." She spoke to him as if he were a child. Her love and grief reached out to him and Peter responded. He pulled her up until she sat on his lap and he buried his head in the softness of her breasts, and she wrapped her arms about his back and smoothed his thinning hair.

It was then that Peter felt an almost electric stab of alarm. Invited though she was, she had almost been an intruder. He saw her that way. The hairs on the back of his neck rose, and despite the warmth from the fire he shivered and thought of Anya. Why, at this precise moment should he think of Anya?

CHAPTER ELEVEN

He stood on the small stone bridge that crossed the mill pond. A low canopy of cloud hung over the trailing path stretching on toward Main Street, and a mist of rain, so very fine that it could barely be seen, washed all in a gray haze of myopia. He had just left the dark red house. He had looked in on Herb only as an excuse to check on Paul and now he felt troubled. He no longer knew how to pray for Paul. But pray he would.

Paul Maple's delivery was dispassionate as he informed his psychiatrist about the abuse, explaining that it had nothing at all to do with his current problems. Although it was completely unnecessary, he was willing to subject himself to a little psycho-babble for the sake of Herb, his long time lover. He was fine. There was nothing wrong with him, only with the relationship, which after all these years needed a little revamping.

It mattered not at all to Herb that the clothes in his closet be arranged by color and style, or that the cups on the shelf have their handles pointing out for easy access, or a thousand other details of organization whose demands put a strain on the relationship. Paul believed that Herb's unwillingness to be tolerant was certainly unreasonable. A symptom only of the neglected state of the relationship, which could easily be repaired with a little attention.

With some reluctance, but amused by his own rendition of the story, and inviting his doctor to be equally entertained, Paul admitted that his need for a controlled, predictable environment might be remotely associated with his experience of being molested as a child. He then apologized for presenting such a transparent and unchallenging case and promptly changed the subject. Child molestation was the new media shocker, and Paul confessed to feeling like a cliché when he discussed the subject.

After some months the doctor suggested hypnotism, which Paul adamantly rejected, convinced that he recalled most of the experience anyway, which was in no way impacting his current problems. The relationship with Herb, he reminded his doctor on numerous occasions, was why he was there. Still it was proving difficult to keep his doctor on track and away from subjects Paul had long since stopped dwelling on, if in fact he ever had. Why think about the past anyway? To what purpose and to what end?

Suddenly therapy was no longer a diversion to appease Herb and had ceased being fun. Nevertheless, Paul continued to return for nearly a year. Herb was worth the effort. He seemed impressed by Paul's supposed sacrifice on his behalf and had threatened to leave if he stopped. Now Herb would never leave, and for a while at least Paul felt safe canceling more appointments with his doctor than he kept.

Still he thought about it. Even as he denied that he did, he couldn't help himself. It was as if therapy and his doctor's gentle, incessant prodding had opened a fissure that would not be closed. At odd moments, when he least expected it, he was besieged by memories, which threatened more memories, and it became exhausting work to monitor that floodgate. Tears would come to his eyes in the most inappropriate of circumstances, which left him wondering about sanity.

As a child Paul had loved the boathouse. It was a large musty building with the ocean lapping under half the floor when the tide was up. The place was filled with long forgotten treasures. There were spools of twine, torn nets, a half disassembled Johnson outboard and even an old lobster cage, and above all, suspended from large grappling hooks, a row of dinghies. Paul was able to climb the ladder at the inside of the building, which went up into the rafters. From there he crawled on hands and knees across a support beam until he could drop into the highest boat. It was a perfect place to be. In heightened excitement, Paul lifted away a corner of the tarp. The outside of the boat was a weathered blue, his favorite color, but the inside was painted a fresh, pristine white.

Paul stocked the interior with supplies. A jar of peanut butter, match box cars and baseball cards; a flashlight, sticks of whale bone from an old corset resurrected from the attic, a rabbit foot, a pocket knife and a few of his favorite books, the current being, "Treasure Island." His mother thought he read too much. She called him a solitary boy and often chased him outside. After Paul discovered the dinghy, he didn't mind at all. He knotted a rope and secured it over the rafters. When it was time to descend, he could swing down and around and land on a pile of nets in the corner of the boathouse.

He got the idea from watching Tarzan, the Jungle Boy. On television this neat trick appeared easy, but on that first day the jarring realization of just how far from the floor he actually was struck Paul with the force of a paralyzing weight. In panic he struggled to regain his place in the hull of the boat, but it swung out from under him and he was forced over the edge. Breath fled from his chest as in a rush of air, and with what seemed like great

130

speed, he found himself standing miraculously below on two legs barely able to support his weight.

It was a frightfully thrilling experience making him feel invincible, intensely alive, and immensely capable. After that first day Paul perfected his technique until he had mastered the fine points of a smooth drop. Some time later Uncle Howard found him in the boathouse.

"I'll have to tell your mother," he said. "She wouldn't approve. It's far too dangerous."

"Oh, please don't," Paul had pleaded.

It started that summer, although Paul could not say precisely which summer or how old he was, but he was certain it hadn't lasted very long. It started with inappropriate holding and then touching. When Paul threatened to tell his mother, he was threatened in return. Uncle Howard would harm his mother, and in order to demonstrate how simple the matter and how this could be accomplished, he began to leave tortured chipmunks for Paul to find in the bottom of the boat. Howard informed Paul that when his mother learned the truth, she wouldn't want him anymore and would have another child. One that she could love better.

But Paul knew that his mother could not have any more children. She had already confided this. If Uncle Howard could be wrong about such an important detail, he could be wrong about everything else.

When the fondling escalated to acts often painful, Paul decided he would go to live with his father in order to both escape the torment and put his mother out of harm's way. What was happening to him? This was confusing and the experience itself painfully humiliating. All the gifts of toys went largely unappreciated because he had plenty, but his mother monitored his diet with a vengeance and so the candy was at first a distraction. Soon he hated to wake in the morning, and nothing could dislodge the stone of immense reluctance that constricted his child's heart and robbed him of peace.

Paul understood something important. Howard wore a mask and when his mother swept into the room and kissed her brother's cheek, she had no idea of the danger she was in. Paul alone, in the entire world, knew that beneath the outward friendliness of that handsome countenance lived the monster of nightmares come to life.

If only his mother could see, then she too would recoil in disgust and horror. But Howard's face remained perfectly disguised. Each morning that calm, impenetrable mask smiled at mother and son from across the mahogany breakfast table, a cunning and constant reminder of the snare that had trapped his spirit and threatened to destroy his mother by mere association.

To have his tormenter under the same roof and all around him, rooted in the routine of any summer, seemed a cruel parody. Paul began to suffer nightmares and unexplained bouts of anger and a penchant for having all in his room arranged in a particular order. This work kept him in the house and out of Howard's reach for precious long hours, and it was this proclivity which dogged him, even into adulthood.

Brenda Maple was rarely in a mood for extracting confidences. She liked to talk but rarely listened and was often busy with her social life, which was for her a kind of career. After weeks of vigilant surveillance, Paul finally found her alone and away from the house at a time when Howard was otherwise occupied.

She sat at the far end of the dock. Paul recalled the incident more clearly than any other of his young life. The tide was out and she had removed her stockings, which sat rolled in a ball in her lap. She leaned back on her arms, her head titled toward the sun, with eyes closed.

As he walked toward her, ever so slowly, putting one deliberate foot in front of the other, he had never been so scared. His neck felt hot and his palms wet, and his breath came uneven with a loud roar to the internal place of his hearing. The sun was behind them, and when he stood beside her she smiled, her blue eyes bright amidst the tan, freckled skin of summer. Paul sat beside her and concentrated on details rather than on what he would say or how he would say it.

His mother was careless with her clothing, and yet it was nothing for her to spend exorbitant sums on her wardrobe. Today she seemed unaware of how the wood of the dock could tear tiny holes in the gossamer overskirt of her dress, but Paul was acutely aware, and he worried and thought of this as he attempted to summon the courage to speak. She wore the white strapless dress from Worth. Paul had been with her, sipping apple juice from a highball glass, when the model emerged from the dressing room. Brenda often asked her son's opinion, and when he said he loved the dress, a word he reserved for the very best, she bought it on the spot, right off the model's back. The white skirt had an iridescent overlay of blue with silver flecks that sparkled when she moved, and her silver sling-back pumps, with the three-inch heels, sat between them like diamonds on the weathered gray planks of the dock.

Brenda would be attending the ritual Saturday dance at the yacht club, and already a recently delivered corsage of gardenias had preceded her escort's arrival. Paul would be ushered in to shake hands with her date, one of several she had known in college or from one club or another, and like a, 'little man' he would stand back and watch as the corsage was affixed to his mother's wrist or bodice.

In the quiet hush of a gathering twilight mother and son looked out at the flats and the gleaming sea beyond, and until she spoke Paul felt certain she had forgotten he sat beside her. "Pretty, isn't it?" his mother asked. "When the tide is out of the inlet, you can almost forget the sea and think we have a river instead."

"I've decided to go live with father," Paul announced.

"You'll be visiting next month, dear."

"No, I mean forever. Go to school there and live there."

"But why, Darling? I wouldn't give you up. You are my own precious boy. You are all that I have." These were the words Paul longed to hear, and yet the monster had made him doubt they would ever be spoken.

Paul kept his voice neutral. He tried to imitate the unconscious tone of authority his mother used when conferring with the help. "I'll ask Marta to pack for me," Paul said and began to stand. "I can be gone by tomorrow if you'll just call and make the arrangements."

An expression of alarm came over Brenda's face. Paul's father was a concert violinist who was rarely home. He and Brenda had already decided to separate when Paul was conceived in one last futile burst of intimacy. They divorced before he was actually born, and each summer Paul spent three weeks with his father and new wife. Immediately the new marriage produced two children who absorbed his father's attention with a devotion that excluded Paul. Eventually, when he was older Paul would refuse the visits and adopt his mother's maiden name of Maple. She did not see why she should object, and his father did not protest too long or too hard. Nevertheless, at this juncture of her child's life, Paul's request seemed very odd indeed.

Brenda coaxed the truth from Paul and was duly horrified, but on some level not surprised. A few months before, Howard's wife had divorced him and for reasons which the family could not understand, Howard had given up all parental rights while paying a fortune in child support and maintenance. Howard had insisted the family have no contact with his former wife whom he accused of driving him to a nervous breakdown. The charges against her were many but on the whole insignificant, and the entire affair was baffling, raising more questions than could easily be answered.

It was true that Howard was harried that summer. He seemed unusually preoccupied, easily angered, and prone to solitary drinking spells that he tried to conceal. Only the sight of little Paul seemed to cheer him. The family believed Howard was mourning the loss of his own son, Peter, and felt great compassion for him.

By the time they left the dock that summer day, the tide was in and the

133

lights from the house came up and fell across the manicured lawn and down to the dock where mother and son sat talking. Brenda's escort had come to the door and been sent away. Now the sea hit his mother's ankles, but Paul, who was small for his age, had to scoot to the edge of the dock and lift himself down while his mother held his arms, just to have it brush the soles of his feet.

She would not allow him out of her sight until her brother left the house late that night. Any fledgling doubt and tendency to denial had been squelched by a candid conversation with her former sister-in-law. With Paul in tow Brenda had sequestered herself in the library, and Paul would never forget the look of utter horror that came over her face as she listened to what was being said on the other end of the line.

Perhaps, Paul had speculated to his psychiatrist, it was because Brenda had handled his experience with such swift and certain intervention that it was easy to forget. She had gathered him into the tight embrace of her arms and informed him that evil people did exist, often appearing deceptively normal, and a child could not be expected to know the difference. When he tried to speak and tell of his experience, she hushed his words in a flood of her own. Over and over again in those first hours, with the library door locked, she encouraged him to think of all that had transpired as a bad dream; a nightmare of no importance that must be put immediately out of mind and never thought of again. To illustrate her point she picked up a book and placed it out of sight, under the cushion of a nearby sofa.

Brenda Maple took responsibility entirely upon herself. "A mother should know," he heard her lament. "Why didn't I know?" The pathetic plea of her voice was a long whine of despair that made Paul think he must be permanently scalded. When she pulled him against her, he stiffened in her arms. Her manner and the convoluted rhetoric of her ranting had consigned his pain to ash and hers to fire. He never trusted her again.

Brenda then picked up the phone and called her father, who was in Manhattan on business. Paul sat under the desk and fiddled with the silver strap of her shoe and counted the lines in the wood grain and the red sword shapes in the Persian carpet. When finally Paul fell asleep Brenda was still on the phone, the emotionally charged tone of her conversation, completely escaping the web of his withdrawal.

Although Brenda thought it unnecessary, Paul saw a psychiatrist in Cambridge, a former classmate of grandfather Maple. From Paul's perspective the appointments were bearable only because his mother allowed a stop at Brigham's on the way home. Here he was indulged with the rare luxury of a huge chocolate sundae with coffee ice cream and a mountain of whipped cream. As he devoured his sundae, his mother sipped her raspberry Ricky and they talked of the Red Sox player she was currently dating and the boat she would buy him when he was old enough. They talked of school and books and a trip to Disneyland. Brenda wanted her 'old happy boy' back, and as best as he was able, Paul obliged.

Almost immediately mother and son had come to a tactical agreement, the complicated details of which never really had to be discussed. After that first evening on the dock where he had finally confided in his mother, they would never speak of the events of that summer again, and so Paul understood that he should also not talk to his Cambridge doctor. He learned to skirt the issues and act the resilient child his mother told him he was. It was the Maple way after all, to bounce back quickly from adversity, or so the Latin phrase on their family crest proclaimed. Dutifully Paul expunged from his mind as much as possible, as quickly as possible, never reckoning a later price for that premature gloss of peace.

Fall was well advanced when Paul and his mother left the fieldstone mansion on the hill. Leaves lay ankle-deep in the wood, and shiny wet trails of red and gold overflowed the gutters of narrow streets. They left the boathouse, the private cove, and most difficult of all for his mother, the luxury of a maid and driver. With a little creative book-keeping, Brenda was able to borrow the money from Paul's trust fund to purchase the house on Mill Lane, and grandfather Maple did his part to be sure Brenda could continue her former life as little disrupted as possible.

Almost immediately Paul met his next-door neighbor as she was outside pruning her roses. Grandmother Fothergill took one look at Paul and decided that he wasn't entirely normal and it was her job to help. She told him he was always welcome and with the literal mind of a child Paul began to spend more time in her kitchen than his own. The next summer Paul met Nora and Lydia.

"I have two little granddaughters who come each summer. You'll like them," Grandmother Fothergill informed Paul over hot gingersnaps and milk.

"Where are they now?" Paul had asked. It had been a long silent winter and hard in that small house to escape his mother's scrutiny. The baseball player had left and she was dating a banker from Boston, a business associate of Grandfather Maple, and for some reason she had taken to confiding in her son details of her relationships that he would have preferred not to know and did not always understand. Despite school Paul felt lonely and disconnected from the world in general, although he often crossed the narrow yard to visit with Grandmother Fothergill. She was a no-nonsense sort of woman who preferred listening to talking. The silences between them were often prolonged, although entirely welcome so that neither seemed to mind.

"They live outside Boston and come for the summer," she answered his question. "They'll be here at the end of June. Those two wouldn't miss the parade and the bonfire and the fireworks on July fourth. Not for the world." Grandmother Fothergill laughed at the thought of her two granddaughters, and intrigued, Paul laughed in return.

With great expectation Paul awaited their arrival. In some ways he already felt he knew the girls, since Grandmother Fothergill had let him play with their toys and he had read many of Nora's books. He and his mother had been invited to join the Fothergills for their traditional Fourth of July dinner of salmon, creamed onions with peas, and strawberry shortcake.

Paul was sitting on the steps when they first turned down the lane. The family came on foot and the luggage followed later in the town's only cab; a flat bed truck that existed solely for the purpose of ferrying the luggage of the summer folks from the train station. Mr. Fothergill wore a suit, and the girls were formally dressed in hats with white gloves. Within the hour the formal clothes had disappeared, not to be worn again until church on Sunday and then the trip home two months later. Paul wondered why they couldn't live all year in Rockport, never dreaming he would someday get his wish with tragic consequences.

What Paul remembered most from that first meeting was that Nora punched his arm so hard it left a bruise, and he tripped her going up the steps, resulting in a scraped knee. Instead of crying she scrunched her face in a fleeting demonstration of pain before bestowing on him a dramatic look of withering disdain. The battle of stares that ensued resulted in a tie, and for the remainder of the summer the two were inseparable.

What Paul remembered about Lydia was that she was beautiful. Her skin was a porcelain shade of ivory, absent the freckles that scattered across the bridge of Nora's nose. Her red hair shone in the sun and was a prettier shade than her sisters', and her green eyes were vibrant and alive.

Immediately she complained of feeling left out, and Paul recalled Grandmother Fothergill patiently explaining that before the summer was out she would find a friend her own age to play with, but Lydia was never satisfied. Red rover, pirate ship off the raft, and stick ball and tag in which the smaller, younger Lydia was often, 'it' was not her idea of fun. She whined when she was not included and cried and complained even more when she was. In all their dealings with Lydia, Paul and Nora unfailingly emerged in the wrong and often found themselves standing side by side as they explained their side of the story. The inevitable result was an enduring lifelong bond of friendship.

One incident concerning Lydia stood out in Paul's mind with certain clarity, and when he thought of her he often recalled it. On a rainy day Nora had taken the train with her mother to see the family dentist. Paul spent the afternoon doing Lydia the very great favor of indulging her with his company. No one but his own mother had ever been so thrilled to have him all to herself. They played with Lydia's Barbie dolls and rearranged the furniture in her dollhouse. They dressed the neighborhood cats in party dresses, tied makeshift leashes to miniature chairs, and served them a special concoction of tuna and milk out of Grandmother Fothergill's green and white breakfast china. Paul was impressed with the scope of his generosity and her admiration.

Later, as though to confirm this impression of himself, Mr. Fothergill had thanked him for entertaining Lydia, as though the whole experience of dressing up the neighborhood cats and playing with dolls must have been entirely abhorrent. Mr. Fothergill had shaken his hand and treated him with a respect that was foreign to Paul.

Paul came to love the Fothergills'. He liked the wonderful cooking smells that emanated from Grandmother Fothergill's kitchen. He liked the structure of bedtime and meals at specific hours. "You better watch out," Nora would mouth behind her mother's back in anticipation of the inevitable warning should one fail to cooperate with clearly defined expectations.

When Nora's mother announced bedtime, Paul got in the habit of returning home and climbing into his own bed. His mother had stopped imposing these sorts of restrictions and the first night thought him lost and never thought to check his room as she rallied the neighbors for an inconvenient midnight search. Nora's mother suggested that he might actually be asleep as all normal children were at this hour. The neighbors crowded the small doorway of his bedroom, as his mother scolded and informed him that only boring people with not an ounce of creativity retired so early.

Paul especially liked Mr. Fothergill, who was a man of few words, always with a book under one arm. He used his cane with the skill of another appendage, which had become a necessity after returning from the war as a young man. At Nora and Lydia's request he would roll up one pant leg and to squeals of exaggerated horror, exhibit the ugly scars that encircled his shattered kneecap and puckered the skin down to his foot in an ugly, trailing burn scar. Sometimes the girls would not pretend horror at all but would ask for an explanation, and he would use that occasion to tell them a story about trusting God. Because of Mr. Fothergill's resolute faith, Paul had never doubted the existence of God.

He had his own corner in the front room with a large leather chair and a pipe stand with gleaming pipes of various woods and each with a different smell. He always had time for his daughters, and since Paul and Nora were inseparable, for Paul as well. They sat on his lap, and he read them books and he graciously limped around the backyard croquet wickets with the three of them. He liked nothing better than to sleep in the sun at the beach, and more agile in the water than anywhere else, he often swam with them out to the raft.

When weekends came and he was expected back from the city, the entire house was hushed and focused on his arrival. Special foods were cooked, and Mrs. Fothergill turned herself out in bright Lilly sun dresses with white lace trim contrasted against her tan, and the delicate scent of citrus trailing in her wake. She was as thrilled as the girls to welcome him but would stand back as they rushed into his arms.

In those first moments, over the heads of Lydia and Nora, Paul noticed that Mr. Fothergill never took his eyes off his wife. That they loved one another was a silent certainty, the glue of their security. It was something to aspire to, but deep inside Paul suspected he could never be clean enough or good enough to deserve a similar prize. This family that he had come to love and wished desperately were his entirely and permanently, could make him forget for a little while the gnawing sense of worthlessness, but not for long. No confluence of carefully-spun logic could convince his child's mind that he was not damaged. Wasn't that the message carefully imbedded in his mind that kept him from telling his mother sooner? Planted in the dark recesses of unresolved trauma, the evil rhetoric of his tormenter was a constant threat.

Sometimes Mr. Fothergill would look at him in mock exasperation and say, "In a house full of women we men must stick together, right Paul?" He pushed Brenda to allow Paul sailing lessons and golf lessons, often saying, "I'll have to have a little talk with your mother," and they had career talks about what Paul would do with his life. Paul listened attentively and appeared to agree. Sometimes he wished he could confide in Mr. Fothergill, but that was not possible. He didn't have the words. He didn't understand enough to begin, and this feeling only increased his isolation.

One year for his birthday Mr. and Mrs. Fothergill gave him a dark blue Bible with his name engraved in gold letters. On the inside cover they wrote words about their love and hope for him, about the love and forgiveness of Jesus Christ and the notation of a passage of scripture. Paul found the book of Ephesians so that he could read the words. *For by grace you have been saved through faith, not of yourselves, it is a gift of God, not as a result of works least anyone should boast (Ephesians 2: 8,9).*

What did those words mean? He asked his mother, who told him that it was nonsense. Everyone knew you had to try and be good enough for God, and if your good deeds outweighed the bad, then you could count on heaven. Paul had never regained any measure of respect for his mother, so he tended to believe Mr. Fothergill, who had encouraged the three children to memorize passages of Scripture. Long into adulthood the words of one particular passage would flash to mind and often when he least expected the intrusion of those words. Immediately he was transported back in time, a small boy taller than Lydia and the same height as Nora standing before a proud Mr. Fothergill and reciting in the sing-song way that children have of joining their voices in unison, confident of praise. *For God so loved the world that he gave his only begotten son that whoever believes in him should not perish, but have everlasting life (John 3:16).*

Mr. Fothergill encouraged him to read his Bible whenever he was lonely or frightened, but submerged in the trials of his chosen lifestyle, Paul had resisted and then forgotten. He knew in the deep recesses of a scarred conscience that certain compulsions, evolved and submerged into lifelong habits, had separated him forever from the ideal of the one man he had wanted most to emulate. Mr. Fothergill would never approve. Nor would he agree that change was impossible.

Nevertheless when he was with Mr. Fothergill, Paul felt he had been admitted to some exclusive club that Nora and Lydia were exempted from simply because they were female. He felt safe with Nora's family and especially her father in a way that made him almost relax his guard. Deep inside he knew that if Mr. Fothergill had really been his father, Howard Maple would have suffered more than banishment from his family, and there was satisfaction in knowing that the world was a better place because of this man and his love and care for his family. Mr. Fothergill was the only male figure in Paul's childhood who loved him easily and truly, and when he roughed his hair or slapped his back or reprimanded him for not being patient enough with Lydia, Paul was happy just to be basking in the center of that masculine attention.

When Mr. Fothergill died of a heart attack four years after Lydia's disappearance, Paul felt he had lost his own father. He was inconsolable all of that long winter and even now visited the gravesite more often than Nora. The loss was one that faded in freshness but never in intensity, and the wealth of good memories sustained and encouraged Paul when depression and sadness threatened to overwhelm him.

CHAPTER TWELVE

It surprised him how the town kept her disappearance close to their hearts. It was as though the crime itself had inflicted a collective wound that never healed. Some whispered that the two families drew inward to protect the only children they had left, keeping more and more to themselves. Others were suspicious and wondered at the isolation and veil of secrecy.

When Herb became sick this last time, Paul stopped making time for his psychiatrist. Regardless of how often he was assured otherwise, he felt certain that when he was gone, Herb tended to do worse and so he made his forays away brief and infrequent. Paul studied the face that he loved. Herb lay with his emaciated frame propped up on a snowy white pillow. He'd lost all of his wonderful glossy black hair and his expressive brown eyes appeared unusually large, the mole above his thin lip oddly misshapen.

"Have you tested?" he asked Paul.

"You know that I have."

"And you're fine?"

"I AM fine."

"You're certain, are you?"

"Very certain."

"Maybe you should get tested again."

Paul suppressed his irritation. Lately Herb's mind had begun to wander. He often focused on an idea or thought, only to need constant reassurance of the same answer. The idea that plagued him today was testing. Yesterday it had been a weather report of flooding in California, but Herb seemed unable to make the distinction that Massachusetts was on the opposite coast. The very worst occurred just before the holidays. A substitute nurse, unaware of Herb's tendency to obsess, had looked out the window and seen the girl who had stood out in the lane for much of the night. She'd waited almost until dawn to tell Paul, but Herb was already upset and demanding that they call the police. For two days he insisted that she was dangerous and made the outrageous claim that she had entered the house and stood over his bed.

Paul had crushed an extra sedative and put it in Herb's tube feeding.

Connor, his good friend and the only doctor in town, told him that the virus had begun to invade the brain, resulting in confusion and subtle personality changes. Paul could not accept this, telling Nora that these symptoms of confusion were only a temporary result of new medications and terrible side effects that sometimes wrecked havoc on Herb's ability to cope.

Paul took Herb's hand. The skin was paper thin and black and blue from endless probes with IV needles. Connor, Herb's doctor, was due to stop by in the afternoon. He was going to insert a permanent shunt so that Herb would no longer be tortured by the painful search for a vein strong enough to infiltrate without soon collapsing.

Paul saw the frown form over Herb's face. He saw Herb struggle to put the words in sequence. Just as he opened his mouth to ask yet again if he had been tested, Paul changed the subject.

"Nora's going to make you that bread pudding you like so much."

"With caramelized brandy?" Herb whispered, the deep masculine tones of his voice now painfully frail. Paul missed that rich, firm voice which had been such an important part of his life for so long. He nodded and tried to smile.

"Nora never liked me."

"Of course she likes you. She loves you."

"Nora loves you, not me." Herb sounded resigned. "She thinks you're too good for me. Just like everyone else in this awful town."

"I thought you liked this town."

"Well, it's not New York, is it?"

Paul refrained from answering. He walked around the foot of the bed to look at the IV bag. He drew into a syringe the correct dosage of an anti-coagulant that would prevent blood clots from forming and inserted it into the catheter. Since Herb's illness, he and Nora both had acquired a host of skills they never imagined they would need.

Paul did not try to reassure Herb that he was wrong about Nora. It was impossible these days to reason with Herb, and in any case he was certain that despite a tenuous, sometimes rocky beginning, she had grown genuinely fond of him. Paul had done all he could to prepare Nora for that first meeting, but still she had looked at Herb in incredulous disbelief, almost as though she were regarding a bizarre science exhibit. Herb was so unlike any of Paul's former partners, and her instant perplexity if not shock was obvious. Paul smiled to think of it now.

"Now I want to remind you," Paul had said. "Appearances can be deceptive and I'm planning to do a complete overhaul."

"What is he, a used part for one of your boats?" Nora had asked as they cut through the cemetery to Peg Legs, where they would meet Herb for lunch.

"Stop being cruel. I love him. Don't spoil this for me by being too practical."

"You just met him. How can you possibly claim that you love him?"

"Three months can be a very long time and besides; you're jealous because you've never been in love!"

Nora punched his arm, and he ducked away. "True, you fall in love too quickly and I not at all. Which I ask you is worse? While you cry and agonize I can at least sleep nights. Just do me one favor, Paul. This time proceed cautiously. Don't commit yourself too quickly. It seems that only yesterday I was sweeping up the pieces of your last broken heart."

"I'm going to ask him to move in. I'm tired of traveling to New York every weekend just to be with him. I hate that city."

"Do you mind if I get quietly drunk at lunch?" Nora asked. "So I don't have to watch you make a complete fool of yourself without a little liquid reinforcement."

"You worry too much, and you've never been drunk in your life, Nora."

"I have to worry. You worry about the wrong things and when it comes to men, you have a blind spot where your common sense ought to be."

"Don't be so dramatic," Paul chided, his tone dismissive.

Nora did not think she was overreacting. Unlike her, Paul could barely tolerate being alone and seemed to need the drama of a new romantic interest on a regular basis. He was able to keep his friends forever, but not so his partners, seeming to reject the more stable relationships, craving instead those fraught with drama and tension. If she was reading between the lines of Paul's glowing description correctly, this great love of his life, the one destined to last forever, sounded like a street punk. Too much like what Paul himself had sometimes characterized as rough trade. A type he claimed he could never be attracted to but had slowly been gravitating towards for a very long time.

Nora had given up trying to stem the self-destructive slide inherent in a lifestyle she neither understood nor approved. But her love and dashed hopes for Paul and herself, the deep and conflicted trauma of their shared past, and her respect for the integrity that colored all other areas of his life was a fierce bond that would not be broken. As a child, whenever Nora would question the injustice of life, Grandmother Fothergill would unfailingly reply, "God has a plan." When Nora was truly tormented by the consequences of Paul's choices and her total helplessness to change him she would pray, "God you must have a plan. Whatever it is please tell me because only you can help my friend."

When Nora turned to God at these moments of trial and uncertainty, she felt guilty. She had spent her life attending church and yet now rarely went. And even as she prayed she knew something more. Her parents and grandmother had shared an intimacy with Jesus Christ that she could not claim, and yet tenuously she held on to the conviction that God was personal and real, and if she could just shed the bitterness of the past and if God could truly forgive her for abandoning Lydia, then He might actually love her the way he apparently loved others.

Herb was already seated at a reserved table when Nora and Paul walked into the restaurant. Herb shook Nora's hand and sensed Paul's scrutiny as he made the introductions. Suddenly Herb realized that the outcome of this meeting was vitally important to Paul, but why Nora's approval should mean so much was baffling. Herb could feel the first talon of jealousy invade his good spirits and was immediately attentive.

From the way that Paul described Nora, Herb had expected a judgmental, surrogate mother of the sort that often attached themselves to gay men. He was completely unprepared for her youthful, no-nonsense beauty. One could almost call Nora cute, and yet she was too formidable and smart to be dismissed so easily. As he took her measure, Herb knew that Nora was in turn assessing him. Her manner was polite and coolly distant, but when she turned to Paul she changed. The rapport between them was deep and extremely close. Almost like siblings, Herb thought, but not enough to quell his jealousy.

Herb wore white jeans with the pant legs tucked into black calf-length boots and a black tee shirt that showed every bulge of his muscled arms and chest. Traces of mascara clung to the top and bottom lashes of his eyes, and Nora was almost certain that he had applied a natural shade of lipstick with gloss. He wore his hair long. It was freshly washed and hung in a straight line to his shoulders, and irregardless of the hot weather a stiff leather biker jacket was thrown over the back of Herb's chair.

Despite the makeup there was nothing feminine or even tentative about Herb. He had a raw physical presence that made Nora think of trapped steam searching for any crack from which to escape. She guessed he could be a tough opponent, but now that she had met him she was relieved. He would never last. A few months were all she would give the relationship, for she was certain he would be unfaithful, and Paul expected his partners to be exclusive while they lasted.

Nora doubted that Herb would do Paul the favor of giving up his life in New York for the quiet predictability of a town like Rockport. The more he talked of his friends and round of social commitments, name-dropping an occasional celebrity, Nora felt relieved. *Yes,* she assured herself. *This relationship is doomed.*

Paul and Nora were dressed almost alike in summer shirts and chino shorts. Nora's shirt was peach, embroidered with her initials in a tone-on-tone color that made the script barely discernable. Herb noticed that she had the sort of warm, effortless glow to her skin that came from slow, natural exposure to the sun, and her chin-length hair was pulled to one side with a flat, tortoise shell barrette. Paul wore deck shoes with no socks and a faded green polo which had the look of having been professionally laundered.

Herb looked at them and wondered how they could look so carelessly thrown together and yet so perfect. Nora wore half-carat diamond studs in her ears and no other jewelry. Herb tended to wear every possible piece he could manage, but now, as he studied Nora, he suddenly regretted the heavy gold chain that hung over his tee shirt. A recent gift, he had actually worn it to make Paul jealous. As he looked at Nora he realized that manipulations which worked with others might back fire with Paul.

Nora had difficulty tearing her eyes off Herb's hair, which was died a peroxide shade of orange. She picked at her shrimp and mango almond salad and with fixated fascination, studied Herb as he scraped up a layer of runny eggs from the top of a charred T-bone. This particular dish had never been on the restaurant menu, but Paul had prevailed upon his friendship with the owner and had it cooked regardless. Anything for a new love. Nora sighed and kept her thoughts to herself.

After lunch they skirted the cemetery and walked up a narrow footpath toward the old mill. Along the way people greeted Nora and Paul and looked at Herb askance. Paul showed off his house, ten neat rooms with a screened porch and a glassed-in, detached greenhouse. The garage was the original carriage house with a black weather vane and four empty stalls. Paul especially enjoyed walking Herb through his garden, which in midsummer was a profusion of vibrant color, and finally they sat around the weathered bench which encircled a massive oak, and Nora departed to make iced tea.

Herb closed his eyes and turned his pale face up toward the sun. He liked this garden. After his cramped New York apartment, Paul's house seemed more like a castle and this town! It was unbelievable. Towns like this really did exist, and if you dressed the part and adopted the role, perhaps one could just manage to fit in. Managing to fit in was a goal Herb had abandoned long ago, and yet he was drawn to the possibility of how happiness might be attained if he were more like Paul and even Nora. Perhaps another try might actually be worth the risk.

Herb had few illusions, but he felt that meeting Paul had been a good omen. If he was a religious man, he might almost say a miracle, one capable of restoring a bit of faith and even renewal into his jaded life. Herb breathed in the faint mixture of wild honeysuckle on a warm salt breeze as it drifted over the cemetery gate and decided that he would no longer ridicule Paul's discreet suggestions for improvement. As soon as he got back to New York, he would ask Mario to color his hair back to its natural color.

Paul could not see what Herb knew. Right now and early on, the relationship was no more than an exotic diversion, a dangerous interlude, titillating, sensual, and brief. If he wanted Paul and the mantle of Paul's life to sooth his own demons, he must get started right away. The attraction Paul felt must become reliance. Reliance was easily shifted to compulsion and then a kind of blind addiction. If layers of manipulation achieved the desired outcome, it would be Herb and Herb alone who would have the power to sustain or end the relationship. And then, in the delusional bravado of imagining himself solely in command, the internal cord constricting his heart might actually relax. Why did he think it could? Why did he hold on to such misplaced hope?

Having identified his prey, Herb was invigorated by the sense of power he would feel if utterly successful. He reminded himself that only a fool would fail to grasp this opportunity. At any time a male version of Nora Fothergill might come into Paul's life or reemerge from the past, and then he would be quickly forgotten.

In New York Herb was fairly anonymous, but in the quaint town of Rockport he stood out like a pariah. To his eternal heartache Herb had repeatedly grappled with the emptiness of his life, and he was tired of losing. Recently he had turned a few tricks in order to supplement his income and a return to old habits terrified him. Flirtation with 'the life' would soon necessitate a suicidal somersault into addiction. Herb had now been clean for eight months but had stopped attending his support meetings and no longer returned the calls of his AA sponsor. All too familiar with the self-loathing that accompanies relapse, Herb knew he did not have the will to wade through that miry clay again.

Herb surveyed Paul's garden. His eyes came to rest on the day lilies. In fragrant heaviness they bent their heads over a long stripe of lavender, which pushed against a yellow and purple border of pansies. The knowledge came to him with unmistakable insistence. The time for change was now or never, life or death. His legs outstretched, he leaned against the gnarled oak and imagined Paul on the other side. Nora returned and passed out frosted glasses of tea with mint and lemon perched at the rim like miniature bouquets. Paul and Nora lived within the borders of an ordered correctness, which Herb had loudly derided but secretly admired and longed to emulate. He had always equated the seemingly effortless beauty of what he saw depicted in the glossy pages of decorator magazines as artificial hype permanently beyond his grasp and therefore an unattainable fantasy. Now he looked about and weighed Paul's world against his own and dared to hope. If he could own that same ordered existence, then maybe the gnawing hunger that seemed always to claw at his heels would be appeased.

As Nora took her place on the third portion of the circular bench, a picture flashed into Herb's mind of how they appeared from the top of the leafy canopy, and he had the distinct impression of being observed from above. They sipped their drinks but said not a word to one another for a long while. "Nora," Herb thought, "is thinking of how she can get rid of me and Paul–"

As though reading his mind Paul moved around the tree to sit beside him. Paul's hand gravitated toward his and held on tight. Herb studied the dappled patches of sunlight over the perfect lawn and felt a rare contentment. That devouring and perpetual uneasiness which haunted his waking hours was momentarily restrained. Almost involuntarily he prayed to that nameless God, the powers that be, the presence he sometimes felt at odd moments, hovering near. This was absolutely a final chance for happiness. Could he manage himself and Paul well enough not to destroy it? He needed Paul's stability and his neat ordered life. He needed Paul with a desperation that would prove hard to conceal beneath the lackadaisical veneer of the one addiction he acknowledged, substituted for the one he could not name.

After a suitable period of apparent indecision, Herb moved into Paul's house and absorbed what he could quickly and deliberately. Among a thousand bits of useless trivia, he learned the appropriate way to spoon his soup away from him and which shape of decanter to fill with what. Nora and Paul were devoted to understatement with an unconscious passion that Herb found contradictory to his own conception of magazine living, and he went on a spending spree, bringing home odd bits of furniture and accessories that later made their way to the basement storage areas. He gave away his leather jacket, which Paul was clearly fond of, and with Paul's Gold Card in hand, he invited Nora to go shopping with him for a wardrobe his partner would approve. Repackaging the outside proved a simple enough endeavor, but refurbishing his shattered and depleted spirit was another matter entirely.

Nora could never entirely discard her distrust of Herb. When she saw that he had become a permanent fixture in Paul's life, she began the search for something to like, isolating those traits in her mind and concentrating on these, rather than the far more numerous others that irritated her.

Herb sensed Nora's ambivalence. He had not survived a childhood in foster homes and on the streets with only his wits to sustain him, without acquiring certain skills. Even as he fielded her polite, deferential overtures of friendship, he gave the appearance of welcoming her inclusion into their lives. Herb knew that Nora would never abandon her friendship with Paul without a fight, and to his great frustration his few attempts to drive a wedge between them had hopelessly backfired.

What, he wondered, *is this indestructible bond they share?* If it wasn't blood or love, then what was it? No stranger to shame, it seemed to Herb that Nora and Paul shared a secret that for their mutual love of one another, they kept well hidden. He thought it might have something to do with the disappearance of Lydia Fothergill, who he knew had been kidnaped while in their company. Paul and Nora never discussed Lydia within his hearing and when he brought the subject up over dinner one evening, expressing his sympathy, the silence that followed was awkward.

"Thank you," Nora had said. "But it was a long time ago and we really don't talk about it anymore."

"Oh, I'm sorry. I was just curious, and I wanted to say that I know it must have been just terrible for both of you." He looked between Nora and Paul, who sat across the table from him over a late supper of cold chicken and salad. Paul glared at his plate and Nora reached for her wineglass, and Herb knew better than to broach the subject again.

The dynamics of Nora and Paul's relationship remained a mystery to Herb. He resented the memories and experiences they shared which excluded him, but he never felt secure enough to openly challenge that bond; and on the few occasions when jealousy had got the better of him, resulting in an argument over Nora, he had unfailingly emerged the loser. Like many other accommodations in life, Herb adjusted to what he considered Nora's intrusive presence, but always resenting Paul's apparent need for her approval and company.

Paul remained oblivious to all the little sub dramas that orbited his new relationship. Herb was impetuous and endlessly entertaining, sometimes verbally abusive, but always willing to apologize and make amends and then there was the passion. Passion fraught with the threat of danger blinded Paul to a multitude of deficiencies and had always managed to pierce his core in a way that nothing else could. The rocky, roller-coaster pattern inherent in all his relationships, which included components of physical and mental abuse, appeased the guilt and shame he could never shed and made him feel alive in some way that ordinary existence failed. Being alive, no matter the cost, was preferable to feeling nothing at all. For in the great mass of that dark void of numbness breathed the threat of something far more terrible which stalked the rim of consciousness.

"I saw you once."

"When did you see me?" Paul asked and straightened a crimp in the IV tubing. He lifted the light blanket and checked the urinary catheter.

"Here in Rockport when we were teenagers."

Paul sighed. Herb was about to go off on another fanciful tangent and seemed even more confused than usual, but at least he was no longer reminding him to get tested for AIDS.

The last time Paul had talked with Herb's doctor he was reminded that this was part of the natural progression of the disease, and all he could do was patiently remind Herb of the truth. There was still so much to know about AIDS, and the drugs in use only managed to contain the symptoms for a brief time. Herb had been on the verge of death twice before but was never as debilitated as he was now. In the past he had managed to snap back and resume his life, although each time his recovery had required more time and he emerged frailer and more susceptible to secondary infections.

"We first saw one another at that off-Broadway production of the Fantastics. After the play Liza introduced us. You do remember that, don't you? We all went to dinner and I contrived to sit next to you."

"Of course," Herb said, "but I'm speaking of a different time. I saw you once before that. I just never told you."

"Okay, I'll bite," Paul was now curious. "Where did you see me?"

"I was with Howard. He was my first real love, you know. I was crazy for that man."

"Howard? My Uncle Howard?"

"You were sailing and we passed by and nearly capsized you."

The incident flashed into Paul's mind. His hands shook as he replaced the covers and tucked the blankets about Herb's wasted frame. Time had suspended its progression, and his thoughts drew inward even as an overwhelming sense of apprehension tore through his body. That one encounter was the only one he had with Howard since the day his mother had instructed the servants to pack his belongings and escort him from the house. It had been abrupt and unexpected. He recalled scanning the deck of the other boat with his binoculars. With difficulty he'd brought his much smaller skiff around, furious at the thoughtlessness of the larger craft, and then he spied Howard on deck.

Herb's face was clouded by an absent, far-off expression which hurt Paul to see. He turned from the bed and walked to the window. Herb had never disguised the fact that he knew Howard. It was one of their first exchanges of information as they sat in that restaurant and savored their onion soup beneath a layer of thick cheese. "Who do you know that I know?" When Herb heard Paul's last name, he asked if he was related to Howard Maple. But the news that they had ever been together well, that was different. Herb had never confided that and Paul had never suspected. If he had....

Herb continued completely oblivious to Paul's change in demeanor. "I said to Howard, 'who is that boy?' Because it seemed to me that he had deliberately passed by so close and then he sped up just to create those swells. He said, "That's my nephew." Howard rarely used profanity, but when he said your name it had that effect. And that's when I knew there had been something between you and that it hadn't gone well. But Howard was hard to read. Of course, you would know that. He was always so polished and careful. My, he was careful, so I knew that there was some kind of problem. Something about you had really disturbed him. I was curious, so I studied you through my binoculars just as you looked at him with yours. When you lowered them I saw the family resemblance, but you were even better looking than Howard was, and it was clear that you loathed him. I saw it on your face and I knew."

Herb's voice trailed into silence. "Go on," Paul prodded. He felt cold and stiff, and the physical sensation of the room evaporated into a dull tintype.

"I wanted to be like you ... lucky. You looked so lucky and blessed to be sailing that boat, and you had a rich family. I couldn't believe my luck when we actually met years later. Somehow I thought Howard's polish would rub off, and he would turn me into someone like you."

"But he didn't change you for the better, did he?"

"No. He was never generous like you. When we met I was already too old for him," Herb replied, his raspy voice wistful, yearning.

The words came at Paul like a whip. He pulled the curtain aside. He had moved Herb to this guestroom when round-the-clock nursing care was required. The furnishings had been his mother's, moved from across the hall after she'd died. Paul had replaced her antique, canopied bed with the hospital bed, but everything else remained the same. Across the way was Nora's house. Paul could see the cemetery and a slice of the sea beyond. The room was wallpapered with pink cabbage roses, matching curtains, and a rose and green Oriental rug which covered the hardwood floor. Green striped chintz adorned the chairs, and Nora had painted him something for the wall. Paul let his eyes drift over the painting and started. There clearly depicted was the boathouse in disrepair, and now he recognized the row of pine trees, which marked the entrance to the cove, and the knoll above where the Maple mansion had once stood.

Paul hadn't realized until this very moment what Nora had painted. It had been so long ago, and the family house was now gone. He wondered if the boathouse was still standing. Well, it had to be, for here it was, weathered and listing and captured just as it must have looked to Nora on that day that she painted it. Paul lifted the painting from the wall. He opened the dark closet and tossed it in. Behind him Herb coughed. Herb hated the décor of this room, calling it too English. Suddenly Paul hated it too.

Unexpected tears pooled in Paul's eyes, but the anger he felt burned them quickly away. The sudden question flashed to mind. Who would take care of him when he became sick? Why must he think of himself now? Why now and not later, and how did Herb get AIDS in the first place? They were supposed to be monogamous. They had pledged fidelity. Paul had cast off the need for answers to all these questions until another time when once again his life would be his own. But how would he live without Herb? Herb was his life. Or maybe not.

With effort Paul kept his voice neutral. "Why did you never tell me about you and Howard?"

The room was so still in the aftermath of the question that Paul could hear the drip of the IV. Then the furnace kicked in, and the sound of the bells from the white steeple over the cemetery wall rang out to mark the noon hour. Nora would be coming home for lunch, and she would poke her head in to inquire how he was. It irritated Paul that she was more concerned about whether he was eating right and getting enough sleep than about Herb. Didn't Nora realize that Herb was dying?

Paul turned from the window. "Why didn't you ever tell me about Howard?" he asked again, but Herb was asleep. His head had lolled to one side and drool slipped from the corner of his mouth. Paul walked to the bedside and dabbed at Herb's mouth. He then applied ointment and straightened the blankets. Gently, ever so lightly, he bent to kiss the paper-thin brow, avoiding a large round lesion. Then he walked from the room.

CHAPTER THIRTEEN

He saw how some insulated themselves from a reckoning with human vulnerability. They had ordered their lives in such a way that when pain came, it threatened every termite invested mooring. Those who believed they should not suffer turned bitter, and so he looked for opportunities to catch that moment, poised on the inner rim of a spiritual void, so that he could talk about Jesus.

Paul stood in his garden where under beds of leaves and strips of burlap his children slept. He felt paternal toward his garden. The night was cold, but the moon was bright and reflected through the low cloud-cover. In the light from the kitchen and back porch Paul paced the yard. He reached up to retrieve a twig half broken and suspended from a narrow limb of the Chinese Maple. He brushed snow from the back of the granite tortoise, which was a permanent fixture amid the Shasta Daisies and the Black-Eyed Susans. He imagined the crocus, the paper whites, and the many tulips that would emerge in spring, and he fingered a sprig of forsythia and then the lilac. No knobby protrusions yet. "Not yet," he said aloud to pierce the stillness of the dark night.

All day, since Herb's revelation about Howard, Paul had avoided the sick room. Twice he had walked to the door but could not bring himself to step over the threshold. Connor came with his nurse, but for the first time Paul was not on hand to support Herb. The cut-down was performed and the permanent catheter inserted into the vein without incident, and now, genuinely confused Herb had not asked for him. Paul mixed himself a whiskey and ginger ale and offered Connor one when he came downstairs.

"You're kidding, right?" Connor said. "I have patients back at the office and a baby due and you know I don't drink."

It struck Paul how much his friends accommodated Herb for his sake. He had taken them for granted and been oblivious to all their many kindnesses, refusing to see that most had never warmed to Heb.

"I don't think I've ever told you how much I appreciate you coming to the house for Herb," Paul said carefully. It made him feel disloyal to say the words, and he thought of the first years of their relationship, before they had burrowed into a kind of settled predictability, which he had adjusted to with far more ease than Herb.

"Glad to be of help," Connor said. Connor had graduated from Rockport High School with him and Nora. His father had been a fisherman and he had married his high school sweetheart while still in medical school, and now they had four children. Often he and Paul engaged in rousing debates, as if the high school debate team had never disbanded. Before Herb's illness they had played a regular game of golf in summer and handball in winter.

Herb never understood the friendship. Connor attended a conservative Bible church and stood for everything Herb hated. After witnessing his first caustic debate between the two, Herb had thought *good riddance,* certain the two would never speak again and so was astonished when a few days later they greeted one another with a warm hug at St Joachim's annual bazaar.

"If that doctor tells me one more time about Jesus," Herb said to Paul one day, "I'm going to report him for medical harassment. He judges us, you know. He hates our relationship. He told me it was wrong."

Paul laughed. "Well, yes.... He's said that to me a time or two. He also told me my life expectancy was lower because of the lifestyle, that I would be more prone to suicide and certain cancers. What can I say? He tells the truth."

"Why do you subject yourself to that? I just do not understand you!"

"We got into the habit of being friends when we were young. We've always disagreed."

"Well, I hate it. I hate it for you especially. And Nora agrees with him, you know. She hates our lifestyle but doesn't say so to our faces." Herb spat out Nora's name with disdain.

"I like that they're honest. I like that we can talk and say what we think and still really like each other because we have a lot else in common, and the sexual preferences are just a small part of that."

"You just like arguing. And repent!" Herb said. "What does repentance have to do with anything? Do you know that Connor actually told me I could beat this homosexual thing, like I was an alcoholic or something? He told me there's a program in Memphis, Tennessee called "Love in Action." He actually had the nerve to offer me the phone number. Do please, let's find another doctor."

"Can't. He's the only show in town."

"What about the experts? He's just a GP, you know?"

"You see the experts. Connor consults with them, and they don't stop by after a busy day just to see for themselves what color your sputum is."

It was Connor who put the question to Herb. The question that was most on Paul's mind, the one he could not bring himself to ask. Did Herb want to return to Boston and expire in a hospital bed after everything possible had been done for him, or did he want to stick with the local hospital and die at home? Herb wanted to die at home, and even if Paul failed to grasp the seriousness of his current state of health, patient and doctor did not.

Suddenly Paul realized that Connor had asked him a question. All through the long day, ever since his conversation with Herb, Paul had found himself replaying in his mind odd, seemingly unrelated portions of his past life. Though he tried he could not silence the voices or quell the disjointed images that sprang to mind with biting cruelty.

"Are you feeling okay?" Connor repeated. "If you don't take care of yourself you'll be no use to Herb, and I'll have anther patient to worry about."

"I'm fine."

Connor put a hand on Paul's shoulder. "Right, and I am a small animal vet. Call me if you want to talk. You know I'm praying for you both." Connor looked into Paul's eyes, seeming to invite conversation. But Paul looked away. "And get some sleep. You look like hell."

The storm door slammed. Paul followed and stood on the step and watched his friend trudge through the snow. His red Jeep could be seen at the head of Mill Lane, which was too narrow for the snowplow to turn around. Once no more than a bridal path, the lane narrowed even more at the crest of the hill before descending to the old mill.

Everyone walked in Rockport. The physical perimeters of the town were small, and many of Connor's patients drove in from Gloucester. People warned Connor that if he didn't set up practice there he would never have enough patients to support his growing family, but he refused to listen. Connor, like Paul and Nora, had never desired to live anywhere else.

Paul considered Connor's assertion that he was praying. He imagined that Connor talked with God often, and if he was asking help for him and Herb, well … that couldn't be a bad thing. Maybe at some point he would give it a try himself, but not now. Right now memories were gathering like storm clouds, momentarily held off, but threatening release and he felt afraid to be alone.

When the night nurse came at six, Paul told her he was retiring early. She nodded her head approvingly, believing that he was finally taking her advice and getting more rest. She'd been on many cases like this, but she had rarely seen a partner as devoted as Paul. She thought that at times his hovering had a manic sort of quality. His almost ritualistic attention to detail regarding each aspect of Herb's care seemed a futile attempt to bargain with the God he'd rejected. She too was praying for Paul and especially for Herb. She'd asked her mother to get her church circle praying, and her three prayer partners, all nurses working in home care with last stage, critically ill persons, met regularly for that purpose.

Paul made himself a tuna fish sandwich on cinnamon swirl bread with watercress and Major Grey's Chutney. He then retreated to his room but not before studying Herb's vast array of medications. He found one labeled 'sleep' and avoiding thought he swallowed the Dalmane with another shot of whiskey floating on top of his ginger ale. He then retired for a bath.

At three he awoke. He looked in on Herb and the nurse. Herb was awake, but Paul ducked out before he was spotted, and now he stood in his garden in the dead of night and shivered. He thought of taking another sleeping pill, but his head hurt and he didn't like the idea of that helpless, artificially induced oblivion. Though he tried he could not recall leaving the bath or his head hitting the pillow.

Deciding abruptly, Paul ceased the aimless survey of his garden and striding into the kitchen he grabbed a set of keys. He let himself in through Nora's back door and climbing what had once been the servants' staircase, he entered the upstairs hall, turned left past the main staircase, and entered her bedroom.

"Don't be scared," he whispered. "It's just me."

"I know. I saw you in the yard. I had that dream again. The one about Lydia."

Paul slipped into bed beside Nora. His feet felt like ice. They both shivered and lay quietly. Paul listened to Nora's even breathing and thought he might drift back to sleep. But first he would have to phone the nurse and tell her where he was. What if Herb needed him? What if the nurse needed him? If he called, the phone might disturb Herb just drifting off to sleep. He'd have to get up and cross the yard in the shrinking darkness, and then he would not be able to return to Nora. Something would keep him away. Paul sighed. He wanted to move, but he did not dare move. He wanted to swallow, but his throat constricted and his limbs felt weighted. Despite the warmth generated by Nora's nearness and the bed covers, he was cold, very cold and he would never be warm again. Never.

Nora spoke. "What are you doing here?"

In answer Paul could not suppress the sob. It came from the deepest place of his soul, emerging raw and primitive. Instinctively Nora turned her body into his and wrapped her arms about him.

"Is it Herb?" she asked. "Oh, Paul, I am so sorry for you. Don't you worry," she soothed. "We'll get through this together."

"You never liked him," Paul accused, great tears staining the front of Nora's cotton gown.

"No, but we both made a valiant effort. Herb and I had an understanding. We had you in common, whom we both loved. We'll have the arrangements to make. I'll help you just as you helped me. Remember when my parents died? You were such a big help to me. I couldn't have gotten through that without you."

"He's not dead."

Nora sat up and turned on the light. She looked at Paul. He remained curled up under the covers, his face averted. "Tell me," she said.

"I can't."

"Come here," she said sternly. Paul put his head in her lap and wrapped his arms about her hips. She stroked his hair and allowed him to cry. It was a long while before he stopped.

"I don't know why I should be so upset. Maybe it's just everything," Paul said. He released Nora and sat up. He punched a pillow behind him and leaned back against the headboard. "It's just the pressure of Herb so sick and the thought that I'll soon be alone and I'll never find anyone like him again. And who will take care of me when I get sick?"

"You're not sick. Connor told me. You're not HIV positive. Nada. Nothing. Comprendes?"

"You can't know that."

"How many times does Connor have to explain this and show you the test results? You did notice that the paper is white and the ink is black? You gave me a copy. I have it around here somewhere. They must be tired of seeing your ID number at that lab."

"I don't know."

"Well, I do know and so would you if you'd only listen to reason. But if you must hear it, I will indulge you and state the obvious. I will take care of you. If and when you get sick and mind you, you won't because you are perfectly healthy if not mentally unhinged."

"I wouldn't expect that of you, Nora"

"Why not? Wouldn't you take care of me if I got sick?"

"Of course."

"Then stop obsessing and tell me what's really wrong."

Into the pause that followed Nora waited. She reached for Paul's hand, but he removed it from her light touch almost immediately. Nora felt a nearly palatable aura of anguish seep from his pores. His skin felt cold to the touch, and so she pulled the down comforter up and tucked it around him. He was suddenly passive; so very still that his chest hardly moved.

"You remember me telling you about my Uncle Howard?"

"The one who molested you?"

"He and Herb were together. They knew one another in New York long before we met. He should have told me! Why didn't he tell me?" Paul's tone was quietly outraged.

"Did you ask him? I hate to say it, but it seems to me that given his history that might have been wise."

"It never occurred to me. I can't help feeling betrayed. I realize how unreasonable I sound, but for years I've nearly succeeded in not thinking of that monster unless I absolutely must, because you know, Nora, I hate him. I still hate him."

"And with good reason," Nora stated with conviction. Paul often apologized for his feelings no matter how justified. It was a habit of his that drove Nora mad. "Did you ever confide in Herb? Did you ever tell him what Howard did to you?"

"I told him I'd been molested, but I didn't tell him who it was. He didn't really react, and I was glad not to talk about it. But listen to what Herb said to me, Nora. This is what really disturbs me. Their relationship ended because he was already too old for Howard. Herb said: I was already too old for him when we met. And that was somehow okay with Herb, so I guess it was the intimation of collusion. The fact that he didn't sound all that outraged. You know what this means, don't you, Nora? Now I must think about it. And I have to wonder about Herb and the choices I've made and the very worst of it. Howard has gone on to molest other young boys and I've kept silent."

"What could you have done? Your mother made that decision and you were just a child."

"I never thought of myself as having a responsibility to expose him."

"Why am I only hearing about this now?"

Paul didn't respond. He went on speaking as though he hadn't heard the question. "Maybe I could have stopped Howard."

"It's not too late," Nora offered, her voice determined.

"He's dead. Remember a month ago when Peter asked me to be pallbearer at his father's funeral and I turned him down? The family was pissed because I didn't show. You and I should have gone to that funeral. Peter wanted us there, but I was almost afraid I might say something."

"What would you say?"

"I don't know. Something like, "Your father was the monster who stole my childhood and altered my destiny forever."

"Do you feel that way, Paul? That your destiny was altered by that terrible crime?"

Paul hesitated. "Maybe."

"Because I've always felt that you didn't have to live this way and be repeatedly hurt as though you were punishing yourself in a cycle of destructive relationships. Because I believe in choice and the liberty to decide that life can be better and even different."

Paul sighed. He reached for the crystal carafe of water that Nora kept beside the bed and poured himself a drink. "Sometimes I think I wasn't born homosexual. That this one event that I do my very best to never, ever think of turned me on anther path. I've thought of it more in the last year than I ever did."

"Why do you think that is?"

"Counseling. I should never have started counseling."

"Counseling has been good for you."

"I haven't had a really happy moment since we finished discussing Herb and our relationship. He had to get into my childhood. And the really scary thing is that I've come to realize how much I pretended that everything was all right. It's like there is more. Something is waiting. Waiting to grab me, and I don't know what it is. So you see, Nora, I couldn't open that door. I couldn't tell Peter the truth, so I just made an excuse and said we couldn't come."

Nora was stunned. "Why would you even consider going? And besides we sent flowers. That was far more than that man deserved. But...." There was a pause and then Nora asked, "Howard. *That* uncle was Peter's father?"

"Yes."

She remembered well Peter's brief visits each summer. Brenda Maple remained close to Howard's former wife, but Peter was as different in temperament and outlook from Paul as two cousins could be and yet, their mothers persisted in the illusion that a close, enduring friendship existed.

The two boys spent their time sailing and playing golf during the two weeks of Peter's annual visit to Rockport that began sometime in July. Nora tagged along only at Paul's insistence. To keep him, he told her, from being bored by Peter's endless chatter, which revolved around sports, girls, and Peter's own inflated accomplishments.

"That uncle was Peter's father?" Nora asked again.

"Of course."

"No!"

"You knew that, Nora."

"No, I did not. And it just surprises me, that's all. The details that you choose to tell me and then the ones you leave out. Don't you think that might be significant? That Howard was Peter's father?"

"Significant to what? Being molested as a child is not a subject I like to

157

discuss," Paul said. "You only know so much about me because you are such a ruthless inquisitor."

"Well, that explains something about Peter, don't you think? Wasn't he here the weekend that Lydia disappeared?"

"He wasn't at the beach with us. He came down with strep, remember?"

"If I think about it.... Yes, I do remember. But, I mean...." There was something more she wanted to say, but in a flood of confusion and uneasiness she changed her mind. She had to think. "With a father like that, I just think we could have been kinder to Peter while he was here."

"Peter didn't meet his father until he was a grown man and besides, that bore never knew we didn't like him. He still doesn't. He thought we'd like to come to his father's funeral! I can understand me. Peter doesn't know what Howard did to me and we're family and all that rot, but not you! When was the last time you saw him, Nora?"

"It's been ages."

"It's been years, really," he answered his own question and continued as though a flood of talk could change something. "And he still expected you to be there. Can you imagine anything more ludicrous? And of course I'm an outcast because I wasn't there, not that I wasn't one already. Appearances are all they care about, Nora, and do you think any of them will stoop to attend Herb's funeral? Do you think if I asked Peter to be a pallbearer at the funeral of my same-sex partner, he'd jet right up to be here for me? Not hardly. But Connor. I've already asked Connor and he'll do it. He believes homosexuality is a sin and I'm going to hell because I'm not a Christian, but he'll be there for me until the end and not just because he has hope he can convert me. No, he really loves me, Nora, and he loves you and even Herb. I don't understand it. How some families will just do what they can to destroy you and talk about love and leave outsiders to really love, because I hate to think of where I would be today if I hadn't known your grandmother and been so cared for by your parents! And without you, Nora? Where would I be if you'd gotten tired of telling me I was wrong and foolish and stopped laughing and crying with me? So you see... I just don't understand it!"

While he was still talking Paul had sat up, letting his legs dangle over the edge of the bed, his back to her. He gulped back a sob. She saw his shoulders hunch and his muscles shake but no more sound emerged. Nora knew that if she could see his face, his expression would reveal a deluge of fear. She'd never seen him like this before and realized that he wasn't actually talking to her. He was venting bottled up hurt and desperation all brought about because Herb was dying. *Well, no,* she thought. *There is more to it than that,* and suddenly sympathy took on an aspect of curiosity. There was something more to know here, but she would wait to learn it.

"Some childhood memories are powerful, Paul," she said instead. "They don't get diluted by the present or amended by reason. I'll send Peter a sympathy card."

"Yes, by all means Nora, do send Peter a card. That'll solve everything!"

Nora slapped the back of his head. "Get back under the covers and don't take this out on me. We can make up the guest room pretty fast or you can go home."

"I'll stay here if you'll let me," he said, suddenly repentant. With that he lay back down and turned his back to her. Even as Nora drifted off to sleep, she knew that Paul was wide awake.

Before Paul had entered her bedroom Nora had awakened from a recurring dream. She had walked with Lydia down Main Street toward the harbor. Across the strand they moved and followed a path, soft with pine needles underfoot, to the high hill that overlooked it all. A ruined boathouse could be seen and out in the inlet the white sails from small boats snapping in the wind with the lobster buoys further out, rising on gentle swells. Lydia's hand lay in hers like a baby bird tucked into a nest. She counted the row of pines and the fingers curled into the shelter of her palm. She counted again and then she realized. Lydia's hand was no longer in hers. She gripped her wrist, acutely aware of that absence, and she woke in a rage of panic, each muscle in her body poised for flight.

Nora walked to her bedroom window. When they were children she and Paul had strung tin cans between the two houses and signaled one another with flashlights. Now Herb lay dying in Paul's old room. After his mother died he'd moved to her larger room, which overlooked the ocean on one side and down the lane toward the old mill on the other. The light was on, and although the nurse would be in attendance, Paul would be there as well. Nights were the hardest for Herb, who was not dying well.

Nora felt she was somewhat of an expert on the subject of death. Her father had died suddenly, but she knew he was not afraid to go. Her mother had died in the knowledge that she was going to Heaven and would be reunited with her husband and perhaps with Lydia. In Heaven there would be answers, while here on earth there were none regarding that one all-consuming desire to know the fate of her youngest child. It was hardest of all for Nora to lose her grandmother. She had been a woman of strong, unquestioning faith, who loved life and people and had an intense curiosity in all around her. She didn't want to die. She knew that Nora still needed her and talked of all she wanted to do and places she had never seen, with genuine longing for a few more good years. Herb in contrast was angry and fearful, and Nora found it difficult to be around him. She did not have the faith of her parents, and it scared her that when her time came she would face it all more like Herb.

Nora's eyes dropped to Paul's garden. She thought she glimpsed a figure there walking, but not until he moved into the light did she recognize Paul. A few minutes later she heard his step on the back staircase. "Herb is dead," she whispered and felt exactly as she expected to feel. Immense relief that, for Paul's sake, the long ordeal was ended.

When Nora woke in the morning, she was alone. The place beside her felt cold although the indentation of his head on the feather pillow remained. The smell of coffee led her downstairs, her bare feet cold over the intermittent spaces between the carpets and the hardwood floors. She found him in the kitchen, huddled in Grandmother Fothergill's rocking chair. He wore thermal underwear and one of Nora's oversized sweatshirts, and his thick nut-brown hair was tousled just as she remembered it from childhood sleep-overs and camping trips.

In the harsh light of morning Paul looked to be drained of color, drained of emotion, and drained of will. He asked Nora to let the nurse know where he was, and after she was dressed and ready for work, Nora returned to the kitchen to find that Paul had barely stirred. He looked at her as though she were an apparition.

Taking matters into her own hands, Nora called the nurse's registry and arranged extra help for the day. When Herb became very ill, it proved difficult to find nurses unafraid of this new disease and willing to care for patients like Herb until more was known. But Connor knew of an independent nurse's registry whose private-duty healthcare workers considered their vocation a ministry, volunteering to work as a team for little or no pay when it was necessary. Paul and Nora had decided to make a gift of funds to them after Herb's death to help a future AIDS patient who didn't have the resources that they did.

Nora crossed between the yards and heard the report from the night nurse before letting her go. Nora sat with Herb until the day nurse arrived.

"I'm afraid that Paul is angry with me," Herb whispered, his voice barely audible. Nora bent her head close in order to hear.

"Paul's not feeling well. You know he can't be near you when he's sick."

"I know, but sometimes I say what I shouldn't. I'm not at all discreet like the two of you. You really know how to keep secrets, don't you, Nora?"

Nora didn't answer. Instead she pretended to read the spiral notebook that held the nurse's notes.

"Is he all right, Nora?"

"He'll be by later, as soon as Connor has checked him out," Nora lied. "And if he's contagious, he can stay at my house and I'll stay here with you tonight. Is that all right, Herb?"

Herb smiled weakly and nodded his head. He slept fitfully. His breathing seemed different, not exactly labored as it had been in the past, but shallow. Those short, quick breaths worried Nora. She gave the nurse instructions for his tube feeding, then called Connor's office and described the change for his nurse. When she crossed between the yards, she found Paul just where she had left him in the kitchen. There was an absent, far-off expression on his face, but his hair was wet from a recent shower. From the cellar he had unearthed a bottle of her grandmother's homemade dandelion cordial, and now it stood open on the butcher block, cobwebs clinging to the fat base. Nora watched as he turned a generous shot into the dregs of his coffee.

"You realize you're taking your life in your hands drinking that," Nora said. She picked up the bottle and read the hand written label. "I didn't know any of this was left."

"There's quite a lot. You've got a small fortune in wine down there, Nora."

"How would you know?"

"Your father collected wine, remember? He taught me."

"You loved my father."

"I did."

"I guess I'll have to get down there one of these days." They'd made small talk long enough. Nora studied his face until, feeling her scrutiny, he looked away.

"Oh please, Nora, let's not have any profound conversations right now. I'll be all right," he stated flatly before she could speak. "And in a few hours I'll be my old self again. It's just that right now I don't want to think or feel anything. Okay?"

"Of course you'll be fine," Nora affirmed.

Paul finished the coffee and poured himself more cordial. Nora noticed that he failed to ask about Herb or express his usual guilt that he was not by the bedside. In the four years since Herb's struggle to maintain some semblance of health, Paul had been beside him every step of the way. He read everything he could get his hands on and drove the Boston specialists mad with his endless questioning. He monitored Herb's care, all the while encouraging and cajoling Herb to bravely face each new treatment.

"I've taken care of Herb," Nora offered. "The registry sent someone who can stay until late afternoon. Why don't you go back to bed?"

"Who did they send?"

Nora told him and he nodded his head, ignoring the fact that she was young and inexperienced and in the past Paul had rejected her as unsuitable. "What about you?" he asked, his voice trailing. "What will you do today?" She saw him swallow hard and thought he might cry again. He was clearly having some sort of breakdown. Nora tried not to let her worry show.

"I have to be at the studio. I'm expecting a shipment so I'm stuck there and can't leave. Will you do me a huge favor?"

"Of course," he said, calmed by the request.

"Bring us lunch at the gallery, but first go back upstairs and crawl into bed. Sleep is what you need, Paul."

Paul looked at Nora and felt as though the world had quietly shifted off its axis. Nothing was right. He felt a rush of terror invade his body, then cold and heat. Nora was stubborn and could be a relentless adversary in defense of a perceived wrong. Last night they had ventured on to forbidden territory, but Nora hadn't seemed to notice, and the moment had passed with the ferment of his nightmare still dormant. Paul took another swallow, this time from the open neck of the bottle.

"Go on then," Nora said as she slipped into the old coast guard jacket. "Go to bed."

"Have you extended that invitation to any other man in this decade?" Paul asked, slurring his words.

"Don't think you can change the subject," Nora chided. "We are worried about you, not me. You've over-extended yourself, and if you don't get some rest you'll be no use to Herb because you'll be in the next hospital bed. And look at yourself. It's still morning and you're inebriated. This isn't like you, Paul." Nora picked up the bottle and poured the remainder of the amber liquid in to the sink.

"I only hope I'm drunk enough," Paul said and felt the sort of immense relief one feels when catastrophe is narrowly avoided. He looked at Nora and felt that he loved her. Regret was a weight of immense and painful longing. "It is not right, Nora," he said, enunciating each word.

"What's not right?"

"That you should be alone and all these years I've had Herb to love."

"You know why I'm alone," Nora said deathly even.

"But why? I don't understand it."

"Yes, you do. I've made the choice to be alone. There is no dignity in living the way you do, Paul. I'd rather save myself the pain, so let's not go there. Okay?"

The atmosphere between them was suddenly rapt with caution. Paul was

162

clearly losing control. Why must he bring this up now? Hadn't she given up her hopes for Paul long ago? Later when she talked with Connor, she would ask him to prescribe a sedative or even an anti-depressant. Something more appropriate than half a bottle of dandelion cordial at eight in the morning.

"When was the last time you had eight hours of uninterrupted sleep?" she asked.

"Last night, thanks to the wonders of modern medicine, and as you can see, it did me not a bit of good."

"Go to bed. Look, I'm taking the phone off the hook. I've instructed the nurse to phone the studio if Herb needs anything, and Connor is going to stop by when he has time."

"If either of them calls, you will come for me?"

"You know I will," Nora said.

Paul stood and walked over to Nora. He was taller than she, although he was not a tall man. The top of her head came to his cheek. He pressed her against his chest and slipped his arms under her coat. She felt his limbs melt into hers and breathed in the mixture of herbal shampoo and cordial and was startled at the intimacy of his embrace. How many times had they held one another with no hint of sexual tension between them?

"Remember the time we made love?" he whispered and gently bit her ear.

Nora remembered. How could she forget? She had once, in her naïveté, believed that the right woman could cure Paul. He said he loved her, so why couldn't he just decide to really love her as other men loved women? It happened without preamble just after her mother had died. They were alone in the house and home from college. They sat on her bed loaded down with stuffed animals and dolls, despondent and sad, discussing the funeral and their parents and how life might change for them with only her grandmother left.

Paul had kissed her and she had responded. Long drought of kisses that sent their senses racing and made her think she might be consumed, but afterwards that first flush of ardor had sizzled like water over bright glowing embers. When he later made light of the incident, referring to his sexual orientation like it was a sort of inevitable condition he was helpless to change, then Nora laughed with him. But her smile was brittle and her heart was pained, and she hid her hopeful wishes for something more behind a wall of sibling like affinity.

"I do," Nora said. "I remember it well."

"I wanted to be like other men. All my life I longed to be like your father, and like Connor. I wanted this ambivalence to just shrivel up and go away. What could I do? We are who we are, but I wanted you, Nora."

Nora disengaged herself from his embrace.

"I wish for that now," he drew her back and leaned in to her for what Nora knew would be a long fluid kiss. Once she would have welcomed that kiss. She felt his breath on her neck and his grip tightened with passion, but Nora gently pushed a space between them and turned her head away. When she looked up there was an odd mingling of resignation in his eyes.

"Like always you'll do anything to avoid facing the truth." Nora forced herself to sound stern. He mustn't know that she was tempted, and that each willful 'no' was followed by a silent shriek of 'yes'. She had come a long way since that day in her bedroom when she dreamed of marriage and a large wedding. She had learned to be alone for one thing. She had her self-respect and her career, and she wouldn't give them up for a risky moment of vulnerability ever again.

"I'd apologize if I weren't drunk," he said and smiled a charming smile.

"I'm not what you want, Paul. We came to grips with that a long time ago. This is really about loss, my friend. This is about grief and pain. Nothing can protect you from feeling it. Not even me."

Paul turned away before she could see his expression. He carried his cup to the sink. *And this is about Lydia,* Paul thought grimly to himself. *This is about Howard and me and Herb and you.* But his retort remained unuttered as it darted against the walls of a locked cavern and everything he'd fought so long and hard to forget.

He heard the door slam and knew that Nora was gone. This house that had so rarely been empty or silent or lacking warm cooking smells, bright greetings, and love seemed strangely full despite the family that was gone. He missed them terribly, but now it was just he and Nora that were left living in parallel homes and with a tragic secret that was as much a bond as a wedge between them. Why couldn't they have something together? A real family with a child and that same kind of full and vibrant exchange of love that was so prevalent in the day-to-day life of her parents and grandparents? Why couldn't they?

How well he knew the answer. They didn't deserve happiness. Not after what they had done. And this Jesus that Connor talked of with such liberality. The one that his friend prayed to and loved could never, ever forgive them. And Paul knew that Nora was every bit as doomed as he was. If God couldn't forgive him, how could he possibly forgive Nora, the only woman he had ever trusted with his heart?

CHAPTER FOURTEEN

At times it was work to stay in touch with Nora. When she looked at him, he knew that she was thinking of that day. Although it was not logical, she resented him for being the last person to see and speak with Lydia. And so he understood that the pain of that shared burden was so very great, that she would avoid him and remain superficial in all their interactions.

Nora made her way up Mill Lane keeping to the worn footpath the neighbors had defined in the snow. Up the rise to the street she stepped. Here the road descended toward Main Street and a granite block remained where people had once hitched their horses. She had a view over the rooftops and although the trees were bare, she carried in her mind the look of a landscape in summer. The light off the water and the towering oaks heavy with shimmering leaves and the black weather vanes and the steeples and the sea gulls circling. She kept to the sidewalk, the snow still pristine and piled neatly along one edge. An occasional car went by and she returned the waves and smiles, but it was an absent wave and a smile preoccupied by worry and doubt.

As she walked Nora thought of the Fourth of July weekend that Lydia disappeared. Peter Maple and his mother had arrived on the heels of her own family and Nora resented having to share Paul so soon with his cousin. She prayed that Peter would get sick and when he came down with strep throat she could only be happy.

Key in hand Nora opened the door to her studio. Soon she was busy mixing colors. Her brush moved swiftly, precisely as she painted in, amid a sweeping branch of pine, the bird nest from her dream of the night before. The stand of pines often figured in her work. Sometimes, as now, she painted all fifteen lined up in a row and the little cove below and then the boathouse. When the painting sold she would wait a while, sometimes as long as two years, before she found herself working on another interpretation of the same scene. The older locals often looked at the most recent landscape and immediately recognized the location. Is this what had triggered her dream? This painting she'd been working on to replace the one a tourist had purchased at the end of October, just as she closed her studio for the winter.

The door opened and a string of miniature mission bells clanked and jingled against the cracked wood. Whittaker Wobus came in with her mail.

"Painting another one, I see," he said. "Why don't you just tell people it's not for sale and leave it in the window? Doesn't anyone complain that nothing you do is original?"

"Not yet," Nora laughed. She made an excellent living from her work and did an annual show in New York and another at a Gallery on Newbury Street in Boston and the rest of the time she worked from her studio in Rockport. Her own work sold too fast so that in summer most of the gallery space was filled with the work of lesser known artists. This allowed her time to stockpile for those shows that provided the bulk of her income.

The year after college Nora worked for an advertising agency in New York. She became engaged to a stockbroker and, until Grandmother Fothergill died, it looked as if her life would be entirely predictable. Nora came home to plan the funeral and as previously arranged, her grandmother was buried alongside her husband and Nora's parents.

Nora recalled standing by the newly dug grave with the other headstones close by and realizing that there would be no room for her. Only four plots had been purchased when her grandfather, a part of the first troops to enter the First World War, returned home in a pine casket. Newly graduated from college he had left his bride and landed in France only to die in a wheat field a short time later. That was long ago, before she and Lydia had been born. Long before Grandmother Fothergill imagined sending the perfect baby she delivered as a widow, Nora's father, to fight in another world war.

During her last meeting at the mortuary Nora made arrangements to purchase another plot for herself and was nearly out the door when she turned to write a second check. No one was more surprised than she to find herself scribbling the name of Lydia Ann Fothergill in the space marked recipient. Although logic said otherwise, perhaps something would be found out about Lydia. Some day. Maybe.

After the funeral Nora stayed an extra week to close the house. The pink and white impatiens had faded, but geraniums languished in the window boxes and the ivy retained a waxy sheen. Most of the summer cottages had been closed though the tourists continued to descend at weekend intervals.

Paul was brisk and short with her as he helped fasten and latch the outside shutters. He found it incomprehensible that she would choose to live in any other place. His reproach was evident, even in his reminder that except in anticipation of a storm the shutters had never been closed for any length of time. Nora was not due to return to Rockport until her two-week vacation in

166

July. That seemed a paltry, meager span and she knew that inevitably, even to her closest neighbors and friends, she would be demoted to the rank of summer folk.

As she sorted and packed, Nora could not escape the view of herself as traitor. She was deserting the neat rooms with the high ceilings that had never been without a Fothergill. Nora spread the dust covers, great billowing tents that obliterated the blue and white of her grandmother's chintz and the green and red stripe of the dining room chairs. Gathering another armload and feeling like an executioner, she mounted the back stairs and could almost hear a moan from the pinks and butter yellow, the reds and harbor blue of the bedrooms as she snuffed from sight her grandmother's love of color. When finished she surveyed the sterile result which spoke to her more clearly of death than the gleaming casket, or the long line of mourners who wrung her hand and kissed her cheek until her face was numb.

Nora began to pack a box to take back to her apartment in New York. She gathered her grandmother's collection of atomizers from the top of her vanity and carefully wrapped the fragile glass in newspaper. Each space no longer occupied rang out to her with a gathering sense of its own absence. Nora moved into the living room to the Limoges boxes, some that she and Lydia had given as gifts, and then the collection of silver snuff boxes and thimbles that had once belonged to her father's great Aunt Nellie, the first Fothergill to live at Mill Lane.

If inanimate objects could speak, they spoke to her now with a certain hollow clarity whose message she fought to ignore until she picked up her grandmother's Bible, open at Psalm 139. Nora leafed through the pages. Many passages were highlighted and notes filled the borders. Tucked between the pages were cards and scrapes of paper; many notes that she and Lydia had written as children. Outside a hovering dusk burned brighter than the room as early twilight slanted bars across the floor. She fought to see, forgetting entirely the light beside the bed.

She didn't want to cry, but the tears came anyway. Lydia's disappearance clung to this room and this book. The echo of her parents' anguish seeped from the walls and she felt the torture of all that accumulated, useless waiting. Diligently they had sought to protect her from the repercussions of her sister's disappearance. Even as they pushed her toward the normal life that was no longer theirs, Nora was grateful to be free. With her grandmother's death that conflicted vigil had mysteriously passed to her and she could no longer escape the guilt of its proximity, or the gravity of its legacy. And yet she could not stay, steeped in waiting and tortured by questions. Her sister was dead. She had to be and it was time to put all that behind her.

Gathering strength Nora stood and wrapped the Bible in tissue paper. On the way out she dropped it on the top of an open crate, ready for the dim hibernation of storage. At the threshold she paused. Her hands felt strangely light and absent of that heavy book. The pull to wrap her hands over the binding and keep it close was nearly physical. Feeling herself on some level very foolish Nora retraced her steps and placed the book back where it had been, on the bedside table in her grandmother's room. It will be there, she told herself, when I return. Must she go? The entire house seemed hushed and pensive; at odds with the very fate that had propelled her far from home. She couldn't stay. She would not stay.

As Paul drove her to Boston in his restored 1954 MG Midget Nora thought of that Bible and wished she could retrieve it. The MG was uncomfortable and with little room for her luggage most would have to be shipped separately. She took the inconvenience personally when he informed her that his mother's Cadillac convertible, which he had inherited, was in the garage. On the way down they fought over Nora's fiance. "He's a jock, Nora. The sort of perpetual frat boy who thinks it's fun to cruise gay bars and pick fights."

"Don't be ridiculous," Nora said. "You hardly know him."

"I know his type well enough and I'm frankly disappointed in you."

"Oh yeah, this from a man whose last boyfriend beat him up and stole his credit cards."

They struggled over grilled swordfish at the No Name Restaurant, for once finding little to speak of, before heading for South Station in Boston's noon traffic. She felt angry. Angry with him and irritated with herself. Even before the train pulled away he had left the platform. She waved from the doorway, but he gave no indication that he saw her and she knew the slight was deliberate. For the first time ever they had not parted as friends.

Nora measured distance outside the fleeting landscape of the train window. She counted thin slices of life and narrow vignettes of canvas through countless small towns, by factories, over rivers and bridges. She had relied on these lengthening miles to mount a barricade between herself and home, finally lifting the mantle of her disquiet.

She slept and imagined the gasps and death groaning of inanimate objects under lengths of white sheeting and all the while the relentless ring of the phone. Persistent and pulsing the sound raced through the abandoned interior of the house on Mill Lane until finally it stopped and all lay quiet. Nora woke in a rush of panic. What if that long awaited phone call finally came and there was no one there to answer? What if the doorbell rang and the house was closed and still? Nora heard the single phrase of her name being called. She wasn't dreaming. No one on that train knew her. And the sound was more clear and resolute than she could ever later describe. "Nora," the cry came.

Before the train pulled into Grand Central she had decided. She would catch the next train back to Boston. And she did.

In her heart Nora knew that Lydia was dead, and yet she could not extinguish the echoing knell of that singular, all consuming question which had haunted her family. What really happened on that Fourth of July weekend? The 'what if' of their anguish now became the impetus that powered her life and orchestrated her decisions and inspired her work with far more clarity and precision than ambition or acclaim or even a significant relationship with a man.

Nora left most of her grandmother and parents' possessions packed and made the house on Mill Lane her own. Without planning she turned her love of painting into full time work. When it was necessary to be away from home she was never able to enjoy herself and preferred her friends come to her, which they did in summer. In winter the town was an entirely different place, settled and genuine with a certain untainted flavor of timelessness. During the off-season, with the tourists and summer residents gone, Nora could more easily imagine a horse and carriage rolling over the narrow streets than a car.

"You know who planted those pines, don't you?"

Nora was startled. She had almost forgotten Whittaker's presence. He looked over her shoulder and studied the painting. "Who?" Nora asked as he dropped his mailbag with a thud and helped himself to coffee. In winter his route took half the time, but no one thought to adjust his schedule. He often passed along bits of news and sometimes a book from one neighbor to another, all the while freely dispensing his Yankee brand of pragmatism.

"It was old Mr. Maple. Paul's grandfather. Was rich, he was. Textiles, I think. He bought the old mansion on the hill below those pines. Summer folks, is what they were," he added in the derisive way the locals have when distinguishing themselves from that other, peculiar class of interloper. "It was he that planted those pines so he could recognize his cove from a few miles out. He wasn't much of a sailor and he kept missing the cove," Whittaker chuckled. "He bought a fine boat though. The same one that Herb ran up on that south sand bar five summers past."

Nora wiped her hands on a rag and poured herself a cup of coffee. She was in for a longer than normal visit and might as well get caught up on local news. Sooner or later Whittaker would get around to giving her a report on the shut-ins along his route and which children were home sick and even a capsule bulletin from the local paper. He often snuck a look at the paste-ups when he happened by the press office. He would in turn report to others that she was at work in her studio and, if her neighbors felt so inclined, they might poke their heads in to say hello and inquire after Paul and Herb.

"That boat was too much for Herb and it was too much for Paul's grandfather. Old man Maple had no sense of direction and would lose his bearings right off." Whittaker chuckled again.

"So what happened?"

"Had to hire old Sean and I to go out with him and eventually pride won out and that beauty sat in dry dock until Paul restored it." Whittaker bestowed his highest compliment. "A fine sailor, Paul. How many boats he have now?"

Paul's work was buying old boats and restoring them. Occasionally he even managed to part with one or two, usually when he needed the space.

Nora shrugged in answer. She thought she knew everything there was to know about Paul. "What happened to Paul's grandfather?"

"He'd be long dead by now."

"Did you know Howard Maple, Paul's uncle?"

"He was a mite bit older than me, but I knew him all right and I don't like to say, but I didn't much like the man. That's all. Someone like him didn't talk to someone like me, if you get my drift, Nora. He was a movie star, you know?"

"No, he wasn't," Nora said, amused.

"He was," Whittaker asserted. "Made two Hollywood skating movies with that foreign film star and that Canadian bombshell. He was a big shot and he knew it. I heard down at the courthouse that Paul inherited that land from him a few months back. And choice property it is, too."

"A movie star, right?" Nora was dubious.

"You can ask Paul if you don't believe me."

"I will," Nora said.

Whittaker walked over to the huge tarp that covered Nora's most recently completed project. "Finished it, uh?"

"Yes."

"Has Paul seen it?"

"I generally keep it covered," Nora said and turned to look at the coffin as Whittaker lifted the tarp. The wood was unfinished ash when Herb had it delivered to her studio and asked her to paint if for him. "Follow your instincts," was his only instruction. It was just like Herb to want something unorthodox, even at his own funeral. Now it only awaited the upholsterer and Herb's choice of satin.

Whittaker replaced the covering. "Sorry about that boy. Sorry he turned out the way he did. The old man would be turning over in his grave if he knew. He wasn't much of a sailor, but there was no doubt he was a man."

Paul was tolerant of such comments, but Nora was not. He often told her that the dubious distinction of being the town's most prominent homosexual was preferable to the anonymity of living in a place like New York or San Francisco. Here everyone had known his family and, following in the path of his mother, Paul was on the town council and a member of the tourist board as well as intermittent president of the garden club.

"Well, I must be on my way. Thanks for coffee Nora, best in town." Whittaker hoisted his satchel over one shoulder. "By the way. How's Herb doing? I haven't seen him about for a while."

Nora decided to indulge Whittaker with news he could pass along his route. A little sympathy was sure to bring Paul enough frozen casseroles and quick bread to last the month. She had just finished returning the freezer containers from Herb's last crisis and knew that Paul hardly ever cooked for himself anymore. "Not well, Whit. He can't eat and needs oxygen most of the time."

"Is Paul still convinced he'll pull out of it?"

"Yes," Nora said simply. "Paul is hopelessly hopeful. He won't even look at that," Nora said and gestured toward the coffin, which sat suspended between two sawhorses.

"Poor boy. This will be hard on him." He sounded genuinely sad and Nora forgave him his earlier comments. The door slammed, the bells jingled and she returned to her work.

Nora wondered why people persisted in referring to Paul as a boy. No one had called her a girl for a very long time. She guessed it was the absence of guile in his personality. A certain quality he projected of being open and uncomplicated. Like his mother, he had a need to be accepted and liked by everyone.

Nora switched on a Van Morrison CD. She sang along with the lyrics of "Ball and Chain," and contemplated the canvas. It was difficult for Nora to call a painting finished. Her agent had been known to physically wrest a piece away in order to include it in a show. Nora liked having the studio to herself. She got her best work done in winter and had knocked out half the ceiling and slanted the roof ostensibly for the light, but really for the view. She liked the water.

The entire town knew that Herb had AIDS within days of Paul and Herb learning it themselves. Most believed Herb would be their first and only loss to this new, mysterious disease. For Paul's sake they were solicitous and kind. When Herb was not well enough to leave the house neighbors visited. The ladies from the church benevolent society took turns ferrying books from the library and doing the grocery shopping for Paul, who was reluctant to leave Herb's side.

"Why don't they bring me a book I can read," Herb would complain to Nora and Paul.

"You've read many of those books," Nora reminded him.

"You need to write those ladies a thank you note," Paul said, adding, "Something suitable to be published in a church bulletin, where, I might add, it will certainly end up."

"What am I, a debutante?"

"Use that nice note paper I bought you for Christmas. The ivory with your monogram in sepia," Paul said as Nora suppressed a giggle.

The ladies often stayed to visit with Herb. They treated him, Nora noted, with the same respectful consideration as Bitsy Faron when she was dying of cancer, and they hadn't liked Bitsy any better. It was her husband Hal, just as it was now Paul, they truly extended themselves for. Each summer Bitsy had chosen a tourist to have an affair with and then was selectively blind enough to convince herself that no one noticed. The town had a way of ostracizing those they disapproved of with a certain benign, but distant politeness that was deadly, but Nora noticed that Herb was largely oblivious.

Even for Paul's sake, and the sake of his mother, who had been immensely popular, most residents could not warm to Herb. He was often sarcastic and talked freely of wishing he could live some other place. He had a way of insulting them and then deluding himself into believing that they were too obtuse to understand the double entendres and half implied slights. Openly they speculated as to whether Herb was truly in the relationship for Paul or was it Paul's money that he liked, or the trips they took, or a hundred other comforts? They especially did not like the manner in which Herb spoke to Paul in public, sometimes belittling him, or his fondness of alluding to money and possessions, or his habit of eyeing their husbands and sons. Paul was one of their own. Herb was not.

Days after learning of Herb's diagnosis Paul returned from a Yacht Club board meeting to tell Nora that news of Herb's condition had leaked to the community. She told him he was being paranoid. "How do you know?" she asked when he insisted he was right. "Because," Paul said. "I've never had my back slapped or heard so many declarations of friendship for no reason by so many men anxious to convey that nothing is wrong. It's like the pack took this consensus and decided to act normal, only they can't. It's a man thing, I guess. Took me about five seconds to figure it out."

Paul's friends watched and waited and took careful note of the fact that his nut brown hair still fell over the smooth forehead with the same luster and although the squint lines around his eyes were deeper and they saw him less because of Herb's condition, he appeared to them no different. If he were HIV positive he would have confided it to Nora. People knew this, but they also knew better than to ask Nora or even Connor, who had recently fired one of his staff for revealing privileged information.

Nora had her own past to contend with and the town was protective of her as well. For several months, and then with decreasing frequency, the disappearance of Lydia Fothergill had placed Rockport on the front page of the Boston Globe and the Boston Herald as well as every news station in New England. Lydia had vanished with such sudden and mysterious swiftness that for a time it affected the tourist business whose frantic flurry in summer supported many through the isolated solitude of winter.

The story that Paul and Nora told was entirely plausible, which made Lydia's disappearance all the more horrifying. Every parent could easily relate to the events of that flawless summer day and suddenly began to keep track of their children with hawk-like vigilance.

One minute little Lydia was with Paul and Nora and the next she was gone. They had walked up the ramp from Front Beach to buy butter brickle ice cream cones from the pharmacy soda fountain. They passed over their quarters, their bathing suits still dripping and their bare feet covered with sand. Outside the weekend tourist traffic was thick; the cars on Main Street moving bumper to bumper and the pedestrians on the sidewalk heel to toe. The following day was the Fourth of July parade followed by a bonfire and fireworks launched over the water. Nora and Lydia had already staked out their seats on the cemetery wall across from Front Beach while Paul had the distinct honor of being one of the children who would ride on the yacht club float.

The children darted between the bodies on the sidewalk and Nora reached back for Lydia's hand. They walked a few feet, but Lydia was lagging and Nora let go. When she turned back at the edge of the ramp that descended to the beach her sister was gone. Completely and utterly gone.

When the mission bells rang out Nora did not even turn around. Whittaker would have forgotten to tell her something or discovered another piece of her mail. She was absorbed in the stroke of her brush. Sometimes it seemed to move of its own accord, but even she could see that this painting was finished. She thought about what size canvas she would like to use next. Often that was how a new work was begun. The size that appealed to her and the snowy blankness that begged for form and color.

Nora did not consider herself a great artist, but she could not understand the television painters whose brushes moved with swift automation as they taught through the prescribed thirty minutes. She guessed the resulting work was okay, but that was all. Nora liked to research a topic. She had to have a feeling and then be surprised by the result. She didn't want to be a good illustrator. She wanted to be an artist and if that emotional connection did not exist and somehow get conveyed, then she couldn't work. Minutes passed and the door was forgotten until she sensed movement.

"Forget something?" she said to the shadow, just at the edge of her peripheral vision.

"Yes," replied a stranger's voice. "I'd forgotten how cute you are."

Nora turned. "You should know that, "cute," is not a description that real women aspire to."

"I'll try to remember that," he said and smiled. He looked familiar, but she could not place him. Then she remembered. He had been in her studio last October. She had seen him in passing as he left with her painting, 'A Stand of Pines', under one arm. The same painting whose subject she had now reworked at least a dozen times over the last ten years.

Nora remembered their eyes meeting and he, glancing away, but most of all she recalled feeling disappointed. Checking the day's receipts she noted that he had paid in cash and the artist who was watching the studio that day explained that he did not want his name included on her mailing list. Nora recalled counting the money, which was too much to have on hand, so she immediately left for the bank.

"I'm Rev Porter." He offered his hand. His grasp was large and swallowed hers. "I was out of town so I'm a little late, but I got your message."

"I know who you are, Mr. Porter. The painting you bought last fall is a little out of reach of a policeman's salary, isn't it?"

"Uh, but you forget. I was Josiah's only heir."

"I'm sorry. I am being rude. I was told you were on vacation."

"Medical leave actually, but sitting around is not my style. It seems I've felt compelled to unearth the particulars of an unsolved case. So when you called, I was glad. After our last conversation I didn't expect to hear from you."

"I'm sorry," Nora said. "It's just that there have been so many disappointments and I didn't want to set myself up for another. But if you think you can discover some new information then I want to be of help. My family would have wanted me to cooperate with any valid investigation," Nora added, with special emphasis on the word 'valid'.

Once more Nora wiped her hands on a rag and cleaned her brush, replacing it tip-up in a red S.S. Pierce coffee can jammed with others. She led Rev to the two down filled sofas that faced one another in front of the large slanted window, but almost immediately, and without explanation, he excused himself and returned from his car moments later balancing in his arms three large filing crates.

"These of course comprise only a portion of the original investigation into Lydia's disappearance." He let them fall with a thud on the old trunk Nora used as a coffee table.

"I suppose you expect me to read all that. A bit presumptuous don't you think?"

He looked at Nora with impatience. "Hey she was your sister, not mine."

Nora studied Rev's face. His expression seemed to add, "So why do I have the feeling that I care more than you?" He stood over six feet and looked to be a man devoted to a regular work out. His dark hair waved slightly over his brow and she thought that if she ever painted him she would have the hair longer. It would create a softer, more vulnerable impression, but would in no way diminish the strength of his features. Nora swallowed the bitter reply that sprang to mind. Even when no more than a voice over the phone she had found Rev abrasive and meeting him now, had in no way altered that first impression.

"Sit down, won't you?" she invited, but he was already seated and this too irritated her.

"Unfortunately your sister disappeared during the Fourth of July weekend." Stating the obvious, he removed the top from one of the boxes.

"You'll have to do better than that," Nora said and noticed the inside jammed with folders.

"The town was thick with tourists and no one could be found who saw anything suspicious," he continued ignoring her comment. "My guess is … Lydia may have recognized the person who took her."

Nora regarded Rev with new interest. She agreed, but had been told that every available piece of information that could have linked an acquaintance or family friend with the events of that day had been thoroughly investigated. Still, Nora knew that Lydia was a strong personality who rather enjoyed too much the drama of protest. If a stranger had grabbed her and forced her into one of the slow moving cars, locked in a one-way crawl up Main Street, that car would have passed her and Paul. Nora was convinced that if Lydia had believed herself to be in any danger she would not have gone to her fate passively. But, if Lydia was with someone that she knew, well this was different. She might have been tempted to spite them over not being included, yet again, in their activities.

"But the authorities told us it was a stranger abduction."

"What else can they say when they have nothing?" Nora did not reply, but

Rev saw that she agreed with him. "You and … who was the boy who was with you?" Rev asked.

"Paul Maple. We grew up together."

"Right. And Paul Maple is still your neighbor and friend."

"If you already knew that, why did you ask?"

"Habit, I guess. And Maple? What did he see?"

"Nothing more than I." Nora's reply was curt. It was as though she couldn't help herself. He irritated her without even trying and she was determined to be just as abrasive.

"And you and Paul realized you'd be in trouble if you returned to the beach without Lydia," Rev prompted.

Nora decided to make an effort. After all, he had come in response to her message though she had clearly overreacted to that girl who had waited all night outside the house. Though she regretted calling him, there could be no real purpose to her rudeness. She sank back against the soft cushion and studied the ceiling as she gathered her thoughts. She leaned slightly forward her arms resting on her knees. It was an inelegant pose, but she felt his eyes on her anyway.

"Lydia put up with a lot trailing after Paul and me. We were best friends and we resented her. Two sisters could not have been more different. Lydia liked to play with dolls and didn't like to get dirty. Sometimes the smaller fishing boats would take us out in the morning, but she would tell our mother and then I would be grounded. After Paul's mother realized the punishment I had been given she would follow suit. I liked to play ball and climb trees and sail. Paul and I were the same age and we preferred to be alone and she was so much younger. A typical sibling dilemma, you see."

"And you feel guilty?"

"Of course. I didn't even want to go back for her, my own sister! But Paul insisted so we retraced our steps. At first I thought she might have returned to get more ice cream. I wasn't worried because even if she tried she couldn't possibly have gotten lost, but the last thing my grandmother said to us was a reminder to stay together. She always thought that if we children stayed in a group there wouldn't be any trouble."

"How much time elapsed while you and Paul debated going back?"

"A couple of minutes. No more. Lydia let go of my hand less than a block from the beach."

"Show me."

The route had been gone over countless times, but no one had ever invited Nora to be a guide. She was strangely moved by the request. She closed the studio door without locking up and they walked in silence until Nora stopped before the clothing store that had once been a soda fountain and pharmacy.

"What do you remember about being here?" Rev asked.

"Nothing helpful."

"Try me."

Between the buildings an invisible blast of cold swept off the ocean. Nora looked down the narrow alley and absently studied how the gray water blended into the horizon and the slender thread of white, which differentiated the two. She pulled her collar up and stepped from between the buildings. She shoved her hands deeper into her pockets and noticed that the cold did not seem to affect Rev. He wore jeans and a bright yellow ski jacket with navy trim and a lift pass dangling from the zipper. Was he skiing when he decided to pick up his messages? An incongruous past time for someone claiming to be on medical leave and simultaneously working on Lydia's disappearance. He didn't appear sick to her or even slightly injured.

Once again Nora regretted phoning Rev and reminded herself not to encourage him by appearing grateful. There was just too much going on right now. It looked as though Paul was at last coming to grips with the seriousness of Herb's health and was perhaps having a nervous breakdown in the process. She needed to focus her energy on him and not on a lost cause.

"I remember incidentals. That we all ordered the same flavor of ice cream. Lydia had been swimming and Paul and I hoped to get away without her, but she was too quick. I remember that she had a red and blue Snow White towel over her shoulders and her hair was wet. We argued over that towel earlier in the morning. I wanted it only because it was her favorite. I was not always nice to my sister."

"As you know I was an only child, but I recall my best friend's elder brother almost killed him once. Now they couldn't be closer."

Nora almost had the feeling that Rev was inviting her to confide something and she thought his comment strange. Putting the thought from her mind she continued as though she had never been interrupted. "The sidewalk was hot, but it was early in the season and our feet were not yet immune. We ran to get inside. I remember that Lydia wanted us to take her sailing later. Paul was not allowed to be out by himself, but we went anyway and she threatened to tell if we didn't include her."

"You were young to be sailing by yourselves."

"We mostly stayed in sight of the harbor and Paul's mother could be pretty dense. She tended to assume Paul did precisely what she asked, while my parents were smarter about such things. My mother was nearly forty when I was born and my father was ten years older. They didn't deserve to lose Lydia."

"No one deserves to lose a child."

"No."

"Go on," he prodded, nearly in a whisper. At the sound of his voice Nora realized that she had been speaking softly and he had lowered his tone to match hers. Now he inclined his head and moved a step forward, ostensibly to hear better. Nora felt he had invaded her space. She turned abruptly and walked back up the block. They came to the ramp, which led down to Front Beach. Across the street was the cemetery and at the crest of the hill were her own house and Paul's, standing side by side.

"We're an easy day trip from Boston. You can't imagine how crowded it gets here on weekends. We have more commonwealth visitors than actual tourists. They hunt the galleries and the antique shops and eat fried clams and stroll down Bear Skin Neck and feel they've escaped the city. After Lydia disappeared my mother and I moved here permanently and my father stayed in Belmont. They always thought Lydia would come home." Nora's voice trailed. Now she sounded truly sad. "You know, they thought they'd open the door and there she would be on the front step and little changed no matter the years. They died with that idea still fixed in their minds."

"And you?"

Gusts of wind whipped Nora's short hair to a frenzy, but she failed to notice. She watched the waves roll over the frozen beach. Pools of steam rose from the shallows where the rocks formed a barrier between one stretch of sand and another. She watched the white vapor dissipate as it hit the cold air and studied the gleaming rocks and the threads of frozen snow and considered Rev's question.

"I firmly believe my sister to be dead and yet I cannot seem to live my life as though she is. God knows I've tried to move from here, but when I go away on business I'm restless and consumed with anxiety to be back."

"Was it always like that?"

"No. In the beginning my family kept that vigil quite well without me. After they died I realized that I was all that was left and this futile job of waiting was left to me. A kind of mandate, if you will."

Rev looked reflective and Nora felt an unreasonable urge to lay her head on his shoulder. *Snap out of it,* she told herself and felt as though a knife were turning in her heart. Too much talk of Lydia brought to a boil so many simmering emotions.

"I understand you were hypnotized in order to recall more detail. Did anything come of that?"

"I never saw the report. In those days sharing certain information with children was not done."

"I'd like a copy of that report. For some reason it never made its way into the police file."

"I imagine there's a copy in these boxes of yours, but you know the FBI didn't get involved because there was no proof that state lines were crossed. Not until it was too late to do any good and the investigation was going nowhere were they called in to consult. I saw a doctor at the Massachusetts Mental Health Center, but I can't recall his name, Gershon, I think. I'll sign a waiver if you need one."

"Was Paul hypnotized?"

Nora nodded. "It wouldn't work. Paul wanted to help and was devastated when the doctor couldn't get anywhere with him. I remember he cried inconsolably and after his final session my parents had to go over to tell him it was all right."

"I want you to go over all the police reports. Have you ever done that?"

"No."

"They had few leads and nothing much to follow up on. It's a lot of reading. Take notes and when you finish, I'll bring more."

"What are you hoping for?"

Rev had the look of someone to be reckoned with, but now a veil lifted from his eyes and he appeared unsure of himself. Still, Nora had the distinct impression that he had anticipated her question and had already selected his words with care. "It surprised me, how little you and Paul were involved in the initial investigation. Reading between the lines, it especially appeared that Mrs. Maple was anxious to protect Paul. I understand she tried to put him out of reach of the police."

Nora nodded. "Until Paul was older he visited his father and sometimes over a long weekend, so that wasn't unusual."

"Yes, but never during July when you and Lydia were here. Without notifying the authorities, she had his plane ticket and his bags packed until the police were alerted by your parents. Brenda Maple was none too happy when they suggested she keep Paul available for further questioning."

"That was a difficult time," Nora said and saw immediately that he was disappointed in her reply. He wanted her to say more, but Nora was numb to such expectations.

"You were interviewed, both in the presence of your parents and out, while Paul was never left alone for a minute. At one point Mrs. Maple even had an attorney involved. It struck me as inappropriate so I looked up one of the old-timers on the original case. He said that no one liked her and if she hadn't been a woman and had an iron-clad alibi, her behavior would have identified her as a suspect. Even to this day he is convinced that she had

179

something to hide."

"I can see why he might think that," Nora said, feeling strangely disloyal to Paul.

"Was she normally overprotective of her son?"

"She was, and often she was not smart. What you describe was completely in character for Brenda. She was short on common sense. There was little discipline or routine in Paul's life, but she gave him plenty of attention. Sometimes she relied on him too much and treated him like he was older. I envied Paul his freedom, some of his possessions, and the unlimited allowance. I never envied him his mother."

"He has a trust fund?"

"He does."

"Must be a significant one if he can call his hobby a job and not worry about making a profit."

"We've never discussed it." It occurred to Nora that Rev probably already knew Paul's assets and hers too.

Again Rev was disappointed in Nora's crisp answer. He wanted more and decided to shift gears.

"The police hardly questioned you and I'm thinking that you may remember more than you're aware of. I'm hoping that some detail in this material may strike you as odd or worth commenting on no matter how insignificant. I'd like Paul to read the reports as well. Read them twice. Once as the adult you are now and then try to remember how you felt at the time. You were a child. Look for something that strikes a chord. Something that feels authentic. Will Paul cooperate?"

Nora resented the question. "Paul loved Lydia as much as I did. He was like a brother to us. You may find him more willing to cooperate than I." Nora turned abruptly and Rev followed until they came to her studio. Just inside the door Paul waited with the UPS man. He had just signed off on two large boxes of art supplies and rolled canvas.

"Did you forget about lunch?" he asked Nora.

"Actually, yes," Nora said as Rev walked in behind her. She introduced the two men.

"You're welcome to join us," Paul offered.

"He can't," Nora said. "He's due back on the ski slopes."

"I'd like that," Rev replied, ignoring Nora's comment. He put on a different face for Paul, amiable and charming, as they chatted over pastrami and dill sandwiches, with Verner's ginger ale and homemade chips. Although Paul was slightly more animated than usual Nora saw no evidence of his drinking. He seemed more like his former self, before Herb's long illness had begun to take its toll. With ease, he repeated much of what she had already related, but painting a more vivid picture. He spoke of lunching on the beach with Nora's mother and grandmother and his and Nora's plans to sneak away for a sail soon after. He described the mix of tourists and summer residents and their childish anticipation of the Fourth of July parade until Nora too was transported back to that hot, July afternoon.

Nora noted Rev's habit of asking a question and then observing each gesture and nuance associated with the response. She watched as Paul warmed to Rev despite the grim topic and grew increasingly uneasy as Paul described that last walk with Lydia trailing behind. Abruptly she decided enough was enough. Paul's words had evoked vivid images of the days that followed as Main Street was closed off and the town fanned out to search for Lydia. Then the coast guard was called in and precious time was wasted as the authorities explored the possibility of her drowning.

Nora left her place by the large window and sat beside Paul. "Have you seen Herb?" she asked.

"Not yet."

She could feel Rev Porter watching her and resented the feeling of being on display, but he had been pulling their strings long enough. She felt like a wooden puppet suspended above a child's painted stage. She didn't want to come alive and feel the pain and anguish of that loss all over again. And the guilt. She looked at Paul and tried to catch his eye, but he was looking at Rev with fresh interest. She imagined that Paul could be easily drawn into another futile investigation and especially now when he so needed a distraction from the larger issue of Herb's pending death.

Nora placed her hand over Paul's. "Why don't you go along? I'll say goodbye to Rev and we can get started on these files later tonight, if you're up to it."

Paul shook Rev's hand. "I hope that I can help you. I've always felt I could have done more," he added wistfully and looked at Nora as he spoke.

"Well, actually there is something you can do. You can allow yourself to be hypnotized again. I understand your current psychiatrist is an expert at uncovering lost memory."

Paul was startled. "You seem to know quite a lot about me."

"Just doing my job," Rev said, suddenly distant and impersonal, without the warmth that had made Paul want to trust him. It occurred to Nora that Rev wielded charm like a weapon, putting on whatever face was called for in order to gain the desired outcome or information. She would never trust him.

"Well, actually," Nora interrupted acidly. "This is not your job. You are investigating a case without actual authority, out of your jurisdiction and on

181

your own time. A case, I might add, that everyone else thinks is hopeless."

"That's all right, Nora. I don't mind," Paul said. "I'm just surprised that Rev took the time to learn that I was seeing a psychiatrist. Of course I'll try again," Paul said earnestly to Rev. "I don't expect we'll find Lydia alive, but I wouldn't want to impede any real investigation. I'll do whatever I can."

Paul was almost at the door. Rev followed him across the floor. "And one other thing?" Paul stopped and this time turned to face Rev with a show of reluctance. "Were you ever sexually molested?"

Nora felt, rather than saw, Paul recoil from the question.

"I hope I haven't offended you," Rev said. "It's one of the first questions an investigator would ask today, but back then, if they inquired at all, it would have been of your mother. With no other evidence, they would have accepted whatever she said."

Paul looked at the floor and then at Nora. "Actually, yes. A relative molested me. It was a long time ago, before I knew Lydia or Nora."

"And what about you?" Rev turned to Nora.

Nora shook her head. "No, never."

"Who was it?" Rev fired the question at Paul without raising his voice, but distinctly changing the cadence. The question came so fast that Paul responded without thinking.

"It was my uncle. My mother's brother, actually. Howard Maple."

"Why does that name sound familiar?"

"He was a movie star," Nora answered for Paul.

Paul looked at Nora, surprised. "Well, no. He was hardly a movie star. He had two or three supporting roles in old skating films from the fifties that enjoyed minor success. Between the times he molested me and now, I only saw him once, and that was when our boats passed out there." Paul gestured vaguely to the view of the harbor outside Nora's window. "I didn't even go to his funeral," he added.

"He's dead?" Rev inquired.

"He died recently. He was old, but I understand it was unexpected."

"Do you have a picture of him?"

"No, but his son would have one. I wouldn't want Peter to know about his father. I wouldn't want him to know about me."

"Don't worry," Rev assured Paul. "I wouldn't betray a confidence."

Nora felt a flush of disdain. Who did he think he was kidding? He was in the business of betraying confidences, but Paul did not seem to grasp this. Again Nora questioned why Lydia's disappearance should be so important to Rev. She disliked his arrogance and Machiavellian penchant for manipulation. He believed he was clever. Perhaps that came with the police work and the jaded view of life one must be daily confronted with. Following in Paul's wake Nora saw Rev to the door.

"Thank you for your time. I just want you to know that I'll do whatever I can." He handed her two cards. "I can be reached by either of you at this number, night or day. Will you give one to Paul?"

Nora nodded and pocketed the cards. "Just don't expect too much. Not from Paul or me," she cautioned.

"I understand Paul's companion is ill. If there's anything I can do?"

"Why do I doubt the sincerity of that offer?"

In answer Rev smiled at her. A crooked smile, which prompted Nora to recall how he had looked as a boy. His eyes were the color of the sea shimmering on a crisp clear morning. She had still not seen any sign of an injury significant enough to release him from the Boston Police Force. He looked perfect to her. His face had the same rugged charm, which had made every female art collector mad for his famous uncle. Nora was annoyed with herself for noticing. Rev was nothing to her and yet there was no denying that she was both attracted and repelled by him at the same time.

CHAPTER FIFTEEN

As Connor ground fresh coffee beans and put water on for his wife's tea he thought of Herb. Herb had rebounded from death so many times that his survival had to be a miracle, fully part of God's divine timing. Even Herb's immune specialist in Boston, a confirmed atheist, had acknowledged this possibility when they discussed the case. He thought of the following verse as he lowered his head to pray. The Lord is not slow about His promise, as some count slowness, but is patient toward you, not wishing for any to perish but for all to come to repentance (2nd Peter 3: 9).

"You've been avoiding me."

Paul ignored Herb's accusation and maneuvered himself between the IV tubing and the catheter. It was March, but hinted spring as the wind came up and hit the swelling fullness of the tide and the white-tipped swells that rolled over the breakwater. There seemed to be no place to touch Herb and yet Paul felt an overwhelming desire to be embraced. Soon he would be alone.

"Why did you never tell me about Howard?" Paul asked and sat cross-legged on the side of Herb's bed. The nurse had been sent to the kitchen for a break. Dusk settled over the room and a dim light brightened on the small chest beside them.

Each time Paul opened his mouth to speak the words came stilted and remote and he felt as though he were impersonating himself in some seedy off-Broadway play. Only the ingrained habit of a lifetime allowed him to maintain the precarious masquerade that all was normal and largely unchanged.

The specter of death had not diminished the essence of Herb's personality. He had always tossed himself into the melee of whatever captivated him with greedy enthusiasm. Even now a certain energy flowed from the ruin of Herb's body. In the mere course of living, Herb had said and done so much that embarrassed Paul, but was conversely exciting. Soon the last vestiges of life as he knew it would pass with the body of his partner into the grave and he would be alone.

Amidst the false cheer and disingenuous trappings of an atypical

Christmas Herb had rallied, relapsed, and rallied again. And through it all Paul had not found the courage to ask what was most on his mind. Though he could prove nothing he knew that Herb had been unfaithful.

"Why didn't you ever tell me about Howard?," Paul repeated and looked into Herb's shrunken face.

"I couldn't. I thought it might end things between us. If I hadn't been confused I would never have told you about Howard and myself. I am so sorry."

"You should have told me. But a long time ago." *In the very beginning, before we ever began as a couple.* Paul added this last, silently to himself. He had begun to think that he'd thrown his life away on someone who had used him, but he didn't want to think of that just now.

"Would it have made a difference?" Herb asked.

Paul was careful with his reply. Careful not to betray the mounting rage that had begun to steal past his defenses when he least expected it. "Never," he lied and Herb seemed to believe him. His lips curled in a smile.

"Because of you I'm a better man," Herb said. Economy of speech had become a necessity, but now Herb pushed himself. "I've lived longer than I would have, because you loved me, and I'm not talking of this illness. Appetites are more important to some people than right or wrong. Consumed with satisfying themselves they're always pushing empty, never satisfied. Howard was like that, you know. You saved me from being like him."

"You could never have been like Howard!" The thought was abhorrent to Paul and he was shaken by the comparison that he himself had made only minutes before.

"No, not entirely." Tears sprang to Herb's eyes. He gasped for breath. Not often prone to introspection, Paul could see the fullness of all Herb longed to say bursting over his face, but he did not want to hear. Ever so gently Paul wrapped his arms about his frail body, careful not to let his own weight rest. Herb was a sand-castle being washed away in tiny chunks by an onrushing tide and Paul wished that despite the certainty of nature's laws, he alone could prevent it.

With his ear close to Herb's chest, he heard how full the lungs sounded and reached for a stethoscope. He felt a stab of guilt that the worsening of this symptom had escaped his attention. Now he noticed that tinges of blue lay beneath the fair, wafer thin skin and Herb's hands were cold. Connor had wanted his patient in the hospital, but Herb had protested and then one of Herb's consulting physicians at Mass General suggested they wait another forty-eight hours and start a new spectrum of drugs.

Paul elevated the back of the bed and turned on the suction machine. Herb shook his head in protest, but Paul ignored him. Putting on gloves he carefully inserted the tubing. Finally he wiped Herb's mouth with a lemon bliss stick and applied more ointment to his lips. Herb started to speak, but Paul silenced him. "It's all right. We'll talk later."

"But there is something more. Something I must tell you."

"We'll talk later," Paul repeated. In reaching for Paul's hand Herb only managed to pluck at his sleeve. In the grip of an immense reluctance, which seemed to impede each movement, Paul turned back. He leaned over the bed. "What do you want to say?"

Herb's face constricted in pain. Tears returned to his eyes. "Don't ever doubt that I love you," he whispered.

"I won't," Paul said. Herb had never seemed more vulnerable and yet Paul could not stand another millisecond under that needy gaze. Suddenly his beloved house seemed oppressive, the gathering gloom of impending death and his own life unbearable to contemplate. If he had his way he would pack a bag and be gone. He would do it now. He could do it now, but at the same time, fleeing his responsibilities was impossible. Paul wondered how his entire perspective could shift so abruptly with the simple news of what he should have guessed at long ago. Herb and Howard had been lovers. Herb was his life partner, his cherished friend and yet suddenly, the fracture of that facade and ministering to Herb seemed an insurmountable task. He had been betrayed. Right from the beginning what they'd called love had really been a complicated mask of manipulation. Paul wanted a drink. Something to deaden the terrible conflict of his emotions. Later he would think.

Paul's house was the oldest on Mill Lane and actually predated the gristmill. The rooms were smaller and the ceilings lower than Nora's with five working fireplaces and narrow, steep stairs leading to the second floor and third floor attic. Paul's mother had extended the back of the house adding on a large sunny kitchen and porch, and later Paul had added the green house. Paul descended slowly and paused momentarily at the landing. He looked across the hall and into the low-beamed living room at Nora.

They had gone to Gloucester for an early dinner and now she was slouched in a chair before the fire. She wore an outfit he had bought her for her birthday the year before. The slim navy skirt was corduroy and the pink cashmere sweater matched the tiny rose buds in the skirt pattern. Her short boots were off and her slender legs, encased in navy tights, stretched out over the ottoman.

His glance lingered. He had seen her in various stages of undress during their long acquaintance and even naked during that one encounter when they had made love. How, Paul wondered could he admire Nora, even be attracted to her, but not allow a different relationship? Suddenly he was submerged in regret. How much different his life would be today, if only they had married. Although they never discussed it, he understood perfectly that at one time she had desired him and even dreamed of marriage. And yet he had slammed the door on that possibility believing that there were no real choices to be made. Why had he felt so constrained by that inflexible belief that a change of habit and inclination was not possible? And was he really re-thinking his options, his bruised heart suddenly longing for a different life style? They might have had children and now he would never be a father. Why, as Herb lay dying, must he lament what long ago, he had willingly embraced with such conflicted longing?

Herb had never given up being jealous of Nora. It proved impossible to convince him that nothing more than friendship lay at the root of their close affinity for one another. Early in their relationship Herb had suggested a threesome and Paul had erupted in anger. "If you think Nora would go for something like that, or that I would let her, then you certainly don't know either of us." Paul's tone was scathing and the intensity seemed to sting Herb, who was silent for a long moment. Almost, Paul thought, in the manner of a deer caught in the glow of a headlight.

Paul had not thought of the incident in years, but he recalled it now. Herb had apologized admitting his jealousy of Nora, but Paul was not sorry for how he reacted. He wanted monogamy and safety and that Herb would consider such behavior in the realm of possibility offended him. For one brief moment he had a glimpse of how his own choices might impact Nora. So often she had verbalized her concern for the consequences of his lifestyle and so often he had laughed and made light of her remarks.

Paul realized that if he had allowed himself to consider the full scope of Herb's past he would probably turn and walk away, but he had decided to love Herb, who had promised that he could change. Still he could never convince Herb that Nora was not a threat to their relationship. This argument, like all others ended in the same way. They embraced, said they were sorry and then went on with life, submerged in the lulling monotony of Paul's routine. That this same routine was the antithesis of all that Herb craved was a threat conveniently ignored by both.

Now Paul and Nora sat across from one another, and shared the same ottoman, their feet sometimes touching. They passed folders and sheets of paper, all so carefully copied and organized by Rev, back and forth. Nora had always shunned the details of her sister's disappearance, but was now engrossed, feeling a great urgency to reclaim lost time. This was in sharp contrast to Paul's own lack of enthusiasm. It was as though the two had

187

executed a role reversal. In the past he had pushed her to learn everything she could about Lydia's disappearance, but now he was preoccupied and reluctant.

The mantle clock ticked loudly, the fire cracked as pinecones sputtered and the occasional start of the suction machine drifted down the narrow stairs. Nora lay her papers aside and studied Paul. He appeared to be absorbed in what he was reading, but she knew that he was not concentrating. During the time that she had drunk half a glass of Pies Porter, he had consumed the remainder of the bottle and was now starting on another. Nora had been surprised when in the late afternoon Paul had suggested dinner. It was a rare occurrence when she could wrest him away from Herb's bedside, but lately Paul seemed grateful for any excuse to be away.

Paul lifted the crystal hock to his lips and glared at Nora over the rim of the glass. "What!" he said irritated. "You've been staring at me all night. Spit it out. What's on your mind Nora?"

Nora did not hesitate to answer. It was as though she had waited for his question. "Why haven't you told Rev that Peter was here the weekend that Lydia disappeared?" Nora scrutinized Paul's face. She had intended to ask the question ever since Rev had interviewed them in her studio. She remembered hesitating over the phone, her hand on the receiver and even considered racing after Rev to tell him on that first day, but something had restrained her. Some inward pull of caution that she could not now explain.

"Don't you think Rev knows? It's here in all this paperwork someplace," Paul said and waved at the files scattered between them.

"Maybe, but no one considered it important. If Peter was here maybe Howard came too. It would have been an opportunity for him to see his son, even if only from a distance."

Paul gave Nora a searching look. "Then you suspect Howard?"

"Don't you?"

"When did you first think of Howard?" Paul asked.

"That night you climbed into my bed and let me think that Herb was dead. Then you told me that the relative who had molested you was Peter's father. I wish I'd known that earlier," Nora said with a quiet stillness that Paul knew was deceptive.

"What difference would it have made?"

"Because we know Howard had an excuse to be in Rockport that weekend and we certainly know he was capable of harming a child."

"But he didn't know Lydia. Why would he take her?" Paul responded, his expression showing the strain.

Nora had thought a lot about this very question, and the answer seemed pretty obvious. "Maybe he wanted you. Because of you the family ostracized him. Perhaps they even disinherited him. The Maple money would be a significant loss."

"He got his share."

"Maybe he wanted to catch a glimpse of the son he'd lost custody of. Hell, I don't know. It might have been a crime of opportunity. Don't you remember? Lydia was the one who fell behind, while you and I walked together. We were inseparable. Maybe Howard was frustrated because he couldn't get his hands on you, or because Peter wasn't with us. If it was Howard, I actually think that you or Peter would have been his logical targets."

"So now it's my fault that Lydia disappeared?"

"I didn't say that," Nora replied evenly, never shifting her gaze from his face.

"This is ludicrous! Will you listen to yourself, Nora? You have no grounds for such a theory. None at all! You could destroy lives with such groundless allegations!" There was an outraged, pleading quality to Paul's voice.

"This is all I have," Nora erupted, extending her hands palm up in supplication. "Look at these blasted files," she shouted. "They didn't even have a possible sex offender to interrogate, and they took their own sweet time about labeling it a kidnaping. There was no ransom note, and as far as I can conclude, the FBI wasn't consulted until it was too late."

"I disagree. They did a very thorough job with this investigation. I can't imagine what more they could have done."

"Are you crazy? Are we reading the same material? For the first time I realize how much time they wasted trying to convince my parents that Lydia was with a friend or relative or had drowned or gone back to Belmont, as if someone on the train wouldn't have noticed a child in a bathing suit. And all the while your mother, and I might add Peter's mother, sat in this house and said not a word about Howard!"

"Why should they? This is wild speculation, Nora, pure fantasy." Paul's tone matched Nora's.

"It's a hell of a lot better than what the authorities had, which, I might add, was nothing. This is at least a theory that makes sense and it feels right. Don't you think it feels right, Paul?" Nora had leaned forward as she spoke, but suddenly she stood, oblivious to the papers that fell from her lap. "Remember what Rev said. He said look for something that feels authentic. Well, this could be it!"

Paul remained silent. He stared at Nora, his face furrowed in exasperation.

"Look," Nora said, lifting a file into the air. "I see nothing in here about

Howard. Your mother never told them you'd been molested! I was the only one you confided in, and I never betrayed that confidence. As a little girl I didn't really understand it anyway. My parents didn't know, so it wouldn't occur to them that your family might have such a connection to a child predator. Maybe the police asked your mother some of those questions and maybe they didn't, but she certainly did not volunteer the information."

"Why should she?" Paul was horrified.

"The appropriate question is why wouldn't she tell them? Why wouldn't she make a connection, in view of Howard's history?"

Paul opened his mouth to speak and then hesitated. He looked at her, almost pleading. "You know the answer to that, Nora. She was trying to protect me."

"At the expense of my sister's life! Need I remind you that your Uncle Howard was a pervert? A sexual predator! We have just learned from Herb that you weren't his first victim or his last. Paul, listen to me! If it turns out he took Lydia, no one would blame you. You couldn't possibly predict such a thing. You were only a child."

"But," Paul stumbled over the words, "it can't be. For one thing, he liked boys, not girls!"

"Who knows what he liked, or for that matter, what he was capable of? I only know that we have to look at the facts. We have to learn more about Howard. I want you to call your cousin, Peter. I want you to ask Herb for information."

"I can't!"

"You must, Paul. Herb will trust you and we need to know before we lose another chance and someone else dies."

At her words Paul visibly winced as though she'd physically slapped him. "As you so aptly point out, Herb is dying. It's wrong to burden him with this, and what do you imagine I would say to Peter? 'Your father molested me when I was a boy and now we suspect him of kidnaping Lydia Fothergill.' Peter came to love his father. He'd sue me for slander."

Nora was dumbfounded. She could not understand Paul's reticence and refusal to see the possibilities. If Brenda Maple had shared this information years before, Howard would most certainly have been investigated and even cleared. Or perhaps not, and her sister would be alive today. Nora had no idea if she was right or wrong. She only knew that she felt an urgent and powerful need to explore the possibilities, and that Paul was not right beside her, helping and encouraging as he always had, was hurtful and even perplexing.

"You were always pushing me to pursue every avenue. Now that we have legitimate information that deserves close scrutiny you won't help," Nora said softly. "Why is that, Paul?"

"Because you have no proof and because Herb is dying. Why upset him over a theory that has no basis in fact?" Paul bounded from the chair and walked to the fireplace. Picking up a poker, he furiously stabbed at the flames and then tossed on another log. Sparks went flying but he ignored them. His neck stiffened, and he seemed to feel the intensity of Nora's gaze on his back.

Nora was baffled. In all the years she had known Paul, he had never been so defensive. "You mean you won't help me? You won't help because you gave Herb the best years of your life and now you know that he was unfaithful. You only have to wonder how often and with how many other men, and when you add Howard to that equation, the possibilities are truly frightening."

"I won't believe that of Herb," Paul asserted lamely.

"Then you're a fool." Nora began to pace. She strode across the long narrow room, stabbing at the air to emphasis her point. Paul began to speak again, but she cut him off with her own tirade. "Oh, please. Then what about this illness? What about the fact that he has it and you don't? Every fight you ever had was an excuse for him to disappear for a few days, and you told me yourself that you began using condoms. Do you really think it remotely possible that Herb would have agreed to such an arrangement if he thought himself capable of a monogamous relationship? What planet are you living on? Wake up, Paul, before it's too late."

"Stop it!" Paul screamed, his face flush with anger.

Nora was suddenly still. She looked at Paul intently. "No, I won't stop it, Paul. He was never kind to you. He was barely nice to you most of the time, and I had to stand by and watch you be insulted because if I'd told you the truth I would have lost your friendship. Isn't it true that in a heartbeat you would have chosen Herb over me?"

"You never asked me to make a choice."

"No, but I should have." Common sense warned Nora to tread softly, but a torrent of suppressed suspicion had been unleashed, and she could no longer hold back. "If Herb loved you, it was a self-centered love that revolved around him and excluded you. He was rude and self-centered and nothing you did was ever exactly right, even on the many occasions when everything was perfect. He couldn't help himself. He had to tear you down, and he often did it publicly because he and everyone else knew he didn't deserve you. For Lydia's sake you have to consider the possibilities, Paul. You have to be honest and demand honesty from Herb before it's too late because at the very least...." Nora's voice broke, but she quickly regained control. "At the very least he may know something about Howard."

191

"Too late for what? What do you think Herb could possibly know about Howard that would help us find Lydia? Don't you see Nora, how deranged you sound?"

"If you won't ask him, then I will!" Nora strode toward the stairs, but Paul intercepted her and grabbed her arm, pulling her around to face him. Grasping her shoulders he almost shook her. "You will NOT ask him anything! I won't have you disturbing what little time he has left!"

"I intend to ask if Howard continued to molest children, because you know what the experts say. These people don't stop! They continue committing these horrid crimes, despite any consequence. And then I'll ask Herb if he thinks that monster was capable of kidnaping, and guess what, Paul? You can't stop me!"

Nora broke free and once more started for the stairs. Paul followed at her heels and was again reaching for her arm, when she stopped abruptly. They both looked up. The nurse stood on the third stair, her face pinched in disapproval and her arms crossed defensively across her chest. It struck Paul that Herb had probably overheard their argument, and in a flood of unguarded feeling, he was glad and happy and relieved all at once. But the onslaught that followed a moment later was a grip of guilt so painful that he felt its reality in a sinking, physical sensation. How could he be glad to see Herb suffer? How had he allowed this conversation with Nora to get so out of hand, and especially now, at a time like this?

"I'm afraid there's just too much fluid in Herb's lungs for ordinary suctioning. I've called an ambulance, so if you'll just phone Dr. Connor and have him meet us at the emergency room."

Paul remained at Herb's bedside and Nora stood at the front door, watching the lights of the ambulance as it backed down Mill Lane. It seemed that every light in the house was on, but overhead it was dark. Wrapping an old afghan about her shoulders, Nora walked across the lane and stepped onto the stone slab at the gate side. She turned and looked at their two houses and thought of the young woman who had remained all night in the lane. This is where she would have waited, for here one could stand or sit and rest against the cemetery gate. She and Lydia had sat here as children with all their beach paraphernalia, impatiently waiting for an adult to take them swimming.

A yellow glow spilled across her boots and up the fieldstone wall of the cemetery. Nora listened to the sound of the ambulance tires breaking through the crusted snow. She recalled Connor describing a living will and Herb declining to consider any course of action that would take his life sooner. Herb would fight, holding on for as long as possible. He was afraid to die. She had seen it almost from that first day that he and Paul had told her of this

192

new and mysterious virus and the fatal lack of a cure. Herb had grown more angry and irritable, but Nora watched him censor his more destructive inclinations and resultant behavior in ways she never had before. She liked him better for the effort, but had no answers. No one, it seemed, could help Herb to face death with anything but bitterness and dread.

That he would not give up more easily and sign the papers that would release Paul sooner had made Nora resentful of Herb. As far as Nora was concerned Herb was, as always, selfish. Paul had suffered enough over the last three years, and Nora wanted to spare him more. She lifted her gaze, faced the wind, and concentrated.

The crest of the horizon was close, the drop of the hill and the white gravestones a milky tilt against the sea. Nora closed her eyes and paced her words in rhythm with the waves. It was awkward to pray. She was out of practice, and yet she had fond memories of praying with her family at meal times with all of them holding hands. Some of the prayers had been formal and others were conversations that she liked better. She wondered if God would hear her after all this time. Was He angry at her neglect and doubt and lack of trust? She had grown away from thinking of things like eternity, heaven, and hell. It had all seemed so pat, so simple a solution to the complications that had surrounded Lydia's disappearance, and she wondered how God could allow such a thing to happen. She hadn't stopped believing, she told herself now; she had just turned her back on God, who seemed distant from their suffering. She had felt herself abandoned, but maybe that was wrong.

Nora had never felt so alone. She felt her need as a helpless dread that culminated in this moment when she might finally learn the truth about her sister. The cold wind snatched tears from her face before they could fall as she pleaded with God for one, just one, last lucid conversation with Herb. For Lydia's sake, a final exchange that would either put the worst of her suspicions to rest forever, or send her off in an entirely new direction.

Paul sat huddled into a corner of the waiting room sofa, his tone curt and distant. "You don't need to stay, Nora," he whispered, although the intensive care unit that had swallowed Herb in a rush of activity only moments before had placed Herb safely out of hearing distance. Paul had never spoken to her with such cold detachment. But then...they had never quarreled so bitterly.

"Will you give us a minute, Connor?" Nora asked, not taking her eyes from Paul's face.

Connor looked in turn at Nora and Paul. He seemed clearly mystified by the tension between them. "Look, you two, this is not the time to fight.

Whatever is wrong, forget it," he advised with his usual directness. They watched his back as he disappeared into the hallway and heard the almost imperceptible swoosh of the wide double doors that opened automatically into the ICU. Almost involuntarily Paul and Nora looked at one another, understanding that they would be sensitive to that sound until they knew the outcome of Herb's fate.

"I have no intention of leaving," Nora whispered so as not to be overheard by another family who kept a similar vigil at the opposite end of the long narrow room.

"I don't want you here!" Paul hissed.

"Why, because I verbalized all your fears? Because I stated the obvious? You can't even say why you're angry at me, Paul."

"I won't have you talking to Herb about Howard!"

"Are you afraid of what he might reveal?"

Immediately Nora regretted her choice of words. She bit her lip and reminded herself to change tactics. Paul was just too distraught to face the possibilities, but if he forced her to leave, she might never get near Herb again. She hated herself for the lie she was about to utter. "Look, Paul, I'm sorry that I overreacted. Don't let my suspicions drive a wedge between us. Not at a time like this. If you don't want me to talk with Herb about anything serious, then I'll respect your wishes and I'll understand."

Paul looked at Nora, seeming to hesitate over a difficult decision that Nora would not give him time to make. She couldn't risk the wrong response.

"Just let me be here for you," Nora spoke, filling the void of his silence. "I'm not angry with you. I love you," Nora glanced self-consciously at the other family and wished for privacy. There was so much more she wanted to say.

Paul stood abruptly and walked to the far wall. He rested his forehead against the smooth surface and studied several air bubbles trapped under the paint. Nora had said, "I love you." Paul could not express the degree to which he suddenly despised the ring of those words. From deep within the recesses of his memory, the distinct sting of a slap echoed. Paul put a hand to his cheek. He reeled from pain revisited and pressed his forehead harder into the wall for balance.

The strain of shielding himself from Nora's scrutiny was becoming more and more difficult. If she knew, if she had any idea at all, she would demand he relate each and every particular. She could always sense what no one else could, and even now might perceive disjointed shreds of memory rising from deep pits of loathing. All logic to the contrary, Paul felt naked and exposed. No one could know all the ways that Howard had abused him. He himself did not know. The experience had not left a visible scar on his face, but this recent deluge of memories made him feel otherwise.

Could Nora be right? Could Howard have taken Lydia? Paul just did not want to think about that. Not now. As the longing for a drink washed over him, Paul consoled himself with the conviction that soon he would stop consuming so much alcohol. Both Connor and Nora had remarked on his drinking, and on some level it had embarrassed him but on another he couldn't care.

Paul spoke to himself sternly. He would promise anything to stem, postpone, or stifle what was coming. As soon as Herb was well enough to leave the hospital, Paul vowed that he would call his doctor and resume therapy, but for now he must simply get a grip on his emotions and stomp these memories back to oblivion where they belonged and where they'd once happily resided.

After all, Paul consoled himself, he was merely experiencing grief and a temporary loss of control. Anticipation of grief was a normal reaction. It did not mean that he wanted Herb to die. CERTAINLY NOT! It only meant that he was preparing for the inevitable. *Oh God,* he thought. *Why now? Why must I remember NOW?*

Nora walked up to Paul and let him feel the firm grip of her hands on his arms. She turned him to face her, his body no longer rigid and fraught with anger, but in a sudden switch of exhaustion, he seemed slack and passive. A wave of guilt assailed her. She was being far too hard on Paul, even brutal, and yet there was no denying the urgency which propelled her actions and roused her to speak. A slim window of opportunity had opened which afforded no alternative. She must shove it wider or risk a lifetime of regret.

Not disguising their curiosity, the other family watched them, but Paul seemed unaware. Nora led him to the sofa. They sat, their thighs touching, and studied the far wall until Paul had lost a bit of that absent, haunted expression which now, for the first time, truly worried Nora. Whatever there was to do would have to be accomplished without Paul's help. She glanced at his profile. His expression was now stoic and remote.

After a bit, they had moved to opposite ends of the sofa. It happened by degrees, with trips to the restroom, for water and on the pretense of reading an outdated *Newsweek*. Their faces averted, as though by design, they hardly spoke, the silence between them alive, their bodies tense and waiting.

Finally Connor joined them. "Herb's awake and resting. I took him off the ventilator and he's breathing on his own. He wants to see you."

"Thank God," Paul said and headed for the door, but Connor put out a hand to stop him. "I'm sorry, Paul, but Herb is asking for Nora."

"I won't have it. You can't let her in there!" Paul exploded with sudden passion.

Connor looked at Paul, astonished at his response. "You can't prevent her. Herb is clearly upset about something that somehow involves Nora. He needs to get it off his chest so he can rest."

"But why Nora? Why not me?"

"You can see him as soon as she has her ten minutes." Connor turned to Nora. "No longer than that, Nora, and don't upset him. He's too weak."

Paul dropped to his corner of the sofa. He fought an urge to draw his knees up and hug his body tightly. There was a time when he had sat like that for long periods and perhaps hours. As quickly as the thought came, he cast off the image and looked instead at Nora. "If you bring up Howard, if you upset him in any way, I'll never speak to you again. Never. Are we clear about this, Nora?"

Nora nodded. She tried and failed to hold his gaze. He turned away as though she was of no more importance than a gnat.

"There is something else I must tell you both," Connor added. "Herb has asked not to be hooked up to a ventilator if he has another episode like the last. He wants us to let him go, so you both need to say your good-byes. It's only a question of time."

"He's in no state to make that decision. His lungs will fill up with fluid and he'll drown," Paul asserted.

Connor spoke gently. Paul and Nora sensed that their friend was happily relieved about something. His attitude caught their mutual attention more than his words. "Herb is perfectly lucid. He and I have prayed together and he understands exactly what he's done."

There followed a few seconds of stunned silence.

"Oh, that's just bloody wonderful! What does that mean?" Paul erupted as though Connor had betrayed him also. "Now Herb's a Christian so it's okay for him to die! We can stop fighting to save his life. Is that what you're saying, you simpering hypocrite?"

"It's hopeless, Paul. He can die tonight or next week, but either way he can't survive this illness. He has finally made his peace with Jesus Christ. Only a personal relationship with a living God can give one peace at a time like this. When you talk with Herb you'll see that he is sincere and you'll be happy for him."

"You've been after him with that religious voodoo since the first day you diagnosed his illness."

Connor shook his head and seemed to regard Paul with a mixture of surprise and pity. Paul had sunk to the sofa. Connor joined him, placing an arm about his shoulders, but Paul pulled away, his eyes on Nora as, grim faced, he watched her walk from the room.

Herb was in a separate cubicle attached to the ICU. Outside the double glass doors, which afforded no privacy, Nora noticed that the trash cart and other disposal bags were a bright cherry red, while those in other rooms were beige. Herb's head was elevated. He had two IV bags running, and instead of a nasal oxygen tube, a mask covered his mouth and nose. Away from the softer lighting of home he truly looked like a dying man, and yet there was something different about Herb. He seemed strangely peaceful and even happy at some special comfort. Was it God? Was it because he had prayed with Connor?

Nora walked to the bedside and took his hand. It felt limp and cold until she felt his fingers curl into her palm and his head turned in her direction, though he failed to open his eyes. He gestured to the mask, which Nora removed and replaced with the nasal catheter. It struck her as odd how, in the last four years, she and Paul had grown comfortable with all this medical apparatus which had once greatly intimidated them.

Herb tried to speak but no sound emerged. His throat was raw from all the suctioning. His bed had been rolled up to waist level. Nora ducked under the tubing, lowered the bed rail, and leaned her waist against the mattress. "What is it, Herb?"

"I heard you fighting, Nora. I'm sorry."

"Sorry for what?" Nora asked and held her breath.

"I'm dying. Must tell you," he whispered. "Must tell someone, but not Paul."

"I'm listening, Herb. Take your time. I'm listening."

"No time."

"Just say what you can."

"There are pictures."

Nora was certain she had not heard correctly, but then Herb repeated the phrase more clearly. "Pictures of what?" Nora asked.

"Photographs. In the walls."

Once again Nora was convinced that Herb was confused. "What about Lydia?" He shook his head. "Herb, you must tell me. Was Howard capable of taking my sister? Out of revenge because he couldn't see Peter or because he wanted to punish Paul for exposing him?"

Herb opened his huge, cavernous eyes. His face seemed stripped of flesh, but again she was struck by a deep inward change in him. He appeared to be looking for something. There was a photograph in a silver frame beside the

197

bed, which Paul insisted accompany Herb whenever he went to the hospital. He wanted to remind the nurses of how Herb had looked when he was well and healthy. Herb was particularly fond of the photograph, which Nora had snapped of the two men on the bridge of the Chris Craft, their arms draped about one another's shoulders and the open sea beyond. They had looked like any two male friends in that photograph. Handsome and smiling with energy that even now reached out to touch Nora, and she was glad that on that day neither of them could guess at the devastation to come.

Nora held it up for Herb to see, but he shook his head. The bleep of the monitor raced faster, and he was becoming agitated. He grabbed a line of IV tubing, but Nora pried his fingers loose. She tried to place the oxygen mask back over his face, but he waved it away with surprising strength. He leaned forward, his body stiff, and Nora thought he might collapse forward like a wooden puppet whose strings were no longer held taunt. "Nora," he whispered, but with an intensity that caught her off guard.

"It's all right, Herb," Nora nearly sobbed. "We can talk later. You must rest," she pleaded, convinced that she had gone too far. Paul was right. It was wrong for her to question Herb at a time like this. Paul would certainly have confided the details of Lydia's disappearance to Herb, but apart from that one instance at dinner, Herb had never again alluded to the events of that long ago summer. At the time, Nora had valued such decorum.

"Pictures of Howard and Paul. You must destroy them, Nora. Paul doesn't remember. I don't want him to remember."

Nora felt the deceptive calmness of all her suspicions jell into one moment. "Where are they?" Nora saw a blaze in Herb's eyes. He was making one final effort to communicate, and now she believed him. He wasn't confused. He was trying to tell her something important, and she was not listening.

"In the walls," he whispered, the brief restoration of his voice lost again. "On which wall? At Mill Lane?"

Herb fell back against the pillow. "No," he rasped out in frustration. "At Howard's." The red dot of the monitor chased itself across the screen, tracing a line of green as the bleep sounded faster before lapsing into one continuous drift of jarring current.

A nurse raced into the room and elbowed Nora away from the bed. Another came and then another. Nora stood helplessly back and watched, stunned by Herb's words.

"You'll have to leave, Miss," the nurse said to Nora. "NOW, if you please," she repeated for emphasis, but Nora stayed. She backed as far as she was able against the far wall of the cubicle and watched as the bed was flattened and another nurse placed a black ambu bag over Herb's face. From just outside the door a red crash cart was hurled to the side of the bed as Connor raced into the room, white coat flying. He waved away the crash cart and removed the bag from the nurse's grip.

When they pronounced Herb dead a short five minutes later, Nora felt stunned by the swiftness of it all. Compared to the long, drawn out drama of a prolonged illness, death itself was an anticlimax and a hollow parody of all she'd steeled herself to expect. Nora remained rooted to the same spot when Paul was finally ushered in. He bent over Herb's body. Gently he pulled back the sheets and placed his palm lightly over the still chest, as though to confirm that there was indeed no heartbeat. Nora noticed that Herb's facial expression was transfixed in death by what could only be great emotional release and even joy. How could that have happened, she wondered. Had he seen or known something just as consciousness lifted away and his heart stopped beating? It wasn't what she expected of Herb and she felt momentarily confused.

"You must have an angel to guard your grave. I want Connor to say a prayer, and we'll ask him to play the pipes. Oh, Herb," he said, his voice breaking. "I wish it was summer so the flowers could come from our garden." Paul's voice trailed into silence, more sorrowful than words. He clearly believed himself to be alone. He crossed his arms and hugged his own body for futile comfort, and leaning forward he stared into Herb's face as though he could will his partner to wake.

"I'll help you make the arrangements," Nora said gently and stepped out of the shadows. "I want to help you, Paul, if you'll let me."

Paul turned in Nora's direction. His expression was tortured and she felt a stab of remorse that they had ever quarreled.

"You won't help me, Nora. I don't want you anywhere near Herb or me."

"But, Paul," Nora started to speak.

"Did you find out what you wanted? Was it worth it, Nora? I begged you not to upset him." Nora could see the nurses behind their crescent shaped desk turn in Paul's direction. Connor put down Herb's chart and walked toward the room. This was not the place to argue. All the other glassed rooms were occupied, and it was only because of Connor that they had been allowed to linger.

"Paul, I'm so sorry and I–" Nora spoke.

"Don't apologize to me. You who never loved him. Don't deny that you ruined his last moments by asking a lot of hateful questions. Leave this room, Nora, or I'll have you thrown out. It's my turn to be alone with Herb."

Herb's body lay outstretched, the clutter of an aborted rescue scattered about. Paul looked for some evidence of Herb's eleventh-hour conversion to faith in that same expression that had startled Nora. But he saw only emptiness and an eloquent stillness, which Paul found reminiscent of gossamer cocoons, suddenly obsolete as they clung to the wet, black branches of spring. He thought of snakeskins lifted from the garden with the prong of a rake, and the empty shells of horseshoe crabs scattered on the shore. Herb was gone. Simply and undeniably no longer at home to the shell of this once vital body. It was a dearth disconcerting to ponder, but to ponder later. Much later.

Nora hesitated to leave. She desired nothing more than to wrap her arms about Paul's stricken frame. She wanted to plead her case and change his mind, but Connor laid a firm hand on her arm and escorted her into the hallway.

"Don't worry," Connor said. "I'll take him home with me tonight, and the two of you can work things out tomorrow."

"Try to understand this, Connor. I know him better than you do. Paul may never forgive me. Not this time." A sob caught and strangled in the back of her throat, and Connor reached his arms around her.

"That's the thing about Paul," he reassured. "He's generous to a fault and quick to forgive. I go to church with a few people who could learn a thing or two from him. And, Nora?"

She lifted her face to look at him, and he held her gaze as though with a child to whom he had something important to impart. "Paul didn't mean a thing he said back there to either of us. He's drunk and in shock and everything will look different after he's had a little rest. You can see him tomorrow."

"If he'll allow it," Nora whispered, unsure. Connor walked her to the ICU entrance, still holding her hand, and there they separated. Her footsteps sounded hollow as she approached the elevator. She watched the reflection of her feet across the floor's antiseptic finish and felt a heightened mixture of triumph and sadness. Nora thought of the coffin she had painted and was glad she had taken the time to get it to the upholsterer. Herb would be amused. He would like the bright, discordant colors and the Celtic scroll design. In a normal world she would be upstairs grieving with Paul, but suddenly her world had shifted, and something more compelling demanded her attention.

Herb had given credence to her theory concerning Lydia's disappearance, which now seemed entirely plausible. Though Paul could not understand, Nora knew that Herb did and she felt closer to him now in death than she ever had in life. Nora slid into her car, turned on the dome light, and hunted in her book for the card Rev Porter had given her some months earlier. She then returned to the pay phone in the emergency room lobby and placed a collect call. When Rev came on the line, he hesitated not at all when the operator announced her name. Sounding groggy, almost disbelieving, he asked, "What's up, Slick? You okay?"

Despite recent events, Nora smiled.

CHAPTER SIXTEEN

Connor looked forward to waking his wife when he returned home. He knew she would not care. She would want to hear all about Herb's conversion, and together they would rejoice and thank God. "In the same way, I tell you, there is rejoicing in the presence of the angels of God over one sinner who repents" (Luke 15:10).

Outside of Gloucester Nora picked up Route 128. Although it was an unnecessary detour, she took the Winchester exit and followed Route 3 through Arlington and into Belmont. She passed down the tree-lined street that had once been residential, looking for the place where her home had been.

At the corner she slowed and locked eyes with an elderly woman walking a cat on a leash. There was something familiar about the woman, who lifted a gloved hand, and Nora waved back. Eventually she came to Storrow Drive and the Harvard lights burning over the Charles River and the Mass Avenue Bridge. She liked Boston.

Nora put Paul and Herb deliberately from her mind. In the shelter of the car, with the streets nearly deserted, she savored a last sane hiatus as Geraldine Farrar's singular voice floated from the best that could be copied from worn-out recordings. Geraldine sang a selection from Carmen as Nora turned left on Marlboro Street, finally skirting the common into Beacon Hill.

Rev Porter lived only blocks from the gallery that hosted one of her largest annual shows and often displayed an original in the window. Life was fraught with coincidence, she reflected as Rev let her in wearing faded jeans torn at the knee and a white t-shirt. His hair was mussed and he was barefoot but looked to be fully awake. In silence Nora followed him into the kitchen, where the smell of coffee was pungent.

On the way through she glanced into adjoining rooms, surprised by the formal décor of period pieces that Nora guessed would be genuine and inherited. A Child Hassam adorned one wall and she recognized a work by Willard Metcalf, as well as the painting of her own that Rev had purchased at the end of her last season. Nora felt proud to be in such good company, but was disappointed to see no sign of Josiah's work and guessed the bulk of it would be on extended loan to museums.

The kitchen was unremarkable, but unlike the rooms she had just passed, which had a starched unlived in look, it was decidedly messy. Dishes overflowed from the sink and a computer sat in a corner. Rev picked up a stack of books from a chair in order to make room for her to sit. Papers, folders, and gray-speckled filing boxes littered the floor. "I have the house cleaned on Thursdays," he offered by way of excuse.

Nora's eyes drifted to a stack of photographs on the farm-style serving table. "What's this?" she asked and then caught her breath. Over the grainy black and white surface was an image of a young woman. Nora knew instantly that she was looking at the computer-aged enhancement of her sister. The family resemblance was obvious as Lydia peered back at her, entirely and completely herself. The effect on Nora was electric. She was looking into the eyes of a woman who lived and breathed and performed ordinary, routine tasks of life just as she did. This was the sister who, in Nora's mind, had never grown up, and yet here she was presumably alive and well and yet Nora knew. She knew what she had always known. Lydia could not possibly be alive.

"She would have been beautiful," she whispered, hardly aware of the tears that pooled in her eyes. "It's odd," she continued, speaking slowly, and Rev knew that she was not at that moment addressing him.

"It's odd how the truth emerges. Not as instant revelation, but ever so slowly, through bits and pieces of random happenstance that may suddenly slip the bonds of obscurity into a particular pattern." Nora finished speaking and turned on Rev a penetrating stare. "Have you ever felt that way?"

Energy flowed out to Rev from that look, and for the first time he thought that he loved Nora. He had been attracted to her even before all this started, from the time that he saw her at a neighborhood showing off her work, but when he sought her out to remind her of their former, brief acquaintance as children, she was nowhere to be found. He knew she had a reputation for being aloof and distant, but when he finally met her, he was unprepared for that tough exterior, the direct, almost defensive way she pushed aside any and every offer of help. It was as though she abhorred weakness of any kind and especially her own. If he'd met her in the midst of an investigation, he would have been convinced that she had something to hide and at the very least, some reason not to see the truth emerge.

That first day that he saw Paul and Nora together he could not help wondering if there was something more than friendship between them. Physically they made a handsome couple, and he knew that Paul was often her escort when she attended various social functions to promote her work. Paul was sociable and friendly, playing off Nora's penchant for distance, and yet they had a way of completing one another's sentences like an old married couple who'd long ago lost the mystery.

On that day at her Rockport Gallery, when Rev had seen Nora painting at her easel and she had been unaware of his watching, he could not escape a vision of her as fresh and uncomplicated, an impression that quickly evaporated the moment she spoke. The contrast was compelling and he studied her now, her short hair gathered behind her ears to reveal the almost porcelain symmetry of a delicate profile. He sensed the absence of boundaries between Nora and Paul that his investigative instincts had unearthed only among lovers or people who shared dreadful secrets that left them in a kind of bondage to one another.

Nora was not the kind of woman he was normally attracted to. Even now as he looked at her, once more appearing vulnerable and yielding, he had to fight an urge to take her in his arms and comfort her. Deliberately he turned away, busying himself with mugs and spoons.

"Have you ever felt that way?" Nora repeated her question.

Rev turned to her with a slight, almost imperceptible intake of breath. "Yes," he said. "Each time I approach an investigation I hope eventually to feel just that way. It's the moment that transforms the ugly chaos of crime into craft." Rev handed her a blue mug with the crest of the Boston Police Department on the outside. Their hands touched and almost unwittingly his lingered seconds longer than necessary, but she seemed not to notice.

Nora glanced past him and out the window and Rev followed her gaze. All was a pale shade of gray under the streetlight and the red brick of the neighboring building a gentle wash of color. Nora took a tentative sip of the steaming coffee, and Rev realized that for the moment she was biding time as she struggled to compose her thoughts. Rev had witnessed this many times in the course of an investigation, although never in his own kitchen. He could see that Nora was loathe to begin.

Often there was that lull of anticipation before the cesspool of many shameful secrets flooded into the light. Finally all those good police instincts and painstaking accumulation of detail paid off as he waited for confirmation of that one theory that was true. In the end, facts had a way of telling their own story, and if you'd taken the time to accumulate enough they drove the reality of crime to its own and sometimes surprising conclusion. And when that moment arrived, the best that a good investigator could do was to get out of the way and wait.

He watched her face but her eyes avoided his. Rev resisted an impulse to shout out a warning. He wanted to urge Nora not to say anything that would bring consequences that might take her from him. But was Nora truly a suspect? Must he really think of her in that context? Years of experience told Rev that he had no choice.

He watched as Nora visibly shivered although it was not cold. Now she focused the full grip of her stare in his direction. Her eyes were dry and clear. "I have a story to tell you. It may be false or it may be true. Are you up to the task of listening?"

Rev swallowed a gulf of dread and nodded. He took Nora's hand in his. That she did not pull away prompted a surge of desire that he wished he could ignore. He'd never before felt anything but a fleeting attraction for a female suspect that was quickly dispelled the moment he contemplated the nature of the crime. Even now, before he heard Nora's story, he could not ignore the possibility that she and Paul may have killed Lydia, or at the very least, concealed an accident they felt responsible for. They'd been young, but even children had been known to commit crimes against humanity. A crime, any crime, had an impact far beyond the immediate circumstances and a way of eroding the freshness of life for those left in the wake of violence.

Still holding her hand he led her to one of two comfortable chairs by the window, and with the other hand he brushed off yesterday's *Times* and *Globe*, letting them fall to the floor. As her hand fell away he felt the absence of her touch and realized that he couldn't protect her.

"Okay, I'm listening."

"I wish I could begin this story as though it were a fairy tale," Nora started. "You know, 'once upon a time' or 'in a far off place.' But I can't. The place was home and the time was real. It might have been yesterday, because it's so very hard to forget how our lives changed. My grandmother buried a young husband and then her son and daughter-in-law. I can't imagine how she bore that and still kept her faith in God. But she did. She was never bitter or angry with God, that I could see. I really believe that if she hadn't had her faith and believed she would see them again, grief would have claimed her also. But she held onto that Bible verse, and you know I don't read the Bible all that much. But she quoted it so often that I remember. *I know who I have believed and am persuaded that he is able to keep that which I have committed to him until that day.* Don't ask me where that verse is because I couldn't tell you, and I'm not sure I have the words exactly right."

Nora paused. Rev thought she might break down but she didn't. She continued. "I'm not proud of that. She wanted me to have the same relationship with her Jesus that she did. She trusted her family to God and she believed that we would all be reunited after death, and that justice would somehow come. If not in her lifetime then in mine, and sometimes I imagine her up there nagging God. Saying something like, "Okay, Jesus, you promised when I was living down there that you would resolve this for our family, and Nora is the only one left."

Nora took a sip of coffee. "My father had to sell our home in Belmont to pay for all the business of chasing down those rabbit trails that always came to nothing. It killed them. Can you possibly understand what a loss this was to my family? I think more often of them than of my sister. I think, if only I still had my father and my mother and how much richer my life would be today. Because you know I miss them every day. They were remarkable and with them alive we were a remarkable family, just living a normal life, and yet extraordinary for that. And then there is the burden of wishing and thinking that if only Paul and I had done this or that differently."

Nora stood and walked to the sink, pouring out her coffee.

"Would you rather have a drink?" he asked.

"No. I need my wits about me. What I'm about to tell you will change everything, and I don't want to miss a bit of it. So I need to get this right. I've only just figured some things out in the last few hours."

"What happened to change things?"

She looked at him. "Herb died early this morning."

"I'm sorry."

"He told me something curious, just as he died. It wasn't Paul he needed to talk to. It was me."

"He wanted to get something off his chest?"

"Yes, and evidently he found faith in Jesus Christ. Hard to believe, because, suddenly, he had a conscience. He found religion, thanks to Connor and he wanted me to know something, and now I'm almost certain that I can tell you what happened to Lydia." Nora lifted her face and looked into Rev's eyes. Her expression was one of barely concealed rage, and he knew that if the object of that rage were anywhere near, she wouldn't hesitate to act.

No more than the rooftops of houses could be seen from the street and sometimes not even that. The beginning of one property was determined from another strictly by the shade of brick in the neighboring wall. They drove slowly, hunting for numbers until they finally settled on an unmarked drive. Rev rang the bell and the gate swung open. They were expected.

Peter was clearly surprised by Nora's early morning phone call. He had not seen her in years and was curious at her insistence that they meet immediately. As Nora introduced Rev, identifying him as an investigator from Boston, Peter eyed him with open curiosity. They sat in an office off the library, a tray of coffee within arm's reach, on a Chinese butler's cart. Without asking, Peter poured them each a cup of the fragrant streaming brew. Cynthia's own blend.

"It was certainly a surprise to hear from you, Nora. Is this a social call?" Peter asked, ever aware of his schedule and impatient to be off. He looked pointedly at Rev. "If you need my legal services we might just as well have met at my office."

"You may want to sit down, Mr. Maple," Rev said in an official tone. "We have some startling news for you." But Peter remained standing and glared at Rev with sudden distrust.

"I understand that despite your father's age, his death was unexpected. Was there an autopsy?" This was not the question Nora expected Rev to ask, but she realized that just as his line of inquiry had yielded results with Paul and herself, it might do the same with Peter.

"I can't imagine why this should concern you, but I will say that I did insist upon one. I am sorry to say that my father's death was preventable. He died of suffocation."

Nora and Rev caught the note of hesitancy in Peter's voice as he revealed this. "Did that seem odd to you?" Rev asked.

"Actually, yes, it did. My father was partially paralyzed and could not turn on his own, so the thought that he could have suffocated seemed ludicrous to me. My wife and I discussed the final report and decided an investigation was not warranted. My father could not speak as a result of his stroke some years ago. He had brain damage, but there was evidence of a seizure, which explained the manner in which a carelessly left plastic bag, which was draped over the bed rail, could have covered his face. His death was ruled accidental. We are considering a lawsuit against the healthcare agency, but they of course claim the attendant is completely innocent and cannot say where that bag came from."

"Did you have any other thoughts concerning the death?"

Peter sat at his desk and placed his palms on the leather-trimmed blotter. He wondered where the conversation was leading. In the first throes of grief he had confided to Cynthia his suspicion that Anya was somehow responsible. Cynthia had no qualms about telling him he was deranged for suggesting such an absurdity. The emotional side of him had thought immediately of Anya, but logically he knew he sounded somehow paranoid, and yet even now as she came to mind he felt a deep chill of foreboding and was tempted to share his thoughts. It would be a relief to tell someone who might listen and even take him seriously. As he wrestled with the idea of bringing up Anya's name an innate cautiousness prevented him from doing so. Thanks to Cynthia he had come to appreciate just how bizarre that theory would sound to sane ears.

Peter found his gaze seeking Nora. Several times she appeared about to speak as she sat at the edge of a jacquard wing chair. He thought her surprisingly unchanged from the young girl he had summered with in Rockport. She had always been a bit of an enigma to Peter, confident beyond her years with a clean sort of prettiness. Peter recalled with some discomfort his attempts to attract Nora's attention. Other girls liked him and thought him handsome and even entertaining, so why didn't Nora? No matter what he did, he could never breach that impenetrable space she affected between herself and others, and perhaps taking her cue from Paul, she had seemed to regard him behind a veil of ironic humor, completely immune to his adolescent attempts at flirtation.

That was long ago, but even today Peter could recall with some bitterness how he had longed to be included in that exclusive world which his cousin and Nora seemed to inhabit. After the tragedy involving Nora's sister that hedge of protection had only grown thornier. She and Paul closed ranks, growing ever more distant and secretive. It galled him that they hadn't seemed to need anyone but each other and now he wondered how that relationship had changed. He felt an almost perverse satisfaction about her sitting here in his home and finally needing something from him.

The last time Paul and he had been at a social function together was at his wedding to Cynthia, where Paul had agreed to be one of the groomsmen and Nora had accompanied him. They were content to let others assume they were a couple, although by this time Peter knew that Paul was gay, so why didn't Nora take the opportunity at his wedding to meet some of the eligible single men who had been present? Some were excellent prospects, Ivy League graduates with family money and good jobs. Isn't that what every woman wanted? What was wrong with Nora? Even Cynthia had been a little mystified, but while they had seen Paul infrequently though the years, they never again saw Nora, and after Lydia's disappearance there were no more summer visits on Mill Lane.

Peter regarded Nora with interest. Could he still be a little in love with her, even after all this time? He had expected Nora to accompany Paul to his father's funeral and was particularly hurt when neither came. Perhaps they had never realized how important they were to him and that ignorance of his feelings was far more insulting than their absence.

Peter decided to change the subject. He was angry with Paul and Nora and felt a sudden wash of self-pity. He would dispense with Nora and her investigator friend as quickly as possible. Whatever problem had brought them to his door could not possibly be as important as the two appointments he had cancelled just to satisfy a childish curiosity.

"Is Paul in some sort of trouble?" Peter ventured. "Because I am hardly the person to help. Perhaps you are unaware that my cousin and I are not on speaking terms at the moment."

"You were disappointed when he failed to attend your father's funeral," Rev stated dispassionately. "You asked him to be a pallbearer and all you got in answer was a sympathy card some weeks later."

"That's right."

"Are you aware of the reason?"

"I can't imagine any good reason and I no longer care," Peter replied, feigning an indifference that he did not feel. "I asked him to take part in the funeral when others were courting me for that honor, and he never even had the courtesy to respond."

"Paul was sexually abused by your father, Howard Maple."

There was the barest flicker of emotion at Rev's assertion. Then Peter's lawyer persona shifted into gear. Nora could almost see him draw into himself. His body straightened in a formal way and his eyes narrowed. "And you have proof of this?"

"Yes," Rev said simply.

"I mean more proof than my cousin's word, because you do know that he is a homosexual and tends to be hysterical."

Nora bristled at the stereotype and bit her lip rather than give voice to the retort that sprang to mind. Rev had insisted on conducting the interview, and now she understood why.

"To your knowledge, has your father ever been charged with any sort of crime?" Rev asked calmly.

"My father was a paragon of respectability. He and my mother were divorced, but he had an illustrious career as a philanthropist. Over one thousand people attended his funeral, and the condolences are still flooding in from three continents."

"In regard to child pornography and pedophilia there are no economic or educational barriers," Rev replied evenly. "You might make a list of those who sent cards and notes for the authorities. They will certainly be asking." Nora realized that Rev was deliberately provoking Peter, just as he had tried to provoke her and Paul on that first day in her studio.

"I must ask you to leave my home," Peter said, pointing a finger at Nora. "These are serious allegations. You damage the reputation of my family in any way and you'll find yourself in court."

"This is your right, of course," Rev said. Nora stood, ready to leave, but

Rev remained. He leaned back in his chair and crossed one ankle over his knee, looking to all appearances like a man ready to settle down with the Sunday paper and his first cup of morning coffee. "A dead man cannot be prosecuted. There would be nothing to be gained by dragging your family name through the mud, and I'm sure your cousin wouldn't want that either. But crimes have been committed and others are involved."

"Let me escort you to the door! Nora, I am disappointed that you would come to my home under the pretext of needing help, only to attack my family name. I thought we meant more to one another than that."

"But I do need your help, Peter," Nora said, entering the conversation for the first time. "You must remember my sister. My sister Lydia?"

Peter leveled a cold stare at Nora. "I can see where this is going," he said. "Many people, my mother and Aunt Brenda included, have always believed that Lydia wandered back to the beach and drowned. The undertow is unpredictable even with the breakwater off Front Beach. So you see how ludicrous to think that a man of my father's caliber would stoop to kidnaping a child. Get out of my house. If I hear from you again, I'll not hesitate to obtain a restraining order. I'll see you in court, and all you think you own will disappear as you defend yourself against slander and defamation of character and a few other choice charges."

The phone rang. Peter walked back to his desk and shouted a demanding, "Yes?" into the receiver. Nora realized that once again Rev had failed to follow her to the door. She turned back to see him calmly sipping coffee as he studied Peter over the rim of his cup.

Irritated by Rev's scrutiny, Peter tried to calm himself as he listened to the voice on the other end of the phone. "I am sorry," he said. "Would you repeat that?"

"Mr. Maple, this is Rowan Greer, with the construction crew, working on the apartment."

Even in his shock over Rev's allegations, Peter was struck by Rowan's stern tone. Rowan and his hired crew had done extensive work for them over the years on various pieces of property. Cynthia was very fond of him. With the title to the New York apartment now firmly in their possession, Peter had given Cynthia the go-ahead to begin a total refurbishing, and they had hired Rowan to begin the first stage. Cynthia had persuaded Peter to purchase the newly vacated apartment on the floor above and Rowan, following the architect's plans, was now combining the two into one. It would make an impressive second home and Cynthia fully expected *Architectural Digest* to feature the finished result in a future issue.

"I know who you are, Rowan," Peter said impatiently and turned his back

210

against Rev's scrutiny.

"We've knocked out the east bedroom wall and have found something here that you ought to take a look at."

"What are you talking about?" Peter demanded. Nora and Paul looked at one another. "You're there to renovate, not explore in places you are not supposed to be."

"This is the wall your architect asked us to remove. Now if you don't get down here within the hour, we'll be phoning the police. I know you never lived in this apartment and I appreciate what you did for my grandson, so I'm giving you an opportunity to get here first. Am I making myself clear?"

Peter thought back. It was Cynthia's idea to arrange for several private interviews, which would assure the boy was seriously considered by several Ivy League colleges, including their own Alma Mater. Rowan's grandson was accepted at Harvard on his own merit just as he had also been accepted at several lesser universities. Cynthia often performed useless deeds for people, which resulted in big rewards.

Peter's voice dropped to a whisper and Rev and Nora could no longer hear. Finally he replaced the receiver with strained deliberation. He rang for his butler.

"Show these two out," Peter said to Lawrence. "Remember their faces. They are not welcome back, and keep your eye on them until they are actually off the premises."

"No need. We're ready to go," Rev said and took Nora's hand, nearly sprinting to the car.

"What are we doing?" Nora asked.

"Intriguing conversational exchange, don't you think? And that body language. I think we owe it to ourselves to find out where he's off to in such a hurry."

"Peter was uncomfortable and understandably anxious to see us go."

"My guess is that his car will be coming from the direction of the garage in just a moment. So we'll just meander slowly up the drive and catch his tail as he leaves."

Nora agreed that Peter's whole demeanor had changed with that one phone interruption. It had not escaped her attention how he had stared at her, allowing his gaze to linger longer than seemed appropriate. She wondered what he remembered from that fourth of July weekend. Had he stayed in bed all day, as was claimed? Had Howard Maple longed to reconnect with his son and been in Rockport on that day?

Brenda Maple had gone to extreme lengths to keep Paul from the police and it was possible that Peter's mother had done the same. It seemed to Nora that these two women had been more concerned with their positions in society, and what others might say of them, then causing risk to future victims. Nora had known Brenda Maple and believed it entirely possible that she might have kept silent. If she had done so at Lydia's expense, then she and Peters mother were certainly culpable. *How terrible,* Nora thought. *How absolutely criminal.*

"He forgot his briefcase. It's a safe guess that he is not going to the office. I think we can learn something here," Rev said as he turned his car down the long drive.

CHAPTER SEVENTEEN

Early the previous morning God had awakened him to pray. He had grown accustomed to waking suddenly from sleep, fully alert and fully called. After praying for his wife and children he began praying for his patients. For Melody who had a baby due and for Arnie who had emphysema but called it an allergy and refused to quit smoking. And then he thought of Detective Reverdy Porter. Rev had come to talk with him months before about Lydia's disappearance. He had seen Rev recently on the street talking intently with Nora. He prayed for Rev, not exactly knowing why God's shielding power was needed.

"Do you have it?" Dex asked as he and Ryan walked toward baggage claim.

"Yes, but if I may be so bold as to ask, what's the mystery? Why do you need Elliot's schedule for the day? Why not just phone like a normal person and invite him for a drink? Hey, and why are you dressed like this?" Ryan asked fingering the material of Dex's lapel. "I might borrow this while you're here. I have a funeral to attend day after tomorrow. I'll be gone overnight, but I'll leave you my keys."

"There might be a compliment in there somewhere. Who died?"

"No one from skating. AIDS, I think."

"Sorry."

"Yeah," Ryan said off-handedly. "I just heard this morning. Haven't seen him since he got so sick, but I need to be there. Now tell me, what's going on with you?" Ryan insisted, changing the subject. As he spoke he handed Dex the network visitor's pass and schedule he'd asked his assistant to surreptitiously obtain from Elliot's secretary. Absently, Dex pocketed the pass but studied the schedule.

"Looks like Elliot has a planning meeting with the northeastern affiliates," he read out loud.

"That would be in the eighty-second-floor meeting room. Not a gathering to interrupt. Only a medical emergency could free Elliot. If you plan on a confrontation, it's far too public."

"Perfect. I just have time to waltz in uninvited and appropriately late."

213

Dex tossed his suitcase into a waiting cab.

"I have a car. What do you need a cab for?"

"This is all I need," Dex said and held up Elliot's schedule. Suddenly he turned serious. "Actually, Ryan, you might want to distance yourself from me for a while."

Ryan eyed Dexter with ironic interest. "I guess you're telling me gently that you won't be staying at my place while you're in town. And to think I made up a bed and everything."

"That would mean you've cleared a corner of that closet you call an apartment and set up an army cot with a sleeping bag," Dex replied.

For over ten years Ryan had occupied a three-room walk-up on a dead-end street called the Mews. The village apartment did not fit what was expected of a young man on the rise, which a consumer culture associates with worth. The lapse of image irritated those who thought they knew him well enough to offer advice. When pressed, Ryan would reply, "I just had the place fumigated, sprinkled and blessed, so why should I move? I'm good for another year."

After sharing hotel rooms with Ryan, Dex knew the truth. No matter how much money Ryan made, he would never move and never acquire much by way of material possessions. Dex had heard stories of Ryan's bizarre sleeping habits, but not until they roomed together while on the world team did Dex take the rumors seriously. While Ryan often began the night in bed, he never ended there. Dex would wake to find him propped in a chair or most often in the bottom of a closet completely ignorant of how he got there and yet sadly resigned to this odd, seemingly unconscious ritual. It seemed that any enclosed or barricaded corner would do, but Dex also noticed that his friend slept most soundly in busy airports, ice rinks, or any public place where he could catch a few winks. Ryan was a man who could not remember his last night of uninterrupted sleep. They never discussed why.

A worried frown crossed Ryan's brow. "If you need someone at your back, I'm not afraid of a little trouble," he said, and Dex knew he was serious. "Besides," he continued, "I don't recall you distancing yourself from me, and I imagine there was a time when you got a lot of that advice."

"True," Dex smiled grimly. "But unfortunately this is not the same. There might actually be some legal implications that the network won't want you associated with. But I appreciate the offer, my friend."

"Oh, but what if I insist?"

"Thank you. It's just that you attract more attention than I want at the moment, but I'll let you know if that changes."

"At least tell me what's wrong! We've been friends since the day you dropped that gold medal in my bag. I owe you."

"There was something more I should have done for you that day. No matter what you said, I should have gotten you some real help. I should have told someone what I saw." The two men held one another's gaze. Ryan shrugged and Dex smiled grimly.

"Where did that come from?" Ryan asked with some discomfort. "Hey, I don't think about that anymore."

"Even if I believed you I couldn't confide in you just yet. Later," Dex said and closed the door of the cab as it pulled away from the curb.

Dex left his luggage at the front desk of the McAlpin and asked that it be delivered to his room. He then took a cab directly to the network building. One of the photographs that he had held back from the flames left little doubt as to the identity of two of the three men on camera. A blinding rage propelled his limbs, and instinct warned that only catching Elliot completely off guard, before he had time to marshal his defenses, would force him to reveal the truth. There were so many questions he wanted to ask. Among them, did Anya have a family, and if so, why hadn't they protected her?

With the yellow pass pinned to his lapel, Dex signed the visitors' log and followed Ryan's directions to the meeting room. A receptionist looked inquisitively his way and then recognized him. Dex could always tell that moment when people realized they had seen him before. A blank expression suspended their features as they questioned their judgment. Sometimes a little notoriety came in handy.

A long table filled the length of the room, as people milled about obviously taking a mid-morning break. Beverages were being served with small finger breads and fruit. Dex saw Elliot, the center of a group of laughing admirers. Elliot could always command an audience. To these people he was a celebrity as well as a successful businessman. Dex walked directly over.

"Dexter, what a surprise. What are you doing here? Allow me to introduce you," Elliot said cordially, as in a rush he made brief introductions to the group standing about. Dex smiled and handed Elliot the envelope as he shook a few hands.

"What is this?" he asked, too poised to reveal his surprise. "Something that can't wait?" Elliot asked with an indulgent chuckle. His manner conveyed that he would be happy to do a favor for a friend. Carelessly he lifted out the photograph and laid it on top of the envelope. Almost immediately his smile shifted to a horrified grimace as he resisted that first stab of comprehension. Then in one frantic motion he jammed the photo back into its sheath, and to hide his hands shaking, shoved them to his side like a marionette suddenly stiff with fear.

There was something about observing the disintegration of Elliot's famous composure that was immensely satisfying. Conversation receded as those closest to him could not ignore the sight of his trademark tan as his skin color sank to an ill green pallor. For the first time Dex wished he had confided in Anya and brought her along to witness this moment. It was her moment, not his, and he stored away the details in his memory for the time when he could tell her.

Elliot's reaction confirmed what Dex already knew, and now he spoke, his voice devoid of indecision. "We can talk here, or we can take what I have to say some place more private."

Elliot walked from the room with Dex following. "What is this? Some sort of blackmail scheme!" he hissed, his tone accusatory, jumping to a first offensive. "I would have thought this sort of behavior beneath you, Dex."

"Would you have preferred I go directly to the police?"

They stood in the privacy of Elliot's corner office. The view was spectacular, the décor sparse and contemporary with several original Miro a focal point in the otherwise monochromatic color scheme. The door opened and Elliot's assistant poked her head in. "They need you back in conference," she said and looked with annoyance at Dex.

"Tell them to go on without me," he said and nearly slammed the door in her astonished face. As he slid the bolt into place the phone rang. Elliot strode back across the room and picked up the receiver.

"I don't care what you tell them," he said, his tone seething. "What do we pay you for, anyway? Manufacture something believable, but under no circumstances are you to put through another call until I say otherwise."

Elliot replaced the receiver and leveled a stare at Dex. It was a look Dex had seen often through the years of watching Elliot cleverly cut people in their tracks with his smug brand of caustic detachment. The look seemed to say; "I know how this competition will play out. I know which judges like you and which think you're an overrated brat." But Dex's competition days were far behind him and he no longer felt his future could turn at the whim of such misplaced power. It had been a paper-thin disguise all along, only as strong as the fears of those Elliot sought to intimidate and control.

"What do you want?" he asked. "Money? A spot with the network? Name it!"

"I want the identity of the other men in this photograph. I want an explanation of how Anya found herself in these circumstances. I want answers."

"I have nothing to say." Elliot reached for the phone.

"I don't think you want to do that, Elliot. I think you want to get this settled here and now between the two of us. No one wants publicity. No one wants to ruin your reputation or cause my wife any more pain," Dex lied. For a brief moment Elliot looked hopeful. "But if you don't cooperate and tell me what I want to know, I'll phone the police. You and I both know that this one photograph is merely the tip of the rubbish heap."

"What about Anya?"

"Anya wants the truth to come out. She wants to see you all prosecuted," Dex lied. "All that is standing between you and a prison sentence, not to mention complete financial and personal ruin, is my good will. So start talking."

Dex could see the hesitation. Elliot stared at the phone as though struggling to make a decision. Twice he reached out his hand before letting it drop back to his side. Dex wondered who he thought of calling - security, a friend, or one of the men who had abused Anya? In a burst of impatience Dex walked over to the desk. "Here! Allow me to make this easy for you!" Lifting the photograph out of the envelope he slammed it face up before a shaken Elliot. "This is you!" he said pointing. "This is Sasha Eymrnov! Now who is this?"

Elliot looked like a beaten man. His voice had suddenly lost the bravado that so characterized his usual manner. "Sasha Eymrnov was executed soon after Anya defected. You didn't know that, did you? It's not public knowledge. I think his government is still giving out progress reports on the cancer that will soon claim his life. They found out a few things about Sasha. Soon they'll have a mock funeral and the skating world will send flowers. They can get away with that sort of thing in some countries, you know."

Elliot sounded envious. "You may have wondered why Anya had such trouble getting permission to stay in this country and why you had to marry her to smooth it all out," he continued. "Our government knew, of course and hoped Anya could give them more details."

"Knew what?" Dex demanded. He had never been physically aggressive, could never recall having deliberately provoked a fight, but now he found himself clenching and unclenching his fists. His palms itched, and it was all he could do to keep from striking Elliot, but if Elliot recognized the threat there was no evidence in his impervious expression.

"It seems your Anya had access to large sums of money, which Sasha wisely invested out of the country. The government claims it was money embezzled from them, others say profits from a vast pornography ring."

"And what do you say?" Dex prompted.

"I say the latter, and if her former country didn't agree, she'd be dead

217

already. When Sasha returned home without Anya, he had no idea she'd betrayed him. If he had, he would have followed her example and defected himself. Anya left detailed information in certain hands, which effectively sealed Sasha's fate, and if you hadn't rescued her, we would have killed her ourselves. So you see, Anya gambled heavily on your Sir Lancelot mentality and was planning to defect with or without your help."

This made perfect sense to Dex. It explained Anya's need to marry in order to stay on in the country and her long interrogations in Washington soon after defecting, but he saw nothing to indicate she had access to large sums of cash.

"An interesting story, Elliot, but not what I want to know." Dex pointed to the man who had been poised over Anya in each of the photographs. "Who is this?"

"You will be surprised. Perhaps even astonished, but then hero worship would never have been your proclivity. I imagine you only admire yourself."

"Shelve the projection and get on with it," Dex said.

Elliot's tone shifted to a certain fawning eagerness. "You are opening a Pandora's box, my boy. Do you promise to embrace the truth when you hear it? Of course, you know you are sealing my fate just as Anya did Sasha's. I am a dead man even as I utter the words."

Dex rushed over to Elliot and brought a fist within inches of his face. "Stop playing with me, Elliot. As far as I'm concerned you don't deserve to live, and I would be perfectly justified in killing you now."

Elliot's voice came wistful, self-pitying. "I imagine the world would agree with you. Your stay in prison would be minimal, but then there is so much more to know. Just the tip of the rubbish heap, as you so eloquently pointed out."

Once again he reached for the phone, but this time Dex spun around with dance like grace and leveled his foot into a blow at Elliot's arm. Elliot recoiled as Dex grabbed him in a choke hold, the white leather desk chair bending back with the weight of them both. Elliot sputtered and gagged, his arms flailing helplessly. The feel of Dex's fingers as they felt fragile resistance against Elliot's fleshy throat was immensely satisfying, a culmination of primitive imaginings interrupted only as the chair toppled over and the two men fell in a heap on the floor. Dex let go. Elliot was right. If he died now the truth would die with him.

As Elliot staggered to his feet, Dex walked to the bar and poured a shot of whiskey. Amber liquid sloshed over the rim of the glass as he slammed it down before Elliot. "Start talking and this time leave your opinion out of it," he said, fixing Elliot with a menacing stare.

218

Elliot pointed to the photograph. "Howard Maple," he rasped simply.

"Howard?" Dex repeated incredulously.

Elliot studied Dex, seeming to enjoy his astonishment. "You recall the party you attended in January at his son Peter's home? You didn't realize that Ryan was there as well, did you? In fact, we came together, because you see, Ryan and I have a long history. Oh, I can see the question on your face. Why didn't you see us, you want to ask? Let me answer that question for you, Dex. It seems you and Anya were otherwise occupied."

"I can't imagine Ryan agreeing to go anywhere with you."

"It's not easy to persuade a cab to drive that far out on a Saturday night. I had a network limo at my disposal, and, although it's been the bane of my existence, Ryan and I do share the same employer, as you well know. Actually, Dex, you might want to consider that Ryan Campbell is not the person you think he is."

Elliot walked to the mirrored bar. Retrieving an ice cube he rubbed it gingerly across his neck. "You, my boy, were the talk of the party." Elliot stabbed at the air with his glass, leaving a spray of amber droplets over the white carpet. In frantic haste he gulped what was left of his drink and poured another shot.

"Yes," he said, as always enjoying center stage. "It was on everyone's lips. How you and Anya locked yourselves in that closet. Very Hollywood, but not in the least bit original. Howard died that same night."

Dex had personally never known Howard. He'd heard him speak at various events and seen him at many of the major competitions, but they had never indulged in anything more than superficial conversation. Dex knew that Howard had sponsored a number of figure skaters, generously picking up the expenses. He was a major contributor to the Winston Skating Center, where Ryan and he had trained, but in the latter part of his life he kept a low profile while continuing to wield tremendous influence behind the scenes.

Ever since Hillary had handed him that envelope in such benign ignorance, Dex had been preoccupied with one thought of revenge. At the hovering rim of each waking thought had been anticipation of that moment when he could confront the gray form of the man who had raped Anya. Each still of that event had been burned indelibly into his brain. For a split second Dex longed for doubt, but as he looked into Elliot's avid face, he saw that this was just what was hoped for and even expected. A shunning of reality that prompts vacillation and a willingness to ignore the facts. The very doubt and denial upon which evil feeds.

Dex felt deflated and disappointed to think that death had placed Howard permanently beyond his grasp. A frustrated weight of rage fastened like a brick to his chest, and he was overcome by a renewed rush of anger. He thought of Anya and their reunion on the night that Howard died. He saw her in that green dress with her red hair shining and the smell of her perfume and the feel of her arms about his neck. He remembered the snow falling and the delay as he waited for her in the car.

"Was Howard's death an accident?" Dex asked with all the calmness he could muster and hating himself for that dawning suspicion that limped its way into words.

"Of course. He'd had a very bad stroke. Much worse than anyone let on. Cynthia Maple wanted to maintain the illusion that he could still influence the skating establishment. She allowed only a handful of his very best friends to visit, of which I was one," Elliot stated proudly.

In spite of himself Dex felt immense relief. How could he think Anya capable of murder?

"But he was a great man," Elliot lamented. "A gentleman, a true intellectual, and there is no question that the skating establishment is diminished without him."

"Skating never deserved a man like Howard!" Dex nearly spat out the words as he thought of the families of some of the children he coached. Good friends with many, he had always been welcomed in their homes. "Howard Maple was a monster who preyed on defenseless children, and he did not deserve the privilege of expiring comfortably in his own bed."

"I don't molest children," Elliot countered.

"I don't know what else you'd call it. You stood back and watched, didn't you? Even if I believed you, I'd have to say that constitutes the same thing. In fact it's worse, isn't it? Because you could have helped Anya and you didn't."

"I couldn't possibly have helped Anya. I'd be dead myself if I tried, and it was all a horrible mistake. Howard had never been so reckless. He intended to take someone else. Someone he could have returned, and he took her instead. Then he panicked and didn't know what to do with her. She was supposed to be a throwaway. I can tell you we all had some sleepless nights."

"And Anya?"

"She wasn't supposed to live, but then we thought of Sasha. He happened to be in town and he liked girls, and the minute he laid eyes on her he wanted her and promised to keep her for no more than a few hours. But Sasha liked to save things, and you wouldn't know it now, but Anya was like a Dresden doll, and Sasha had this most remarkable collection of memorabilia."

Elliot spoke in a rush, caught up in the web of his own evil mind and perhaps revealing more than he intended. Dex felt sick. He bit his lip, willing himself to keep silent as Elliot stood and walked to the window. He pressed his cheek against the triple pane and then turned his head and stared out at the row of empty flower boxes that lined the walled ledge.

"Howard's mistake was trusting Sasha, but we'd done business with him before without a problem. Only a man with Sasha's monumental ego would risk taking a trophy like that out of the country, and the next thing we knew she had this whole other identity. She was an orphan, and there were plenty of those in his country, so I guess no one took notice of one more. Suddenly she was Sasha's Pygmalion, and he was teaching her to skate. He was rubbing our faces in it. He'd always been an outsider, and now he was forcing his way in and we were helpless to stop him."

"And that worried you?"

"Yes, you idiot, that worried us!" Suddenly Elliot sounded truly angry with Sasha for putting his friends at risk. "When Howard confronted Sasha, he told us that Anya had completely lost her memory. Howard threatened him, but Sasha was holding all the cards and used every one of them. As long as Anya remained alive, Howard was firmly under Sasha's control. Before that no one wanted much to do with him. He was too crass and too opinionated. An undisputable liability, but suddenly he started attending all the important skating events, and he was appointed to international committees and boards so he got to leave his country more often. You could almost say that under duress Howard took Sasha under his wing and people noticed. We got him to modify his behavior, but that Bolshevik was always going to be a loose cannon."

Elliot turned and leveled a stare at Dex. "Didn't you ever wonder why a skater of Anya's talent rarely competed internationally? Sasha had to keep her away from Howard. She was his insurance policy, so if she turned out to be temperamental and a little crazy, well that only served his purpose. Howard would have killed her in a heartbeat, if only one of us could have gotten close enough."

Elliot's eyes burned into Dex's. "There is only one reason, one reason alone, why Anya is alive today, because if Howard had been well, the two of you would never have crossed the Canadian border."

Dex hardly heard. He was stunned. Elliot was telling him that Anya was an American. Vividly he recalled his first conversation with Anya in Sweden, after he'd rescued her from an evening trapped in the rafters of an empty ice rink. Now he knew that leaving her there would have been a kinder fate than insisting she return to Sasha, her abductor and abuser.

"I know Boston," she had said. "I want to go home," she had said. That little girl voice, devoid of the usual accent, rang in Dex's ears. He struggled not to let his emotions show as he pointed to a place off camera. "Someone took these photographs. I want the name of that person!"

An evil grin tore across Elliot's features. Dex had never understood the phrase 'chilled to the bone', but now he understood it perfectly. He felt that he was standing on the precipice of evil and looking its substance and design firmly in the face. Elliot seemed to have no idea of the impact of his words, but Dex was now beyond anger. He was looking into the face of a rabid dog, and he appreciated how one could rationalize murder. He felt he would be doing the world a favor if he killed Elliot rather than allow the legal system to deal with him. This was no longer just about Anya. There had to be other children whose treatment demanded retribution, and it didn't matter that he didn't know their names. The burden of that knowledge, no longer an abstract to briefly remonstrate over, would galvanize him into future action and change his life forever.

What rankled most about Elliot's delivery was his apparent lack of awareness of how his words sounded to civilized ears. If Elliot had begun life with a conscience, it was now totally obliterated. Dex thought of Howard, Sasha, and now Elliot. It seemed that depravity ran in packs, just like dogs, but who was the fourth dog? He had to know.

Despite his apparent poise Dex noticed that Elliot's eyes were shadowed by anxiety, and his hands had never lost the tremor that had arrived with a first glance of that photograph. His fading blonde hair was streaked with gray, and his Nordic blue eyes regarded Dex warily. There was no evidence of remorse. Elliot was only sorry to be found out.

Elliot spoke. His words were resigned, as though he suddenly realized he could not persuade Dex to another course of action. "There's nothing more dangerous than an honorable man and you have always been so predictably ethical. It's boring, Dex. You are boring. Wouldn't you rather give people a little mystery to guess about?"

"Not your kind of mystery."

"It is with great sadness that I must say, I'm glad people like you don't dominate the human race, because if you did no one would have any rights at all. You're probably one of those born again Christians who champion non-profits that have religious agendas. You probably want internet access restricted in libraries and so called pornography to be fully prosecuted. I hate people like you. People like you are dangerous."

Dex could hardly speak. If the evil he saw in Elliot was real, there had to be a God to overcome it. Otherwise there would be no goodness, nothing to live for, and no purpose or dignity to his existence. He hadn't intended to pray, but words flashed to his mind, rising from some deep place of need within himself. *God, please help me. Please let me know you. Please rescue children like Anya from men like Elliot.* He had questions, but those questions about God and destiny and the eternal fabric of life would have to be grappled with at a later time. Elliot continued.

"As we've been chatting I've been racking my brain, wondering. What can I offer Dex in exchange for silence? The answer seems painfully obvious? I can offer you nothing. Is this not correct?"

Dex nodded his head.

"Well, then. Where do we go from here? Are you going to destroy Anya? Or will you allow her to go on and enjoy the success and acclaim she's won for herself because you know the press will have a field day with this when it gets out."

"You make it sound like Anya has something to be ashamed of. Make no mistake, Elliot. I'll not keep silent to accommodate you. Somewhere out there Anya has a family and a past. I'll help her reclaim it. I'll blow the whistle so loud your ears will explode." Dex stepped threateningly into Elliot's orbit. "I won't ask you again! Who took this photograph?"

"I dread to tell you," Elliot said and backed away. "Especially because it seems I shall gain nothing for my cooperation." He smiled again, a fevered approximation of joy. "Except perhaps to hurt you, dear Dex. Pour me another scotch, will you. Straight up and neat. Then I'll do what I must."

Dex walked to the bar. He lifted the crystal decanter and heard the sound of glass sliding against metal. A March wind, an incongruous whiff of thawing ground that promised budding trees and grass easing into green, even in mid-town Manhattan raced like a freight train through the room. Why had he not registered the empty pots enclosing a wide ledge into a patio?

Before the crystal had shattered against the marble rim of the bar Dex had sprinted halfway across the room, but all he managed to grab hold of was the fabric of Elliot's sleeve as it slid like a paper burn across his palm.

CHAPTER EIGHTEEN

Connor could not explain his day. For the first time in memory there were no babies due, and although he was on call to a small drop-in clinic convenient for working fishermen, the usual suturing was not needed. Several appointments canceled and the rest went smoothly. He even had time to stop in at the local Methodist Church, where communion was offered on Wednesdays. He wasn't Methodist, but they didn't seem to care. He liked the pastor, who was part of the grassroots confessing movement that sprang up in an effort to return Methodism back to their Wesleyan roots, and the two often prayed together. Once there he felt so very strongly that he needed a prayer partner. He looked up from the pew where he knelt, to see his friend's smiling face.

Rev had difficulty keeping up with Peter's black BMW. He drove wildly, dodging traffic and twice occupying the right shoulder. Just before the bridge Peter was stopped for speeding. Rev pulled ahead waiting for him to pass, but Peter gave no indication that he noticed them following.

Once in the city Peter's car disappeared into an underground garage while Nora and Rev were left to hunt for the impossible in New York - a parking space. "I'll pull over and let you drive. After you've parked you can join me inside," Rev told Nora.

"How will you get in? This is a secured building," Nora said, noting the elite address.

Rev flashed his shield. "I'll let them know that my assistant will be following."

Nora grabbed the badge as Rev double-parked. "No," she said, "I'll let them know my assistant will be following." Impulsively she leaned over and kissed his cheek. She felt suddenly buoyant and hopeful. It seemed an odd little burst of emotion that could not last. "Don't even think of trying to talk me out of this," she said when she saw his face cloud over. He would have but it was too late. She was already gone.

All eyes were on Peter as he walked into the apartment. Half a dozen men stood about in work coveralls, and a film of dust particles floated in the air. Although it was early, most were in the process of packing up their equipment for a quick departure. Peter noticed that none of the men would hold his gaze, but quickly found some useless object to consume their attention.

"What's going on, Rowan?" Peter asked.

"This way, Mr. Maple." Peter followed the large-boned, middle-aged grandfather into what had once been two bedrooms. The area was now gutted with partial walls removed and only a supporting beam left in place. Rowan pointed to a four-foot depression in the floor. Peter allowed his gaze to follow the depression toward the remaining wall, where stacks of what looked like canisters of old reel to reel movies and the newer variety of video tapes were wedged into shelving from floor to ceiling. Color-coded files and rows of folders clearly labeled with a series of numbers ran along the depression in the floor and were meticulously arranged to fit precisely the depth. Rowan picked up a folder and handed it to Peter.

"These numbers correspond to others on some of these old reels and tapes," he said. "This operation has been going on a long time. It was your father who used to live here, wasn't it? That's what your Missus told me."

"Oh my God," Peter cried out audibly, his words an anguished plea of shock. As he leafed through the photographs, he felt contaminated and defiled by the little that he looked at. It was horrifying to think that there was more, and yet there was. Even he felt overwhelmed as he considered the impossibility of imposing much damage control. He took a deep breath. He had to try.

"Have the police been called?" Peter asked.

"Not yet," Rowan responded. "Looks like invoices over there," he pointed. "Had a profitable little business going on. Something to see him through retirement," Rowan's tone was contemptuous.

Peter took a deep breath and steeled himself to speak. "Stop those men from leaving. We can destroy all this within the hour. I'll do anything. Give them money." Peter's legendary composure was disintegrating. He removed his jacket and rolled up his shirtsleeves as though to begin the work of destroying evidence immediately.

"Your troubles are just beginning," Rowan replied sympathetically. "After we found all this," Rowan waved his arm to encompass the room, "some of the men went looking for more. I told them to wait for the authorities, but I'm afraid it was already too late. Come this way."

The cold chill of disaster pricked at the hairs of Peter's neck, and his palms felt hot with a sudden blood surge of apprehension. With great reluctance he followed Rowan deeper into the apartment. Rowan pointed to a wall and spoke with the professional tone of any contractor explaining why some whim of thoughtless design could not be carried out.

"Looks like nothing, doesn't it? But this...." He pounded his fist against an outcropping in the wall and a hollow sound reverberated. "This is not on the architect's plans and doesn't lay flush on the other side. Here," he said, leading Peter by the arm. He pushed at a panel that swung open. The room was small and lifeless. A cot lay on the floor and old Disney posters lined the wall. For a long moment Peter refused to see anything unusual. *So what*, his mind soothed. *So what*, until his gaze took in the miniature leather restraints lined with lamb's wool. As though in a dream Peter bent to pick one up. It was small and slender with openings, as though for belt loops, and at the center a large ugly buckle. With false composure Peter noted the inventory of characteristics until suddenly, as though burned, he threw the restraint from him. The inside cuff was stained brown, the color seen in police evidence rooms; shades of old blood.

"It seems to me you've got no choice, son. You've got to phone the authorities. It will look better for your family if you do it yourself."

Peter turned to see Rowan's crew standing in the hallway opening. He realized that even though they had prepared to depart they were drawn to this macabre drama like moths to a flame. They observed his reactions with cautious wariness, clearly wondering if he were somehow involved. Peter knew that this kind of crime had a way of clinging to and contaminating anyone associated, no matter how innocent. When he spoke, Peter was stunned at the calm, concise quality of his voice. He was back in law school, role-playing one of the criminal cases he'd decided was not his sort of law. Gearing up for arguments, confident that he would prevail, he was, for the moment, only interested in the quickest course to resolution. "None of you are rich men. How does half a million dollars sound, divided equally between the seven of you?"

"Most of us have children. You think we could sleep nights knowing a place like this exists and we haven't told anyone?"someone said, and the others nodded and murmured in agreement.

"My father is dead. He can't hurt anyone else. As you can see, I had no idea."

"How do we know that?" "Maybe not," came duel responses and then a concurring murmur.

"Do you think I'd turn this place over to seven strangers to tear apart if I even suspected the truth? Not to mention the architect and my wife's decorator and her team of assistants."

"I don't know," someone wavered, and for a second Peter let himself think he was winning the room.

"How does seven hundred thousand sound? That's a cool hundred grand for each of you, and all you have to do is walk away. Don't any of you have mortgages or children you'd like to put through college?"

"What about all the people he corresponded with? All the people he sold this wickedness to?" one man asked. "From what Rowan claims, your father had no time to cover his tracks. Somewhere around here there must be a mailing list that ought to provide the authorities with lots of work."

"On the day my father had his stroke, all this died with him," Peter tried to reason.

"I know you're scared, Mr. Maple," Rowan said. "But taking a bribe is not my style. Now I tried to do you a favor, but I can see this has all been too much of a shock. One of us will be calling the police in the next couple of seconds. Who will it be? You or me?"

"No, wait," Peter said, grabbing Rowan's arm, now desperate. "We can work something out. I am a rich man. I'll just come up with more money, and all you have to do is walk away."

"I'm afraid there will be no more of that." They all turned at the sound of a woman's voice. "You can't protect your father's reputation, Peter. Or anyone else involved for that matter. Rev will be here in a moment and he'll call the police."

Those blocking the door moved aside as Nora stepped up to the threshold. Peter was struck by how small she was, and yet there was a certain noble polish to her demeanor that commanded attention. He couldn't help thinking that she would make a good witness. A jury would believe her. It was a good thing for his family that his father was dead.

Tears glistened in Nora's eyes as she spoke. "My sister may have been imprisoned in this room. That could be her blood on those restraints," she said and stooped to pick up the cuff that Peter had earlier thrown down in horror and disgust. She turned it over, almost lovingly in her palm. Unlike Peter she seemed loath to relinquish this thread to what could possibly be Lydia's fate.

Taking in the scene at a glance, Rev came up behind Nora and gently took the cuff from her. Ever the professional, she noticed that he had put on gloves and wondered where they came from.

"This is a crime scene," he pronounced. "I'll have to ask you all to move into the next room and wait there without touching anything until the New York Police arrive. "You," he pointed sternly to one of the workers getting ready to depart, "will be going nowhere."

Peter slumped to a nearby chair.

"Don't you think I have a right to know what happened to my sister, Peter?"

At the steadiness of Nora's gaze, Peter flinched. Abruptly the reality of his father had rudely shattered all those carefully constructed fantasies which he had fabricated to form the illusion of the complete family that had never been his. He had been a fool for indulging such sentiment and wondered what Cynthia would say. He would call her. Her instincts were so very attuned to furthering their causes. She always knew the correct posture and position, the right spin to diffuse a difficult situation.

Peter looked into Nora's face and attempted to conjure up an image of Lydia Fothergill, but it was difficult, for she was now just a vague memory of a child with red hair, who continuously complained and whined as, much like him, she chased after Nora and Paul.

Peter recalled that he had been sick in bed the weekend that Lydia disappeared. His last glimpse of the trio had occurred as he looked out the guest bedroom window. Lydia complained of carrying the beach ball instead of the picnic basket and Nora's calm reasoning voice explained that she, as the eldest, would carry that basket. Paul had finally settled the dispute and appeased Lydia by taking it himself. Peter watched enviously as they stepped onto the rock slab at the side of the gate, too old to open without difficulty, and jumped into the cemetery for the usual short cut to Front Beach.

Arms laden with bright beach paraphernalia, they disappeared down the hillside, amidst the granite headstones and burnt grass of summer. Despite his illness Peter lingered at the window until the last of their voices, suspended on the hot sea air, could no longer be heard.

There was no escaping the truth in Rev's allegations. It would remain to be proven if his father had anything at all to do with Lydia's disappearance, but that Howard was guilty of unspeakable and shocking acts could not possibly be in dispute. Peter felt a profound sadness displace his initial panic. In a desperate attempt to recapture and rewrite the past, he had loved a helpless stranger and called him father. He had invested him with all sorts of attributes and sentiment that had been nothing more substantial than a mirage off in the shimmering distance of a vast wasteland.

Was there any father who ever lived up to the expectations of their children? There was Father God. When people prayed they sometimes said those two words, "Father God," and how odd that he should think of that now. Peter almost felt that on some deep soul level he was being invited to pray. Feeling foolish, he resisted. He needed to get control or the events of this day would destroy every wonderful achievement he and Cynthia had built. He thought of church and the minister he hardly knew. He and Cynthia went to church to be seen and to establish useful acquaintance, but.... he'd think of all that later. Right now he wanted to withdraw someplace safe and discuss with Cynthia a course of action. And ... he felt helpless and so profoundly disappointed. He wanted to cry. Peter stood and realized he was dizzy. He staggered slightly and Rowan caught his arm.

"Forgive me, Rowan, for so foolishly trying to compromise your ethics. Now if you will excuse me I have some phone calls to make." The others stepped aside as Peter exited the room.

Dex walked through the old world charm of the McAlpin's lobby. He had come here as a boy for his first Eastern competition. The staff had known his mother and still called him by his first name, but recently the building itself had been sold. Beyond the height of its former popularity, the hotel was clearly outdated, like a resurrected bottle of wine from a lost crate in the cellar, and this was part of its ambiance, but for once Dex's concentration lay elsewhere. He failed to register the gilt and marble, the fresh flowers or the unwavering courtesy of the staff. He did not reflect on the gas light fittings, which remained still operational in the hotel restaurant that his mother had so appreciated, or the fact that he was never to return here again.

Upon entering his hotel room Dex filled the massive marble tub with steaming water. He felt drained and exhausted. Fragments of Elliot's conversation, the scope and horror of his revelations, replayed in his mind as he shed his clothes and settled himself into the bath. Dex felt somehow contaminated by Elliot. He had looked over the white blocks of the terrace and seen Elliot spread-eagled on the pavement below, and he had not been sorry. From far up Elliot could be sunbathing or resting, and there was no hint of the twisted broken body splayed on the pavement below with bystanders helplessly gathering.

It was no casual impulse that compelled Dex to lie to the first two officers at the scene. He described the locked door, the exchange with the secretary, and Elliot's obvious discomfort as they left the meeting room. Any temptation to explain the truth was only fleeting. He had to think of Anya. Claiming to have no idea why Elliot would suddenly decide to kill himself, Dex remained vague but acutely aware of how conspicuous his omissions sounded to reasonable ears. There was no note, no reason any of his co-workers could give to explain Elliot's shocking plummet from the balcony ledge of the network building. Judging by the shock and grief on the faces of Elliot's co-workers as they suspiciously looked in his direction, Dex surmised that even though the police had not named him a suspect, they certainly did.

After two detectives arrived, the polite inquiries took a more assertive bent. After interviewing those in the boardroom and Elliot's secretary, Dex was asked if he would voluntarily supply his fingerprints. Outside on the street it had begun to rain, a straight invisible drizzle, which lent a purple cast to the drifting winter skyline.

"We'd like you to take a lie detector test. Maybe this evening," the younger of the two detectives told him and then wrote down the name of the hotel where Dex was staying.

But Dex was evasive. He certainly had wanted to kill Elliot and could not be sorry that he was dead. He wondered what it would be like to answer a barrage of questions about Elliot's last hour, as an impersonal machine interpreted data on his pulse and respirations. He could not risk a lie detector test. He had too much to hide.

"I'll let you know after I've consulted my attorney," he said, trying not to sound as nervous as he felt.

Although he could not hear the conversation, he knew a debate was raging as to whether they should bring him back to the station for a more formal interview. This might be postponed but would certainly happen. Perhaps his mention of an attorney made them realize they would not get anything more from him, and they had the fingerprints to compare. Dex tried to remember how much of the ledge he had actually touched as he tried to stop Elliot.

Getting up from his place in the outside hallway he walked to the reception area off Elliot's office. Through the open door he watched as a lab worker dusted for fingerprints around the window ledge and balcony door. Dex had the impression of events careening out of control while he futilely struggled to keep pace. He decided to leave, noting that everyone else interviewed by the police, including Elliot's secretary, had been told they could go. It was time to test the waters. Either those two detectives would stop him and haul him down to the police station or they would not. He walked toward the elevator.

"We wouldn't want you to leave the city without letting us know," one of the detectives reminded Dex before the elevator door closed off his face.

As he sank deeper into the warm water and felt his muscles ease, he switched channels, catching bits and pieces of the evening news. The local networks reported Elliot's death as an apparent accident. No mention was made of the police investigation and no other explanation was given, but Dex knew that could not last. He was only thankful that for now he could postpone calling Anya. He did a mental calculation of where she was right now. Her round of interviews completed, she would be flying from Atlanta to Kansas City to join Glen Winston's tour. He expected her to call soon after checking into her hotel room.

Dex closed his eyes and leaned his head against the padded neck-rest of the ivory bath and allowed his concentration to drift. He was nearly asleep when the ring of the phone jarred him back to the present. Sandalwood bath oil dripped from his arm as he reached for the receiver.

"What room are you in?" Ryan demanded, his shrill tone jarring Dex back to the present. "I'm coming up."

Dex recited the room number, wrapped a towel around his waist, and went to unbolt the door, leaving it ajar. He was just belting the hotel robe when Ryan burst into the room.

"It's time to stop holding back, Dex. I just drove by Howard Maple's old place and at least six police cars are out front, and then I get paged that Elliot has jumped to his death with you in the same room and the door locked. Did you push him?" Ryan demanded. "I hear you pushed him. Did you?" Ryan leveled an indecipherable stare at Dex. "Because if you did, I can't actually say that I feel anything but jubilation. We'll just have to hire the best defense attorney in the city, that's all."

It surprised Dex that Ryan was so clearly relieved that Elliot was dead. There was no grief and no remorse for all the harsh words during their long rivalry and sometimes-public feud. Dex regarded Ryan with interest. His pupils were dilated while his body exuded an intense energy. Could he have had some sort of relapse and be back on drugs? Dex hoped not, but knew it was entirely possible.

"Do you want dinner? I'm actually starving," Dex picked up the phone and dialed room service. "Lamb okay? It's excellent here." Ryan's impatience was evident as Dex calmly ordered lamb with new potatoes, green beans, and sorbet.

"I've wanted to kill him a thousand times over. So just tell me if you killed him, because if you have to know, I can't imagine Elliot sorry enough about anything to actually take his own life. So just tell me," Ryan demanded, clearly desperate the instant that Dex replaced the phone.

"It seems to me your dislike of Elliot goes beyond a simple personality conflict. This is all somehow connected, and for Anya's sake I need you to tell me the full story."

In answer Ryan gave him a wooden stare.

"Don't you trust me, Ryan?" Dex prodded and pulled a pair of wrinkled cargo pants from his suitcase. Pulling them on, he ran his hands through his damp hair, trying to think clearly. His question hung in the air like lead. He turned to look at Ryan, surprised that there was no response. He knew that his

231

friend had much to contribute if he could just be persuaded to talk openly, but that was something Ryan had always resisted.

A sudden stillness enveloped Ryan and he averted his face. "I think you know. I think if you've spoken with Elliot and as a result he actually killed himself, well then. You could probably enlighten me about a few things."

"Humor me."

Ryan sat at the foot of the bed. He turned his hands over and studied the lines in his palms as though deliberating and then coming to a wrenching decision. "My parents were rich, but Howard Maple paid for my skating. My father got into some sort of trouble representing a criminal type who was connected in some way. I don't really know the details, but pornography and maybe drugs were involved. Dangerous characters anyway. If not for Howard, my parents would have lost everything. Howard stepped in. He helped my father by somehow getting these people off his back. I don't think my parents meant to lose me in the process. At least, that's what I like to think, but the truth is they never went against anything that Howard, and later Glen wanted to do. Those two ran my life and my career, and when I was too young to fight back or even understand how it started, I was spending a lot of time with Elliot and then it was Howard. They molested me."

"What about Glen?"

"I don't know about Glen. He physically abused me, but he didn't molest me. He seemed to know my breaking point. Sometimes he even found excuses to keep Howard away, because he was nothing, if not ambitious." Ryan's tone had shifted. He spoke in a flat, mechanical manner, almost as if reciting. "Their manipulation of me in order to insure my silence grew more sophisticated as I became older. Howard had pictures that chronicled my life. Not the sort you'd put in silver frames on the grand piano, you understand. Just the thought that those photos would surface if I told, was pretty effective blackmail until I decided I'd rather die than go on. That's when I realized I could turn the tables on them. They actually had far more to lose than I."

"Why didn't you tell anyone?"

Ryan's expression shifted to one of withering contempt, and Dex wished he could retrieve the question. "There is always some fool who must ask! Why did you marry that person? Why were you walking by yourself at night? Why did you dress the way you did, why not run or scream? Why not leave Ireland when food became scarce or escape Germany when friends began to disappear? As if every outcome can be foretold, and that one minor mistake of judgment that sets you on the road to destruction justifies the consequences. If it's my fault, then you can delude yourself into thinking that evil could never touch you or someone you love. Well, Dex, it has touched

232

you. I suspect it has rammed into you like a runaway train. And you did nothing to invite it, did you, Dex? But you sure as hell spent some time denying and doubting your instincts. Everyone does."

"I'm not asking about everyone. I'm asking about you."

"I don't think of myself as a victim. I hate that word."

"Ryan," Dex pleaded in desperation. "Just tell me."

"Every child tells or tries to tell, or leaves clues that no one wants to see. Don't you believe that? Isn't that the core message on every daytime talk show?"

"I'm sorry, I–"

"Once I told a visiting coach who didn't want to get involved. I think rumors must always surround those who abuse children. Too controlling or verbally abusive or stepping over some line, but no one ever thinks to investigate. I told my parents. I even had the audacity to call the police, but I was eleven and they thought Glen had just hit me a little too hard. They told me to behave. Somewhere a police report exists, but I figured that if no one would hold the great Glen Winston accountable for his behavior, how much more they would disbelieve anything I had to say about Howard. And for a long time I really believed that I was somehow protecting my parents and that they couldn't know what I was suffering. Hell, you know with skating it's a fine line because a certain level of training is already abuse if you don't really love it and some parent and coach aren't forcing you along."

"What about Howard?"

"Howard is on another level entirely. He had this whole persona in the skating community that would have challenged everyone's judgment and effectively shielded him. I was an easy kid to label 'out of control' because I was out of control. Glen cultivated the notion that he was doing me a favor, and everyone believed that without him I was nothing. Just a bad boy, gone bad again. I decided the best revenge was to do well."

Ryan continued, speaking more slowly now. "I had rich, negligent parents and some people like to denigrate that stereotype before they look at the facts. People believed Glen was the only positive influence in my life. I would have killed myself if I hadn't wanted to keep skating, and finally Howard left me alone. Not because of my success, but because I got too old for him. A kid like me, if he can just learn to survive and live long enough without permanently losing physical and mental health–" His voice trailed until he was silent. The moment lengthened, and then he came to himself and his body trembled. "It's a long shot. Not many make it," he added, as though he was speaking of someone else.

Dex had a thought. "That funeral you're going to. Is that another of

Howard's victims?"

Ryan laughed. His tone was derisive and bitter. "We're a secret society of sorts. We often recognize a fellow member by the invisible scars of brother and sisterhood. You can hide from the world forever, but not from a member of the club."

"You escaped by deciding to do pairs," Dex prompted. Ryan had stopped talking. The silence between them stretched into minutes as almost hypnotically he stared at a fixed point across the room. Dex followed his gaze and saw that he looked at nothing. He had retreated and was gazing inward through a portal to which Dex was denied access. Under normal circumstances Dex would have waited and gently tried to coax Ryan, but there was no time.

"That's when you left Glen and decided to do pairs," Dex repeated.

At the sound of his voice Ryan actually shook himself. His wide shoulders straightened and then he shivered. The haunted expression on his face frightened Dex.

Ryan nodded. "I deliberately chose an obscure rink and a coach no one had ever taken seriously. Then I absconded with a little insurance. Although I was a minor I hired myself an attorney and threatened to emancipate myself. I was sick of their world and wanted nothing more to do with it, and since I was no more use to them. Of course I left certain evidence with a conservative attorney. He wanted to go to the police, but I wouldn't let him. I let him know that if he did they'd kill me. That man was the first adult who believed me and then tried to protect me. Pretty soon it was a stand-off with five-six shooters pointed at the two of us from across an invisible corral."

"And the evidence?" Dex had to ask.

"It's still there with instructions to open it if I should die prematurely. Not very original, as Elliot pointed out at the time, but still effective." For a moment he looked pensive, almost worried. "If the police are clearing out Howard Maple's old apartment, they won't need the little that I can offer."

"I'm surprised they didn't kill you."

Ryan leveled an ironic look at Dex. "They did. Do you wonder why I live alone? Why I've never had a significant relationship with a woman? It's because I can't get close to anyone. On some level I just don't feel. I'm a shell. They did that to me. It's part of the insurance they count on."

Dex was disturbed. He put his hand on Ryan's shoulder and squeezed. "You and I are close," he asserted, wanting more than anything to deny the significance of Ryan's words. Anya could just as easily have parroted that same sentiment. She could be just as damaged, a hollow shell of a person walking through a life denied, but Dex refused to believe this was true of either of them.

"Maybe we are close," Ryan was noncommittal. "I can't explain that, except to remind you that we safely live on opposite coasts and see one another in small controlled doses. If you hadn't met and married Anya, you would not have stumbled on the truth, and I sure as hell wouldn't have volunteered. We've never exchanged any deep, soul searching secrets or confidences."

"You can't believe that. You know everything about me worth knowing. You've told me about yourself. Not everything, but enough for me to guess that it was worse than I could imagine. I hope you know that you can trust me, Ryan … and what do you call the conversation we're having right now. Idle chitchat?"

"Sorry, Dex, but I call this damage control."

"I am your friend. You've been my friend. It's a relationship we've sustained over time. That should count for something," Dex insisted, needing more than ever to stem his growing uneasiness.

There was no evidence that Ryan heard him. He went on speaking. "It's not true that all can be forgiven, forgotten and healed. Not in this lifetime anyway and how can you forgive people who will never make any kind of apology and believe that their addictions are normal? I decided a long time ago that I wouldn't go there. In the end you just have to learn to live with the consequence of memories or lack of them, and convince yourself that change is possible. Certain experiences separate me. I'll never be completely free. That's why they didn't kill me. They count on a slow annihilation of all the traits that make us human. It's a force to overcome, every day. At a young age you are introduced to blatant evil, wearing a human face and walking about in a human shell. It threatens to kill you or suck you in and you believe that these are the only choices. I fought a battle to hold on to my identity as a man. I decided I'd rather die than be like them."

"Who exactly is 'them'? I mean … I know about Elliot and about Howard, but there is another person involved?"

Ryan gave Dex a hard stare. "I was speaking in a metaphysical sense. I mean evil. The evil one. If there is a God, then there is a Satan, and this is his work."

Dex was startled by Ryan's words. He looked intently at his friend. "I was thinking along the same lines as I confronted Elliot. It was chilling to see him without that mask of sheer normalcy. I thought you didn't believe in God?"

"Oh, but Dex, I do believe in God. I've longed to be clean. That lawyer I told you about. He told me I could be washed clean in the blood of Jesus. If I would just confess my sins, God would forgive me. More than once I've just about made up my mind to give that a try. I just feel dirty. I can't imagine a righteous God wanting anything to do with me, and then there is the question of authority. I'm not sure I can give authority over to anyone else ever again. Even God."

"What are we going to do?"

"I don't know."

"Speaking of authority, I guess we'll have to call the police eventually and tell them everything we know."

"I can't do that."

"They'll understand. You couldn't help yourself. You were a child."

Ryan shook his head vehemently. "I'd rather follow Elliot out that window than open my past to all that scrutiny."

"We need to help the authorities. Silence isn't a luxury we can afford, Ryan. There's been enough of that already."

"If you thought the police could help Anya, you'd be there right now, spilling your guts, telling them everything you ever imagined. You had a perfect opportunity this afternoon and you let them run with that bogus theory that you might have actually murdered Elliot. So don't hypocritically talk about the authorities and lay the responsibility on me."

"I need your help, Ryan."

"You didn't go to Elliot without proof. I know that." Ryan leveled a hard stare at Dex. "I've made a life for myself. I talk the language and make the right moves and it's all just a carefully choreographed parody and I an imposter miming my way through. But I make a pretty good salary for all the pretending, and it's my life. The only way I know how to live. I won't give it up for you, and certainly not for Anya."

"There were photographs of Anya. There are photos of you. We can't predict where or how they'll turn up. But after the day I've had, I can guarantee the police will be looking very carefully at Elliott."

"If it comes to that, I'll deny they are of me, and I'll keep on denying until no one cares. Everything grows old, and besides, Anya has already seen to Sasha and Howard, and you, thank God, have taken care of Elliot."

The cold simplicity of Ryan's assertion slammed into Dex's consciousness. He could accept that Anya had arranged for Sasha's downfall. He wouldn't have hesitated to do the same, but that she had actually killed Howard? That was murder!

Dex thought of the evening that Howard had died. For a moment he was back in that car outside Peter Maple's house. He saw the snow as it fell, obliterating the lacy pattern of frost on the window, and he heard the drone of the engine as it paced the rhythm of his waiting. All he could think of was the tender reunion that lay ahead of him and Anya. Soon after they would marry, and all that was lost, all that was so abruptly interrupted, would be restored. Just thinking of that second chance for a life with her had made him happy. He could feel Ryan scrutinizing his expression.

"There were three men in the photographs that I saw," Dex stated, forcing his concentration back to the present. "I figured I was being set up to be blackmailed, and I couldn't wait around for something to happen. I had to learn as much as I could. Those three were Sasha, Elliot, and Howard. All are dead. So now I have to wonder who took those photographs. I expect I'll hear from him soon enough."

"Anya will get around to him soon enough."

"Do you know who it is?"

Ryan lifted his face up to the ceiling. He shrugged his shoulders and then brought his gaze back, as though seeking the eye contact that was lost. "No." Ryan shook his head slowly.

There was a knock at the door and the tray of food was wheeled in. Suddenly Dex was no longer hungry, but Ryan was. He poured himself a drink and cut into the lamb with relish. Dex watched as he spooned out a generous helping of the mint and ginger chutney that the hotel restaurant was famous for.

Dex felt a cold sweat break over his brow. Time seemed to pause at the threshold of realization, like horses at the gate before a race. He gathered the courage to ask. "Are you saying that Anya killed Howard?"

Without responding, Ryan laid aside his fork. His chair toppled over as he made a mad dash for the lavatory. Dex listened to the sound of Ryan's retching and felt a numb quiet steal through his body. When Ryan emerged he was pale, his face drawn and almost empty in a stunned sort of way. He paced back and forth across the room.

"Are you deaf? To what extremes are you going to take this denial thing?" he suddenly erupted, his voice dripping ridicule. "Of course that's what I'm saying. Anya killed Sasha, she killed Howard, and you saved her the trouble of taking Elliot out of the picture. She might not thank you for that."

Turning his back on Dex, Ryan walked to the window seat. He drew up his legs and sat looking out at the city lights and the street below. Not since those brief tears of rage, which marred Ryan's performance makeup on that long ago night at the nationals, had Dex seen Ryan cry, and he was not crying now. Instead he seemed beyond tears, fiercely determined to avoid any further display of emotion.

Far below traffic melded in a blurred river of brilliance as miniature stick figures moved about. From here the world looked manageable, and one could almost imagine a God-like invincibility that would never be the province of man. Dex thought of all that Ryan had accomplished in the intervening years. Overcoming great odds, he had survived a childhood, the ramifications of which he could only guess at. Dex had always been loved and protected by his mother. During the worst of the conflicts with Thierry, he knew his father cared, and he had skated, not to escape or survive as Anya and Ryan had, but because at some point skating had become his choice and he had loved it.

As he thought of Ryan, a picture of Elliot's face flashed to mind. Ryan was not like Elliot, and yet the hint of a new wariness rose in Dex and he was loath to make a comparison that reason mocked was absurd. At the end, finally unable to hide the truth, Elliot had defended himself by speaking a foreign language in which an entire range of emotions like empathy and culpability had been replaced by qualities one could not humanly relate to. Elliot's only true lament had been that Sasha had not murdered Howard's throwaway child as he had promised, and now Anya had reemerged to become a monumental inconvenience and threat to him; to Elliot. There was no comprehension of the pain and havoc that had been reaped in Anya's life. Ryan was right about evil. Evil was bent on the destruction of those qualities that make humanness possible. It was a miracle that he and Anya had survived at all.

Dex looked at Ryan and it seemed to him that his friend had never appeared so isolated. Always there had been this tough, no-nonsense shell and the sarcastic barbs and humor to ward off any real conversation and too often he had let Ryan get away with that. A real friend would not have been afraid to demand more.

Dex sat behind him on the narrow window seat and joined his arms about Ryan's chest. Ryan pulled away, but Dex drew him firmly back. As he felt Ryan's body stiffen, he felt drawn into a great sadness, like the blending of watercolors on a wet page. Against the inevitable melding of spirit Dex held on tight, refusing to let go. Ryan's heart was pounding dangerously fast against his palm as unsung sobs strained against the boundary of flesh. By degrees his muscles eased and his breathing returned to normal. In a rare abdication of all those dearly-won defenses, Ryan let his head drop back against Dex's shoulder. Minutes passed and Dex knew he held a child and not a man. He would not be the first to let go.

"Life has a way of making us all a little crazy," Ryan finally spoke, his tone detached and suddenly restored. "Will you go to that funeral with me?" Ryan sat up and twisted on the window seat. They looked into one another's eyes.

"Why?" Dex was surprised.

"Trust me. If you want to know the full story, you should go to that funeral with me."

"Where is it?"

"Rockport, Mass."

Dex started to speak. He wanted to ask more about Howard and that fourth man. He wanted to ask about Anya, but Ryan stopped him. He moved to a chair close by. "I think that's about all the male bonding I can stand for one day," he said.

Dex swallowed his impatience. It rose to his throat like bile, but he bit back the words that flashed to mind. He wanted answers now and not later and wondered at Ryan's motivation in hesitating. Dex thought of the detective's parting reminder not to leave New York. *Forget it*, he thought. Time was running out. He felt its urgent march, the measured breath of demons blowing at his neck. He was on the trail of truth. If he dropped the ball and retreated, as he would truly like, the storm would come regardless.

"What are you going to tell Anya about Elliot?"

"About Elliot ... I don't know. I'll call her tonight. Right now she's at practice getting ready for tomorrow night's performance. I'll call her later."

"What I mean is, what are you going to tell her about you and Elliot? About why you were there when he killed himself."

"The truth, I guess. I'll have to tell her the truth, but not over the phone. After that funeral I'll fly to Kansas City ... if you really think I should go. I don't want to waste time."

"It's up to you, but yes," Ryan said. "I think I know what you're after and you should be there."

"Why can't you just tell me now?"

In answer Ryan shook his head. He stood to go and Dex remembered Ryan's comment at the airport about borrowing the suit that was so much out of character for him to wear. "If you borrow my suit, what will I wear?" he asked instead, retreating to the same meaningless banter that had preserved their friendship in countless awkward moments.

"You can wear the suit. I'll wear something else," Ryan said as though his closet were not already full of such attire.

Dex had demanded an explanation and now Anya wondered what she would say. All she could do was practice, reciting words until she found a few that seemed right. The more she spoke the more her life sounded like an unbelievable web of soap-opera lies, and she felt an overwhelming reluctance to begin. The surrender of self was a heady force, both reviled and admired for the polarity of extremes that defined chaos and made control possible.

239

How could she explain the lapses in time that would never be recovered? She could not bear the thought that Dex might think her insane or worse still … disbelieve her story.

Exposure lay at the root of her fear. She was well aware that Dex might reject her, perhaps not immediately but certainly over time as he grasped the true nature of her pathology. He was a man whose life was molded by standards and her instinct to trust him on that first encounter in Sweden and then later in Montreal had been right. He was a good man, and some part of her had awakened to that goodness. Now she wanted him to accommodate and appease her fears by allowing her to remain the same, but could their love survive with that great gulf of secrecy between them? The answer seemed obvious, and those dual choices … to tell him or not to tell him … rife with the sharp laceration of consequence.

Anya rehearsed the words of an explanation, beginning with what could be recalled of her early life with Sasha, but felt the paralyzing weight of an overwhelming reluctance. Just the thought of unleashing the past by giving it a form and definition through the power of words called forth a whole army of warring factions.

Was it too much to expect that Dex would understand if she couldn't tell him everything? Anya made her decision. Though dead, Sasha could still win. She wouldn't let that happen. She would have to risk the words, because the thought had already come to her and had stayed with her, and neither that Other or the Lie or Mocking had managed to dislodge it, although they had all tried. Crazy was going out. She could almost feel the fissure widen in the top of her skull, even as love was coming in. And with Dex's love came hope. For the first time in a very long while she dared to hope and in hoping, to risk those dangerous words of illumination.

As Dex became more a part of daily life, the Anya personality had grown sharper, refining and pushing the original Anya to the forefront of consciousness with a definition not seen in years. As Anya lay in the arms of her husband or walked with him through the predictable routine of a life spent between skating and the vineyard, there was no need for that pervasive vigilance, that constant wariness and attention to the mired signals that warned of danger.

Immune to reason and numb to attachment, that Other remained suspicious and suddenly alive to the threat of an ever-stronger Anya. The very excess and extremes of prevailing that had blunted pain and blurred boundaries now threatened the precarious balance of a multiple existence that had made it possible for Anya to live. And always, through the collective soul of nightmare imaginings, that Other maintained a constant, often paranoid surveillance from an ever-narrowing slit of power.

From the airport Anya took a cab to the Weston Crown Center Hotel, only a ten-minute drive from the skating arena. After today she could look forward to riding the bus from one city to the next with the other skaters. Once over her initial fear of the unknown Anya welcomed the opportunity to fine-tune two new programs before live audiences. She should be concentrating on her skating and looking forward to the weeks ahead, but all she could think of was Dex. She wanted to wrap her arms about him and have him embrace her in return. She wanted to be assured that in spite of everything he still loved her.

When Anya arrived for practice, the other skaters had already assembled with the choreographer. She had been sent a video to familiarize herself with the group routines, but a mental run through in her mind and actually skating were not the same. Feeling awkward and out of place, she skated through the number with few errors but lacked the unconscious fluidity which distinguished the performance of the others, who had the advantage of frequent performances before live audiences. No more than a quick run through of this simple number was all that was needed for a cohesive group of professionals accustomed to skating together, and so Anya knew that the practice was to accommodate her.

If there was any ill feeling about her last minute addition to the show, none was evident. The other skaters were curious about her life and seemed to welcome the opportunity to get to know her better. Anya maneuvered her path about their friendliness like footfalls in a minefield.

For the remainder of the afternoon she practiced two other group numbers and then performed her two solo performances for the choreographer, who suggested only minor changes. She was just finishing and was due for an appointment with wardrobe when she caught a glimpse of Glen Winston. He had been a brooding presence in and out of the rink area during much of the practice but had yet to greet her. It was a surprise to all when the music was suspended and Glen's voice boomed out over the ice.

"For those of you who have not yet heard, I have some tragic news. I regret to inform you that the rumor is correct. Elliot Smythe is dead as a result of an accidental fall from a balcony just this morning. The show will go on as planned. We will dedicate tomorrow night's performance to his memory. Those of you who imagine that we will cancel any engagements so that you can attend his funeral should think again."

There was a prolonged moment of stunned silence and then a drone of whispering began. As Anya skated toward the boards she caught snatches of conversation.

"Fell from his balcony?" "There has to be more to this story," another voice echoed. "Dexter Arujo was with Elliot when he fell," one of the principal male skaters offered and glanced at Anya as she skated by, his voice dropping to a whisper too late. Anya could not help but hear the speculation as she slipped her guards into place and headed for the closest exit.

"Leaving?" Anya looked into the face of Glen Winston and blinked. "I understand that you have a fitting in wardrobe."

Anya had forgotten. All she could think of was the comment that Elliot had been with Dex when he fell. Could that be true? Anya had not spoken to her husband since parting at the airport, but she knew that he and Ryan should be heading north from New York in pursuit of some good fishing.

"Thank you for reminding me," Anya said. "I am sorry to hear about Elliot, Mr. Winston. I understand you were good friends."

When he failed to answer, Anya began to retrace her steps, but Glen remained in her path. She had rehearsed this moment countless times but could not escape the dreaded nervousness which enveloped her in a cloud of uncertainty.

"After the fitting I thought I'd return to the hotel for a rest before tonight's performance," Anya said, reaching for the futile blanket of words to cover her discomfort.

"Good idea. Shall we leave passes with the gate for your husband tonight?"

"I don't think so. Dex and Ryan have gone fishing somewhere in Maine. But I know he'll call tonight and he'll catch up with us later in the tour."

"What a treat!"

Glen's sarcasm was clearly directed at Dex and not at her. Didn't he recognize the far larger threat that she presented? Even Howard Maple, that shriveled-up excuse for humanity, had opened his eyes and been horrified to see her leaning over him. For the mere heartbeat of seconds, as she looked into his face, Anya wondered if she had been right about Glen Winston. All that she knew of him had been bolstered by Ryan's recollections. In spite of that she suddenly doubted that Glen was among those monsters that had exercised full reign over her childhood nightmares and the thought was disconcerting. Could memory be manipulated? Should she doubt Ryan?

Anya looked into Glen's face. She had yet to meet anyone who did not like and admire her husband. She opened her mouth to speak but found that she could not. Instead, that Other projected alien words over that mysterious flash of splitting in which the multiple, if only briefly, occupied the same spot of constraint, poised at the threshold of emergence to become separate and whole.

"May I say, Mr. Winston, that I have looked forward to working with you," that Other replied.

"Do you have to be so defensive? Do you want him to suspect what we're really here for?"

Anya heard the bitter retort of that Other and did not welcome that safe cave of oblivion beyond pain and scheming. This splitting inwardness had always been a haven of coma-like retreat, and she had rarely hesitated to go there, happy not to suffer the consequence of mental and physical abuse. But now her ambivalence festered. She was, after all, the owner of this body. A girl named Lydia had been born to house this mind and soul, but Lydia had never grown beyond the age of six or seven and was an entity incapable of responding appropriately to any of life's challenges. The fact was that Anya hadn't seen or talked to Lydia in a very long while. Her stunted and shadowy persona might have completely expired except for the little hand that sometimes rested in hers. The same hand that waved Anya forward, choosing life over death.

"Then we are not enemies?" Glen asked.

"Why would we be enemies?" that Other responded as Anya listened and watched, knowing that she was hated more than ever for that failure to retreat completely.

Glen noticed that Anya's accent had suddenly become more pronounced. He looked at the woman before him with open curiosity. There had been an odd shift. Her tone had strengthened and even her facial expression had jelled into one of haughty confidence. It seemed as though she knew him, really knew him. Inwardly he squirmed under that imagined inspection.

Glen told himself that he was being foolish. This sudden impression was too much at odds with the preconceived notions of who and what Anya Szcepanik was, and so he ignored the collective subtleties of the changes he'd noted. Inwardly Glen breathed a sigh of relief and chided himself for an overactive imagination.

"I have to admit that at first I didn't think you were right for the show," he said in response to her question. "And I always speak my mind. I'm surprised Dex didn't tell you."

"Dex is far too protective of my feelings, so no," that Other paused as though clinically considering the behavior of a rat in its maze. "He would have thought my knowing this unnecessary. I only hope I can prove you wrong. I want to be an asset to the show and I expect us to be friends." She smiled the perfect disguise of that Other, unruffled and cool, impenetrable, invincible, and dangerously devoid of scruples. That Other looked at her watch. "As you have so kindly pointed out, I am late for an appointment. Now if you will excuse me."

The Other placed a cool hand on Glen's arm in a familiar, even suggestive manner that made Anya cringe, and as though suddenly making up his mind, Glen turned and walked away. That Other watched until he was well out of sight and then dropping the skating bag with a thud, sat to remove their skates before heading toward the back of the arena.

Measurements had already been forwarded to the seamstress, but fittings took longer than one expected, and she hated the tedious wait and uninspired conversation, as pins were inserted and seams ripped out. That Other thought of abandoning the field to the Lie, who loved the feel of a new costume, but immediately thought better of the idea. The Lie could never skate as Anya did. When the Lie was catapulting those limbs in her exaggerated and exhibitionist style and operating that mouth as though she were a giddy teenager with nothing but marshmallow for brains, she drew too much of the wrong kind of attention to them all. The Lie had been useful when Sasha was alive. It was the Lie that Sasha liked best, but that time had passed, and that Other suspected she ought to get rid of the Lie forever as she had other useless and immature victim entities that emerged from the formless void of Anya's young despair.

"Yes," the Other decided. These were dangerous times for splinter personalities, and they certainly didn't need any more to manage. Far better to remain alert and fully in control, for Anya had grown increasingly assertive and independent, stepping to the threshold of consciousness far too often and with far less trouble. And to make matters worse, her seething resentment and dissatisfaction had gained a foothold like the insidious burgeoning of a cancer, which threatened to become a serious problem with the inevitable result of undermining the current balance of power. That Other could not help wondering if the solution hadn't been there all along. There had to be a way of getting rid of Anya without harming the host body. It was a novel thought, intriguing and delicious with possibilities. That Other smiled a rare smile, and a rink worker, who happened to pass and witness that stiff facsimile of human joy, actually recoiled in a flutter of disquiet.

CHAPTER NINETEEN

*Something about playing the pipes gave him great comfort. A similar sound
had sent plaintive notes over ancient lands, accompanied explorers far from
home, and spurred men into battle. Today he would play for Herb, and he
would imagine the vast crowd of angelic witnesses and risen saints who
would sing along in joy. "Therefore, since we have so great a crowd of
witnesses surrounding us, let us also lay aside every encumbrance and the sin
which so easily entangles us, and let us run with endurance the race that is
set before us" (Hebrews 12: 1).*

Nora stood beside Paul in the front living room. The house was congested.
Like water seeking its own level, people spilled into all the first floor rooms
as they jockeyed for space and eyed greedily each occupied chair. The
evening was milder than normal, but still an Atlantic bite lingered off the
coast and sent a moist chill over the granite gray of the headstones, across the
fieldstone wall that bordered Mill Lane.

Herb's last minute, deathbed conversion to Christianity, was viewed by
some with a jaundiced eye. They had boycotted the visitation, which was just
as well. Paul had set up an open bar, and friends from the garden club had
graciously offered to organize and serve the eclectic stream of dishes which
steadily arrived on the dining room table, now pushed into the library to make
room for the casket Nora had painted. The mourners demonstrated their
appreciation by making frequent trips to the buffet table to refill plates and
glasses with overwrought abandon.

Nora glanced at Paul. It felt good to be standing beside him, shoulder to
shoulder. The night before, she and Rev had driven back to Rockport from
New York, arriving late. Settling Rev in Lydia's old room, Nora undressed
and slid between the flannel sheets of her own bed. She dozed intermittently,
but real sleep eluded her. First light, just easing the March sky, drew her to
the window, and she looked out over Paul's backyard. The greenhouse door
was open. Her heart beating fast, Nora slipped into faded jeans and, tucking
her nightgown into the waistband, moved quietly down the stairs. In the
darkness her feet found the back door Wellingtons, and grabbing the pea coat

she went to investigate.

Washed in the gray blue of a breaking dawn, the greenhouse felt decidedly empty and Nora was disappointed. Prepared to endure Paul's wrath in whatever form it would take, she had steeled herself for this first meeting since the debacle at Herb's hospital bed. She needed Paul to understand that her actions were not personally directed at him in order to hurt. She just had to know the truth before it was too late.

As she walked deeper into the glassed enclosure, tears burned in her eyes. Dropping her head Nora wrapped her arms about her own slim body as though for comfort. Defeated, she turned to study the house beyond, where no light burned, until her startled gaze picked Paul's form out of the dimness. Wrapped in Herb's crocheted Afghan, he sat on the top of an empty bedding table, wedged into a corner and with his eyes straining for the last morning star.

"Hi," Nora said and noticed the clay pots and the hoses neatly coiled and the late winter onions sprouting next to the spinach, carefully divided by wood barriers. The brick floor, sloping toward a drain, was dry. Overhead bunches of dried flowers, which under normal circumstances would have been recycled into flower arrangements and wreaths to give away, still dangled from a low-slung rafter to brush the top of her head. In all seasons the greenhouse overflowed with the activity of new life sprouting and old recycled, but with Herb's last relapse there was little time, and it was now eerily empty of its usual thriving profusion.

"Hi," Nora said again, thinking that Paul had not seen her. He seemed stiff, almost catatonic, and when he finally turned in her direction she had the distinct impression that she had called him back from a very far place.

"Are you all right?" Nora asked.

"I'm hanging in there. This seems to be the phrase of the moment and so everyone's been saying, "hang in there, buddy." So that's what I'm doing. An apt phrase really. I'm hanging." Paul's tone sounded tentative and his voice cracked in the way it does from prolonged disuse.

Nora nodded, letting a little silence gather in acknowledgment, and then she took a deep breath and spoke. "I need to tell you something but I don't know if you want to hear or if now is the time."

"Now is the time," Paul stated flatly, and so Nora told him.

Paul hardly responded as she related Peter's reaction to their charge that Howard had molested him. Sliding up on the opposite table and propping her feet across the narrow aisle, she described the unfolding police investigation, which was for now centered on the massive amounts of evidence uncovered in Howard's apartment. "The detective told me that if they find any connection between Howard and Lydia's disappearance, it'd be fairly certain she'd be dead."

The pause was long as Nora awaited Paul's reaction. "If Howard hadn't had that stroke, do you think he would have destroyed everything?" he asked.

Nora had expected him to say something sympathetic about Lydia. "Maybe not destroyed it, but certainly moved it or turned it over to someone else. He had a pretty good business going there. I hope he had the mental capacity to agonize over the possibility of discovery each and every day that he lay immobile in that bed and speechless in that wheelchair. They'd had several break-ins and attempted break-ins and had doubled security, so now they actually think someone was trying to get into that apartment."

Paul turned his attention back to the sky above the geometric configuration of the greenhouse windows. The air was warmer, somehow heavier, and Nora knew that by mid morning the sun would burn through a milky haze and the snow would melt into wet pools, which would freeze again by nightfall, turning the lane into a treacherous pond. Spring thaw, just a hopeless pipedream the week before, now seemed a certainty, and even the trees and gulls and night sounds appeared to express faith in its arrival, and yet March could be a cruel month. No true New Englander ever counted on March or April.

"Paul, do you forgive me?" Nora asked. "I said some harsh words to you."

"We've always told one another the truth, haven't we? We've lied to everyone else, but not to each other."

"There's more I need to tell you, but it can wait until after the funeral." With renovations begun on that apartment this was all going to unravel, and the photographs of Paul, that Herb begged her to retrieve, would certainly surface. Did Herb also guess that his request on Paul's behalf might lead her to the truth about her sister? Did he know of the existence of that secret chamber, and was he aware of the international scope of Howard's child pornography business? Rev had reminded her that if Paul did not already remember, she had a responsibility to tell him before the authorities arrived with all their harsh, intrusive questions. But she hesitated to tell him now, with the loss of Herb so fresh. Still there was a resignation in the set of Paul's face that made her think he was less fragile now than at the hospital two days ago.

"You seem to be doing okay. Better than I expected," Nora offered.

"Well, there's nothing more I can do for Herb, is there? When he was alive he needed me. Now he's gone."

"There is something more we can do. Herb never wanted a somber event for a funeral. I imagine half the town will show. Will you let me help?"

Again Paul was silent for long seconds. It seemed almost that his body rhythms had slowed. "Herb looks nice," he finally said. "I have him in that gray suit he liked, with my college tie and the emerald earring I gave him our first Christmas together. You want to see him?"

Nora nodded her head as Paul moved stiffly off the bedding table. Draping their arms around one another they walked back to the house. The sky was lighter now and Nora could see Paul's face more clearly. The night sounds had faded and the first birds could be heard singing in the bare branches of the trees.

"Are you hungry?" he asked. "I'll boil us a couple of eight minute eggs and toast bagels, and then we can catch a few hours of sleep before people start arriving. You haven't slept, have you?" he looked at her sternly. Nora felt a thrill of joy at his reproach. She hugged him and would not let go until he hugged her back.

Nora and Paul had slept until noon and then she had slipped back across the yard to shower and dress. All afternoon plants and bouquets of flowers arrived until they were required to shuttle the excess over to her house. There was little to do because Paul had already seen to everything. He had arranged to have their first Christmas card reissued by the local serigraph artist who had done the original. A printer friend had inscribed the inside with the twenty-third Psalm and placed Herb's photograph on the last page as a memento. Then Connor had suggested adding the following words, which Paul agreed to, only because it seemed dishonest not to validate in some way Herb's last hours.

"Before he breathed his last, Herb made a profession of faith in Jesus Christ and is, at this very moment, glorifying his Savior in Heaven. *Come to me, all you who are weary and burdened, and I will give you rest. Take my yoke upon you and learn from me, for I am gentle and humble in heart and you will find rest for your souls. For my yoke is easy and my burden is light (Matthew 11: 28, 29).*

All afternoon Nora and Paul stood by the fireplace and followed the bright holiday flash of those cards as they greeted guests. "Do you think Herb would have approved of all this lack of piety? I mean, since he discovered religion and all that?" Nora asked.

"Not to mention drunkenness." Paul added. "It's very possible that you and I, and of course Connor, and maybe those two late arrivals over there," Paul gestured, "are the only sober people present."

Nora glanced toward the dining room, where Herb lay, with his head on a satin pillow in the colorful coffin she had painted. After a quick trip to be embalmed at the funeral home in Gloucester, most wakes or visitations in Rockport were still held in people's homes. Tomorrow morning a hearse would back down Mill Lane for the casket and a short ride to Connor's church. After the services Herb was due to be buried in the Maple family plot.

"Herb liked nothing better than a good party, but I think even this would have stunned him a little," Paul said, allowing his gaze to scan the room. It was an intriguing group of people who had assembled with little advance notice. Friends arrived from New York, Boston, and as far away as San Francisco and Taos.

"Are you surprised?" Nora asked.

"I'm surprised that so many people came with such little notice and that I can't claim to have met many of them. You were right, you know. Herb had a whole other life."

Nora wore a slim black dress and jacket trimmed with matching satin and Paul wore black trousers and a black wool shirt with silver buttons. Though his face was pale and his eyes rimmed red, Nora thought he looked very handsome.

"Then you forgive me?" she asked.

"I'll consider it, only after you explain what HE thinks he's doing," Paul said, inclining his head toward Rev, who seemed to be making a concerted effort to personally speak to as many of Herb's friends as possible. "I would never have thought Rev could be such a good host. And this isn't even his party."

"He definitely has an agenda, but you might want to wait a few days for an explanation."

"You know, Nora," Paul said, turning suddenly serious. "I am sorry that Herb is gone, but I feel somehow lighter, and I have this notion that he is happy. As I was sitting in the greenhouse last night, I felt that he was looking down at me from a better place. I know this sounds strange, but I felt that distinctly and it was comforting."

"Then you're not sorry that Connor prayed with him?"

"Herb was always so defensive of the lifestyle. It just seemed a betrayal of everything he stood for, and it seemed to me that Connor took advantage of that moment and had robbed him of the dignity of staying true to what he believed."

"But Herb was scared. He was afraid to die. Could it be, that in the end, that radical pro-gay stance he was so vocal about just wasn't going to replace his need for God? His death was a long slow process and he had plenty of time to reflect."

"Maybe, and I sure didn't have any answers for him. In the end it was

Connor whose belief system never wavered. Maybe you and I should look at that, Nora. I've been thinking that Herb and I were never honest with each other. How can there be love without honesty?"

"Maybe in the end you'll only remember that you loved one another very much."

"That's a nice thought, Nora, but if I find that Herb had any involvement in Howard's activities, I shall have to hate him."

"I suspect that Herb, too, was exploited by Howard."

"Perhaps, but that's not the point, is it? There are lots of victims in the world and most of them don't become perpetrators. If I had known the truth, I would never have committed myself to loving Herb. In fact, I could not have loved him because there are absolutes in life that should not be rationalized, no matter how seductive the rhetoric."

"But you loved one another. I saw that love. It was real, Paul. Up to the very end it was real."

"Was it? Let's not shade the truth just because we have a funeral. And are you forgetting everything you said the day we took him to the hospital? You said he never loved me. And how does that stack up against all the emotion that I invested in our relationship over the years?"

"I don't know," Nora acknowledged. "We don't have to think about all that right now, Paul."

"Oh, but I have been thinking about all that. Ever since he acknowledged knowing Howard in less than the casual and superficial way that he first implied. He lied to me. When you give someone your youth and later you find that love was never reciprocated, you can't take it back. What does that say about me? That I was stupid to trust him? That I was foolish not to have guessed? Or that he was despicable for not telling me the truth about Howard because, even if he wasn't involved in Howard's activities, he did tolerate his behavior? I think that Herb made the decision to deceive me because he knew the truth would have ended things before they began."

"Paul," Nora began, but he cut her off.

"He robbed me of choice, Nora. And yes, you were right. He was unfaithful and with more than one person in this room with the abominable lack of taste to share their own grief, implying and telling more than I want to know. They didn't live with him and meld their finances with him and operate like a couple, trusting that the relationship was exclusive, did they?"

This tortuous questioning was just beginning for Paul. Nora wanted to stop the process and save him the pain, but knew that she could not. Nothing could hurt and then heal like the truth. Paul went to the kitchen and returned with two glasses of ginger ale. He had stopped drinking as suddenly as he had begun. He handed Nora a tall glass.

"I may be in love, you know," Nora said, changing the subject. She squeezed Paul's arm, simply grateful to be back on speaking terms. What would she have done, Nora asked herself, if Paul had really cut himself out of her life? That wouldn't have happened. She wouldn't have allowed it to happen! They watched as Rev introduced himself to the two late arrivals. Both looked familiar to Nora, but she couldn't place them.

"In love!" Paul said, amused. "How do you know?"

"I'm quite familiar with the symptoms from watching you, thank you very much. He hasn't said that he cares for me. Still, I think that everything he does is absolutely marvelous and endlessly entertaining. Yet I can't help arguing with him at every turn and indulging a certain thrill of heightened reality when he looks at me. That's what you had with Herb."

"That's what we had in the beginning, always in the beginning," Paul acknowledged wistfully. "Only you could come up with such an analytical definition of love. Well, Nora, I'll be happy for you if I must. A little jealous. Yes, definitely jealous," Paul said as though weighing his emotions. "But decidedly happy for you, and if he hurts you in any way I'll pound him into oblivion. Well, no, I couldn't actually," Paul said, eyeing Rev, who stood across the room speaking to a very handsome stranger who did not seem to be keeping up his end of the conversation. "But I'll hire someone."

Nora laughed. "Jealous. How could you be jealous?" she cajoled.

Paul was reflective. "I've had you to myself all these years. Now I'll have to share you at a time when I'll be alone for the first time in my life. I ran from loneliness. To me it was the most horrid state in the world, and yet running only brought heartache. Don't you think there's a certain fateful symmetry in the reversal of our lives?" Paul's hand found Nora's and he held on tight.

"Let me ask you something," he said and hesitated.

"What?" she prompted.

"Did we ever have a chance, you and I? If I had just tried could we have had a life together and maybe children? Because it seems to me that you would have tried and that you might have been waiting. And I wasn't listening or seeing. Is it too late for us, Nora?"

Rev was intrigued from the moment they entered the room. The man more formally dressed, in dark suit and tie with a black raincoat over one arm, held back as the other approached Herb's casket. Neither followed the protocol displayed in near identical manner by the other mourners. They did not greet Nora or Paul, nor did they kneel and say a short prayer at the casket. Despite the fact that they were offered a pen, they declined to sign the guest book that stood on a podium at the entrance to the dining room, where Herb's last bed sat festooned with baskets of flowers, wreaths, and plants.

Only the second man, dressed informally in jeans and cashmere blazer, actually approached the casket. Placing one hand on the rim of the raised hood he leaned forward and gazed for long moments into Herb's face. Some close by noticed his wooden stance and tense manner. They glanced in his direction and then uneasily turned away, for suddenly the length of that prolonged scrutiny seemed irreverent.

"What is he thinking?" Rev asked himself, but the coffin stand had been wheeled and locked against the far wall, and it was impossible to see his expression. Rev turned his attention back to the first guest, who remained at the threshold. He made no attempt to speak to anyone and yet was not awkward in the way of people with nothing to say and no one to visit with in a group. Others noticed him as well, but there was something unapproachable in his manner, and he struck Rev as being completely at ease with himself. Rev thought that he looked familiar. Actually, as he thought about it, both men seemed familiar, and suddenly he was certain that he had seen them before.

"Rev Porter, I don't think we've met," Rev said, intercepting Ryan as he finally turned from Herb's casket.

Ryan cast Rev a disinterested look. Whatever he had been thinking as he peered into Herb's inscrutable face was now safely hidden from view, but Rev was instantly alert. There was something to know here, and he could feel the distinct but formless hint of a taunting outline.

Ryan shook Rev's hand. "Ryan Campbell, and this," he said, gesturing to include his companion, "is Dex Arujo."

"You two stand out and I'm trying to decide if we've met before? I've got it. Television, right? You work for one of the cable news shows," Rev said as Ryan's identity suddenly flashed to mind.

There was no fleeting look of irritation, and yet Rev felt it just the same and knew that Ryan had taken an instant dislike to him. If he played his cards right, he could exploit that momentum. He always had. Now, reluctantly Ryan nodded his head. Rev was not making a good first impression, but he didn't care. He had circulated all night among Herb's friends and found nothing more unexpected than too many former lovers, rapt with fear as they considered the nature of Herb's illness and death. Ryan struck him as cold and distant, and he knew that this sort of defensiveness did not exist with irrational paranoia. He'd seen Ryan many times on television, and he didn't like him then either.

"And you," Rev turned his attention to Dex. "Are you a friend of Herb's or Paul or both?"

"A friend of mine actually," Ryan interjected before his friend could answer, and Rev had the feeling he was deliberately deflecting attention away from Dex. "And what about you? Are you a friend of the deceased, because I don't believe I've ever heard Herb mention your name?" Ryan asked.

"I'm a friend of Nora's," Rev admitted and nodded toward the meager receiving line where Connor had just joined Paul and Nora. He stood between them, a hand on each of their shoulders and the three laughing at some joke. Ryan and Dex glanced into the next room, but Dex seemed unable to tear his eyes away. Finally he looked back at Rev.

"And Nora is Paul's wife?" Dex asked.

"Sometimes I wonder," Rev chuckled wryly. "But, no. I'm sure Ryan can tell you that Paul was Herb's companion and Nora is a close friend." He looked at both men. "Did you know Howard Maple?" he asked and then noticed that Dex was gone. Without preamble he had turned and walked toward Nora. Rev started to follow, but Ryan recaptured his attention.

"Yes, I knew Howard Maple." He let his eyes roam about the room and even coolly nodded towards a few people. Again Rev had the impression that he was being occupied so that Dex could be free, but he decided to play along. This was at least a straight answer to a question he had been asking all night. When he pressed the few who admitted to knowing Howard, he sensed a wary defensiveness and a common unwillingness to shed light on Herb's association with Howard. As news leaked of Howard's crimes, they would be even more hesitant. Rev had seen the process at work time and again. As an investigation heated up and the reality of someone's life confronted the carefully constructed facade, most people shut down, while others nervously sprouted useless trivia, all of which must be sifted and evaluated for pearls of truth.

"How did you know Howard?" Rev asked.

Once more an expressionless shade fell over Ryan's face. "I'd say at least a dozen men in this room knew Howard, but I imagine most have had the good sense to peg you as a cop and have denied it."

"Busted," Rev smiled. "I'm not here officially, but I guess it still shows. Yeah, I'm a cop," Rev admitted.

"I guess there's a lot you think you know."

"Enough to know there's reams more."

"And I imagine you'd like to compare notes."

Giving Ryan a measured look, Rev slowly nodded his head.

Later Dex would be unable to explain how he knew that Nora was related to Anya. He just knew. It was the way she lifted her glass, the familiar heaviness of those sleek red strands that bobbed about her chin. It was the tilt of her head and the line and posture of her body, which made her appear taller than she actually was. Put together, it was a thousand details of persona and spirit which drew his eye and jelled to inward certainty.

Dex shook Paul's hand and, for the moment, avoided looking at Nora. His heart pounded as the caustic chill of discovery threatened to paralyze his limbs. "I'm sorry for your loss," he offered awkwardly.

"Thank you. Were you a friend of Herb's?" Paul asked, as he had already inquired of the steady stream of out-of-town mourners who entered his home and walked to the coffin before speaking words of condolence to him and Nora. Paul felt at an awkward disadvantage as he shook those hands, surprised at the number of people Herb had kept in touch with through the years, and then how full his life had been away from Rockport and their life together.

"I'm a friend of Ryan's," Dex said and looked over his shoulder at where Ryan and Rev continued in conversation. "I hope you don't mind my being here?"

"Not at all. There are actually quite a lot of people here that I've never met. One more doesn't matter. It's turned out to be a lively bunch," Paul offered when he realized that Dex was not going to move off as the others had. "We didn't intend a party, but it seems we have one anyway."

"It's nice," Dex said and looked about the room as though for the first time. The atmosphere seemed surreal. "I think I'd like something like this for myself when I die. Old friends meeting after a long absence, a bittersweet tribute that's not false or over-burdened with ceremony. I don't imagine something like this can really be planned. It just happens."

Paul seemed pleased by Dex's observation. He smiled warmly. "How did Herb and … Ryan, is it, come to know one another?"

"Through Howard Maple, I think. Did you know Howard?"

"He was my uncle," Paul replied, all trace of friendliness suddenly vanished. Nora stepped closer and took Paul's arm. Dex caught the protective gesture and glanced briefly in her direction. Nora fascinated him, yet just looking at her raised the hackles on the back of his neck, and he was reminded of his mother's phrase to explain such a feeling. "Someone just walked over my grave," she would say.

"I'm sorry if I upset you," Dex offered, tearing his eyes from Nora's face with difficulty.

"How could you possibly know enough to be sorry," Paul replied, a razor sharp note slicing the last trace of warmth from his voice.

Unbidden, those horrid photographs of Anya sprang to Dex's mind. He spoke carefully, already knowing that he must risk the words. He looked searchingly into Paul's eyes. "Because Howard was an evil man and I do not use that word lightly. I am sorry he was related to someone as nice as you seem to be."

Paul's face clouded over. He opened his mouth to speak, but Nora interrupted. "He WAS an evil man," she asserted. "Did you know him well?"

For the first time Dex turned fully in Nora's direction and let his gaze linger over her face, unable to disguise his interest. This woman was somehow related to Anya. Dex could not conceal his scrutiny. He couldn't afford to be gentle with her and ease into the many questions that flooded his mind. There was no time for such luxury. "I'm sorry. I don't mean to stare, but it's uncanny how you remind me of my wife," he began tentatively.

"Did you know Howard well?" Nora asked again, clearly impatient for the answer and ignoring Dex's statement.

"I knew him because of our mutual profession. I was not a friend of Howard's."

"But you knew him. I mean," Nora hesitated and seemed to struggle over the words. "I mean, you knew ABOUT him."

"Forgive me," Dex heard himself ask Nora. "Do you have a sister? Because you look like someone I know very well and I want to ask you—" His voice trailed.

A certain feeling descended, like the calm heaviness that precedes a storm. Nora thought of the silver-backed leaves in a summer wood turned up against the impending rain. She thought of mackerel gulls gathering inland for protection before the wind rises and the surf pounds. She registered the closeness of the room and the voices. Connor had left them, and now the sound of a tin whistle, a fiddle, and Eulian pipes erupted from back toward the kitchen in sudden impromptu harmony. Connor would be back there playing the pipes he'd inherited from his Irish grandfather. Nora recognized the tune. 'It Keeps Right on a Hurting Since You're Gone'.

Nora studied Dex. He had asked her a question and she somehow knew that this was not an aimless inquiry prompted by a banal intent.

"I have a sister. She disappeared when she was six. We think she was abducted," Nora replied, breaking her own best rule against volunteering information to strangers. But she'd answered his question as though he deserved an explanation and now she watched for his reaction, rather than turn away in anger as she would normally have done. And at what point, she reprimanded herself, had she stopped speaking of her sister in the past tense?

255

Did she really think that Lydia could possibly be alive?

Dex looked about. A stack of magazines, the *New Yorker, Art News, People* and *Newsweek* sat in a basket under an end table. Finding what he wanted, Dex shuffled through the pages and folded back the magazine. He handed it to Nora, who glanced with impatience at where his finger directed.

Paul looked over Nora's shoulder. "This is you. I didn't know we had a celebrity in our midst," Paul said and pointed a finger at Dex's glossy face on the upturned page. As it turned out they had not made the cover, but he and Anya had been satisfied with the article nevertheless, although Dex was not thinking of that now as he watched for Nora's reaction.

Nora's face drained of color. If she registered Dex's image on that glossy page at all it was doubtful. Instead the full weight of her gaze was riveted on the face of Anya Szcepanik. How did he know? Nora looked beyond Dex and tried to catch Rev's attention, but he seemed to be concentrating on a wary Ryan. With shaking hands Nora reached into the inside pocket of her jacket. With one swift movement of her arm she sent the Wedgewood box, silver-rimmed photos, and two abandoned glasses tumbling to the floor. Exhibiting far more care she unfolded a piece of paper and spread it over the cluttered end table.

Others looked their way, embarrassed. One of Paul's friends from the garden club scooped up the fallen items and cast Nora a puzzled look. Not noticing and with trembling hands, Nora placed the folded black and white photo next to that of the magazine article. Dex and Paul looked over her shoulder.

"What is this?" Paul asked, baffled by the unexpected twist of events. They were looking at the age progressed photo of Lydia and then at the magazine image of a smiling Dex with Anya leaning slightly against him as they sat on the veranda of Dex's house in California. The resemblance between the two women was striking.

"Lydia Fothergill," Dex read the print beneath the age-enhanced photograph.

"And who is this?" Nora asked, her voice trembling as she pointed to the magazine page of Anya's smiling face.

"My wife," Dex replied, his voice hushed as though in church. "I imagine she remembers little about her true identity."

Thinking of the same event, Nora and Paul looked at one another. "No," Paul said. "I think she knows exactly who she is. I think she was here several months ago and stood out there, watching Nora's house." Paul pointed out the window toward the lane. "It was just before Christmas and it had snowed in the early morning hours." His voice trailed and Nora knew that he was pondering something. She nodded her head in stunned agreement.

Almost involuntarily Paul's eyes drifted to the hallway. Herb had asserted that a threatening figure had stood over his bed that morning. Clearly he was frightened and now Paul wondered if he had recognized Anya, for he could no longer believe that Herb was merely confused. He recalled the snowy footprints on the rug when he had returned with his newspaper after talking to Nora and telling her about that girl who had remained the entire night outside. Which house had she really been studying? It wasn't Nora's home she chose to enter. Had she known Herb? Known that he was there? Was there some connection with Howard and had she truly intended to harm Herb?

Irritated, he had retrieved a rag from the kitchen and blotted the rugs, assuming those melting footprints belonged to the nurse assigned to take care of Herb that day. She was on her break in the kitchen, and if she had walked out the front for any reason he would have seen her. How blind he had been! Was such stupidity and refusal to assess the obvious a defense against having to face the truth? Paul shuddered. It was all unraveling and he could sense the phantom breath of discovery teasing all the missing pieces together.

CHAPTER TWENTY

When he did not know what to pray ... when there was no compelling burden, he had learned to speak the Scriptures back to God. Today the thin pages of his Bible fell open to the book of Psalms. He read these words. "The Lord is compassionate and gracious, slow to anger, abounding in love. He will not always accuse, nor will he harbor his anger forever; he does not treat us as our sins deserve or repay us according to our iniquities. For as high as the heavens are above the earth, so great is his love for those who fear him; as far as the east is from the west, so far has he removed our transgressions from us" (Psalm 103: 8-13).

Peeling off her practice clothes, Anya took a hot shower and dressed in chino trousers and a loose sweatshirt. She wore no makeup. In a few hours she would be applying the heavy stage makeup expected for the first evening show. She called room service and ordered cranberry juice, pasta, and a small salad. That task completed, she lay on the bed and ran through her breathing exercises, but it proved impossible to relax.

Tormented by anxiety, she desperately regretted not asking more questions about whose funeral Dex was attending and where he and Ryan were actually going. And she hadn't really understood his explanation of why he had been in Elliot's office on the day that he killed himself. Just the thought of Dex spending any time with Elliot frightened her.

Although she had already left numerous messages with his service and knew that the gesture was futile, she called Ryan's number yet again. Her rage mounted as she imagined his empty apartment and the shrill sound of the phone coursing through those few small rooms. Where was Dex when she needed him? For that matter, where was Ryan? She had lost count of how many times she had phoned Dex's New York hotel and then Rosa at the Vineyard. No one could tell her anything more than what she already knew. Ryan and Dex had postponed their fishing plans. They had gone to a funeral and were expected back in New York the following day. From there Dex would catch a flight and join her in Kansas City just as they had planned before leaving California.

Anya phoned the airlines to confirm, yet again, that Dex had not cancelled his reservation, but the knowledge that he still planned to join her afforded hollow comfort. As Anya listened to a national weather station, which reported a thaw and then unexpected, freezing temperatures and possible snow in the Northeast, she wondered if Dex would have difficulty flying out the following day.

A strong sense of impending disaster threatened to overwhelm her senses. And then … that sudden pressure at her temple let her know that release was near. This was not an unpleasant feeling. She felt her lungs being compressed as her brain began to float. Anya took a deep breath just as the Lie blew out a noxious stream of carbon dioxide so powerful that it could wilt plants and melt plastic. She had to stay out of its way. She had to flee.

Immediately the Lie walked to the mirror and brushed at Anya's long hair. She looked at her nails. It was a good thing she'd arrived, for this body needed a major overhaul, and yet there was not time for a salon facial, body wax, manicure, and massage. The most that she could manage was a quick hot oil treatment for the hair and appointments for the following day. It didn't matter that these appointments conflicted with Anya's skating obligations of which she was blissfully unaware.

That completed, she walked to the mini bar with key in hand. It occurred to her that in such extreme circumstances a drink was warranted, but first she would order room service.

"Room service, room service is what we need," she sang into the receiver. "I *need* some chocolate cake. Do you have chocolate cake? You do? Prekrasno! I want a big piece. As opposed to a small piece. You know … large with a generous scoop of French vanilla ice cream and two shrimp cocktails and one oysters Rockefeller. Oh, and guylyash. Do you make that? What is the word? You know … beef stroganoff only Russian. No … well, you should. Okay then. This is it. Please, and be quick. Pronto. Good day."

Then she remembered. They had drugs. Where were they?

The Lie rose from the bed and rummaged in suitcases. She riffled through the makeup bag and pockets and crevices of clothing leaving chaos in her wake. The Other had hidden those drugs well, and she wasn't even certain what they were for, except perhaps to kill Glen Winston who, no matter what anyone said or did, would certainly die.

Heaving a helpless little-girl sigh, she let her gaze survey the room, shifting from ceiling to floor until her eyes locked on an oddly bunched place in the beige carpet just beside a corner wardrobe. Walking directly over she peeled back the rug and pad to find what she was looking for. The drug was wrapped in a plastic bag and covered with tin foil, which she removed to

259

reveal a white powdery substance that she immediately recognized as coming from Howard Maple's home on the night that Other had snuffed out his life.

Gingerly the Lie sniffed at the powdery substance and immediately her nostrils flared and began to burn as her eyes watered, and she ran to the bathroom to gag and choke as she splashed cold water over her flushed face. Then carefully approaching that place where the ripped plastic lay, she scooped up what she could, careful not to let any come in contact with her skin. With great deliberate strides and feeling a thrill of determination, she walked to the toilet and flushed that horrid, burning substance from sight, acknowledging as she did so a tremendous rush of accomplishment that surprised and thrilled her.

Taking a deep breath the Lie stretched her arms wide and lifting her head, she waited in the hollow shelter of the shower stall for her punishment. Minutes passed, until it finally dawned on her that the Other had not been aware of her actions. Fire was not going to rein down from heaven just yet. The world was not going to tilt on its already tilted axis, and the very least that she expected from that hateful Other; a torrent of wrath, the rage of banishment, never surfaced to usurp that precious space that the Lie occupied in Anya's body. She could hardly believe her luck. For now the hotel room was as silent and empty of competing cries of outrage as the small church at the vineyard where she sometimes woke to find herself standing in the dreaded stillness of night. Perhaps that Other was not so all knowing and omnipresent as they had all imagined. "Maybe," she spoke aloud. "The emperor really does have clothes."

For something to do, the Lie propelled the limbs back and forth across the limited space of the hotel room. She did some stretching exercises until a knock came, and she looked with bewilderment at the salad and pasta that Anya had ordered. She opened her mouth to protest just as another tray was delivered.

As she ate she wished Anya hadn't been so quick to turn down an invitation to do some browsing at the Plaza shopping area with some of the other women from the show. And this thought prompted another. She would change her clothes. She walked to the suitcase, although almost everything had already been dumped out on the floor while searching for those drugs. She examined the few items hanging in the closet. It was clear that Anya had packed. There was nothing, absolutely nothing that she could possibly be seen in.

Now she had no choice. She had to go shopping, a task that Anya hated. Anya never wanted to have any fun. And this hotel? My goodness, it wasn't first rate, now was it? Maybe she should pack the bags and check them into the Ritz. That seemed a good idea. The Lie gathered their belongings, none too neatly, and exited the room with a bellhop trailing. Was there a Ritz in Kansas City? And where were the credit cards? She had forgotten to check Anya's wallet. Oh well. Everything would work out. It always did, although she never stayed around long enough to find out just how.

The Lie thought back to that last confrontation when Dex had pulled his car off to the side of the road and demanded that Anya confide in him. She hadn't been present herself, but still when she heard about it she felt the snare of fear and loss tighten its icy grip on her emotions. She was suddenly scared. Why must she be scared now? It wasn't her job to experience fear.

And Ryan! Why couldn't Ryan imagine what she was going through at this particular instant and call to let her know that nothing had changed? Once again she racked her brain. What friend did both Ryan and Dex have in common that had been so sick that death came knocking? She was relieved to discover that she could think of no one.

The Lie began to cry. Little-girl sobs and whimpers with great tears falling as she drew her knees up under her chin. The cab driver turned to look. "Are you all right, Miss?" But she had already switched. Abruptly the crying stopped. The skin tightened over her face, and she literally snarled at the cab driver, who recoiled in astonishment.

Seconds later it was the much-feared Other who stepped from the cab and surveyed the gray stone facade of the Ritz Carlton Hotel with haughty contempt. Another mess to unravel, another immature personality to rescue, and then she'd have to get back into the former hotel room in order to retrieve their murder weapon. Even she had to acknowledge that when Dex was near there was far less maintenance to be done. The Lie didn't act out as often, and Mocking pretty much kept her mouth shut, and all those others tended to let Anya smother their fears under a blanket of useless platitudes.

A passerby caught the drawn and haggard expression on that Other's face. Anya's eyes, normally so clear and transparent were narrowed slits, and although beautifully dressed, that Other muttered through clenched teeth unintelligible words deranged with hatred.

Secrets, Dex thought, casting Ryan a disgusted look. He was choking on secrets and he was sick and tired of weighing the damage. It was now after midnight. Connor and his wife had remained in the role of host while Paul, Nora, and Rev along with Ryan and Dex, had retreated to the quiet of Nora's kitchen. Nora made coffee and for something to do she defrosted a pound cake, but no one was hungry. It sat on a round plate in the center of the table, and for long minutes they all looked at it rather than at one another. Across

261

the yard, Paul's house had finally become dark, the last light extinguished from the hall as Connor followed the last mourners out the door to join them in the kitchen.

Rev had pulled a notebook and pen from his pocket and had finally succeeded in getting the process started with a few questions. Over the last two hours, all but Ryan had been intensely caught up with discussing and piecing together the past. Ryan, in sharp contrast, had been quiet, almost sullen and contributing very little, even to those events which Dex knew he was painfully familiar.

"You brought me here to learn the truth. You could have saved us all a lot of trouble and simply told me, but no. You had to sit back and let me discover all this for myself. Why?" Dex spoke in a low, furious whisper. He had pulled Ryan aside so as not be overheard by the others.

"What were you thinking?" he demanded again when Ryan did not immediately answer. "You sent me those photographs just to get the ball rolling in some sick game of yours, didn't you? You let me think that Anya and I were about to be blackmailed when really, you could just as easily have picked up the phone and called me."

Ryan shook his head. "I didn't send you those photographs and I have no idea who did. Hell, my instinct for self-preservation is far too sophisticated for that."

"Then why?"

"Can't you see that these people are not our friends," Ryan said and pointed to where Rev, Paul, and Nora remained at the kitchen table going over Rev's notes. Only Connor stood aloof from the process of discovery, seeming to observe them all with a quiet intentness. At times he turned his head away to close his eyes, and Ryan wondered if he was praying. He didn't know Connor, had hardly spoken to him, and yet there was something about the doctor that drew him. Perhaps later he could explore that feeling, but not now. Right now he was in protective overdrive, and he couldn't fully understand Dex's anger. Why couldn't his friend see the danger?

"You are NOT going to suck me into this. No one can quote what I refuse to say. I'm not the one with a self-destructive mandate to understand everything," Ryan shot back in answer to Dex's question. "I'd rather die than see the past dissected in the tabloids, or worse still in a court of law."

"Ryan, you must realize that it's already too late to contain all this. You can't stay anonymous. Anya … Lydia," Dex caught himself, "will need you to substantiate her story and help provide a defense."

A cynical expression crossed Ryan's face. "Incorrigible Boy Scout that you are, Dex, as usual you're assuming too much. The skating community will not have their icon defrocked and I will not testify to explain the actions of four dead men."

"Last time I counted there were only three."

Ryan laughed. The sound was hysterical, barely controlled. In alarm the others looked his way. "Will you listen to yourself? How quickly we become immune. Only three," he repeated.

Though clearly intruding, Rev joined them, but both Ryan and Dex seemed unaware.

"We've already been through this, but let's do another body count, shall we?" Ryan condescended, the brief display of his laughter having dissipated on the air like the sharp echo of glass exploding in a fire. "We have Sasha, who was probably tortured and executed by his government. Political expediency, you understand. This has nothing to do with Anya, because no one can prove that she set him up. We have a second man, who, unless you admit to having pushed him, has accidentally fallen off a balcony in a drunken stupor, because my guess is, the drink you and Elliot shared wasn't his first of the day. Finally, we have a hopeless invalid. A man revered and honored, cut down before his fine work could be completed by a tragic stroke that left him incapacitated. Howard Maple. This paragon of respectability died of an artificially induced seizure and because he couldn't turn himself over, he suffocated on a pillow, or was it a plastic bag? Unless you're insane, or suicidal enough to give the authorities reason, no one will question any of this."

"That's three," Dex said and held up three fingers.

"Assuming Glen Winston was the fourth man in those photographs, which I know you suspect," Ryan said to Dex, and looked questioning into his eyes as though for confirmation. "Can you really imagine Glen is long for this world? Don't you know that Anya is crazy? Ask her the right questions and push the right buttons, and she'd be easily certifiable." Ryan glanced at his watch. "No, my guess is that Glen Winston will be dead by now. I vote for cocaine laced with strychnine."

Dex was too stunned to speak immediately. "What are you talking about?"

"Cocaine is readily available, and Anya, sorry to say, was privy to all of Sasha's dirty tricks. Following Sasha's example, Howard adopted the habit of keeping a supply on hand. Last time I checked, Howard's little stash was missing."

Almost against his will Dex remembered the glimpse he had of Anya as she slipped something colorful into her pocket before turning to him in the limousine outside of Peter Maple's house.

"Where did Anya get strychnine?" Rev asked. The two men looked at him

263

as though only just aware of his nearness.

"Howard kept it in a miniature Chinese apothecary jar. I'd seen it at Peter Maple's in the past. As far as Peter was concerned it was just part of his father's extensive collection. I tried to solve the problem by offering to buy the entire collection months earlier, but Peter refused. When I arrived at the party, Howard was already dead and you and Anya had just made your memorable exit. Striking coincidence, wouldn't you say?"

"How did you know, at that point that Howard was dead?" Rev asked. "Peter told Nora and me that Howard wasn't discovered until after Cynthia Maple went up to say goodnight. That was some time after the last guest departed."

Ryan looked at Rev with withering disdain. "Maybe I was going to take Howard out myself, and save Anya the trouble. Maybe I went up to his room and he was already dead," his tone was bitter.

"Because you knew about those video tapes and photographs. You knew about the vast collection and distribution of pornography and you, like Elliot, realized Howard probably hadn't had time to destroy incriminating evidence before his illness. You were photographed by Howard."

Ryan turned abruptly from Rev. He was halfway down the hall with jacket in hand when Dex caught up with him. Turning him about and slamming him against the wall, he raised his fist and hit the wall with a resounding thud barely an inch from Ryan's face.

"You will answer his question, Ryan. You will tell him what he needs to know, because if you don't you can forget that we were ever friends. So if you really don't care, if you're really as dead inside as you claim, then you're useless. You might as well keep walking when you cross that lane, right through that cemetery and into that ocean out there." Dex stabbed in the direction of the door. The two men stared at one another, their faces nearly touching.

"You want to let Howard and Elliot win? Then don't help us, don't change, just keep hiding from yourself and everyone else who wants to be your friend."

What seemed like a long time was actually less than a minute. Ryan pushed Dex back, and breathing hard, perspiration running down his neck as though the decision he had to make was physically as well as mentally taxing, he finally spoke. Ignoring Dex, he turned to Rev.

"There's nothing I can add that you don't already guess. Everything you suspect and more is probably true. Where you're wrong is that Sasha was always a much bigger player than Howard ever intended to be. Sasha liked the West. He had aspirations and dreams, but a non-capitalistic and restrictive government hampered him, so he was glad to take Anya off Howard's hands. As long as she was alive she was cheap insurance. It was Sasha who turned Howard's proclivities into a thriving international enterprise. Howard became chairman of the board and vice-president of American operations, and he never even applied for the position. Of course, no one was ever going to read a quarterly report or see stock issued."

"And why would you want to kill Howard if he hadn't abused you also?" Rev asked, ignoring the change of subject, suspicion sharpening his tone. "You don't strike me as a man who would do such a favor for a friend. No, I don't believe you would have said to yourself, I'll just murder Howard," Rev imitated Ryan's broadcasting voice, "so Anya won't have to bother."

Ryan looked at Rev. "You have a decision to make. You can play cop and pretend this is a real interrogation with a little muscle at your back, or you can let me tell you the little that I'm about to reveal, which, I might add, is more than you'll voluntarily get from anyone else."

The two men looked at one another and it seemed that both were determined not to break eye contact. Rev hesitated to answer. He did not trust Ryan. Experience had taught him to run with a certain instinct that teased at the back of his skull and raised the hackles of awareness a notch or two, but he decided to let Ryan Campbell win this pissing contest.

"I'll stop," Rev said, "but I won't stay silent. Not if I discover you had anything at all to do with Lydia's disappearance or profited in any way from Howard and Sasha's operation."

"You already think that. You don't know anything about me, but you've already made up your mind. Everyone you want to attack is either beyond reach or dead, so I suggest you take your blinders off and stop playing at what you'll never be. A smart cop!" Ryan shot back at Rev. Dex put a restraining hand on his shoulder, but Ryan shrugged it off.

"Oh, and one more thing." Ryan looked about the room making eye contact with each person. "Any of you quote me later in print or otherwise and I'll make sure you never do so again." Ryan took a deep breath. "And that goes doubly for you," he said and raised his chin in Rev's direction.

"Sounds like a punk threat to me," Rev said.

"When you guess at where I've been, you'll understand that I can get just about any job accomplished and be miles away with an ironclad alibi." He walked back into the room, throwing his coat over Nora's butcher block before seating himself at the table. Nora, Paul, and Connor had been standing by the stairs, their own conversation interrupted by the altercation between Ryan and Rev. Suddenly Ryan turned in Nora's direction, and his stare was a silent invitation for her to sit across from him.

"You want to know about your sister?" he asked.

"Please," Nora said simply. She perched herself pensively on the edge of the chair and leaned across the table, wishing she could instantly assimilate everything he knew.

"I only saw her once and I'm not going to make excuses. I couldn't help her. I was just a kid myself and I'd have been dead if I'd tried, and I wasn't free to leave that place either."

Nora reached across the table and touched the back of Ryan's hand. "I'm sorry for what you must have suffered," she said gently, surprising everyone with her words of sincere condolence.

Ryan looked uncomfortable and stared down for a long moment at the back of Nora's small white hand as it covered his. She wore no nail polish, and he noticed cobalt blue paint embedded around her cuticle and lodged in the tiny lines of several fingers. Her hands looked older than they should have, from all the years of cleaning them with turpentine. He focused his attention on the blue paint and resisted the urge to peel it away. Then slowly, as though extricating himself from the open jaws of a tiger, he withdrew his hand and joined it to the other, out of sight and under the table.

"I knew she was in that room," he continued and looked her full in the face, though she could tell he didn't want to. "And then they gave her to Sasha, but I didn't know that until later. I'd assumed they'd killed her, because that's what they said they planned to do. I didn't even know this is how they solved their little problem until Elliot told me much later. He was threatening me, always threatening. It was like, behave, or we'll give you to Sasha too."

"You know what happened to her there," Nora stated. It was almost a question, but not quite.

"You don't want to know the details."

Nora opened her mouth to protest, but Ryan cut her off. "Because really that's up to your sister to tell you or not to tell you. She's an adult today and not a little girl. She has the right to privacy and dignity and not to have everything known."

"But I need to know so I can help her," Nora said, stifling a sob.

"You only think that because you imagine that by knowing you'll understand. If you can only understand, you can repair the damage. The best you can do for Anya or Lydia, or whatever you end up calling her, is to realize right now that you can't change a thing. No amount of therapy or love or money or guilt is going to give back to you the person she would have been if she'd never been taken. She's screwed up. Big time, and what's wrong with her very few professionals have had any luck at fixing, and most who claim they can do the job are not dealing with the real thing."

There was a long pause as Ryan and Nora regarded one another. "You believe in God?" Ryan asked, surprising them all and unable to resist a quick glance at Connor, who caught his eye and nodded.

Nora also looked at Connor. Suddenly she realized that she did believe in God, and she wanted to say so. She especially wanted to tell Connor, who so often had tried to engage her in conversation. But she had kept him at arm's length and safely superficial. It was true that she hadn't entirely lost her faith. It was just that she didn't know much about what she believed. She didn't know the person of Jesus ... that name that Connor so readily called upon. Maybe her grandmother's Bible was the place to start, and she was suddenly glad that she had not packed it away on that long ago day when she had tried to flee her life on Mill Lane.

"Because only God can start the process, and if you do some smart research you just might find her the right doctor."

Rev could not resist. He laughed derisively. "I doubt very much you believe in anything other than yourself. Don't talk to Nora about God."

Ryan ignored the sarcasm and considered the words. This habit of his angered Rev. He'd baited Ryan and Ryan had seemed oblivious.

"I know that I was somehow rescued over and over again. I think the Bible says that angels watch over us and I really think that God sent them to watch over me."

Rev snickered and started to speak, but Connor stepped from the shadows. "I think the verse you are speaking of is Psalm 91: 11, 12. Would you like me to tell you what it says?"

Ryan looked at Connor, surprised. He nodded his head.

For he will command his angels concerning you to guard you in all your ways; they will lift you up in their hands, so that you will not strike your foot against a stone.

Ryan appeared to consider the words. "I had a lot of close calls. There were times when circumstances conspired to protect me, and I felt that was God. And I really did want to die, but some spark kept me going, kept me fighting for survival. But I was also filled with hate. I wanted to get even. I wanted them to suffer all that they had inflicted on me." Ryan had been speaking to Nora, but now and then he glanced at Connor. Nora nodded her head as though she really did understand, encouraging him to go on, but Ryan realized that the anguish of discovery was just beginning for her.

"Like Dex, I saw her sometimes at foreign competitions and we even managed to speak a few times. She pretended not to know me, but I found out later that she remembered very well." Here Ryan looked over Nora's shoulder at Dex. "Remember when you asked me to say hello to Anya for you in Canada? I hadn't seen her in a couple of years. I walked up to her, and I could see right away that she thought I was the enemy. She thought I was one of them." An absent expression crossed Ryan's face, and Dex was sure he was reliving that moment.

"It was crowded, lots of people around, and she had a bodyguard, but Sasha was watching the last skater on the ice and everyone was distracted. I could tell she didn't really care how she placed in that event or any other, but she knew she shouldn't be talking to reporters and especially someone associated with Howard Maple. She knew he wanted her dead. So I told her right off that I was just like her, that anything she said to me wouldn't be repeated and that I hated them just as much. She seemed to believe me when she realized Dex and I were friends."

"And just like that she trusted you," Rev said, his few words contemptuous and dripping sarcasm, but Ryan seemed not to notice. He considered.

"Trust? Hardly. But we did look into each other's eyes, and we understood something about each other. We didn't have to pretend with each other. It was only a few minutes. I told her I had a message from Dex, and she handed me that patch so quickly I almost didn't know I had it until I'd walked away. After that our relationship sort of evolved into friendship."

"What do you mean, relationship?" Dex asked, suddenly wary.

"Well, no offense, Dex, but she couldn't play me the way she did you. She didn't always like that and she could be absolutely scary. Me, I was actually afraid of her sometimes and if you had any sense you would have been too." Ryan looked carefully at Dex as though weighing how much to say. "That time you called me in New York to ask if I'd keep an eye out for her. Well, she was actually staying with me for a couple of days, but she couldn't deal with you just then."

"Why not?" Dex asked, clearly hurt, but Ryan pretended not to notice.

"She was hot on the trail of Howard and had just figured out that Peter Maple was his son and she was out to learn as much as she could from him."

"How do you know this?" Rev asked.

"Because, stupid, she told me. She was having some bogus legal work done, thinking she could get to Howard through Peter. She was furious with me for not telling her, but you know, I didn't feel I'd been given an edict to reveal everything I knew, and she wanted revenge. I didn't want to be part of that."

"But you hated them?" Rev prompted.

Ryan looked at him. "I did hate Howard, almost as much as I hated Glen.

But I didn't want to be a party to murder."

"Was that because you didn't want to be on her hit list?" Rev asked, but Nora gave him a look clearly asking him to remain silent, and Rev suspected that in this instance she was right. They might learn more from Ryan if he kept his mouth shut, but Ryan answered his question anyway.

"Yes. I knew she planned to go down that list and coolly check off each name like groceries going into a shopping cart instead of a grave. And yes, I could have ended up on that list. After we heard what really happened to Sasha, Elliot was scared out of his mind. I'm not surprised he killed himself."

Dex felt that Ryan had betrayed him. He thought back to those desperate days after Anya had left him without explanation. He had turned to his friend for advice and sympathy, but Ryan had kept silent as he poured out his love for Anya and went through the long litany of everything he had done to drive her away. Was Anya sitting right there listening to him go on and on about how worried he was as he agonized over her leaving and wondered where she was at that very moment?

Suddenly Dex felt jealous. It was the use of Ryan's word 'relationship', and the way he'd said it. "Did you sleep with her?" he asked, already knowing the answer.

Ryan gave him a hard look. "You don't want to know this."

Dex stepped forward, but Rev put a restraining arm on his shoulder. "Did you sleep with my wife?" he asked threateningly.

"You weren't married to her at the time. But no, I didn't sleep with her. I slept with someone else."

"What are you talking about?"

"I didn't sleep with Anya and I wouldn't even say it was consensual the first time, because I didn't want her that way."

Despite himself, Dex remembered how aggressive Anya had been with him on that first night in Maine and with a physical strength she only rarely exhibited after. "If you don't start making sense...." Dex stepped forward, but once again Rev caught his arm.

Ryan smiled. "It's not like you to be so combative, Dex. But okay. I'll say this as clearly as I can. The woman you know is probably the closest to the original Lydia that you will ever find. She's almost sweet and she wouldn't hurt a fly. She would never have deliberately plotted the murder of her enemies and then taken enormous pleasure in seeing her intricate scheme for Sasha's death come to fruition. But Anya is not alone. She's alive today for only one reason. The same reason that is now motivating her to seek revenge. She's a multiple."

Anya sat straight up in bed. Something had propelled her out of a deep sleep. She threw her robe over her shoulders and jumped from her bed. As though for safety's sake, she nearly ran to the window and pressed her palms against the cool glass. She took a deep breath. She didn't recognize the room. Where was she? She had to think.

Over the last few months, Dex, who told her everything, had failed to mention anyone who was so sick that they were actually dying. But there was Herb. She would have killed him, but he was already dying. Again she savored that moment when she had stood over his bed and looked into his pale face. It was fully in her power at that time to take his life, but clearly he looked to be in the grip of more suffering than she had time or inclination to inflict.

Still she had wanted him to open his eyes and see her face. She wanted him to recognize the danger he was in and to experience the torment of hell just a little sooner than God had planned. "Herb," she had whispered and reached out to shake his shoulder. His sticky eyelids fluttered in that ravished face, but just as his gaze focused she stepped back. If he remembered her at all, he would imagine he was dreaming.

The muffled sound of thick-soled nurses' shoes came to her from the back stair. The nurse was returning. Silence itself, Anya slipped out of the room like a ghostly apparition and settled her straight frame into the shadow of the stair. She felt no fear of discovery. She studied Paul as he walked into the hallway below. It pained her to see him. He was a man now, but she would have known him anywhere. How keenly she had desired to be his friend. He clutched his newspaper and looked down at her footprints of melting snow on the rug, and she resisted the nearly overpowering urge to call out to him.

"It's me, Paul. It's me! Do you remember?"

That inclination to reveal herself sent a warning knell of anxiety into the far reaches of the inmost cavern. Anya felt an imbalance in herself. A dizzying sensation, and her head hurt. She was becoming small while someone more powerful was becoming large. It took a great effort of will to stay aware.

Paul never looked up, and the moment passed and she was no longer in control. Still, there was work to do. A task to accomplish that was far from finished, and when finally completed no one from her past would want her back. Anya felt sad and wondered at the feeling. Did she actually hope? Did she dare to hope that the child she had been could emerge to reclaim a past that was dead? A great deluge of fear descended. The feeling of imbalance grew stronger as she fell into herself, retreat an irresistible and well-practiced lure.

A moment later she had switched, but Anya fought to watch, her presence muffled by distance, her emotions entwined in a cloaking numbness. Paul mumbled something about needing a rag just as Herb's nurse turned the corner into the sick room. In that moment Anya's body had been within full sight of both. It was true, the alter proclaimed. They were invisible and completely and utterly protected. Nothing at all, not death, or discovery could touch them. Anya knew this wasn't true, and then the thought came to her. How did she know this wasn't true? She felt that she had removed a brick from a very high wall, letting in a restless beam of light.

Nearly tripping over a chair that shouldn't have been there, Anya walked back to the bed and fell to her knees with her hands folded. Something in that pose sparked a memory which she ignored. She tried to think, but her thoughts were too scrambled with competing voices and she fought the demand to switch. And where was she anyway? Nothing looked familiar. Anya turned on the television set and caught the date and time at the bottom of the screen. In ten minutes she was due at the ice rink for the night's performance. Anya flew into practiced action and was very soon hailing a cab.

She settled back against the seat and wondered if Ryan would be so reckless as to have Dex at Herb's funeral? Yes, she thought, waking the others to a chorus of alarm. Dex knew! And if he knew, they no longer had the luxury of time. That Other would kill Glen Winston tonight, and this time, she would help.

CHAPTER TWENTY ONE

"We hate him. We hate all who are stained with His blood." And the reply was, "He belongs to the Father, you cannot touch him." Connor woke then, slipped out of bed and stole down to Paul's kitchen to make coffee, picking up empty dishes and glasses as he went. The lid to Herb's casket had been lowered and he admired how Nora had so beautifully painted the surface. He had no doubt that the voices he'd heard were real. He prepared to pray against the forces of evil working to destroy someone called by God. He would begin by praying for salvation ... and then protection. "The angel of the Lord encamps around those who fear Him and He delivers them" (Psalm 34:7).

No one disputed Ryan's assertion that Anya suffered from multiple personality disorder, but the others looked to Dex as though for a conflicting opinion. She was, after all, his wife and he would know. Dex felt the weight of that inspection, and as much as he longed to deny that it was true, a dreadful chill of certainty clutched his heart.

The two friends regarded one another. Ryan could almost see Dex's mind at work as he thought back to all the shifts of personality and absence of memory for what had preceded a recent event or circumstance. The signs had been there all along and yet Dex had never thought to connect Anya's behavior with anything other than the abuse she had suffered under Sasha's coaching. Suddenly he was more frightened for her than ever. Turning abruptly, he grabbed his coat.

"Where are you going?" Ryan asked in alarm, taking a few steps after him.

"To Kansas City. This has to stop."

"Why stop it? Let Anya kill Glen. Tell him," Ryan erupted and turned to Rev. "You're an officer of the law. You know these people are predatory animals. They cannot be rehabilitated. Tell him that Anya would be doing the world a favor and no court in the land would convict after what she's suffered."

"Doing the world a favor?" Rev probed. "Or doing you a favor?"

Rev wished he could feel sympathy for Ryan, but something prevented him. Ryan's connection to Howard and now Herb, during a time when he was young and vulnerable, seemed to indicate that he too had been victimized. Ryan would have been twelve at the time that Anya was taken. Young people committed horrendous crimes in today's world, and he could not shift from viewing Ryan as anything but a suspect. At least not until he knew more. If Ryan had anything at all to hide, why had he brought Dex to this place? Either Ryan's behavior reflected a callous arrogance or he had a self-destructive need to have the truth known, not only about Anya but about himself as well, for the two seemed inexplicably tied.

Dex cinched the belt of his black trench coat and pulled on leather gloves. He took a few steps towards the door before looking back at Ryan. "You said you couldn't be a party to murder, and yet your silence has paved the way for just that. I guess we have less in common than I thought, because no matter how despicable the target, murder is not a solution I can live with."

"Where are you going?" Ryan asked again.

"I'm going to charter a plane and get to Kansas City as soon as possible. Maybe what you say is true and no one will ever connect Anya to Howard's murder, but I hope to prevent another that could possibly send my wife to jail and make it impossible for her to have a reunion with the little that's left of her family." Briefly he glanced at Nora before turning once more to Ryan. "And you, more than everyone else in this room, should understand that."

"I'm afraid you won't be going anywhere tonight," Paul interrupted.

They turned to look at him. He and Nora sat at the kitchen table holding hands. Despite himself, Rev felt a stab of jealousy and wondered if he and Nora would ever be as close.

"You may not have noticed, but the rain turned to snow a few hours ago. Snow on top of ice is not good. My guess is the highway patrol will be blocking travel on 128 until late tomorrow morning, and that lane out there is a river of ice. The roads will be just as treacherous up and down the coast from Portsmouth to Boston. I doubt we'll even get Herb to the gravesite tomorrow morning."

Nora came back downstairs to shut off the lights and put the dishes in the dishwasher, but the table was already clear and all else put away. Paul had left with Ryan, Connor, and Dex to spend the night at his house, and Rev would stay with her as he had the night before. She saw him in the small sitting room off the kitchen and walked in just as he replaced the receiver.

"Thanks for straightening up."

"Happy to help." He smiled at her. They had been smiling at one another a lot and for no good reason. Nora felt foolish. He had abandoned his suit jacket hours before, and his tie hung loose around his neck. She thought him remarkably handsome.

"I was just talking with Peter Maple," Rev offered.

"I'm surprised he took your call."

"He's scared. I really think all this has ambushed him."

"What more could he possibly have to contribute?"

"I wanted to ask him if Ryan was a frequent visitor at his house before Howard's death, and it seems he was. Ryan and Elliot were among the few of his skating contacts that Cynthia allowed to interact with Howard. They often arrived together."

Nora paused before speaking. "I thought Elliot and Howard hated one another. Not only was their feud public and ongoing for many years, but Elliot had good reason to be afraid of Ryan. He knew the truth."

"I don't know," Rev said. "It just seems there was a lot of collusion there, if for no other reason then certainly for damage control. Peter told me that Elliot was after them to buy Howard's apartment, but Cynthia Maple did not want to sell."

"But Dex said that Ryan hated Elliot. I can understand Elliot maintaining contact with Howard, but not Ryan."

"Ryan and Elliot had plenty of motivation to be fearful of where those photographs and all that evidence would surface. They both had high-profile careers that would be jeopardized by all that information falling into the wrong hands. Those two were perfect blackmail targets, and Peter did say that Howard's New York apartment was broken into several times. Someone was trying to recover that material."

"And you've concluded it was Ryan." Suddenly Nora sounded irritated and Rev was instantly alert. He didn't understand why Nora felt the need to defend Ryan. He was the last person to have seen Lydia as her family remembered her, and maybe that was the reason. Rev looked at Nora carefully, neither of them smiling any longer.

"Have you considered that at some point Ryan knew that Lydia was alive? Not only that, but he knew where she was living and yet never went to the authorities. And you think I'm being too hard on Ryan?"

"I think that Howard, Sasha, and Elliot are all dead, and Ryan is all you have. I also think he's suffered as much as Paul. So maybe we should reserve judgment until we know more."

"You seem to forget that reserving judgment is not my forte. If detectives took that bleeding-heart view of potential suspects, no one would ever get arrested."

For now Nora did not want to think of Ryan and Elliot or for that matter,

Howard Maple. She felt exhausted and yet nervously elated. Tomorrow she would see her sister, and she could not imagine how they would greet one another. Would Lydia know her? Did she harbor anger and still feel she was abandoned on that long ago summer day?

"Let's not disagree about anything more tonight," she said, and Rev perceived a frailty in her that she rarely showed. He stood and walked toward her and would have put his arms about her if she had not turned away and seemed so preoccupied. He felt a momentary stab of disappointment.

Nora and Rev shut off the lights, he automatically helping as her own father had often helped her mother. Together they walked up the stairs. At the entrance to Lydia's old room they paused, and Rev kissed her cheek before closing the door behind him.

Still feeling the fresh impression of that feather kiss on her cheek, Nora took a few steps into her bedroom and wondered if he would be warm enough. The temperatures had dipped below zero, and under the light of the windows, frantic snowflakes swirled and pummeled the windowpanes. Nora was almost grateful for the delay of weather. She wanted time to sort out her thoughts and prepare, and yet she knew there could be no true preparation for what was coming. She perched on the edge of her bed and thought about tomorrow's promised reunion. Anya. She would have to call her sister by this other name, at least until they got used to one another and she found out which was preferred.

A blast of wind through the trees and the sudden rhythmic pounding of Paul's garden gate jolted her alert. Nora returned to the hallway, opened the door to the linen closet and removed two wool blankets. Without thinking she opened the door to Rev's room. He had just removed his shirt and hesitated before turning in her direction. The scar was clearly visible and caught her eye immediately. It was long and curved like a sickle and came from below his shoulder to his waist. The red was fading, but fresh scar tissue molded the line of angry flesh. Nora reached out and traced the healing suture line. "Does this hurt?" she whispered.

He shivered slightly and turned his body, his face inches from hers. He smelled of mint toothpaste and the fresh milled guest soap in the hall bathroom, and she noticed the evening stubble on his face and that his lips were just a little dry. "Not at all. Fortunately one can live without a spleen, and I had two kidneys, both in good working order."

"I'm sorry," Nora said. "When you said you were on medical leave I had no idea. What happened?"

"Came up against a bad guy I couldn't get to before he got me."

"Will you go back to work?"

"I always thought so, but now I'm not so certain." They looked deeply into one another's eyes. Nora was suddenly flooded by insecurity. What if she had only imagined a mutual attraction? It had been years since anyone had held her. Years since she had been passionately kissed. He saw the hesitation. She drew back, almost involuntarily and from habit, but he held her fast.

"I'm going to kiss you," he whispered against her ear. "If you plan on objecting now is the time." He paused a moment, but Nora said nothing as he stepped directly into that silence. He bowed his head and wrapped his arms gently about her.

His kiss was at first tentative. It was as though he had been waiting for her to stop him, and guessed the scope of her ambivalence. Then his lips softened and her body awoke to an eruption of senses, and yet, another feeling came over her as well. This was not right. She knew what she had always known. All the years of her self-imposed isolation now had a purpose and timing beyond the incidental happenstance of chance. This was not her man. She'd really only loved and wanted one man almost her entire life, and what they had suffered and survived together was far more enduring than mere chemistry. She pulled away.

On the flight out to Kansas City Nora sat beside Rev. She did not know what to think about the night before. He was comforting her now as a friend and had graciously accepted her rejection. She could no longer think of him as a potential partner and hoped he felt the same. A door had closed and she was glad to have had her own feelings clarified. Eventually they would talk about it, just not now.

Alternately nervous and frightened she was also elated, a jumble of emotions seesawing in anticipation. She wished that Paul had been able to come, but he had stayed behind in order to see Herb buried, and Connor had agreed to come in his place, should a doctor be needed.

Nora felt lonely. Only Paul could know the depth of her uncertainty. A reunion with Lydia should be as important to him as it was to her. Once more that old familiar resentment surfaced that he had chosen this last obligation to Herb over her own needs and wants.

What would be different in the future? She would have to take a long hard look at this question. As soon as she got back she would tell Paul everything she felt and thought about their relationship and its marvelous potential to begin the healing process, not only for them, but for Lydia as well. If he rejected her again, if he hesitated even for five minutes, she would do the unthinkable. She would sell the house on Mill Lane and concentrate on Lydia. Perhaps she would even move to California and live with her sister and Dex, if they would have her.

Nora felt frightened at the prospect of losing Paul. And yet ... the ultimatum she had always hesitated to issue would have to be clearly stated. She could ... she would have a life apart from Paul. No matter what it took, she would abandon him to the lifestyle she hated, no longer passively assisting him to sustain what she knew to be destructive to his body and killing to his spirit. That, after all, wasn't love.

Rev noticed that Ryan seemed to avoid him. He sat beside Dex on the chartered Cessna. His body was turned toward the window, and he avoided eye contact. Ryan's trademark humor, so often a buffer and frequent vehicle for communication, was absent in a way that made him seem intrinsically empty. Ryan had to be frightened. The unexpected resurrection of all his childhood traumas could all too easily be sensationalized and misinterpreted. The threat of that exposure, which would certainly re-victimize him, had to be exerting strong influence.

Dex had told him that behind the numb exterior, Ryan was in pain and hurting. The explanation seemed a little too pat and Dex himself too anxious to explain away Ryan's obsessive need to control the flow of information at everyone else's expense.

Dex seemed determined to protect his friend. Despite the strong words of the night before, Rev noted that Dex had reverted to a kind of passive approval of Ryan's outrageous behavior. Ryan had clearly betrayed the friendship when he slept with Anya. In addition, Ryan had lied to all of them each time he withheld crucial information that would have saved them all a lot of time, not to mention heartache, and this too was overlooked by Dex.

Was this just his personality? Was Dex simply a forgiving sort of person and was his only agenda the preservation of his marriage and this friendship at any cost? None of this seemed healthy, but Rev felt no obligation to help Dex see things differently. After all, he was not a counselor. And yet he had concluded, through his extensive police work, that people who successfully managed to maintain secrets over long periods of time attracted personalities who opted for blindness at any cost. For now he would give up the probing and questioning, but he would keep his eye on Ryan in the same way he would a hissing cobra.

Ryan insisted on driving the rental car, explaining that he knew the way to the arena, but Rev suspected that driving would allow him the opportunity to avoid further conversation as he concentrated on the route they would take south on 29 and across the Broadway Bridge into the city.

A late wash of daylight reflected off metallic puddles that dotted the wet streets. Spring had arrived in this part of the country weeks earlier than the Northeast. Here the snow had melted, and the air was rife with the promised riches of color and new things growing. A low sun burned on the horizon as a pale moon brightened with the streetlights. If they were lucky, they would be on time for the first evening performance.

Dex wanted Nora to see Anya skate. Although it made no sense to anyone else, he thought it would somehow ease her nervousness and help her recognize the kind of person he knew Anya to be. Not crazy as Ryan described, or to be pitied as he could see they all pitied her, but as a survivor with an inner strength and beauty which superceded the entire trauma and tragedy of her life.

If it was true that Anya intended to kill Glen, then Dex had to stop her because Ryan was right. The deaths of Elliot and Sasha could be explained, while the facts surrounding Howard's demise seemed dubious and might not continue to appear accidental under close examination. New light would be cast in their direction as the police continued to investigate the contents of Howard's New York apartment. A final death among the key players might prove impossible to explain and Anya would emerge the prime suspect.

The arena was in a low well of a place in sight of two connecting overpasses. In the fading twilight, Dex could see the river below the levies, and overhead the bridge they'd recently crossed into the city. Old warehouses lined the narrow streets, but the wide berth of parking was filled to overflowing. Ignoring the signs and barriers, Ryan pulled the car to the front of the building and parked illegally below the many steps that led up to the arena. Rev placed his business card on the dash and another under the window wiper and hoped security wouldn't tow the vehicle.

They crossed the wide corridor that encircled the interior, ignoring the souvenir and refreshment stands that dotted the outside rim. The show had already begun, and as they pushed open the wide doors, they looked down on a large oval surface of gleaming ice. As though on cue, Anya's name and skating credits were announced and a single spotlight picked her out of the darkness, center ice.

She wore a white dress, which sparkled silver under the light. As the first notes of music pierced the air, she began to glide. Nora's first thought was that her sister looked like a swan, floating weightlessly over a frozen pond. With stunning competence she landed a triple-flip, double-toe combination to an eruption of applause from the audience. Rev came up on one side of Nora and took her hand, but she was oblivious to his presence, her eyes riveted on the small figure of her sister as she executed an elegant spiral sequence.

It all looked so beautiful, fluid and effortless, but at the same time difficult in an exotic merger of athleticism and artistry. It occurred to Nora that there was no other sport with that same mix of compelling elements as figure skating. She had never followed skating and could not tell the difference between a triple flip and a double-axel, and yet knew that she was witnessing a remarkable confluence of talents. *This is my sister,* she thought and tried to imagine that it was really true.

"I'd know her anywhere," Connor whispered in her ear, and Nora felt closer to him in that moment than she ever had, for he had spoken aloud the very words that rang in her heart and momentarily replaced her anxiety with a surge of pride.

"Let's go," Dex urged and led Nora, Connor, and Rev across the stands and down to ice level.

So glamorous from above, here the spell of fantasy was quickly dispelled by the cold block walls and slab flooring. They were stopped twice by security guards until Dex was recognized, and now Nora noticed that Ryan was not with them. She wondered why, but it was only a passing thought. She was about to meet her sister, and yet in the grip of so many conflicting emotions, there was a lingering anxiety that this long awaited reunion would never take place.

Nora noted that there was a crisp, moist quality to the air at this level, and as a change in music bellowed out over the unseen arena, she imagined her sister abandoning the spotlight. As they made their way down a tunnel like corridor, another group of skaters filed from the dressing area in bright costumes, as others went through a routine of stretching in order to keep their muscles warm and limber. Several smiled or waved in Dex's direction, but he barely acknowledged the greetings. More than anything else, Dex's single-minded air of urgency struck new fear into Nora.

"Wait here," he said and walked ahead to where the other skaters were disappearing into the spotlight, but Nora would not be put off. She followed and stood close by, knowing that Rev and Connor also had joined them.

"Did you notice where Ryan went?" Rev whispered in her ear, but Nora shook her head impatiently. Rev's treatment of Ryan had disappointed her. She felt that like Paul, he had suffered more than anyone could know, and she was willing to wait for answers before she formed a judgment, but she could not think of that now. Over the music she struggled to hear what Dex was saying.

"Have you seen my wife?" Nora heard Dex ask a man with a clipboard, but she could not hear the answer. She had learned to live with the guilt of that moment when Lydia's hand had slipped out of hers seemingly forever.

She had accepted the sad fact that forgiveness could never be asked for and then given. Although her feelings were not logical, now only minutes from seeing her sister with limited physical space between them, she could not escape the sneering doubt that this was all a cruel joke.

"Have you seen my wife?" Dex asked the ice monitor.

"She's supposed to be out there." He pointed to the arena, lit bright under roving spotlights of pink, green, and red. The animated flow of performers alternately skated and jumped to a fifties' rock and roll medley, their dance like footwork impressive to watch.

"You may not notice, but there is a gaping hole out there. When Glen hears about this he'll be livid. He didn't want her joining the show so late. He said she was unreliable and something like this would happen."

"Where's Glen?" Dex demanded, nearly choked by impatience.

"Well," the man hesitated and looked about as though suddenly baffled. "He's usually close by, but I don't know. You might check back there," he waved vaguely in the general direction from where they'd just come. "We lost some of the set in transport and Glen might be checking it out."

"When was the last time you saw Anya?"

"Look, I have a job to do." The man started to walk away, but Dex deliberately stood in his path.

"Hold on," he said menacingly. "I asked you a question and I expect an answer."

"I saw her right here," he stabbed a finger at the ground. "And she was supposed to do a quick change and be out there," he pointed at the ice in disgust.

Dex was growing weary of the program monitor's response. This man was typical of the sort of person Glen surrounded himself with. Inadequate types who blindly reflected Glen's opinions while they successfully deflected criticism away from him. He would not be popular with the other skaters and yet would make Glen look like a saint in comparison. "Which way did Anya go?"

"When she stepped off the ice Ryan Campbell was here. I guess Campbell thinks he's grown so important that he can divert an ice show with an interview. How should I know where they went? I have better things to do; I have a show to run."

"If you worked for me I'd fire you," Dex tossed behind him as he turned away.

"Yeah, well, I guess there was no reason to think the ice princess wasn't professional enough to do the quick change required of her and get back out there for that group number. Yeah, like Glen and I didn't call that one," he shot after Dex, who was already jogging down the corridor.

Dex was frantically trying to remember the layout of the arena. It had been years since he had skated in Kansas City, and he could not be certain that this was the same place.

Nora, Rev, and Connor followed Dex. "What do you think is wrong?" Nora could not help asking. "Where is my sister? Why isn't she here?" But Dex did not answer her questions, and his expression of single-minded anxiety alarmed Nora.

"Don't worry," Rev said. "We'll find her. Why don't we split up?" he suggested. "Connor can check the dressing area, and I'll talk to some of the other skaters as they get off the ice. Nora, you can–"

"I'm going with Dex," she said, already turning away and then running to catch up with Dex, who had just disappeared up a staircase.

"Aren't you going to shoot him?" Ryan spoke to Anya with a flatness that struck fear into Glen. She pointed the gun in his direction and he had backed as far as he was able into the corner of an abandoned receipt office.

"Shoot him," Ryan demanded. "Shoot him NOW," but Anya stood as still as a deer transfixed by headlights.

"Ryan, I don't understand," Glen pleaded. He somehow knew it was useless to address Anya. She had a dead, glazed look on her face, which frightened him almost more than the gun itself. If she wanted to shoot him, she would do so and nothing could stop her. Nothing except Ryan, who seemed to be telling her what to do, as though she had been programmed to do his bidding. As he contemplated her expression in a haze of panic, it occurred to Glen that she might even relish that bloodthirsty prospect.

"Ryan," Glen tried again, his voice breaking. His legs felt as though they'd been stripped of muscle, and he wasn't sure they would continue to hold him upright. "Please, Ryan, whatever I've done let's talk about it. You've always been my favorite. I loved you as though you were the son I never had. Didn't I protect you and take care of you? Oh, maybe I was too hard on you sometimes. Maybe I hit you too often, but I only wanted the best for you. Ryan! Listen to me! I–"

"S-H-U-T U-P, shut-up," Ryan erupted, his tone seething hatred, as his handsome face contorted in a kind of tortured rage. At the sound of his voice, Glen heard the unmistakable sound of the gun being cocked, and he imagined that impersonal steel bullet gliding into the greased chamber. In anticipation of death he squeezed his eyes shut and wished he could pray.

The sound when it came was deafening. It echoed off the walls in hollow agony, and he waited for the searing pain and felt he would die in the torment of anticipation. It took him a moment to realize that the cry he heard was not his own. Laboriously he forced his eyes open, as chilling sweat dripped off his brow, and a warm trickle of urine slid down his leg.

He could hardly believe his luck. Anya had swung the gun away from him in a deliberate arch. Glen pressed his back harder into the wall and inched a few steps toward the door. He felt certain that at any second she would turn in his direction, re-aim and shoot again, but for now she had the gun leveled at Ryan. She shot off another blast and Glen saw Ryan's body spin around and drop to the floor. He wasn't dead. Incredibly he wrapped his arms about his middle and glared up at Anya in an odd grimace of astonishment and pain.

"It was you," she said. "It wasn't Glen. It was YOU!" Shock at having uttered this revelation was clear in her voice, all her senses straining towards that one conflict of realization as her fingers tightened on the trigger. She stood in stockinged feet, dressed in her shimmering white costume, with an iridescent silver ribbon braided into her long hair.

"No," Ryan struggled to speak, his hands attempting to stem the blood flow from his wound. "We've been over this a thousand times, and now you're confused again. Anya, you know it was Glen. He held the camera, set up the lights, and tightened your restraints."

"I can see it now," Anya said. "You all counted on me losing my memory. But I remember how you argued with the other men. You could have helped me escape. There were opportunities."

"And what did we argue about, Anya? Think. We argued about you. I begged them to let you go."

"But they didn't, did they? They forced you to go along with them, knowing it would make you as despicable as them. You could have helped me. You could have!"

Once again the click of the chamber. Glen knew that if he chanced to live, he would hear that unforgiving sound in nightmares for the rest of his life, but this time it freed him to move. He ran blindly, careening around the corner and directly into Dex. Others hurried behind, summoned by the sound of the gun and Ryan's scream of pain. Dex took in the scene at a glance and put up his hand for the others to stop.

Connor was grateful that he had brought along his black bag, and he clicked off in his mind the contents, hoping he had everything he would need until the paramedics arrived. And yet it was clear to him as he observed the scene that they were all in danger, and they might never reach Ryan before Anya shot off another round.

Connor held Nora back as Rev reached under his jacket and removed his gun. Nora gave a gasp of disapproval and fear, but he waved her back. She looked at him stubbornly, a fierce gleam in her eyes, and shook her head. Nothing was going to stand in the way of Nora being there, not even the threat of her own death.

Dex stepped further into the room, ahead of Nora and Rev, while Connor pressed his back against the wall and inched closer to Ryan. They all noticed that Anya seemed oblivious to the commotion. She was bent on one task and one task alone as she stared down at Ryan's suddenly still form. Ryan was deathly pale and he had grasped his shoulder in an attempt to stem the flow of blood, but to no avail. Dex knew that Ryan would die if he couldn't get through to Anya, but as he studied the set of her familiar features, he realized that he had never seen this woman before, and he wondered if she knew him.

"Anya."

She heard his voice and hesitated.

"Wait, Anya."

"Dex?"

"Yes, it's me." He stepped into the room and walked a few steps forward.

"You heard, did you hear? Now you think you know everything, but you can't possibly," Anya stated, her voice suddenly tempered by confusion. As he watched, her composure seemed to dissolve like melting ice in a firestorm, and there was a wild look in her eyes, which he had never seen before, but at least she knew him and had spoken to him.

"I know enough, Anya. Enough to know we can beat this thing and I don't care," he emphasized. "I only care about you. I'll help you. Give me the gun." He stepped forward, almost close enough to reach out and touch her. She had lowered her weapon, but now she raised it back in the direction of Ryan's skull.

"Stop right there," she said to Dex, in that odd tang of an accent that came and went for no good reason. It occurred to Dex that he had heard that accent only when they argued or the few times that she had been aggressive in a combative way that had unsettled him, and especially in Washington when she was fighting to stay in this country. He thought about Ryan's claim that Anya had multiple personality disorder. What did that really mean? He would think about that later. For now he refused to be afraid of his wife, even as she held the gun to Ryan's skull with murderous intent.

"Stop right there," she repeated. "I can kill you too. I won't hesitate."

"You won't kill me, Anya. You can't kill me, we have a life together." There was a pause. Anya stood unwavering as Ryan moaned in agony. It was then that Dex saw that Ryan was far worse off than he first thought. There were two wounds and a wash of bright, slick blood pooled from beneath the place that Ryan lay on the hard concrete. The fear had left Ryan's face, and

Dex realized that shock was setting in. He moaned again and attempted to shift his position, and that sudden movement captured the full intensity of Anya's stare. Once more she swung the gun in his direction.

"Anya, I want you to think about something. Imagine Ryan's face at that time. It was the face of a boy, and that's why you didn't recognize him when you met him years later. He wasn't much older than you were, and Howard was trying to blackmail him by involving him in their dirty games. They had to ensure his silence because they did the same to him."

"What he did was wrong! I begged him to help me, but he wouldn't lift a finger! And he protected Sasha. I don't care what you say. He could have gone to the police. He could have told them where I was."

Her voice was savage, almost inhuman as she spat out the words. It was still that same cold voice with the disturbing accent. How could he call forth the Anya that he loved? The one he had laughed with and discovered a sweet intimacy with that had seemed to make both so very happy. There had to be something he could do. *Think,* he told himself silently and uttered a swift prayer of desperation. Dex concentrated on her face. It was still the face he remembered; the face he loved, and he held on to that knowledge like a drowning man to a life-raft.

Over her shoulder, Dex saw Rev approach, but Anya caught the shift of his attention and swung about, and in that moment as she turned away, Connor slid to the ground beside Ryan. With expert swiftness he pressed a bandage to the bleeding shoulder, even as he ran his hands over Ryan, searching for the second wound.

Rev couldn't believe the risk Connor had taken. He didn't seem to be afraid of Anya, but was now intent on his patient. The gun fired and ricocheted off the wall, and if he'd counted right Rev estimated that Anya must be almost out of bullets.

Anya lifted her arms to the ceiling and pointed the gun above her head. She swirled around and began to lower the weapon back in Ryan's direction. And then she hesitated. She looked into Connor's face and lifted her hand to her temple as though in pain. The expression on her face was momentarily blank, and then a look of surprise followed one of recognition.

"I know you. Do I know you?"

"I haven't seen you for many years, but yes. You do know me," Connor said, still working over Ryan. "We were friends long ago. But now you need to let me help Ryan. Will you put the gun down? Just lay it down here on the floor."

Connor spoke gently and Dex took a few hurried steps in Anya's direction. There was no time to bridge the distance, for she stepped back and once more lifted her weapon, seeming to ignore Nora, who had remained in the hallway, a look of grief and fear clouding her expression.

"Anya, think of us. We have a life together and your sister is here."

"Nora?" Her response was a question followed by an animal-like whimper.

"Nora wants to see you and get to know you again. Don't you think you both deserve that opportunity? Don't let what Ryan did so many years ago rob us of a future. Let Ryan live with his own demons."

Slowly Dex had begun to bridge the gap between them. He was inches from her when he reached for the gun, surprised that she released that sleek heaviness with such ease. Almost in a heap Anya collapsed against him, and he wrapped his arms about her as they sank in unison to the floor.

Dex kissed her and held her against his chest. He brushed wet strands of hair away from her face. She was a tortured soul, struggling against the cruel assault of contradictory infringements, her fragile defenses quaking inward against a deluge of treacherous muttering, that he could never know.

Dex's eyes searched for Nora. She took a few steps forward and stopped, unsure of herself. He smiled at her. It was comforting to know that he would have some help.

"The paramedics will be here soon," Rev said to Connor who was still bent over Ryan, loosening clothing and then covering him with his own jacket.

"I'm cold and I'm going to die. I don't want to die." Ryan whispered.

"You said you believed in God," Connor said, removing a compress soaked in blood and pressing another to the wound. "Would you like me to pray with you?"

Ryan whispered 'yes' and Rev was stunned. Why, he wondered, was Connor taking the time to pray when he had a patient who might die? Rev had seen lots of gunshot victims, and as he studied Ryan he doubted recovery was possible. The second bullet had clearly lodged somewhere they couldn't see, and there had to be internal bleeding.

But as he prayed Connor continued to minister his emergency medical expertise. In the distance they heard sirens and knew that help was on the way.

"*Dear Jesus. You love this man. He has acknowledged to us that you have rescued him many times from disaster and an early death. And yet perhaps he has never actually prayed and asked you into his heart. Perhaps he doesn't really know God's Son and His Holy Spirit. And so, Jesus, we issue that invitation to you now.*

Ryan, don't try to speak. Just say these words in your mind, and no matter what happens to your body, you will live. *I believe, Jesus, that you are God."* Connor paused for Ryan to pray, repeating the words. *You are the promised Messiah, who died on the cross to save me from my sins. Come into my life now. Forgive me for all that I have done that has grieved you and been wrong. I am sinful, and only you, God, are good. Be for me the comforter and teacher, who will never leave me or forsake me. We claim your words Jesus as true:* **for God so loved the world that He gave His only begotten son, that whoever believes in Him shall not perish, but will have eternal life (John 3:16).**

Dex felt the weight of Ryan's gaze turn in his direction. He wanted to go to Ryan, but he held on to Anya, who seemed to melt into his protective embrace as though to hide. Now, perhaps close to death, that air of being separate and unaffected was gone. Ryan was as pale and gray as the concrete slab he lay against. His lips moved soundlessly, and despite tears that glistened in his eyes, Ryan attempted an unruffled smile of perfect ease that seemed to echo down the long corridor of their past. But this smile was different. It wasn't a barrier meant to put off any that would penetrate a hard exterior. No, Dex thought. This was a smile of relief and even peace.

Connor bent to whisper in Ryan's ear something they could not hear. For a long moment Ryan and Connor looked deeply into one another's eyes. Connor grasped his hand until Ryan's grip fell loose and his eyelids fluttered and then closed forever on this world.

THE END

Dear Paul:

I could so easily pick up the phone ... and tell you how pleased and privileged I feel at your invitation to be the best man at your wedding. I could so easily pick up the phone ... but I would so much rather write you a quick note because then the answers to all my prayers for you and Nora, and seeing this in writing ... make me all the more joyful for you.

I know that your Savior, Jesus Christ, has protected you through so many trials and difficulties too numerous to count and too hidden to know ... until eternity. I'm so proud of the changes that have come into your life as a result of your willingness to peel back the layers of a horrid past. Because of you, I truly understand these words, "and the truth shall set you free."

I want to share a verse with you from Scripture. If you will memorize this verse it will remind you over and over again of God's power to protect us from evil. And I'd like to recommend a book to you called Enemies in the Camp *by Alexandra F. Clair. You can order this book anywhere online or directly from the publisher.*

And of course I will be your best man. And I will know that it is a brother, not just in spirit but in Christ, that I stand to support on such a momentous occasion.

Because He lives,
Connor

*

Who will separate us from the love of Christ? Will tribulation, or distress, or persecution, or famine, or nakedness, or peril, or sword? For your sake we are being put to death all day long; we were considered as sheep to be slaughtered. But in all these things we overwhelmingly conquer through Him who loved us. For I am convinced that neither death, nor life, nor angels, nor principalities, nor things present, nor things to come, nor powers, nor height, nor depth, nor any other created thing will be able to separate us from the love of God which is in Christ Jesus our Lord. Romans 8: 35-39

Printed in the United States
19231LVS00005B/55-102